BTU Alumni #5

WRITING DIRTY

BTU Alumni Series Book #5

ALLEY CIZ

HOUSE OF CRAZY
PUBLISHING

Also by Alley Ciz

BTU Alumni Series

Power Play (Jake and Jordan)

Musical Mayhem (Sammy and Jamie) BTU Novella

Tap Out (Gage and Rocky)

Sweet Victory (Vince and Holly)

Puck Performance (Jase and Melody)

Writing Dirty (Maddey and Dex)

Scoring Beauty- BTU6 Preorder, Releasing September 2021

#UofJ Series

Cut Above The Rest (Prequel) <—Freebie for newsletter subscribers.
Download here.

Looking To Score

Game Changer

Playing For Keeps

Off The Bench- #UofJ4 Preorder, Releasing December 2021

The Royalty Crew (A #UofJ Spin-Off)

Savage Queen

Ruthless Noble- Preorder, Releasing June 2021

"I've always been her shelter in the storm."

Hockey players.
MMA fighters.
Rock stars.
The boys in blue.
Even sexy SEALs have all offered to slay my dragon—or in my case, my stalker.

Why can't they get it through their thick, *stubborn* heads that I can take care of myself?
I'm no damsel!
But...
What if the real villain in this story is me?

Now the one person I've never been able to resist has appointed himself as my protector.

I don't know what's more at risk—my life or my heart.

WRITING DIRTY is an interconnected stand-alone of the BTU Alumni squad with scenes steamy enough to inspire this romance writing Covenette. This laugh out loud rom-com features a cast of characters who don't know how to stay in their lane, a heroine who refuses to be a damsel, and a hero determined to prove he can deliver one hell of a happily ever after.

Writing Dirty (BTU Alumni, Book 5)

Alley Ciz

Paperback ISBN: 978-1-950884-09-4

Ebook ISBN: 978-1-950884-08-7

Cover Designer: Julia Cabrera at Jersey Girl Designs

Editing: Jessica Snyder Edits, C. Marie

Proofreading: Gem's Precise Proofreads; Dawn Black

❀ Created with Vellum

For Buke,
My own personal Trident. You are my faithful writing buddy…even when you use my leg as pillow and your snoring is so loud I can hear you over the music on my headphones.

And even though you don't actually know how to read, you can brag about the fact you got a book dedication before your dad.

Author Note

Dear Reader,
Writing Dirty can be read as a stand-alone but it is interconnected
in the BTU Alumni world. You do not need to read Power Play,
Tap Out, Sweet Victory, or Puck Performance *first but they*
might help you keep track of the crazy cast of characters as large as
The Coven and their guys.

Prepare yourself to hop aboard the crazy train that is Maddey's
brain.
XOXO
Alley

Text Handles

The Coven

    Maddey: QUEEN OF SMUT
    Jordan: MOTHER OF DRAGONS
    Skye: MAKES BOYS CRY
    Rocky: ALPHABET SOUP
    Becky: YOU KNOW YOU WANNA
    Gemma: PROTEIN PRINCESS
    Beth: THE OG PITA
    Holly: SANTA'S COOKIE SUPPLIER
    Melody: BROADWAY BABY
    Zoey: DANCING QUEEN
    Ella: FIDDLER ON THE ROOF
    (Honorary) Sammy: THE SPIN DOCTOR

Donnelly

| Ruth | Robert | --sister-- | Eileen (aunt) |

| Ryan | Jase (T) | Jordan (T) | Sean |
| | | Dog- Navy | |

Donovan

| Jake Sr | Sarah |

| Jake | Carlee |

McClain

| Jack | Babs |

| Justin | Tyler | Connor | Maddey |
| | | | Dog- Trident Yellow Lab |

Reese

| Tracy |
| Becky |

Stone

| Peggy | Dad (Deceased) |
| | Dex |

Samson

| Lyle | Kyle |

Hawke

| Jamie | Sammy (Rhodes) |

Steele

| Vicki | Vic | --brother-- | Mick | Hope |
| | | | | Gemma |

| Vince | Rocky |

James

| Gage | --cousin-- | Wyatt | Beth |
| | | | baby |

Donovan/Donnelly

| Jake | Jordan |

Lacey (IT)	Lucy (IT)	Logan
Dog- Navy	Black Lab	
Dog- Stanley	Chocolate Lab	

Donnelly/Brightly

| Jase | Melody |

James/Steele

| Gage | Rocky |
| | Ronnie |

Steele/Vanderbuilt

| Vince | Holly |

Other Covenettes

Skye Masters
Zoey
Ella

Fighters at The Steele Maker

Deck (Declan) Avery
Ray
Griff-- Simone (GF)
Nick
Damon

Other Hockey Players

Tucker Hayes- Chicago Fire
Chance Jenson- NJ Blizzards
Wade Tanner- LA Lions
Nate Bishop- Boston Bruisers
Chris 'Cali' Callahan- NY Storm

Others

Paul- (Justin's SWAT Partner)

Playlist

*

"That's How You Know"- Enchanted Soundtrack
"Electricity"- Silk City, Dua Lipa, Diplo
"Overprotective"- Britney Spears
"Bibbidi-Bobbidi-Boo"- Verna Felton
"Woman Like Me"- Little Mix
"Circle Of Life"- The Lion King
"Part Of Your World"- The Little Mermaid (Jodi Benson)
"Go The Distance"- Hercules (BYU Vocal Point)
"Let It Go"- Frozen (Idina Menzel)
"Be Our Guest"- Descendants
"Friend Like Me"- Aladdian Broadway
"Everything You Want"- Vertical Horizon
"Word Up!"- Little Mix
"I'll Make A Man Out Of You"- Mulan
"A Whole New World"- Aladdin
"Fixer Upper"- Frozen
"One Kiss"- Calvin Harris, Dua Lipa
"Kiss The Girl"- The Little Mermaid
"Work It"- Missy Elliot

"Hatef—k"- The Bravery

"Blow Your Mind (Mwah)"- Dua Lipa

"Shots"- LMFAO

"Tequila"- The Champs

"Move"- Little Mix

"What I Need"- Hayley Kiyoko, Kehlani

"Say My Name"- Destiny's Child

"Youngblood"- 5 Seconds of Summer

"LoveGame"- Lady Gaga

"Drinking Alone"- Carrie Underwood

"Ruin The Friendship"- Demi Lovato

"Liquid Dreams"- O-Town

"I Put A Spell On You"- Annie Lennox

"When You Wish Upon A Star"- Pinocchio

"What A Man Gotta Do"- Jonas Brothers

"Sexy Dirty Love"- Demi Lovato

"Just Around The River Bend"- Pocahontas

"Hakuna Matata"- The Lion King

"How Far I'll Go"- Moana

"Tell Me You Love Me"- Demi Lovato

"One Jump Ahead"- Aladdin

"Every Breath You Take"- The Police

"My Oh My"- Camilla Cello, DeBaby

"Love Me Less"- MAX, Quinn XCII

"Prince Ali"- Will Smith

"The Bare Necessities"- The Jungle Book

"Colors Of The Wind"- Tori Kelly

"I'm On A Boat"- The Lonely Island

"Cross Me"- Ed Sheehan, Chance the Rapper

"Beauty and the Beast"-Ariana Grande, John Legend

"A Girl Worth Fighting For"- Mulan

"So This Is Love"- Cinderella

"I Won't Say I'm In Love"- Hercules

"Pony"- Ginuwine

"Single Ladies (Put A Ring On It)"- Beyonce
"A Dream Is Wish Your Heart Makes"- Jessie Ware
"Can You Feel The Love Tonight"- Pentatonix
Available on Spotify

Chapter One

"**D**on't you *dare* think of stepping one foot inside this house in gray sweatpants, Ryan Donnelly." I point an aggressive finger toward the glass sliders leading to the back deck, all while not looking up from the computer screen in front of me.

"Don't be like that, Madz." Ryan pouts when I finally look. It's not a look a twenty-seven-year-old man should be able to pull off, but with his Chris Evans good looks, he totally does.

Not for the first time—perhaps for the millionth, for that matter—I curse my stupid heart for not being able to get its shit together and accept his proposal. *Nooo*, it had to stubbornly, *stupidly* insist on not being able to figure out how to love.

Well, that's not true. I love my family, my friends—Ryan included—and my dog, but I haven't figured out what it actually means to be *in* love.

Sure, the voices in my head can tell me how they feel. My characters pretty much craft all sorts of shouty-capitals-worthy happily-ever-afters in my books themselves.

I'm constantly having to tell them to stay in their lane

when it comes to whose story it is, but when I try to phone a friend with them, they're all, *New phone, who dis?*

"Don't even try it, mister." I wave my finger side to side, still not fully looking up. "You do and I'll sic my attack dog on you."

Warmth leaves my lap as Trident, my yellow lab, lifts his head, knowing I'm talking about him. He may be able to teach a master class on being a well-behaved canine and can scare off any would-be attackers (aka the mailman and such) with his bark, but he's a big ball of mush for Ryan and my other friends.

He lazily lumbers to his feet and heads straight for Ryan, only further proving the point.

The NHL golden boy bends down to love up on my fur child while actually following my orders and staying in the open doorway, the breeze from the ocean bringing in the comforting scent of salt and sea.

"Who's a good boy?" Ryan wraps both hands around Trident's ears, scratching behind them. "You are, aren't you, Tri? Yup, I know you are. You're keeping your mommy company while she ignores her real friends for the ones in her head, huh?"

My "attack dog" has a hind leg scratching in the air and is melting into an almost-hundred-pound puddle right there on the floor. Granted, I'm not super far behind as I watch the display. Why did I have to look up?

No, Madz. The question you should be asking yourself is why aren't you with this sweet, sweet man?

Jiminy can be a real son of a bitch.

Really…is it my fault I can't get my heart to fall in line?

"Can you please stop telling my dog lies? I'm not *ignoring* you guys. It's only six in the morning—almost everyone is still sleeping."

Over the head of my blissed-out dog, blue eyes a few shades darker than my own find me. "Yes, but if *you're* up at six *AM*, it means you've been up all night and will end up ignoring us to sleep."

Is it wrong that I kinda wanna hit him for being right?

"Semantics."

The sound of joints popping as Ryan rises to stand fills the silence before he finally braves going against my orders and walks into the house. He lifts my feet from the chair they're resting on, settling into the seat with them in his lap.

"What are *you* doing up this early anyway?" I ask, reaching down to pet Trident as he retakes his spot at my side.

"I came to pick up my running partner before I set off."

My gaze automatically falls to watch the way the muscles in his arm pop and flex as he stretches to run a hand down Trident's back. My dog lets out a sigh, and I can't blame him. I have firsthand knowledge of how good it feels to have that particular body part do the same to me.

Stop that right now, Madz. You do not get to think those things anymore. You and Ryan are only *friends now.*

God, I need sleep. It's only when I'm overtired like this that I beat myself up over what at times I think are my bad life decisions. I really am fucked in the head.

"You do realize it's the offseason, right?"

There are days I question if the word offseason is even in his vocabulary with the way he trains year-round. His work ethic rivals that of my brothers, and their *lives* depend on their physical fitness.

Hmm…

I saw Justin just last week and he'll be down the shore again this weekend, but when was the last time I spoke to Tyler or Connor?

Tyler is stateside right now, but it's been a few days since he responded to the family group chat. I'll bug him later.

Connor's team is currently deployed, so his additions to the chat are few and far between. I shoot off a quick email—

since that is sometimes more reliable—asking when we can video-chat again. Hopefully the conversation will end on a better note than the last one.

A girl gets herself an overzealous fan and everyone is all up in arms about it.

I swear I'm too old to still be dealing with big brother overprotectiveness.

They have a point, Madz.

Oh, leave her alone, Jiminy.

Yeah—the Die Hard Trilogy needs to take a chill pill.

The metal of Trident's collar tags jingles when he tilts his head at my growl.

Bed.

I need bed.

"We're not gonna bring the Cup back to Jersey without putting in the work," Ryan says, answering my earlier question.

I'm surprised my dog is the only one he's enlisted to run with him. What about his teammates?

"Jake and Chance are lucky I didn't pull their asses out of bed." It's scary how well he can still read my thoughts.

"I agree about Chance since you live in the same house, but I call bullshit on Jake." He arches a brow at the mention of his brother-in-law. "There's no way you would risk facing the wrath of your sister if you woke up any of her babies."

I don't bring up the fact that it's weird for a group of professional athletes—multi-millionaire athletes—to share a shore house together, even if it is a mansion. Those comments fall on deaf ears anyway. No use wasting trash talk on it.

"You got that right. I would prefer not to be the victim of one of JD's revenge plots, thank you very much."

"Plus, you run the risk of seeing her naked since she and Jake like to—"

"Not cool, Madz. Not cool at all." He is quick to cut me off before I can go on about his sister's sex life. Torturing brothers is one of my favorite pastimes, one that is also enjoyed by some of my fellow Covenettes.

Who are the Covenettes, you ask?

Only the most awesome women in existence. It started with the original six—the founding members, if you will—but we've added to our ranks the last few years.

"If you want, I can text her to see if it's safe?" I reach for my phone only to have it snatched away.

"No way. I don't need to be the topic of a Coven Conversation this early."

I snort, like I do any time one of the guys uses the name they assigned to our group chat. I highly doubt Ryan's brother Jase—Jordan's twin—and his best friend Vince knew what they were getting into when they gave us our nickname in college. Too bad for them we're the type of women to take the ball and run with it.

Plus, those Coven Conversations are life. It is seriously the best thing to happen on my phone, and that's saying *a lot*. Think about it; I write romance—can you imagine all the *research* I've conducted on it?

"Don't be a baby," I tease, poking him in the side.

"Let me see what you're working on anyway." He slides my MacBook Pro toward him as he squirms away from my tickling touch.

"Nope." I slam the lid shut before he can get a peek. Only my girls get to read the rough, hasn't-been-edited word vomit I come up with.

"No fun." There's that damn pout again.

I pop a shoulder and bite back yet another yawn.

"Come on, you." He takes one of my hands in his and pulls me to stand. "Off to bed." He cups his hands over my shoulders, turning me in the direction of the stairs that will take me to my bedroom.

"But—"

"Nope." He cuts off my protest, the captain in him taking

charge. "I'll drop Trident at JD's after our run so you can sleep as long as you need."

Gah! Again he has to go and be perfect. I really am an asshole.

Pausing at the bottom of the stairs, I turn to watch my ex-boyfriend-turned-bestie corral my dog, wondering how I can be so good at writing other people's happily-ever-afters when I can't figure out my own.

Chapter Two

Dex

Pulling into the driveway of the robin egg blue shore house, I need to take a moment to absorb what I know has to be a seven-figure piece of realty. Jersey Shore homes go for a pretty penny, especially on the water and in these more secluded areas with private beach access.

I'm well aware of the success of Maddey's writing career, but I can't wrap my head around this being feasible.

That's an issue for another day.

The first order of business is to do a perimeter check. I need to have intimate knowledge of every point of weakness and where Maddey's vulnerabilities lie.

Yeah, maybe don't *use the words 'intimate knowledge' and 'Maddey' in the same sentence, at least not if you like your balls still attached to your body, Stone.*

This entire scenario has clusterfuck written *all* over it.

When Justin called to inform us Maddey had herself a stalker, both Tyler—her middle older brother and my fellow SEAL teammate—and I were ready to charge full steam ahead and destroy anyone who dared threaten the youngest member of the McClain clan.

The feeling only intensified when Justin went on to

explain how long it had actually been going on and how our little Tink was refusing all attempts at protection. I may have visualized wringing her pretty little neck.

Maddey doesn't just physically resemble the Disney pixie she earned her nickname from growing up; she has the temper to match, too.

I also know firsthand how damn stubborn she is. Her three older brothers have been my closest friends since birth, and obstinance is practically a chromosome in the McClain DNA. It doesn't help that she bucks their overprotectiveness any chance she gets.

Or that she can charm her way out of any situation to suit her needs. It's why I'm being brought in. I'm not a brother or an ex she can manipulate as she sees fit.

That's right, you're not *her brother. Good thing, bro, because the thoughts you've been having about her would be illegal if you were.*

Those thoughts are also why I've been keeping my distance more and more over the years. Madison Belle McClain has been like a little sister to me since she was born. Things were fine, chugging along as they always did, until they didn't.

Since the summer before Maddey started college, I haven't been able to see her as Baby McClain anymore. God, even eight years later, I can't shake the memory of that day.

She was playing football with her best friend Sammy and some of his teammates on the beach in an electric blue bikini. When she spotted me, she spiked the football like she was in the end zone, her short legs ate up the distance between us, and she launched herself into my arms, wrapping a body full of curves I'd never really noticed before around me.

I may have hugged her to me a little tighter and longer than necessary, but what man wouldn't when they have a half-naked woman in their arms? And from that day forward, that's how I saw her—as a woman.

Denying my attraction has been an issue ever since. Not a

good problem to have when you are one of the people who helped her brothers scare away any guy who came sniffing around her growing up.

Shaking off all inappropriate thoughts before they can take root, I focus on the task at hand. I learned early on in life never to underestimate the McClain men, so I have three weeks of consecutive leave to figure out who is stalking our girl. *Shit! Not* our *girl, Stone.*

Slamming the door to my truck harder than necessary, I round the hood to get started, hoping if I keep busy enough it will banish any thoughts that would get my ass kicked *Full Metal Jacket* style.

I start off with the front door, pleased to find it locked up tight. The same can be said for the garage and the doors leading to both the lower and upper decks wrapping around the house. *Good girl*, I think as each window check renders the same result.

As diligent as she is with her locks, Tink needs to learn to shut her drapes. Clear as day there she is amongst a kaleidoscope of colorful sea turtle bedding—she's always had a thing for sea turtles—one bare foot hanging out the side, a multitude of anklets adorning her ankle, including the Tinker Bell one I gave her years ago.

What the hell is she doing still sleeping at eleven in the morning?

Time for Sleeping Beauty to wake up. I just got here and already the Disney references are starting inside my head.

Making my way down to the main level, I key in the entry code and disengage the alarm. Stepping inside, I'm hit by just how much the space eclipses every fantasy she had for the perfect beach house growing up.

Later I'll take the time to appreciate the decor for more than the kitchen chairs painted in various bright colors and the sea glass pendants over the island.

Where's the pooch?

Jack McClain made sure Trident had extensive training to be a "guard dog" for his baby girl. He should have come barking his head off the moment the door opened.

On silent feet, I make my way upstairs. Surrounded by a riot of blonde curls, a crooked-lying Maddey takes up more space in the king-sized bed than any person barely over five feet tall should.

There is more bedding than human in the bed with her sheets, puffy comforter, and countless pillows, including the main one she has her arms wrapped around as she sleeps. It's been so long since I've seen her not through a computer screen, I can't help but take a moment to study her.

God she's beautiful.

Her blonde lashes fan across her cheeks, and her pouty lips have the tiniest pucker to them. She looks so peaceful I almost don't want to wake her—almost.

There's a rogue curl slashing across her face, and I give in to the urge to tuck it behind her ear. Hooking a finger under the silky locks, I brush the soft skin of her forehead on the way to setting them back in place.

Being lost in my own musing is the only excuse I have for what happens next. One minute I'm watching her sleep—not like a creeper…okay, maybe a little—wishing our circumstances were different, and the next there's a shooting current of pain in my balls and I'm convulsing on the floor.

Son of a bitch.

Chapter Three

P rior to the last eight months—when the first of my "gifts" showed up—I slept like the dead. Being able to sleep through pretty much anything less than a tornado blowing through the room came in handy those years I dated Ryan. The guy may be one of *People*'s sexiest men alive, but holy crap, as his brother Jase would say, "Homeboy's snores could wake the dead."

Honestly, the way he saws wood like a professional lumberjack is one of my favorite things about him. Ryan is so damn perfect in every other way, and I always thought it helped remind the world he actually *is* human.

Thanks to what I attribute to a heightened sense of self-preservation, I wake the instant I feel another's presence in my bedroom.

I know better than to react carelessly, and I continue to feign sleep until I have the best opening to evade whoever is creeping in my personal space.

Most people would automatically assume the person is any one of the number of people with the code for my house, but I'm able to rule out that possibility immediately—my people don't really grasp the concept of keeping quiet.

So, no. The person lurking on the side of the bed is foe, not friend.

Hidden beneath the fluff of my pillow, I shift my hand ever so slightly and stealthily until it's wrapped around the taser I keep under it.

Thumbing off the safety, I keep my finger over the on switch, waiting for just the right moment to strike.

The scent of the ocean fills my nostrils as the intruder moves closer. There's something familiar about it, but the haze of sleep hasn't lifted enough for me to place it.

A finger trails across my forehead and over my temple. Repressing a shudder of revulsion is harder than not rolling my eyes at Jase Donnelly, the most ridiculous human being on the planet.

I promise myself I'll bathe in a vat of Purell after this as a reward for my Oscar-worthy portrayal of a sleeping woman when this creep moves his finger down my cheek to tuck some hair behind my ear.

Now, Madz.

Keeping a firm hold on the hard plastic, I thrust my arm free, earning a grunt in response as I hit my target and shoot him with fifty thousand volts of electricity.

"Oof." Down he goes, and I'm already scrambling from the bed to press my thumb on the scanner of my bedside drawer to retrieve my gun.

I know my resistance to protection makes some batty, but *Hello people!* I'm not some defenseless damsel here. I've been taught self-defense and straight-up defensive tactics since I was single digits, and it's not like any of my teachers were your run-of-the-mill Joe Shmoe variety either. They have all been Navy SEALs, police officers, or professional MMA fighters.

I'm tiny but mighty, dammit.

With the comforting weight of my Smith & Wesson M&P

Shield in my hands, I sidestep around the end of my bed to the now rolling, cursing, and groaning intruder.

"Son of a *bitch*." The words barely come out distinguishable.

My chick Rapunzel wields a frying pan like a pro in *Tangled*, but I think I'll stick with my trusty 9mm. Shuffling my feet, I inch closer, keeping it trained on my target, prepared in case of attack.

The man, though large, poses zero threat while curled in the fetal position holding his family jewels.

Ooo, look at how his back muscles stretch his white t-shirt. They would look good on a cover. I must be more hard up than I realize because those are *not* the thoughts I should be having at the moment.

"Fuck me!" The slap of his hand beating my hardwood floor rings out, causing me to jump.

"Move and I shoot." He can't see me since he's still rocking in pain. "And I promise, I always shoot to kill." Not that I've ever shot at anything other than targets and beer bottles, but this asshole needs to know I mean business.

"Son—of—a—bitch."

Wait…

I know that voice.

Is that…

"Dex?"

"Fuck, Tink." Sure enough, it's Dexter Stone writhing in agony.

What is he doing here?

Ohmygod.

I just tased Dex in the balls.

It must be some type of karmic retribution or something to accidentally maim my childhood crush.

Seriously though—did I really just tase him? And in the balls, no less?

Holy shit. I couldn't make this shit up if I tried, and I write fiction for a living.

Easing my grip on the gun now that there's no threat, I let it fall to my side and drop to a knee next to his prone body. "Are you okay?"

He rolls to his back with a groan, his melted chocolate eyes rising to me with a *did you really just ask me that?* look.

"Dammit, Tink." Unlike when my brothers—and subsequently my other male friends—use my childhood nickname, it doesn't annoy me when Dex does. Sure it's probably—*definitely*—from residual puppy-love brain, but coming from him, it sounds like an endearment.

His hands still cup his package, and I wonder how he would react if I offered to kiss it better. *In your dreams, Madz.*

You got that right. I've lost count of the number of times I've dreamed about going down on Dex...him going down on me...us sixty-nine-ing...

Yeah, stop those thoughts right now, missy.

Oh, stuff it, Jiminy.

Yeah, don't be a prude.

We live *for the dirty details.*

Let's hear all *the ideas.*

Jesus. This is so not the time for me to get lost in my own head. Be a writer, they said. It's fun, they said. Yeah, well the part no one tells you is that your characters start to take on lives of their own and talk to you *all* day. It doesn't matter how inappropriate the time may be.

"You should know better than that, Hook." It's my turn to bust out the old-school nicknames. Even before he enlisted in the Navy, I always thought he had a roguish pirate appeal.

"Don't try to be cute right now." It's clearly meant to come out as a threat, but it falls flat with the hint of a whimper the words hold. "I think you just ruined my chances of ever making baby Dexes."

I rub my free hand over my heart as if the words are a

physical blow. Taking a hit to the chest from Vince, the current UFC's Light Heavyweight Champ and one of my closest friends, wouldn't hurt as much as the idea of Dex having children with some faceless woman.

Dramatic much? You've said so yourself—countless times, I might add—that you aren't in love with him either. So riddle me this, Batman…why does the thought of Dex making babies with someone else bother you so much?

Fucking Jiminy. Just because I was thinking of Vince, my conscience thinks it can go and hit me with one of his lines.

Can I ask something without you taking it out on me when you get to my book?

Even if she says no, you have to ask now.

Agreed.

You know how much I hate to agree with the cricket—*side-eyes Jiminy*—but you've never had a reaction like that about the idea of Ryan procreating.

"Come on, tough guy." I hold out a hand to help Dex up. "Let's go get you an ice pack for your booboo."

He growls, the sound hitting each one of my lady parts like a pinball ricocheting back and forth. Padded bras and panties are going to be a must for however long he's planning on being around if I'm going to have any hope of hiding the physical effects he has on me.

I thought you didn't do meaningless sex? I mean, isn't that the whole reason you haven't had sex in—

Shut. Up, I shout at Jiminy. I know *exactly* how long it has been since I've had sex with someone other than myself, thank you very much.

Shit!

You know what? I blame Dex for setting my hormones off. I may have gotten over my puppy love, but *damn* if he isn't one of my favorite tropes. Who doesn't love a good brother's best friend? Or in my case, brothers' best friend since he's close with all three of mine.

"Oh stop being a baby." I pop him in his hard, sculpted, can-he-please-take-his-shirt-off-so-I-can-properly-admire-it chest when we stand. "I feel like I should write a letter to the Navy because they *clearly* need to up what they put you through in BUD/S and SERE training if you're not able to just shake this off."

I blink innocently as I cant my head back to see his face. *Oooo, someone is mad.* He's all clenched scruffy jaw, flared nostrils, and narrowed eyes. Is it wrong that I want to poke fun?

"You. Tased. Me. In. The. Nuts."

I shrug and have to roll my lips in again to stop another laugh. Oh, I'm going to get some mileage out of this.

I duck, evading his arm when he reaches for me. I'm sure him still being slightly hunched over is the only reason I'm successful.

"I guess I should be grateful it wasn't this under your pillow?"

The delicious drag of his calloused fingers skimming down the back of my arm is distracting. It takes a moment for my imagination to stop running away with thoughts of his touch moving to my back, across my stomach up to my now heavy breasts—or even better, slipping underneath the band of my sleep shorts to cup my throbbing center.

Shit! Focus, Madison. He asked you a question.

Oh it's *never* good if I'm calling myself by my full name.

What did he ask?

Right—my gun.

"I would say so. You can barely handle a little electric shock—I shudder at the thought of your bitching if it was a bullet." I rub my arms, feigning being cold to drive my sarcasm home.

"Why'd I agree to do this?" He digs into the ridge of his brow with his thumb and the knuckle of his forefinger. "I forgot how much of a smartass you can be."

"I learned everything I know from you, scallywag." Scooping up the taser, I round my bed again to return both it and my gun to my bedside drawer, making sure the lock on the built-in safe beeps closed. I may sleep with one of them under my pillow, but I would never leave them out where anyone could stumble upon them.

"Wait." I turn to face him, folding my arms over my chest. *Did he just…?* I shake my head. *No, of course not. Except…* "Agree to what?" Every ounce of skepticism I feel bleeds into my words. Why do I feel like I might have put my gun away prematurely?

A set of twin parentheses brackets his kissable mouth as the first smile since I stunned him appears. Outside of making my lady parts bibbidi-bobbidi-boo, it also spells trouble.

"You didn't hear?" The joyful lilt in his voice has my gut clenching.

"Hear what?" I ask through gritted teeth.

"Oh, my dear Tink. I was called in to slay your dragon, or"—he tilts his head to the side—"in Hook's case…" His pause only adds to the butterflies filling my stomach. "Catch your crocodile."

Sonofabitch.

I need to ask Gemma for a recipe for frog legs, because I have some frogmen to murder.

Chapter Four

The Lost Boys Group Chat

DEX: Just to let you know, when my mom starts bitching at me for not being able to provide her grandchildren, I'm sending her your way, assholes.

CONNER: Puh-lease. You know I'm Peggy Stone's favorite.

TYLER: First off, why are we talking about your reproductive capabilities? Second, how is your lack of them our fault?

CONNER: Yeah, bro. Why are we to blame for you not being able to get it up?

DEX: I didn't say ANYTHING about not being able to get it up, thank you very much.

JUSTIN: That is more than I needed to know about your dick, bro.

DEX: Fuck you, Just. You're mostly at fault for me potentially never being able to procreate.

JUSTIN: The fuck I do?

DEX: I don't know…

DEX: Maybe you should have told Tink you asked me to help catch the asshat harassing her. Or you know…at least told her I would be arriving today.

TYLER: Oh shit.

CONNOR: You know what? Service is spotty over here in the Sandbox, think I might lose you guys.

JUSTIN: I'm afraid to ask…

JUSTIN: But I take it she was pissed?

DEX: PISSED?

DEX: Yeah, you could say that.

TYLER: Shit. I'm putting my phone on silent. Good luck with that, Just. At least there are 300+ miles between Tink and me. You're fucked, bro.

CONNOR: Never thought I'd see the day I'd prefer to be deployed, but shiiiiiit. Since Tink became friends with Jordan, our little sis has really upped her revenge skills.

JUSTIN: What did she do?

DEX: Oh, not much…

CONNOR: *GIF of John Stewart leaning forward saying, "Go on."*

TYLER: ^^This. Because I'm still trying to figure out the whole grandchildren angle?

DEX: Oh, I'll tell you, Ty.

DEX: Because Tink had NO IDEA *side-eyeing your punk ass, Just* I was coming, I didn't get the usual greeting of flying squirrel hug. Nope...today I got a taser to the balls.

TYLER: Oh shit!

CONNOR: *GIF of Mike Tyson cracking up*

CONNOR: You're fucked, Just.

Chapter Five

Turning on my heel, I flip the lock on the French doors of my bedroom and step out onto the upper deck, leaving Dex inside. I need to take a breath or I'm liable to reach for my taser and zap him again. Though it's entertaining to do so, he's not the one who should be subjected to my ire.

The Die Hard Trilogy—aka my brothers—better watch their six.

Gripping the railing in front of me, I take deep lungfuls of salty air, letting the gentle cadence of the waves crashing soothe my soul. This is my happy place, and I'm getting sick and tired of people trying to ruin it.

I can respect the impulse to keep me protected, but I don't appreciate the method. Who the hell am I kidding? There is not one thing about this I like, including the part where I was kept in the dark.

And why, for the love of all things Nora Roberts, is Dex the one sent to play protector?

He mentioned changing tactics to a more proactive approach and catching the creep who's invaded my life. If they all think I'm going to hide in an ivory tower while they do all the work, they are delusional.

First things first, I need to gather as much intel as possible.

I'm gonna need help. Time to call in my fellow Covenettes.

Shit. Where's my phone? Downstairs? Rookie mistake, Madz.

Avoiding facing Dex again, I use the stairs connecting to the lower deck and plug in the code for my house, leaving it unlocked for those who are actually invited.

From the Group Message Thread of The Coven

QUEEN OF SMUT (Maddey): *GIF of the Bat Signal*

MOTHER OF DRAGONS (Jordan): *GIF of a cartoon Batgirl dropping onto a roof*

MAKES BOYS CRY (Skye): *GIF of Batgirl from the 60s TV show turning with hands on hips*

ALPHABET SOUP (Rocky): *GIF of Alicia Silverstone's Batgirl*

PROTEIN PRINCESS (Gemma): *GIF of Batwoman*

YOU KNOW YOU WANNA (Becky): *GIF of Harley Quinn*

YOU KNOW YOU WANNA: ^^I'd much rather be her.

YOU KNOW YOU WANNA: Sorry not sorry.

THE OG PITA (Beth): Oh me too. Gotta appreciate a woman who's just a little bit crazy.

BROADWAY BABY (Melody): No wonder you recruited Zoey.

DANCING QUEEN (Zoey): HEY?!

BROADWAY BABY: Do I lie?

FIDDLER ON THE ROOF (Ella): Aren't you glad at least I'm normal, Mels?

SANTA'S COOKIE SUPPLIER (Holly): I feel like Vince has grounds to break up with me over not finding an appropriate Batgirl GIF response.

YOU KNOW YOU WANNA: Nah.

YOU KNOW YOU WANNA: Take your clothes off—he'll forget all about it.

THE OG PITA: *GIF of man pointing up saying, "This."*

DANCING QUEEN: You should get some Batman lingerie to make up for it.

ALPHABET SOUP: Can we not? I really don't like being involved in the discussion of sex clothes for my brother.

PROTEIN PRINCESS: I second this.

MAKES BOYS CRY: *bangs gavel* Motion passed.

THE SPIN DOCTOR (Sammy): Shit, it must be serious if I was included. I'm not always brought into the Coven Conversations.

MOTHER OF DRAGONS: We are literally the worst. *facepalm emoji* *squirrel emoji* Madz, what did you need?

QUEEN OF SMUT: Rally the troops. I need whoever is free to convene at my place.

YOU KNOW YOU WANNA: *rubs hands together* Oooo…what are we plotting?

DANCING QUEEN: Mels, you tell those boys to hustle up moving your stuff. A trip down the shore is in order again. We're missing out on all the fun.

FIDDLER ON THE ROOF: *GIF of Mickey Mouse throwing clothes in a suitcase*

FIDDLER ON THE ROOF: ^^See what I did there? Disney GIF just for you, Madz.

SANTA'S COOKIE SUPPLIER: Lyle wants to know if he could be of assistance, aka he's being a nosey Nelly.

QUEEN OF SMUT: The answer is YES!! We could use his partic-ular set of skills.

MAKES BOYS CRY: Wrong movie reference, Madz. You're *Die Hard*, not *Taken*.

With backup called in, it's time for the second thing needed to be able to handle the shit-show that's about to go down—coffee.

Grabbing my favorite blue *Tears of my Readers* mug, I pop in a pod of caramel coffee. It isn't until I'm stirring in my cream and sugar that Dex finally makes his way downstairs.

"Quasimodo doesn't suit you the way Hook does." I can't help but tease at his hunched posture.

"You're *sooo* funny, Tink."

"I know." I blow a kiss and toss a bag of frozen peas,

which he catches with ease. Even injured, his reflexes are impressive. "Now you sit there"—I point to my circular reading chair—"and ice the boys while I go put on some clothes."

"Because...what?" One of his dark brows rises, making him appear extra roguish. "The clothes you have on come from the emperor's collection?"

The nod to one of Tyler's favorite children's stories makes me giggle. I mean, I *am* an author—I love me a good literary reference.

No, the clothes I have on are very real, but I'd rather not deal with a houseful of people in a pair of skimpy boxer shorts and a faded BTU Titans hockey t-shirt.

Taking the stairs two at a time—a real feat when you're only five foot one—I make a beeline for my room. In under two minutes, I'm changed into a pair of denim cutoffs, a sports bra—padded, of course, because it seems my nipples like to do their best impression of a pop-up turkey timer whenever Dex is around—and a Disney tank that reads *I'm a Disney Princess, unless the Avengers need me.*

These boys need a reminder that I can take care of myself.

Chapter Six

Thank god no one is around to witness my embarrassment. The whole holding a bag of frozen vegetables to your junk thing kind of clashes with the tough Navy SEAL image I'm known for.

No sooner do I finish thinking this than a flood of people enter Maddey's house.

Unsurprisingly, Trident is the first to notice me, and Navy, Jordan's black lab, follows close behind. There's a chocolate lab—I think his name is Stanley—milling around too. He's not as concerned as the other two, leaving me be as the other two try to inhale me with how intensely they sniff me.

An earsplitting whistle rings out, followed by Maddey shouting, "Boys, leave Dex alone. He's...*injured*." The way she snickers around the word makes me want to put her over my knee and spank her.

Fucking hell. I *cannot* think like that.

Protecting Maddey won't be an issue. Neither will figuring out who her stalker is once and for all.

Nope, the problem for me will be keeping my dick in my pants. I don't even want to contemplate what the Die Hard Trilogy would do to me if I don't. You know how in the movies, the geeks get shoved into lockers? Ever seen it happen to a giant lacrosse player? I have, when Danny Baker made the mistake of commenting on how hot Maddey looked in front of Tyler in the locker room after lacrosse practice.

Why do I feel like I should be turning in my trident?

The dogs obediently do as they're told, lying down on the nautical-themed dog beds spread around the room, while two blonde-haired toddlers I recognize as Jordan Donnelly-Donovan's (no, she didn't actually hyphenate) climb on their backs.

Female after female filters in, each exchanging a hug and a kiss with Maddey before making herself at home, the once quiet house now a hubbub of activity.

They may be talking a mile a minute, but outside of exchanging hellos with those who greet me, I stay silent. You can learn so much by sitting back and being a spectator. Plus…they are *a lot* to take in.

It still amazes me that Maddey, the girl who barely had any actual *female* friends growing up, now has an entire—and very aptly named—coven of them. The Tink of the past is almost unrecognizable now, though not in the sense of having changed *who* she is. No, she's still the same bubbly, charming, you just want to be closer to her because she makes you happy type of person, but now she's…more.

Fuck. This was a mistake. My ass should have never left Virginia Beach. I know, I know—there was no way I *wasn't* coming with her in trouble.

The things the Admiral in my pants wants to do to her are going to get me into more trouble than all the not-Geneva-Convention-friendly things I want to do to her stalker once I get my hands on him, and I *will* get my hands on him. This fucker has harassed her long enough. This is one mission I will not fail to complete.

"How are the boys doing?" Maddey perches on the armrest of the chair, her long blonde curls tumbling around her face as she peers down at me.

I'm *never* living this down.

"We haven't heard anything, so I'm guessing they're still alive," Jordan answers, walking in with what I'm guessing is her newest baby strapped to her chest. It's been a while since she's been around during my video calls with Tyler and Maddey.

Whenever I first see the two of them together, I have to do a double take. There are enough similarities between them that they could be mistaken for sisters, but Jordan has never made me feel like I'm trying to smuggle a rocket launcher in my pants like Maddey does.

"Not the boys I was referring to." Maddey points to Jordan with a wink. "But maybe we *should* check in with them."

"On it," a voice calls out from somewhere else in the house.

"I was asking about his"—she points to the bag of frozen veggies—"boys. I kinda"—she closes her thumb and fore-finger until they are barely an inch apart—"tasered him in the bro-varies earlier."

"Shit, Madz—*bro-varies*? That better be in a book," someone says.

"You know it is, Beck." The smirk dancing at the corners of her kissable lips tells me she's laughing at my expense, even if she's not doing it out loud.

I'm really starting to question my decision-making skills. Agreeing to protect the youngest McClain without her being informed of the plan might end up being more dangerous to my health than hunting insurgents.

Skye, Maddey's other college roommate, saunters into the room, wiggling onto the armrest next to Maddey. "Did you really tase him in the balls?" she asks out of the side of her mouth.

"Yup," Maddey says with pride, and I press back into the

Writing Dirty   29

soft cushions underneath me to keep from kissing the beaming smile off her face.

Fuck me.

Yup, definitely not making it out of this alive. If I do, I doubt I'll have my recently jumpstarted family jewels still attached. Locker-stuffing was child's play compared to what the Die Hard Trilogy could come up with after being trained by the military.

Skye winces, but like with Tink, there's zero remorse in it. I swear these women are enjoying my pain.

"That can't have felt good." And yup, there's definitely an evil twinkle in the strawberry blonde's blue eyes.

"Well it didn't tickle," I grumble.

Another wave of laughter flows through the group and I grind my teeth in frustration, knowing it's at my expense. My fellow Lost Boys are dead. D-E-A-D.

"I can take a look if you want." Rocky joins us, because there definitely weren't enough people involved in the conversation already. Seriously people, is nothing sacred? Talk about sinking a guy's battleship.

"Blue." Gage—Rocky's giant, UFC Heavyweight Champion husband—growls, coming up behind her and wrapping an arm around her middle. Dude is huge, and coming from a guy who has gone through what most people would say is the toughest special operations training in the world, even I wouldn't want to mess with him.

Like Jordan, Rocky is also sporting a baby on her chest, this one slightly newer than Jordan's latest addition. Maddey jumps to her feet, liberating the baby from his blue octopus-printed wrap.

The sight of her cradling the dark-haired baby against her does funny things to my chest, specifically the heart region, and hearing her coo how he's "such a good nephew" doesn't help. If she can be this way with a baby who isn't technically a blood relative, I can only imagine how amazing she would be with our son.

Shit!

Did I just say *our*?

I'm so fucked. Aircraft-carrier-sized fucked.

"Relax, Champ." Rocky spins in Gage's embrace and wraps her arms around his neck, pressing her body against him now that there's no longer a tiny human in the way. "I only meant in the professional capacity." She places kisses to the underside of his jaw, and I kind of feel like a voyeur watching the intimacy of the act.

Shifting my attention back to the evil pixie, I rap on Maddey's knee. "You and I need to talk."

"*Ooo*, so ominous, Hook." Her dimples peek out as if to say *Don't be mad—you know you're charmed by us.* I hate that they aren't wrong.

"Madison," I growl.

"Relax." She waves me off, not the least bit intimidated. "Don't go around full-naming me, *Dexter*."

It's cute how she thinks using mine proves some kind of point. I level her with a look that has made many a sailor quiver in their boots.

"Fine," she huffs when I don't give her the reaction she wants. "Come with me."

Gingerly, I rise from my seat, handing off the peas to a smirking Skye, and follow Maddey upstairs, leaving the rest of her squad to fend for themselves.

The wall along the stairs has a gallery-worthy display of photos. The crazies from downstairs are featured in them, but what surprises me is my own presence in several of the images.

I may have kept my distance physically from Maddey by not returning home much through the last handful of years, but that hasn't meant I've been absent from her life. Tyler was always dragging me into their video chats, and her friends downstairs rotated through most of them.

This display is a visual representation of all the things Maddey holds dearest in her heart. Each picture of me is a shot in the feels.

I snort when I spot one of us from Halloween almost twenty years ago. Maddey is dressed as Tink, me as Hook, and Tyler drew the short straw of having to don tights to be Peter Pan while Connor and Justin got away with dressing as Lost Boys. Ah…you just realized how we got our nickname?

I'll need to remember to spend some time looking over the rest later.

Passing bedrooms and bathrooms has me wondering again how she's able to afford so much house. At the end of the hall, she turns left, not to the right for her bedroom.

Curious, I step into the room, not at all prepared for what I see. Like her bedroom, one whole wall is made of glass, with the same French doors leading to the attached deck. In the corner is a chrome and glass desk with a large hot pink leather chair behind it.

Another wall comprises three large white bookshelves filled with copies of her books and what I'm sure are some of her favorites. There are Funko Pop! dolls along with mugs and frames of modern Disney pop art.

Holy shit! She has cardboard cutouts of the guys, and even a Team USA hockey jersey signed by the entire Olympic roster.

Maddey heads for the dove gray couch on the wall opposite her desk, leaving me to inspect her inner sanctum without comment.

This space couldn't be more her if it tried.

Looking at Maddey sitting on the couch, one leg bent under her, a throw pillow with *Just one more chapter* written on it hugged to her middle, and framed pictures of all her book covers in an artful collage on the wall behind her, the pride I feel for her is staggering.

With the hitch in my step finally gone, I make my way over. My arm drapes over the back of the couch as I angle myself to face her, our close proximity making my body hum.

We sit in silence, each waiting for the other to be the one to break it, both of us having been taught you learn more by holding your tongue.

For all her earlier bravado, the longer we sit, the more her cracks start to appear. There's a little V between her blonde brows, the corners of her blue eyes have a slight squint, and I'd recognize that McClain clenched jaw anywhere. She's pissed, but it's the way her fingers pick at the seams of the pillow that tells me she's scared too.

She's put up a good front, not wanting to seem weak in a family made up of tough military men, I'm sure, but what she doesn't realize is being scared and asking for help when some creep starts sending you "gifts" doesn't make you weak.

There's a reason SEALs operate in teams and the US military has a no-man-left-behind policy. Time to teach her why.

Chapter Seven

ight months.

That's how long I was able to bury my head in the sand, pretending nothing was wrong and I could take care of myself.

I must have put up a good front, because it's only now that the kid gloves have come off and Justin has called in the big guns. Guess having your stalker send things to your home instead of your PO box changes things.

Who knew?

Silence stretches, and if my Jiminy really were a cricket manifestation of my conscience like Pinocchio's, he would be chirping his ass off right now.

I like the strong silent type as much as the next girl, and holy hell, don't even get me started on alpha men—that and alphaholes are all I write—but I have a feeling I'm going to be itching for my taser *a lot* while Dex is here.

Well played, Justin.

My pain-in-the-ass, *I know he means well but I still want to punch him* brother *had* to go and call the *one* person who has never backed down from challenging me or been charmed into indulging my whims.

Sammy, my oldest and dearest friend? Yup, I totally played that card to keep him from pushing me.

Ryan? We've had a number of fights about what I should do, but I know just what buttons to push with him to maintain my independence.

Paul, Justin's SWAT partner, was the easiest to turn down. Plus, I'm pretty sure he just offered in an effort to keep the peace between my brother and me.

Nope, Dexter Stone only ever does what he wants, and no flashing of dimples or puppy dog eyes will sway him. Hell, even the Halloween costume he wore in the picture I caught him looking at of when he dressed as Captain Hook was one he donned willingly, practically saying, "Hell yeah I'll be a badass pirate." Well…without the *badass* part, because he was nine and Peggy Stone—always Peggy Stone, never just Peggy —would have smacked him for cursing.

Tap-tap-tap-tap.

His fingers drum pinky to forefinger on the back of the couch, waiting me out.

Tap-tap-tap-tap.

My nose twitches like a bunny with the effort of not being the first to break.

Tap-tap-tap-tap.

I will *not* be the one to give in. No, nope, not happening.

Tap-tap-tap-tap.

I drop my gaze, unable to look into his chocolatey eyes without melting. They have always been one of my favorite features on him, even when he would scoff and say they were doo-doo brown.

Instead I focus on the bend of his knee…except I get more distracted the longer I look. The hems of his shorts are pulled taut, stretched by the hard muscles of his thighs, the tan material scrunched across the tops of them from sitting.

Do not look at his dick, Madz. Do not *do it.*

I look at his dick.

What? It's not my fault. The wrinkles in the khaki are like bookends to his package. See? Fashion is to blame.

Plus, I haven't had sex in a long time—a *really* long time, like I'm practically revirginized and the only thing keeping my hymen from growing back is my vibrator.

Not gonna lie, I hate my friends just the *tiniest* bit when they tell me how they need to jump their men after reading one of my sex scenes. I mean, I love them dearly and having people love my words is *everything*, but my water bill is a bit out of control with the amount of quality time I spend with my shower massager.

I feel like I should write a thank you note to Uncle Sam for the body he helped mold with the rigorous special ops training. Holy hell, the way Dex's white t-shirt is stretched across his muscles is practically indecent.

Where's a bucket of water when a girl needs it?

I wonder if I could convince the guys to have a wet t-shirt contest under the guise of needing teaser pictures.

Yes please.

I'm all for you filming your own 'Guys Gone Wild' type video.

Who needs a bucket when we're friends with Wyatt James? Beth would totally ask her husband to spray them all down with one of those fire hoses.

Firemen—more men in uniform…

You might want to check your chin—you have some drool going on.

Not wanting Dex to think I'm checking him out—I mean I am, but I don't need him knowing it—I shift my focus to the ink decorating his right arm.

The short sleeve of his shirt prevents me from seeing where enlarged stars of the American flag start, but I can see where they wrap around his arm to his elbow while the stripes of Old Glory continue down to his wrist.

The head of an eagle follows the contour of his shoulder, displayed proudly on the front of his bicep. With his arm bent to rest on his leg, I can see the frog skeleton climbing up the inside of his bicep on the other side, which he got in remembrance of a fallen teammate.

He rolls his wrist, the joint cracking from the movement. Whoever did his artwork in Virginia is extremely talented, the flag waving and rippling like it's blowing in the wind with the sinew of his forearm.

Every time I've seen Dex—which hasn't been a whole lot in the last few years except through a computer screen—he's had more added.

I catch a flash of something inside the ink, and I reach out and grab his arm as if on instinct. Smoothing my thumbs over the area, I take in the pirate's hook piercing the flag. My gaze snaps to his even as my thumbs trace the most notable feature of Captain Hook.

"What?" A devilish smirk quirks Dex's lips when he meets my gaze. "You couldn't be the only one to bear their nickname."

I suck in a breath when he ghosts his thumb over the miniature silhouette of Tinker Bell at the top of my collarbone and the words *She flies by her own wings* trailing like fairy dust at an angle down the line of the bone.

My body is all *Nants ingonyama bagithi Baba* like it's the beginning of *The Lion King*, and my heart is beating faster than fairy's wings while my characters are screaming, *He's touching us, he's touching us!*

I'm in trouble here. Big, *big* trouble.

Neither one of us has removed our hands, both our touches lingering. The part of me that used to believe I loved Dexter Stone is belting out the words to "Part of Your World" better than Ariel.

But the older, cynical part of me shuts that side up as effectively as the sea witch who stole the mermaid's voice.

All at once, Dex blinks away the glaze in his eyes, drops his hand as if burned, and clears his throat.

"Alright, Tink." The change that comes over him as he straightens in his seat is staggering. "Tell me what's been going on"—he holds up a finger, stopping the lie of 'Nothing' before I can utter it—"and don't even *think* of leaving anything out."

A puff of air escapes as I squish the pillow into me. I don't want to have this conversation. I've avoided it with everyone else, but the steely look in his eyes tells me that ship has sailed like the Jolly Roger.

"Didn't Justin tell you?" I hedge, avoiding the topic as long as possible.

"Yes." He nods. "But I want to hear it from you. I have a feeling you haven't admitted to everything."

Damn him.

"Let's hear it, Tink."

I want to tell him about what has been going on as much as Merida wanted to get married—as in I don't. Nobody likes to be confronted with their stupidity, and I can admit, at least to myself, that withholding information was dumb. In my defense, I spent my entire life having my brothers and Dex overprotect me, emphasis on the *over*. I didn't want to let some creep make me lose the independence I've cultivated the last handful of years.

Even if it could cost you your life, Madz?

I hate when I have to admit Jiminy raises a valid point.

Slumping against the pillows behind me, I blow out a breath and pull on my big girl panties. This princess may not need Prince Charming to save her, but a swashbuckling pirate could come in handy.

"It started out innocently enough, little gifts sent to my PO box, and at first I didn't think anything of it."

"Why not?" Dex's tone is hard, more command than question.

"I've gotten things from readers before. It's one of the reasons I have the box."

"What happened to make you think these…*gifts*"—he struggles with the word—"were different than the others?" The lack of judgment I hear makes it easy for me to continue.

"They started to get too personal, too Maddey McClain and not Belle Willis."

"Tell me about the progression."

Is it wrong that I think this whole detective vibe he has going on is hot?

"First it was about once a month. Then every few weeks. Eventually they stopped coming to the box, and instead something would show up at Espresso Patronum or The Steele Maker." It was a little scary to receive packages when I was writing at Lyle and Kyle's coffee house and the gym where the fighters train.

"What about the cops?"

"We filed a report." *See? I'm not a* complete *moron.* "Dad called in a few favors since it's technically not his jurisdiction, but all the packages turned out to be dead ends."

"What about Justin and Paul?"

"Same thing. One, it's not their jurisdiction, and two, neither of them are detectives." It's my turn to stop the next question. "I'm pretty sure Jamie has some of his security detail trying to find out what they can."

"Sammy's husband?"

I nod.

"Okay." He inhales deeply, and I shamelessly watch the way his chest expands, the shadow of the Budweiser tattoo showing through the cotton.

"Here's what we're gonna do." Dex's voice breaks me from my musings. "First, I want to see the one that got sent here." He points down, indicating my home. Again, I should be focusing on the seriousness of the conversation, but instead I'm captivated by how realistic his tattoo is.

What? I have a thing for ink. Don't judge me. Plus,

remember, I told you it's been a *long* time. And Dex? Well, he's pretty much my OG fantasy.

Yes, lick that ink!

Lick it?

Why not? Wouldn't you?

*Well... *shrugs with a nod* Yeah, you're probably right, I would.*

It's not even Thursday. It's like a bonus.

Tattoo Thursday is my favorite day of the week.

"Tink." There's a hint of amusement bleeding into his tone. He may not know what I'm thinking about, but he's well aware of how easily I squirrel-brain.

My cheeks puff out with a frustrated exhalation and I drop my head to the back of the couch, peering up at him through my lashes.

Listen up, universe—you and I are about to have some words, because this shit just isn't funny anymore.

There is not a color-coded to-do list big enough to help me manage my fucked-up life.

Creepy stalker whose identity and actual end goal we cannot figure out? We'll put him in red.

Irrational guilt that likes to creep in from time to time due to breaking a good man's heart? Blue for that one.

Sexual frustration from lack of sex due to previously mentioned guilt? A big ol' orange highlight.

Whatever. I'm a big girl. Give me coffee and I can handle anything.

So what changed that means the universe and I are going to have words?

Well I'll tell you.

The universe is using karma as a beta reader, and that bitch is giving her all kinds of notes on how to up the angst in my life. And what does the universe do?

Oh, just decides the person I'm going to be forced into close proximity with for my protection is the man who inspires lust so strong it fucks with everything else I have going on. It's truly the only reason I can think of for why I'm allowing *him* to stay on as protector when I've bucked everyone else.

I was only seven years old when the way I saw Dexter Stone changed.

We were at a playground near our house when a group of fifth graders decided to bully me. Seeing as at twenty-six years old I'm the height of your average twelve-year-old, at age seven my bullies seemed like massive giants.

Sammy and I were on the swings, and they wanted mine. I was pushed off and my arm hit a rock on my way down, resulting in a gash from elbow to wrist.

Dex saw what happened and rushed over before my brothers even had a chance to back him up. Did he care that the kids were two years older and bigger than he was? Nope. He went full-on *yippee-ki-yay* when I was pushed off the swings.

My little Disney-loving heart saw him going all Prince Phillip slaying Maleficent or Prince Eric fighting Ursula and I was done. D-O-N-E, done.

Unfortunately, puppy love does not equate to me singing about how I can go the distance like Hercules.

So let me ask you this: how the hell is a girl supposed to meet her deadlines when she's dealing with all this?

"Damn." Dex's manly chuckle does all kinds of things to my girly bits. "I lost you already." He taps a finger to the middle of my forehead. "Come back from Neverland, Tink."

I swat his hand away with a curl to my lips. I hate and love that he is so well versed in Disney knowledge. Not even Sammy uses Disney-speak with me the way Dex does.

"What?" I ask, and he arches a dark brow. "You said first, so I can only assume you have a list of what you need. Let's hear it. What else do you need to keep me from walking the plank?"

He scrubs a hand over his face in an attempt to quell what I'm sure is the urge to laugh again. While he wages a battle with his amusement, I fight one against the drive to rub myself against the stubble I hear scratching his palm.

Is it soft? Prickly?

Would it take away from the soft pillows of his lips when we kiss?

How would it feel between my thighs?

Aaaand holy Dory I seriously need to learn how to stay on topic.

Nemo isn't the only thing we need to find; my self-control seems to be missing too.

I call back my wayward thoughts and hormones like Snow White calling to her animal helpers and settle in to listen to Dex's plan.

Why do I get the feeling my stalker might be the least of my problems?

Chapter Eight

Dex

I n the last hour, I've learned more about Maddey's stalker from the things she *hasn't* said than those she has. It's cute how she thinks she's spinning me this tale of overreaction to an overzealous fan and that she's fine.

Yeah, right.

She can't even fool herself—she has no hope of fooling me.

Her shoulders were hunched when she looked over all the items she'd received, and I had to put my hands in the pockets of my cargo shorts to keep from massaging the tension away.

I about punched the wall when she flinched at the loud bang heard from downstairs. She's spooked, even if she won't admit it.

Justin may have called me because Maddey has a better chance of getting Trident to meow than of talking me out of protecting her, and yes, one of the qualifications I completed with my SEAL training was in High-Threat Protective Security—but those things aren't what's really important.

The simple truth is I've been protecting her for the majority of my life, and I don't see any reason to stop now.

Schoolyard bullies? *Pfft*, piece of cake.

Guys who only wanted to get into her pants? It's not my fault their pansy asses were too scared to challenge me and her brothers.

Participated in the Die Hard Trilogy's stay-away-from-our-sister interventions? More than a dozen times.

All those were handled when I was still a punk-ass kid. Now? Well the US government has invested quite a bit of money to make sure I can handle myself in the most godawful situations, and even more to enable me to protect heads of state if needed.

At five foot one, this curly-haired blonde with eyes such a pale blue they remind me of Genie, the husky I had growing up—and yes, before you ask, Maddey did name him—should be a piece of cake. Yeah, maybe if that cake was last year's stale fruitcake.

She can't sway me from playing bodyguard, but she damn sure charms me every other way possible. My carefully crafted plan of keeping my distance just hit an IED.

Madison Belle McClain might very well be the death of me.

"Enough." Maddey steps back from the desk we spread everything out on, burying her hands in her hair, making the curls flounce about.

Her nickname may be derived from a pixie, but her hair has always made me think of mermaids the way it cascades around her to the dip at her waist. It's long and lush, the perfect length to wrap around my hands, holding on while I drive myself in—

Are you out of your fucking mind, Stone? My conscience scolds me before I can complete the lustful thought.

Fuck! She tased me; I don't even want to imagine what the Die Hard Trilogy would come up with if they ever caught wind of the majority of my spank bank material.

The tasing may not be an experience I want to repeat any

time soon—or ever—but I'm so damn proud of Tink's instincts.

"I can't take any more of this." She waves a hand over the desk. "I'm going downstairs to see what Gemma cooked."

"Tink." We aren't done here.

"Don't." She cuts me an icy glare. "You're just going to make me go over it again with Justin and Paul later. I'm done for now."

"Maddey." I don't want her running away from this anymore. She needs to confront it.

"Dex." She folds her arms over her chest, pushing up her cleavage in a mouth-watering display.

Shit! Get your mind out of the gutter before you get us sent to the brig, sailor. She's Baby McClain, not some frog hog.

Life was so much easier when I *only* saw her as Baby McClain and not a…woman. Fuck me I'm screwed.

"Maddey." Her name comes out gruffly, my voice rough from barely restrained lust.

"Dex," she singsongs back, not intimidated in the least.

Damn if her internal fire isn't the most attractive thing about her. Yeah, yeah, she's all curves made to hold on to, big blue eyes worthy of any of her beloved Disney princesses, and pouty lips begging to be kissed—but it's her spunk that makes me want to go AWOL just so I can spend my days getting into all kinds of shenanigans. It's why with each chant of our names, the small distance between us has diminished to scant inches.

"Hook, if you don't channel your inner Elsa and let this go so I can eat, *you*"—she arches a blonde brow in challenge— "are really going to be walking the plank."

She turns on her heel, proving once again that she doesn't give a fuck that I'm bigger, stronger, faster, and a whole lot deadlier than her.

"You may not have come home all that much in the last few years"—that's a dig if I've ever heard one—"but in case you need the reminder, I get hangry if I'm not properly fed."

No truer words have ever been spoken. I even spotted the warning sign she has hanging in her kitchen.

Hangry (han-gree) adj. A state of emotional turmoil caused by extreme hunger; a lack of food resulting in a negative change in personality and possible angry outbursts.

Experience with such outbursts has me throwing an arm around her shoulders—and if I enjoy the feel of her body snuggled against mine a bit too much, we just won't mention it to her brothers—and lead us downstairs.

I didn't think it was possible, but the noise volume has increased in the time we were gone. Rounding the corner into the open-concept back of the house, I can see why—the number of people has doubled.

"Oh, Gem, it smells *amazing* in here," Maddey gushes, heading straight for the kitchen island.

The sweet and tangy scent of peppers and onions fills the house along with the sizzle of chicken cooking on the skillet across the stove's burners.

"She made *fajitas*!" says Holly, one of the newer additions to their Coven, snapping her fingers and gesturing with her arms like a flamenco dancer.

Maddey giggles, the sound melodic and doing funny things to my insides. "Is that your first *Friends* reference of the day, Hol?"

"Yeah right." Gemma scoffs. "It's already after noon—she has to be close to three or four by now." She makes up a plate and hands it to a salivating Maddey. Perks of having a personal chef as a friend.

"Dex! Bro." Sammy beams when he spots me, coming over to pull me into a back-slapping hug, the force of it knocking the breath from my lungs. It may have been years since his high school football days, but he hasn't lost any of his linebacker build, that's for sure.

"Hey, Samz." I return the welcoming embrace. He and Maddey have been attached at the hip since forever. Naturally, we grew close as well.

Honestly, if not for the fact that he and Maddey have the same taste in men, I wouldn't have been surprised if they had gotten married.

"What the hell are you doing here?" Taking his life in his hands, he reaches over Maddey's shoulder and takes a pepper off her plate.

"Oh, you know…" Maddey waves a hand in the air. "The Die Hard Trilogy brought him in to play bodyguard."

The glare she sends me has my balls tingling in both the *Holy crap she's sexy* and the *Shit, she's gonna tase us again* way.

"Oh, that's hot," Lyle says.

"Ooo, can we read a bodyguard romance for book club next?" Becky bounces over to lean across the counter. The Admiral in my pants salutes the suggestion, but as she is the eternal troublemaker of The Coven, he should be wary of where it's coming from.

Sammy ignores them, instead turning to ask me, "They did, did they?" He arches a brow, decades of knowing Tink giving him a good idea of how well that went down.

"Yup," Maddey answers with annoyance.

This whole scenario is going to be an uphill battle, and Maddey's stubbornness? Yeah, it's going to turn it into a full-on ruck run.

"Man," Sammy whistles. "What I wouldn't give to have been here when you told her that." His gaze shifts back to me. "Did she yell?"

"She tased me in the balls," I deadpan.

"Oh shit." Sammy coughs, sputtering through his laughter. The rest of the room experiences a similar reaction while Maddey continues to eat like it's just another day.

"If you need any help with them, I volunteer as tribute,"

Lyle calls out from where he's coloring with the Donovan twins.

"Kyle, get his travel cage." Skye snickers at Lyle's innuendo.

Personally, I find Lyle *highly* entertaining. He's always reminded me of Jack from *Will and Grace* whenever he would crash the video chats Maddey took at his coffee shop.

"But he's just so cute." Kyle kisses Lyle on the cheek.

"Do you offer your ball-handling services to all the guys?" Holly takes the spot on the couch across from them.

"Only until they're taken." Lyle gives Holly a wink. "Don't worry, Sweets—I'll leave Vince's in your very *capable* hands."

"Just try to keep it out of the kitchen, will ya?" There's a teasing tilt to Kyle's lips.

"Did *nobody* think to tell me it was Dex Madz was with upstairs?" Sammy's complaint is brushed off without any concern from the ladies.

Maddey spins on her stool, a smile peeking around the edges of the fajita shoved in her mouth as she looks around her house full of crazy. Then those icy eyes rise to me, and the slight narrowing at the corners tells me all I need to know.

I'm in big fucking trouble.

Chapter Nine

The way Dex's dark eyes flare when he meets the *Be afraid, be very, very afraid* death glare I send his way has a kernel of satisfaction blooming in my belly, but I'm still too fucking pissed to enjoy it.

Of all the highhanded, overprotective, always thinking they know best things my brothers could have done, calling in Dex takes the cake.

I get it. Really, I do.

I haven't been the most receptive—okay, I haven't been receptive at *all* when it comes to suggestions on what to do about my...situation, but to just bring someone in without my consent...

For that person to be Dex—*DEX!*

Holy crap. I don't even want to contemplate what this means.

A familiar weight settles against my leg, and I drop a hand down to scratch Trident behind his ear. My boy is always able to sense when I need his comfort.

Rehashing everything with Dex has to have been one of my least favorite things I've done this year. It's a miracle I'm able to eat right now, but...

1. It's Gemma's cooking.

2. It's fajitas.

3. It's food, and I'm *starving*.

"Oh, man. I'm missing fajitas?" I spin the rest of the way on my stool to see Tucker's pouting face on my television. Guess they decided video chat was the best way to check on the progress the guys were making.

"Yup." I shove another bite of spicy chicken goodness into my gullet. "Soooo good," I mumble.

"Save me some?" He perks up.

"Not likely."

"Madz." This time there's a whine to go with the pout. "Come on. You know I'm your favorite."

I slap a hand over my face when a piece of pepper burns my sinuses from snorting it out my nose.

"Yeah right, Tuck." Sammy leans on the counter next to me, folding his arms across his chest. "You don't even make top five with Madz."

"Blondie." Tucker scans the room for Jordan, looking for backup.

"Sorry, BB3." Jordan shrugs, baby Logan sleeping through the movement. "Madz has three big brothers of her own, and he who would be BB4 already took a taser to the balls when he got here. Do you *really* want to see what she would do if you tried to be her BB5?"

Tucker hisses and covers his junk as if protecting himself from receiving similar treatment.

"Damn, Madz. No wonder you dated Cap—you are a full-on Black Widow badass."

I shift my gaze to where Dex settled himself at my kitchen table, giving him a *See? I can take care of myself* glare. I probably shouldn't like how he meets it with a *Nice try, never gonna happen, Tink* one right back.

Damn this man for never backing down from me.

"Do you guys have a lot left to move?" Jordan asks, voicing the question that was the true reason for the call.

"We're done." Cali, Jase's teammate and neighbor, pops his head over the back of the couch to answer. "My brother-husbands and I are highly efficient."

There's a collective eye roll at that statement.

"Not sure if efficient is the correct word to use, Cali," Jase's girlfriend Melody says from somewhere off camera.

"Then why use us, Broadway? You act like my man can't afford to hire movers for you."

"Not to stroke your ego or anything." Zoey, Melody's best friend, steps up beside Cali, running a hand down his arm like there is *something* else she'd like to stroke.

The sexual tension between those two is the type of thing that burns the pages in the books I write. Already I'm twitchy to take notes.

"Oh, ZoZo, you can *stroke* anything on me you like."

See what I mean?

"I bet, big guy." Every set of eyes in my house is locked on the screen like we're watching the latest episode of *The Bachelor*. "But if we hired movers, we would have no guarantee what they looked like, and you boys are just so nice to look at without your shirts on."

Amen to that.

I might not want to actually sleep with the two trouble-makers on the screen, but anyone with lady parts—and those in the room who swing their way—can appreciate every inch of hard, hockey-hunk muscle on display.

I use them as cover models for a reason.

Which reminds me...

"Cali." I stand up and move closer to my television.

"Maddey." He beams ear to ear. "What's cookin' good lookin'?"

I'm surrounded by the most ridiculous people on earth, and I wouldn't change a second of it.

"You're still coming down this week right?"

"Yup. Coming with the brother-husbands when we leave here." He casts an uncertain look over his shoulder before turning back and dropping his voice. "Though I gotta say, if Griff weren't such a loyal Storm fan, I'd be afraid he'd kick my ass for you pairing me with Simone."

I shrug, not even sorry for a second. Sure, when my photographer takes my cover and teaser photos, I try not to split up the existing couples if they are letting me use them as models. Every now and then, though, I have to. Plus, it's not like Cali is going to be macking down on Griff's girlfriend Simone. He'll live...I think.

By the time Justin and Paul arrive, I've worked up one hell of a mad.

Since we came downstairs almost two hours ago, I haven't spoken to Dex. Well, not with words. My eyes? Those have read a freaking novel to him.

I anticipate a late night of writing with at least one character getting killed off. I already feel bad for the beating my keyboard is going to take as I work out my frustrations.

Not it. *puts finger on tip of nose*

I'm your favorite, remember?

Any time you write a scene with me in it, the words flow. Please, please keep that in mind.

"Dex, my brother," Justin calls out, his tone slightly more subdued than it'd normally be when greeting him after being apart. I have a feeling Dex already clued him in on what went down when he arrived and Justin is worried about retaliation —especially since I've been radio silent.

There's lots of back-slapping, bro-hugging, and macho-man-love. Through the years, it's been hard to pinpoint which one of my brothers Dex is closest with. He falls between Tyler and Connor in age and is teammates with Tyler, but he and Justin have always had a special bond.

The fact that Justin called Dex in to help is proof enough of how highly he thinks of his friend.

Land meets sea as Justin's green eyes catch mine over one of Dex's broad, drool-worthy shoulders. He may be a big, badass retired Navy SEAL turned SWAT officer, but I catch the slight flinch at my chilly gaze.

There are snorts, snickers, and giggles from the room as they witness the exchange.

Plus an "Oh shit" from Rocky and an "It's about to go down" from Skye.

Followed by "Gem, make some popcorn" from Becky.

I tune it all out and wait for my brother to make the first move. As pissed as I am, I'm curious to see how he's going to play this out.

"Tink," Justin starts, taking a step in my direction.

My brows rise at his attempt to use my nickname, and he falters in his approach.

"Madz," he tries again.

I fold my arms over my chest and narrow my eyes.

"Maddey."

My nostrils flare, each casual brushoff stoking the flames of my ire.

Don't punch him. Sure, he might deserve it, but he is *still your brother and he* was *only looking out for you.*

Jiminy can take a page from Elvis and leave the building right now.

Hands drop to each of my knees, and I look down to see both Jordan and Skye are lending me their silent support.

"Justin." My tone could give Elsa a run for her money it's so cold.

"Maddey."

"I would choose the next words out of your mouth very

carefully. I already tased one man today—I'm not opposed to doing it to another."

Every male in the room winces.

"Tink." It's Dex who speaks this time, and though I put up one hell of a front about what I did to him, I *do* feel guilty for it.

My shoulders slump and I surrender.

With a huff that could rival ones emitted by the two-year-olds building with blocks behind me, I rise from the couch and head in the guys' direction, keeping just out of Justin's reach to avoid hugging him—for now.

"Hi, Paul." I greet my brother's partner because, as much as I think I am, I'm not a complete asshole.

"Hi, Maddey." His lips tip up briefly but he sobers quickly out of respect for Justin. The two of them have been partners since Just graduated the academy last year, so he's familiar with wading through the murky McClain waters.

I also have a hard time holding on to my mad when it comes to people who spoil my baby. Even now, Trident ambles toward Paul to see what treat or new toy he has for him. Today's selection: a squeaky Dory fish.

"Can we get this over with?" I cross my arms, staring Justin down like he's not over a foot taller than me. "I have much more fun things I could be doing with my night, and I would like to get to them."

"Whatever you want, Madz," Justin concedes with a bow of his head.

I scoff. "If that were the case, we wouldn't be doing this." I circle a finger in the air and stomp over to my kitchen table, letting the wooden legs of the teal chair screech across the tile floor when I pull it out.

"Here." I arch a brow when Jordan places Logan in my arms. "You're less likely to commit murder if you have to take the time to put a baby down first." My gaze bounces from the top of my nephew's dark head back to my first true female friend. "Trust me."

God this woman is straight up my soul sister. We've bonded over so many things through the years, and not even the Navy can compete with the strength of our ties.

Older brothers who think they know best and make it their mission to "protect" you? Check.

In love with your brothers' best friend? Not true for me anymore, but for a chunk of my life, I believed it.

Will drop everything if one of us needs the other? Always.

Then there's the fact that not *once* did she make me feel guilty about breaking her brother's heart. Sure, she likes to tease me about how she wishes I was her sister-in-law, but she always follows it up with how as long as she gets to keep me as a sister of the heart, we're good.

Bringing my nose to the top of Logan's head, I breathe in that intoxicating baby scent and let the true meaning of his presence in my life set in.

Growing up, I only really had Sammy. Sure, I had other friends when I was younger, but I spent most of my time with my brothers and Dex. Then once teenage hormones came into play, I learned real quick that most girls only tried to befriend me as a way to get close to my brothers. There was also the fact that none of the guys in school would come near me for fear of what the idiots in my life might do.

This? Finding my Coven, my tribe—it is *everything*.

"You finally ready to discuss the best strategy for keeping you safe?" Holy shit does Justin look like Mom with how his left brow arches just so.

Yes, I can admit that the turn things have taken is creepy, but I still think it's an overreaction saying I need to be kept *safe*.

Am I creeped out that this person has figured out where I live? Of course—who wouldn't be? My home, my inner sanctum has now been tainted, but to say I'm in danger? That's a stretch.

Yes I use a pen name.

Yes I keep my author profiles separate from my personal ones.

But, come on.

Is it really such a stretch to think someone would be able to figure me out when both my personas show up tagged by some of the top players in the NHL and titleholders in both the UFC and WBO? A first-grader can do that math.

"I don't really have much of a choice now do I?" My head flops to the side to focus on Dex, who has settled in next to me. There's a flash of hurt that passes through those melty eyes, but it's gone so fast it must have been a trick of the light.

You know what's not?

The way that rugged jawline is clenched, jutting out from beneath his dark scruff. Or that vein pulsing just above his right eye—I like to call it the Tink Train, because it only pops out when I *really* push his buttons.

I flutter my lashes. Flash my dimples. Nothing. The only time his I'm-a-hardass-Navy-man-hear-me-hooyah stare softens is when I absentmindedly kiss Logan's silky hair.

"As much as it pains me to admit it…" Dex lifts a leg, his knee brushing my thigh and setting off all kinds of sparks that shouldn't be happening. My heart may have gotten over its brothers' best friend love trope, but my body is all *Let's take this to infinity and beyond, baby.* "…has more than proven she can handle herself."

Wait—what?

I missed something. I missed something big.

Did Dex just…

No.

Did he?

I might have zoned out in my lustful thoughts too much to be fully aware of what was going on, but like the bestselling fiction writer I am, I'll fake it till I make it—the *it* being keeping my independence.

"See, Just?" I shrug my shoulders the best I can with a four-month-old cradled to my chest. "Like I keep trying to tell *you*"—I stress the pronoun—"you've taught me well, so *please* stop overreacting and let your guard dog get back to protecting the country. The Navy needs his particular set of skills more than I do."

"Don't use a *Taken* reference. It's beneath you, sis." Justin rolls his eyes like he didn't just throw down the gauntlet.

"Oh my god, I said the same thing to her earlier." Skye throws her arms up like she's calling a touchdown.

I bite back a chuckle, because if I give these fools an inch, they will run for a mile. Damn overachieving special operators.

"Look." I make sure to make eye contact with all three of the macho alphas doing their best to intimidate me into acquiescing their requests. Sorry—been there, done that, have the collection of t-shirts for it in my closet. "I know you want me to be all *Welcome to the party, pal*"—I cant my head, waiting for Justin's nod of approval for the proper movie quote— "but…come. On."

"Tink." My body automatically shifts to face Dex at the sound of his rumbly voice. I think I'm seriously going to have to consider tracking down a sea witch to see if she can cure me of this instinctive attraction to this man. It is highly problematic.

The volume of my hormones singing "Be Our Guest" only increases when he brushes an errant curl from my face, leaving his hand curled over my shoulder, his thumb circling over the skin of my neck. There's nothing overtly sexual about his touch, but tell that shit to my body. It's acting like he's rubbing my lamp, getting my inner Genie ready to pop out à-la-"Friend Like Me" style.

"When Just called, I knew it wasn't a *Come out to the coast we'll get together have a few laughs* type of situation, and"—he holds a hand up, cutting off my objection before I can make it —"yes, I know my nuts have enough of a charge to power your phone right now"—I snort, I can't help it—"but you *do* need me."

"Hook—"

"No."

"Hook—"

"No." He's resolute.

"But—"

He gives the barest of squeezes on my neck, not enough to hurt, more like how Trident's mother would do to keep her pups in line. Holy talking snowman Olaf, the move shouldn't make my panties flood, but it does.

How about instead of killing us off, you get *one of us off instead?*

*Pick me. *raises hand**

*No, no. *shoves to the front* Pick me.*

Look who's all about volunteering now.

Another neck squeeze brings my attention back to the conversation happening outside my head.

"You may not need me to protect you, but you do need me to catch this fuckwat and put an end to this bullshit once and for all."

I hate that Dex is right.

Chapter Ten

Dex

T he pulse under my thumb flutters like the wings of the pixie my girl is nicknamed after.

Shit! Not my girl. Not my *girl. Not* my *girl.*

No matter how many times I remind myself of this simple fact, I can't stop thinking it.

What else?

Oh, yeah, that would be me *still* touching her. *My* hand is still curled around *her* shoulder, stroking the silky-soft delicate skin of her neck.

What makes it worse?

Her brother—one of my closest friends in this world—sits not even three feet away across the kitchen table from us.

Sure, I've touched Maddey like this before—and no there is nothing inappropriate about what I'm doing—but the way the Admiral in my pants is letting out a *hooyah* at the goosebumps dotting Maddey's skin and the way the tiny hairs on her arms are now standing on end—*that* is what is going to get me tossed off a skyscraper like Hans Gruber.

I need to pull myself up by my bootstraps and focus. The point I'm trying to get across is too important, and Maddey is too headstrong for this to work if she's going to fight me every step of the way. I understand my fellow Lost Boys' reasoning for enlisting my help, but I also see how their methods are setting me up to fail the same way John McClane killing the only terrorist with feet smaller than his sister's did.

The silence around the table screams more and more the longer we wait out Maddey's response to my declaration. The full circle of white showing around the extra-thick black border of her icy blue eyes is the only indication she was not expecting my particular stance on the situation.

Her throat works with a swallow, and I don't think about all the times I've imagined how that particular action would look after she took every drop of my cum I had to give her.

No.

Nope.

Not at all.

You, sir, are a dirty rotten liar. You are also a dead man.

A chorus of barking commences and there's a clatter of nails skittering across the hardwood as, once again, the door to the deck opens and a new flood of people enter Maddey's home—this time the male counterparts, along with two more canines.

"Party's here!" Tucker Hayes and Chris 'Cali' Callahan cheer, alla-Snookie style.

The celebrity clout in Tink's tribe is staggering. The combined net worth now inside the walls of her home is enough to buy a small country, yet you would never know it when spending time with them.

"Just because we're down the shore doesn't mean you need to channel your inner *Jersey Shore*, M-Dubs," Skye says from the kitchen.

I'm a sailor, so talking shit is pretty much a requirement among my brothers in arms, but nothing my fellow frogmen sling compares to the easy way the BTU Alumni do it. Case in point—Tucker's nickname M-Dubs, aka shorthand for man-whore.

"Don't be like that, Bubble." Tucker slaps her ass as she walks past, earning an *if looks could kill, no one would be able to find his body* death glare in return.

"You mean it's not *T-shirt Time*!" Cali cups his hands around his mouth for his Pauly D battle cry.

Tucker and Cali fist-pump together as they chant, "GTL! GTL! GTL!"

"The show has been over for years—why are we still quoting it?" Becky asks.

"I would think you would get all the mileage you could out of a show your fair state is known for." Chance Jenson, another player from the NJ Blizzards, starts unloading a case of beer into the fridge.

"Shows what you know, *Canada*." Gemma's lips have twisted down into a frown I can't recall the happy chef ever wearing with their friends. "Most of the cast wasn't even from Jersey."

"My humblest apologies, Princess." If Chance's sarcasm wasn't thick enough, the mocking bow he does certainly is.

"Can you even spell, let alone tell us the definition of humble, Rookie?"

The tips of Maddey's hot pink fingernails jump on Logan's back as we—now awake baby included—watch each of the sexual-tension-heavy exchanges play out. Without her saying a word, I know she's itching for a pad and pen to take notes for one of her books.

If she were a cartoon, this would be the point where they would show an internal shot of the hamster running on a wheel to represent her mind spinning with the possibilities.

Realizing my hand is *still* on her neck, I drop it, missing her warmth immediately.

As knuckle bumps and cheek kisses are exchanged, Justin drums his fist on the wooden table, anxiously waiting for the opportunity to get back to the task at hand.

"Madz," he calls out, trying to get her attention. Like I told her earlier, there is no getting out of having this discussion.

"Just," she deadpans.

My friend's nostrils flare, and if he doesn't stop clenching his jaw so tight, he's liable to crack a tooth.

"We need to talk about this."

"How many times do I have to say I don't *want* to talk about it?" she huffs. "Whoever this is will get bored eventually and move on."

"The fuck they will. They are already escalating—that is the opposite of 'getting bored'." He puts air quotes around the words before folding his arms across his chest in what I'm sure is a move to prevent himself from reaching over and strangling her.

"Just—"

"When are you going to stop being so selfish?"

"*Excuse* me?" Color creeps from her neck to her cheeks, staining her skin with a color not far off from the one on her nails.

I sure as shit hope Justin knows what he's doing, because we are approaching Maddey's full-blown Tinker Bell mode.

"Did you ever once stop to think how this affects the rest of us?"

"Of course I hav—"

"Or what it could mean for *some* if this asshat continues to escalate?" Justin barrels on like Maddey didn't even speak.

"Of cour—"

"Or how about how the mom to that baby in your arms looks a lot like you and could get caught in the crossfire if they mistook her for you?"

Maddey goes from Jersey tomato red to paper white in a second, all the color draining from her face as she whips her head around to where Jordan and Jake are canoodling against a wall like teenagers.

If this guy—my gut says it is a male, not a female—is as

obsessed with Maddey as we think, he wouldn't mistake Jordan for her. They look a lot alike, but there are enough differences to tell them apart.

Yes, they are both attractive short blondes, but that's where the similarities end.

Maddey is a few inches shorter than Jordan, her hair is a few shades lighter from all the time she spends paddle-board-ing, and it hangs longer in curls instead of straight.

If that isn't enough, all the fucker would have to do is look at their eyes. Sure, Jordan's eyes are a pretty golden color, but Maddey? Fuck her eyes are otherworldly in their intensity. There's a thin layer of cerulean surrounding her pupil, but the bulk of her iris is such a light blue it's almost white until it hits another thin circle of cerulean on the outside. And I would bet my life the black border around the entire thing is thicker than any other human's on the planet.

"Tink." I hook a hand over her hip, anchoring her to me to pull her from the worst of the panic overtaking her.

I wait for those eyes to meet mine, and then I wait another beat until she is seeing me and not the nightmare I'm sure she's writing like one of her books.

I kind of want to reach across the table and punch my friend for scaring her like this, especially after having *felt* her fear while we went over everything earlier, but I restrain myself.

"I told you…this is why I'm here. Will I protect you? Abso-fucking-lutely, but catching this fucker before he gets the chance to hurt you—or *anyone* else—is my main mission."

Her chin dips and she blinks rapidly.

I tug her a bit closer, breathing in the sweet scent of coconut I've always associated with her.

"I"—another tug—"got"—a squeeze—"you." I brush a thumb over the jut of bone at the top of her shorts.

She shifts Logan to one arm and drops her freed hand to

my forearm, her fingertips skimming along my tattoo before latching on.

"I know."

The assurance, the complete lack of doubt as she utters those two words makes me feel ten feet tall.

I'd burn the world down before I let anything happen to Madison Belle McClain.

Chapter Eleven

My home may be almost three thousand square feet of prime Jersey Shore realty, but right now it is *suffocating*.

I need air.

A break.

A moment to myself.

Anything to help shake off the guilt that has blanketed me for the last hour or so.

My thoughts are acting like they are employed by *Monsters, Inc.*, picking a new thing to feel guilty about like choosing doors to kids' bedrooms.

Rejecting offers of help.

Refusing protection.

Putting Jordan in danger.

Lusting after Dex.

It's a hot mess inside my head.

I may be the shortest in our group, but I'm damn sure the biggest asshole.

Trident follows me outside and settles himself at my feet as I stare out at the vast ocean in front of me. This time of night, the water looks black, but the rhythmic crashing of the waves has already started to soothe me.

I love the beach. Growing up in a shore town, it has always been my happy place. Any time I needed to get away, to escape, sitting on the sand while watching and listening to the cadence of the ocean was where I could be found.

Curling my fingers around the railing of the deck, I tip my head back, closing my eyes as I let out a large exhalation.

You should have accepted help earlier. Then you wouldn't be in this situation.

Jiminy is as much of a jerk as the characters in my head.

Hey!

I take offense to that.

What did we do?

My conscience isn't wrong, though. Then again, I'm sure he's yucking it up with karma right now, because she's also a bitch.

I hate that I need help, and I hate that the person who has been brought in to help me is Dex. Most of all, though, I hate how being around him opens up a guilt-filled can of worms.

The whoosh of the sliding doors sounds behind me before a presence I'm more than familiar with stops at my side—Ryan.

Resting his elbows by my hands, he leans forward, getting closer to eye level. He's silent, taking a moment to study me before asking, "What's wrong, Madz?"

"Nothing," I answer automatically.

"Yeah." He scoffs. "I know you too damn well to believe that." *Damn him.* "Now spill."

God. Why does he have to be right?

"Really, Ry. It's stupid."

Besides, he's the last person I should be talking about this with.

Fucking Justin had to go and add to the already Everest-sized mountain of guilt I'm feeling.

How *dare* he insinuate I don't care what happens to my friends, to my people.

Why the hell else does he think I wouldn't let them get involved in this shit?

"If it's bugging you then it's not stupid. Now stop trying to drag out the story. Don't make me get your editor on the phone."

I shake my head. I wouldn't put it past him.

"I hate this," I say vehemently, thrusting an arm out at the house behind us.

"What? The house?" The baritone of his deep laughter rumbles through me. Unlike my best friend, I am *not* amused. "Sell it then. I put the deed in your name. You can do whatever you want with it."

Dammit. Why does he have to say shit like that? It only makes things worse. Because, yes, I live in the house *he* purchased for us, a home *we* lived in during the offseason before he proposed. Of course he didn't let a little thing like me turning down said proposal take away what he knew was my dream home. No, instead he signed it over to me.

Seriously, what person in their right mind takes a two-million-dollar piece of prime beachfront property and gifts it to the person who just dumped them?

If there is such a thing as angels on earth, Ryan Donnelly sure is one of them.

And you're paying him back by putting his sister in danger?

Fuck!

"You know that's not what I meant." I side-eye him.

"Okay. So…what?" He pauses like he's deep in thought. "Hanging out with your friends?"

I fold my arms over my chest.

"The beach?"

"No."

"The outdoors?"

"Ryan," I growl.

"Oh, I know!" He snaps his fingers. "You mean you hate that we finally found the *one* person you *couldn't* stop from protecting you?"

That may be something I'm not happy about, but it's not what has me looking around for Jiminy because fuck if that damn cricket isn't making my conscience chirp at me.

"I hate you."

"No you don't, Madison." I can *hear* the smile in his voice.

Damn him for being right.

Arms wrap around my middle, bringing me back to the present with a squeeze.

"Madz…" Ryan prods.

"God." I heave a heavy sigh. "What the hell is wrong with me?"

There's another chuckle. "I'm assuming that's rhetorical?"

Olympic medals and World Champion titles abound in our group, but we *all* could win a trophy for sarcasm.

Yes the question was rhetorical. If anyone else from our squad was standing next to me, though, they would have taken the small opening and pried until the floodgates of potential shit-giving opened up.

Ryan, though? No, he is the *one* person who wouldn't take it.

"Talk to me, Madz." His arms squeeze me again.

I couldn't count the number of times we've been in this exact position, my back to his front, head tipped back to rest on his strong chest, safe in the cradle of his body.

Turning my head to the side, I look over the bulge of his biceps, my gaze once again finding the cause for my melancholy. I have been *beyond* blessed in life, yet in this moment, all I want to do is scream *It's not fair!* and stomp my feet in a tantrum so epic it would put my nieces to shame.

"Madz?"

I step out of his hold.

Justin was right—just don't *ever* tell him I said that.

I'm selfish, a world-class bitch. Why the hell Ryan cares, let alone remains my flipping *bestie* of all things is beyond me. He is too good, that's for damn sure.

Now here we are, him comforting me over something he should hate me for. We were a couple during the time Jordan's ex-boyfriend stalked her and came close to killing her. Why isn't he yelling at me for putting her at risk again?

I'm such an asshole.

I don't deserve to be comforted. No, I deserve to prick my finger on a spindle and fall into an eternal sleep.

"You know none of us believe you are putting JD—or any of us—in danger, right?"

I scoff. Fucking Justin and his big mouth.

"Madz, talk to me." Ryan reaches for me, cupping his hands over my elbows and spinning me to face him.

"It's just…" I drop my head, unable to look him in the eye. "This"—I circle my finger in the air—"makes me question if I did the right thing or not."

"You mean not accepting help with your…situation sooner?"

My head snaps up to see Ryan's denim blue eyes glittering with humor as they watch me.

"You're a jerk." I shove his shoulder playfully. My smile falls as quickly as it appeared and I drop my head again, my hair falling forward, shielding my face from view.

Here we are, years later, me no longer believing I'm in love with Dex because once upon a time I fell for Ryan.

Still…not thinking I'm in love with him anymore isn't going to make these next three weeks any easier with Dex living in my house.

"Do you ever wonder if your life would have been better if you never asked me out?"

Would I feel different about Dex being here if I believed I still loved him?

"Now you're just speaking nonsense." Ryan tucks an

errant curl behind my ear. "I wouldn't change a thing about the last five years."

"*Riiiight*." I scoff. "Not even the part where I said no instead of yes when you proposed?"

"Well…" He chuckles. "Maybe *one* thing."

More than his words, the soft smile he gives me tells me everything will be alright. I can't help but return it with one of my own, albeit a smaller one.

"Seriously though." He waits until I make eye contact. "In the end, it's a risk I would take every time."

"Stop," I beg, another tear falling.

"No." His tone turns hard as he uses his captain voice on me. "Shit, Madz. I have half a mind to tell my sister to kick your ass."

"Pfft." I wave my hand, unconcerned. "If you really meant that, you would have threatened me with Rocky."

The tension between us finally breaks as we share a laugh over our badass friend.

"I mean it, though. Outside of my siblings, you are my best friend. You can't ask me to give up my *bestie*"—his lips quirk—"just because of a little broken heart."

There's nothing *little* about his heart, as made all the more evident by this conversation, but I don't want to argue. Instead I wrap my arms around him, holding on to my elbows and embracing him as tightly as I can.

He mirrors my actions, curling his body down to rest his chin on the top of my head.

With a deep breath, my cheek resting on his chest, I look past his arm and into my house again. Dex is still talking to Justin and Paul, and I'm startled to find him looking this way. His dark gaze burns and a shiver skitters down my spine at the intensity in it.

"And maybe give the guy a break." Ryan follows my line of sight, jerking his chin at Dex. "He's only trying to help."

I know he's right.

Conversations about my stalker aside, I haven't felt safe the way I have for the handful of hours since Dex showed up in *months*.

The longer I hold the stare of those dark eyes, the more my heart aches like the Evil Queen herself is reaching inside my chest and squeezing it.

I have zero doubt Dex will keep me safe. Why do I feel like it's my heart that's the one at risk?

Chapter Twelve

Dex

I think I'd rather have my nuts tased while the Die Hard Trilogy took shots at them in between jolts than have to watch Maddey seek comfort in the arms of her ex. The worst part is Ryan is genuinely a good guy.

Needing to shake off the irrational feelings of jealousy, I rise from my seat, on the hunt for a cup of coffee.

Three weeks might seem like a lifetime compared to the amount of liberty I usually take in one shot, but it's like a drop in the bucket when you think of how long this stalker has avoided discovery while messing with our girl. I'm not wasting a second of my time here. A late night it is.

Maddey may have a more than decent security system already installed, but it's still getting an upgrade. Plus, with the stalker's escalation, it's time to use it for a little bit of offense.

Tyler—our team's resident tech guru—hooked me up with camera and audio equipment small enough to be hidden and hopefully help us finally catch the person in the act.

I don't like how long this guy has been able to avoid discovery and how well he's been able to cover his tracks. It's time to start thinking outside the box.

"You know…" Sammy sidles up to my side, eyeing first my white-knuckled grip on the mug's handle then the couple I was eyeing—again.

I arch a brow, choosing to stay silent. This is Maddey's bestest friend, after all; who knows what could come out of his mouth.

"If you were ever going to make a move, now's the time."

"Come again?" Where is he going with this?

"Now, now." He pats my shoulder. "You may be a sexy SEAL, but I'm a happily married man, Stone. Save the dirty talk for someone else."

Coffee sprays the counter in front of me as I sputter. What? Did he…? Shit, I did mention he's Tink's best friend, right?

"Fuck I missed you Sammy." I pull him in for another back-slapping hug. He's always been one of my favorite non-McClains. It probably has something to do with the fact that he's been out so long I never had to worry about him trying to get with my girl.

Shit!

This 'my girl' shit is happening at dangerous levels of frequency.

Also…

Like my eyes are magnets and Maddey and Ryan are made of metal, they track back to the former lovebirds. Fuck they look perfect together.

"You know she's not in love with him, right?"

I startle at Sammy reading my mind. "What?"

Smooth, Stone. Real smooth.

"That"—he jerks a chin at the glass doors—"is one friend comforting another. It's just like if I were out there."

"Except she didn't almost marry you," I say, under my breath but not low enough for Sammy not to hear.

"This is true, but you said it yourself."

Why do I feel like he's speaking in riddles?

"What?"

"*Almost.*"

Again…what?

"She never said yes." He claps me on the back and circles back around the counter. "You ready, Jam?" he asks his husband before shooting me a *Think about it* look over his shoulder.

Chapter Thirteen

After a late night hunched over my laptop pounding out my frustrations on my keyboard, I need yoga day more than anything. Pulling on my favorite pair of Disney villain leggings, I can't help but smile at the memory of every shouty capital message I've received from my girls that led to them.

One of the greatest joys in life is making my best friends curse me out for leaving them hanging by going to bed after sending them a chapter that leaves a story on a cliffhanger.

From the Group Message Thread of The Coven

MOTHER OF DRAGONS: You are evil. That is all.

MAKES BOYS CRY: Yes!! So evil.

PROTEIN PRINCESS: Why are we friends with you?

YOU KNOW YOU WANNA: *GIF of Maleficent laughing*

SANTA'S COOKIE SUPPLIER: For reals. Here I am, thinking,

"Holy shit I get to beta read for one of my favorite authors," but you, madam, are a sadist.

BROADWAY BABY: Screw this. I'm off to bed. You guys enjoy the Queen of Smut *cough cough* Evil Queen *cough cough* punishment.

DANCING QUEEN: Shit, man—haven't you heard of a thing called instant gratification?

FIDDLER ON THE ROOF: *GIF of girl waving a hairbrush angrily*

THE OG PITA: *GIF of woman miming strangling someone*

ALPHABET SOUP: You remember this chapter you left us on when I have you bent into some crazy pretzel during yoga in the morning. YOU'VE BEEN WARNED.

See what I mean?

It's the simple things in life.

It comes as no shock that Dex is already up when Trident and I make our way downstairs, nor does the way my hormones perk up, going *humina-humina-humina* at how yummy he looks.

At least he's not wearing gray sweatpants, said hormones supply helpfully—or not so helpfully, depending on your definition of the word. They are right, though—no lady-porn gray sweatpants in sight, but he *does* have on a well-worn, super-soft from years of washing, gray Navy t-shirt.

You know the type, right? The kind that displays athletes and military men in all their muscle-rippling, seam-stretching glory.

Focus, Madison. Ah shit, I'm calling myself by my full name again. Not good.

What *is* surprising is how *right* Dex looks drinking coffee in *my* home.

What the…?

It's also completely unfair how bright-eyed and bushy-tailed he looks when I know for a fact he was up just as late as I was installing all the tech Tyler sent him with—brownie points for cluing me in on what he was doing—but Mr. Badass SEAL doesn't let little things such as lack of sleep get him down like us mere mortals.

"Did you eat?" I ask, pulling out one of Gemma's pre-made parfaits from the fridge.

"Yes."

Okay, good. One down, one to go.

"You want to eat or go out?" I tilt my head at the shadow by my feet.

"Didn't you just ask me that?" Dex eyes me like I've lost my mind. To be fair, it usually is a chaotic squirrelly mess with a bajillion characters talking to me throughout the day, but I promise you, I'm sane—mostly.

"Not you, Hook."

Undeterred by the confused human in the room, my fur baby walks over to the stand holding his bowls and sits down.

Food first.

I give him fresh water then scoop out his kibble from the container in my pantry.

"Egg, cheese, or hot dog?" I ask, inquiring as to what he wants added to his breakfast.

Woof! Woof!

"Cheese it is."

Breaking up half a slice of cheese, I mix it with the kibble and set the dish in the stand, taking my own food to the table while Trident devours his behind me.

"You always talk to your dog like he's a person?" Dex chuckles, and I do not notice how tempting his lips look curling at the edges. (Lie.)

"Of course. That's my child right there. Besides, you heard him—he totally understands me."

Those kissable lips disappear from view as they are tucked between his teeth, and I tell myself I don't miss them. (Another lie.)

"You feeling better today?"

No.

Sometime around one in the morning, after my heroine's brother had an unfortunate encounter with a batch of laxative-filled brownies, I decided I will be fine.

Dex will play his military book boyfriend role to perfection, he'll catch the bad guy, ruin some panties, and maybe steal a heart or two in the process.

Even yours, Madz?

Fucking Jiminy.

He'll ruin some panties alright.

Ruin them? He can have them. Here. *hangs thong from finger*

"Madz." He stretches an arm across the table, waiting for me to place my hand in his upturned palm. "I *will* catch this guy, and I *promise* I will keep you safe until then."

There's that weird pang inside my rib cage again, but I nod. I meant it when I said I know he will. It's just having him here, in my home, in my space, being all sexy and chivalrous, reminding me of all the reasons why I crushed on him so hard growing up—it's doing my head in.

My life is one banana peel away from spinning completely out of control.

Done with his meal, Trident ambles over to my side, licking his chops, and drops his head into my lap, leaving a streak of drool in his wake.

Life of a dog mom. So glamorous.

A thumb ghosting over my knuckles brings me out of my musings—damn I really do get distracted easily. I swear I'm as bad as the dog in *Up*, saying one thing one moment and the next yelling *Squirrel!*

"I know it may not seem like it given the reception you received when you showed up, but I'm grateful you're here." Finally, my first truth.

I swear to god his chest swells to twice its size at my words.

Yoga (noun): a discipline that uses the practice of a series of postures and breathing exercises to achieve tranquility and control of the body and mind.

Yoga BTU Alumni style: a complete and epic shit-show filled with trash talk, side-eye from Rocky, less than perfect form, and tons of laughter.

Who needs Bikram? Not us.

"You guys have got to be some of the worst yogis I have ever seen," Dex says from the yoga mat next to mine.

To be fair, most of us take our weekly session seriously the majority of the time, but things tend to spiral out of control more in the offseason when we get back those we miss during the regular NHL season.

I flop my head to the side to see him, not willing to move more than that from my sprawled-out position. The stress of everything and the erratic sleep schedule I've been keeping is starting to catch up to me. Plus, the sand underneath my mat is warm and feels so good on my recently stretched muscles.

"If I didn't know any better, I would doubt most of them are professional athletes."

"Blasphemy," Jake cries.

"Who let the new guy in?" comes from Cali.

"I'll show you." Even from my position, I can see Tucker flexing like a bodybuilder.

"You *do* remember Dex is trained to kill you with his

pinky, right?" Ryan can't keep the amusement out of his question.

"You Americans think you're so tough," Chance comments.

"Says the Canadian who chose to stay with us instead of returning to his country this summer," Gemma taunts.

"There's only one of him—we can take him." The guys all cheer Vince's battle cry.

"Maybe Lyle isn't the only one who should be kept in a cage?" Holly says off to my right.

"Cupcake, if you want to be restrained, all you have to do is give me your panties and I can make that happen...again." The sound of skin being smacked rings out, and I don't have to see it to know Vince just got popped in the chest by his girlfriend.

"*Ooo*, Ky." Speak of the barista devil. "I think I might need to start channeling my inner Gumby if there's going to be all this glorious naked man-meat on display."

Sure enough, when I push up onto my elbows, I see every one of the guys have lost their shirts during the course of the workout. Talk about hero inspiration.

"You know..." I look at my OG inspo as he speaks. "It is still so weird to me that this is your life now, Tink."

"Hockey players and MMA fighters?"

Not the most intelligent question, but I'm a tiny bit distracted by the miles of naked flesh, bulging muscles, and swirls of ink on display for my viewing pleasure.

"Growing up, you pretty much just stuck with Sammy. Seeing you with such a massive squad now is"—he looks out at everyone in various stages of leaving—"nice."

I've long since gotten over how lonely I was outside of my family, Sammy, and Dex before I found my tribe. The memories I've made in the last eight years have overwritten most of the ones from the six before them.

"It's not nice, Hook." I can't stop a goofy smile from forming. "It's the *best*. Getting paired with Jordan and Skye as roommates altered the entire course of my life."

"What changed? You've always been such an outgoing person. I've never understood why you didn't have a crew like this growing up."

If I had heard even a *hint* of judgment in his tone, I probably would have shut down the line of questioning, but there is just general curiosity, so I'll answer.

"When I met them"—I point to Jordan and Skye's retreating backs, the former tucked securely under Jake's arm and the latter slapping Tucker's hand away from her ass—"I was Maddey."

"You've always been Maddey." A V forms between his dark brows, and I resist the urge to smooth it away.

"Ah, but that's the thing—I've always been Maddey McClain."

"Are you officially going by Belle Willis now and I missed it?"

That sense of pride I feel any time someone references my pen name washes over me. Romance is my life, current lack of love life notwithstanding. Making a career out of crafting stories that bring people joy is literally what dreams are made of.

"Smartass." I push to stand and start to roll up my mat. "What I mean is, I learned pretty fast that most of the girls who tried befriending me were hoping to use their newfound close proximity to the McClain household as an in for access to my brothers"—I drop my gaze to the sand squishing between my toes—"or you."

"Bullshit."

I shake my head, wishing it wasn't true. That's the thing about the queen bees of the world—they think they own it and don't always check to make sure there aren't feet visible beneath the doors of bathroom stalls before they confer with their minions.

"Shit, Tink."

I shrug. What else am I supposed to do? Saying I'm over it isn't just some platitude; I really am over it.

"Fuck 'em." I snap my gaze to meet Dex's narrowed one. He's trying to sound lighthearted, but the flaring of his nostrils and the appearance of the Tink Train tell another story. "It's their loss for not recognizing how awesome you are."

The younger me who believed she loved this man back in the day preens under his praise.

I whistle for Trident so he knows it's time to head home, and he immediately falls into step beside me.

As we make the trek across the warm sand, I do notice how Dex doesn't bring up the lack of *male* attention I received in high school. I've had my suspicions on that front, and his silence only goes to further confirm it.

The distinct voice of Mario saying, "Woohoo!" and the tinkling sound of a power-up box being collected hit my ears before we even make it onto the lower deck of my house. It comes as no surprise to find Sammy and Jamie already in a heated battle of Mario Kart on my outdoor entertainment system.

One corner of the deck has a covered roof to protect it from the elements, and under it I have oversized cube seats in tan with teal cushions that can be arranged in whatever couch setup suits our purposes best. There's a coffee table in the middle, the top of which slides off to turn into a fire pit. Edison bulbs are strung across the beams, and there's a large flat-screen mounted in the corner.

I pause so they don't notice us, throwing up an arm to stop Dex's forward progress and ignoring the rippling of his muscles along my forearm where it's pressed against his torso, and then I reach for my phone.

Before either of them can move, I snap a picture of the drool-worthy display of both men playing video games in board shorts—only board shorts—and backward hats. They have the furniture set up so Sammy has his back to the couch, with Jamie sitting in the cradle of Sammy's spread legs and my oldest friend's arms wrapped around his husband's body.

My ovaries pretty much explode on the spot at all the hotness happening in front of my eyes, and none of my lady parts seem to give a damn that neither one of them would do me if given a hall pass.

Curse my lack of penis.

Wait…what? Did I really just think that?

Guess it's finally my turn to get a book.

Yay! *waves hands in air* I love MM romance.

Give it to me.

The way I'm grinning like a fool while scrolling through the shots I took gives me away as I take a seat.

"What did you do, Madz?" Sammy's eyes remain focused on avoiding the banana peel on Koopa Beach.

"Just going through the teaser pic gold you guys just gave me. Thank you for that, by the way." It's one of the many reasons I'll never complain about the amount of time they spend at my place instead of at theirs on the bay side.

"Careful, man," Sammy says to Dex when he joins us. "This one will have you posing half-naked on a book cover before you leave if you aren't careful."

"Can't have this"—I pinch Dex's chin between my thumb and forefinger—"pretty face on one while he's active duty."

Those chocolate eyes bore into me with such intensity my breath catches in my lungs. Holy smolder Flynn Rider, it just became Niagara Falls in my pants.

My breasts grow heavy, my nipples could cut glass despite it being a balmy eighty-five degrees out, and if I don't have a date with my shower massager in the next two point five seconds, I'm liable to launch myself at him and ask this pirate to plunder my booty.

Hold on. *holds hands up in a T* I know you've been on this sex *embargo since breaking up with Ryan, trying to be "honorable" or whatever bullshit about not wanting to "cheapen" the breakup by having meaningless sex with strangers, but—*

I mentally roll my eyes.

Wait, wait—hear me out. Dex isn't just some guy. At one point we thought we loved him. What if…you jumped on his magic wand and let him take you on a magic carpet ride?

Hmm…it's not like Jiminy to give me this type of advice. Usually he's all about laying on guilt trips longer than Mr. Toad's Wild Ride.

Could I do it, though?

Could I…could I have sex with Dex?

Bitch please—you are a trope slut. This whole scenario has you written all *over it—no pun intended.*

clears throat

Here, let me count them for you.

You have brothers' best friend—so hot!

Then there's your forced proximity/roommates for the next three *weeks. Three. Weeks!*

Don't forget the super-hot bodyguard/protector trope thanks to Justin butting in.

And of course, mi-li-tary, they singsong.

cups hands around mouth Trope it up.

I do love me some tropes.

And…

Maybe…

Hmm…

I already proved I don't actually love Dex by falling for Ryan, so it's not like I'd have to worry about catching feelings if I did sleep with him.

Right?

Chapter Fourteen

The Lost Boys Group Chat

CONNER: You still alive? It's been radio silent over there.

TYLER: Truth. Com check, one-two, one-two.

JUSTIN: Hold on—I have proof of life.

JUSTIN: *picture of Dex playing Mario Kart with Maddey, Sammy, and Jamie*

CONNER: ^^You see this shit? Asshole is over here giving us shit and he's sitting pretty on a Gucci mission.

DEX: *middle finger emoji* Fuck you, assholes.

TYLER: Our little Tink did electrocute his balls, so…

CONNER: Fuck that. Dex is a kinky fucker. It was probably fore-play for him.

DEX: The fuck?!

JUSTIN: Can we maybe not use words like "kinky" and "foreplay" when the subject matter is our sister?

TYLER: You've read her books, bro…

JUSTIN: Jesus Christ. How did Mom not give you away when you were a baby?

CONNER: Puh-lease. I'm Babs' favorite.

TYLER: WRONG! That honor goes to Madz and you know it.

CONNER: Only because she lives the closest.

JUSTIN: And what am I? Chopped liver?

TYLER: …

CONNER: New phone, who dis?

JUSTIN: Assholes.

DEX: Was there an actual point to this conversation?

CONNER: Just wanted to make sure Tink didn't make you walk the plank, Hook.

Chapter Fifteen

Dex

Maddey has been acting…strange?…since yesterday morning, and I can't quite put my finger on what changed. I doubt anyone else picked up on it, but when it comes to Maddey McClain, I notice everything.

Like the way her sports bra pressed together those glorious tits she's not supposed to have because she's Baby McClain.

Or how good her ass looked bent over in downward dog during yoga.

Or the generous swell of her hips emphasized by the nipped-in waist displayed by the high band of her printed leggings. Fuck me if they weren't made for my hands to grip while I drive myself so deep inside her from behind she would feel me in her throat.

And don't even get me started on how perfectly she arched her back during the cow stretch.

Shit! Now I'm hard.

One would think after having the least helpful group chat ever with the Die Hard Trilogy, I wouldn't be suffering from a constant case of spontaneous erections. Unfortunately, the only thing it did was remind me of the steamy novels my girl has penned instead of the fact that she is the sister of my best friends.

Oof. I did it again—thought of her as my girl.

Sure, I've thought of Maddey as *my girl* throughout the years, but doing so while playing house is a recipe for disaster.

Remember how I said I noticed she was acting weird? Well, ever since her friends left last night, I've gotten the sense she's been avoiding me. I know she's awake—I heard her having a legit conversation with Trident this morning.

So where is she?

There was movement upstairs while I was reviewing the video feeds from yesterday, so I'm assuming she's in her office. I don't want to interrupt her work, but I need to pick her brain again, see if there are any clues or details we might be able to garner from her memories.

I know it's her least favorite topic, but it is necessary. Plus I figure with Justin and Paul working, she'll be more receptive.

I love my best friend and he's a smart guy, but he has tunnel vision when it comes to Maddey.

Voices filter down the hallway as I crest the top of the stairs, and I wonder which of her friends she's talking to now. The team and I watch a lot of *How I Met Your Mother* reruns—a fact that endears me to Jake and Jordan—during our down-time on missions and deployments, but Maddey and her people take codependent to entirely new levels.

"Come here."

I stop in my tracks at the sound of a male voice.

"You're holding me right now—I'm not sure I can get any closer to you."

Who is Maddey talking to? I don't recognize the voice.

"You have such a smart mouth. The things I want to do to that mouth…"

The fuck?

Every possessive instinct inside my body snaps to attention. The only person who should be talking about doing things to Maddey's mouth is me, not whoever this asshat is. Maddey is *mine*.

What about Ryan? I choose to ignore that particular thought.

I'm not able to hear everything that is said. I need to be closer because what the actual fuck?

"I bet if I slide my fingers into your pussy right now, I will find you soaking wet."

Fuck you, asshole. The only one who will be sliding into her pussy is me.

"Oh fuck, baby, you definitely like it when I do that because your pussy just tightened around my fingers."

That's it. I'm done. I don't care if I come off looking like the world's craziest asshole; I can't listen to one more second of this.

I slam through the partly open door, Trident on his feet in an instant with a growl at how I barreled into the room. *Good dog.*

"Dex!" Maddey startles, a Blow Pop hitting dead center of my forehead at the same time she shouts my name. I'll need to remember to commend her on her aim—and thank her for not having her taser—when I'm not in the throes of wanting to murder the man finger-fucking her.

"Don't stop. I'm so close." A breathy voice moans...a voice *not* belonging to Maddey because she is still currently gaping at me like a fish.

SMACK!

Right after his skin comes in contact with the swell of my ass, he moves his hand around to put pressure on my clit.

"Oh, shit!"

"*That's it, baby. Let me feel you lose control.*"

Wait...what?

Wrangling my raging libido and jealousy, I finally take in the rest of the room: there's no one else except Maddey and Trident.

And that's what I do. My body shakes as the orgasm rips through me. I'm pretty sure I black out at one point. I am still coming down from my high that I don't even realize Zach has stripped out of his pants and retrieved a condom from the night-stand until I feel him thrust deep inside me.

"Fuck, Hails, you feel so good. I love being deep inside you."

Holy shit, she's listening to an audiobook.

And is he ever. Oh my god! Only a few strong thrusts and I feel another orgasm coming on. Oh shit!

"Harder, baby, harder."

My wish is his command. The grip he has on my hips is almost painful as he plunges deeper and harder into me.

"Mine," he growls over and over, and he's right—at this moment, I am his.

A hot-as-fuck audiobook.

As the hero in the book lets out a pleasure-filled curse, Maddey blinks out of her own shocked stupor and cuts off all sound with the push of a button.

"Dex? What's wrong?"

I don't say anything, still trying to comprehend what I just heard.

Fuck a duck. Is that how Maddey likes it in bed? Would she want me to grab her and plunge into her from behind like the heroine in the book?

Lord knows I've pictured that particular scenario more times than I can count through the years.

My heart is pounding against my chest likes it's trying to imitate Tarzan from inside my body, and I'm hard. Like, my dick could serve as an aircraft carrier if an F-18 needed some-where to land hard.

Still I stand there without saying a word. Sticky lollipop residue smeared across my forehead, pulse pounding, nostrils flaring, hard behind my zipper, seeing Maddey bent over the desk and not sitting behind it like she is now.

BANG!

The hot pink chair crashes into the wall behind it from her jumping out of it before rounding the end of her desk to close the distance between us. "Did..." She swallows. "Did something else..." Her eyes dart around the room in a panic. "Get delivered?"

I hate, *hate* how scared she sounds. The hesitancy, the doubt, the *fear*—each is like taking an AK round to the flak jacket.

Thinking she was in here fucking some random, my adrenaline is all jacked up like I just completed a HALO jump. It's messing with my instincts in a way I've never experienced before.

I clench and unclench my hands, shaking them out to dispel the tension coursing through me. I need to punch something, preferably some*one* in the face—repeatedly.

I wasn't thinking when I barreled in the room like the door-kicker I am.

No...wait.

That's a lie.

I *was* thinking—murderous thoughts about the person I assumed thought they had the right to put their hands on what is mine. And, yes, before you say anything, I know, *I know* Maddey isn't mine and I have no claim on her.

But you know fucking what?

The heart isn't always known for its rational thinking.

Sorry not sorry.

"Dex?"

Those pale, pale eyes blink up at me, the flare at where they slant up at the edges screaming for someone to keep her safe.

"De—" She chokes out a sob, her hands coming up and clutching my shirt at the center of my chest.

Coconut hits me full force as the heat from her body presses into me.

Trident lets out a whimper, his weight settling itself on my foot as he leans against both our legs. For a civilian canine, he is more cognizant of the emotions in a room than some humans.

Maddey's uncharacteristic display of vulnerability breaks the last of my resolve. I reach out, cupping her face in my hands, tunneling my fingers into her hair and causing the pen securing her bun to come loose, the silky curls brushing against my forearms as they tumble around her.

"No." I pause to clear my throat of the lust and rage blocking it. "Nothing came. I haven't even checked to see if you have mail."

My thumbs caress the jut of her cheekbones, her lashes fluttering closed as if my touch alone is enough to soothe away all her worries. The complete and utter faith she has in me is a heady thing to experience.

"Then what the hell had you charging in here like you're Rambo?"

There's that sass I adore.

"Rambo was a Green Beret, babe."

She rolls her eyes, ignoring the endearment that slipped out.

"*God*, I forgot how butthurt you all get when we get your branch of the military wrong."

"Well…when you're the best, you want to make sure it's recognized."

"Who's to say SEALs are the best?" She arches one of her blonde brows.

"You did."

She rears back, gasping in mock shock, placing a hand over her heart as if offended, her jaw dropping for effect. Her playful side is one of my favorites, and I focus on that and not how tempting her mouth looks forming a small O.

Or how badly I want to bring my hand forward and slip my thumb inside the space, telling her to suck before pushing her to her knees to do the same to my cock.

Instructing her to keep those ethereal eyes on me while I feed her every inch of me, keeping my hands buried in her curls like they are now to guide her up and down my length...

Fuck me.

Thank god she shifted back to be dramatic; if she hadn't, she would be able to feel exactly where my thoughts have wandered off to.

Focus, Stone. This is no time to ring out.

I didn't come close to ringing the bell during BUD/S and quitting; I'm not going to let wayward thoughts of fucking my best friends' little sister break me now.

What were we talking about?

Oh yeah—how I know Maddey is a true Navy brat.

"You're trying to tell me a person who names their dog Trident isn't a frog hog at heart?"

This time her gasp is genuine, the blue in her eyes blazing as they throw grenades at me.

"Refer to me as a SEAL slut again and my taser will be the *least* of your balls' problem." Said balls tingle, perking up at her spunk, not heeding the threat she lobbed at them at all. "And I named him after Ariel's dad." She pats Trident on the head while he watches as if he understands what we are talking about.

"Ariel's dad is King *Triton*, not Trident, but nice try, Tink."

She emits the cutest fucking growl known to man and pinches my pec. Pushing her buttons is one of my favorite pastimes.

"Damn you and your Disney knowledge."

I keep my hips rolled back as she shifts back into my space. Bantering with her has me ready to wave my pirate flag.

"You only have yourself to blame for that one." I tug on one of her curls, brushing it behind her ear. "Then there's also how you helped Jordan name Navy...well, Navy."

She beams at the mention of her friend's dog. Maddey treats Navy like he's as much her nephew as baby Logan. It probably stems from playing mom when the girls got him during their sophomore year of college.

"You're right." Her hand splays across where I have the Budweiser tattoo inked on my chest, her fingers contracting and extending. "My heart belongs to the sea."

Her eyes attempt to close as I stroke the line of her jaw with my thumbs and massage the tightness at the base of her skull with my other fingers. An *mmmm* escapes, and I need to know all the other ways I can get her to make that sound.

Her tits brush my chest with each deep inhalation she takes.

I continue to massage and stroke, content to stay like this for days if it means having her this close. Eventually her eyelids lose the battle and shut, her blonde lashes fanning across her cheeks as she luxuriates under my ministrations.

She's so damn beautiful I can hardly stand it.

She sways in my hold.

Tits brushing.

*Mmm*s singing in her throat.

Fingers contracting on my muscles.

There is zero trace of her earlier panic.

Her head lolls to the side, falling deeper into the hand cupping it.

Her lips part ever so slightly.

I want to kiss her.

I *need* to kiss her.

Need to learn what her lips feel like under mine, what she tastes like.

What will she do? How will she react?

I can't imagine she would be a passive kisser. She has too

much fire inside her to not meet me kiss for kiss, stroke for stroke, nip for nip.

There's a hint of shine on those plump pillows.

This is it.

I'm doing it.

After years of imagining what it would be like to kiss Maddey McClain, I'm finally going to know what it's like.

My thumbs press under her chin, tilting her face up higher. A whiff of watermelon hits my nose when I'm centimeters from her mouth. *Ah, her lollipop.*

Closer.

I lick my lips in anticipation.

Closer.

A deep inhalation.

Closer.

This is it.

I close my eyes.

Woof! Woof!

Maddey and I both jolt from Trident's impromptu contribution.

Fuck!

Was I really about to kiss Maddey?

Maddey McClain?

The same Maddey McClain who has three older brothers?

Justin, Tyler, and Conner McClain—those older brothers?

Also known as my best friends?

The ones I've helped scare off anyone who tried to get close to her?

Fuck! Fuck, fuck, fuck, fuckity-fuck!

What the hell was I *thinking*?

Not good. Not good at all. Just over forty-eight hours and I'm ready to forget the reason I'm here.

To protect her.

To catch her stalker.

The Die Hard Trilogy doesn't trust many people when it comes to keeping Maddey safe, and they chose me.

I can't break that trust by making a move on her.

Abort mission. Head for the LZ.

It's time to listen to the orders coming from the command in my head and make tracks. I need to put distance between Maddey and me before I do something I can't take back.

Ignoring the questions swimming in those blues and the furrow between Maddey's brows, I spin on my heel and flee like I'm still a tadpole and not a badass frogman.

Chapter Sixteen

From the Group Message Thread of The Coven

QUEEN OF SMUT: HOLY SHIT! HOLY SHIT! HOLY SHIT!

MOTHER OF DRAGONS: What happened?

MAKES BOYS CRY: Whose ass do I need to kick?

ALPHABET SOUP: Isn't that my line?

YOU KNOW YOU WANNA: *GIF of Jimmy Fallon saying, "Oh, snap!"*

THE OG PITA: Shhh. Don't distract her. I want to know what happened.

SANTA'S COOKIE SUPPLIER: *GIF from *Grease* with "Tell me more, tell me more."*

FIDDLER ON THE ROOF: *GIF of Willy Wonka saying, "Please, tell us more."*

BROADWAY BABY: Yes. Please don't take advice from Aaron Burr and talk less. Give us the deets.

DANCING QUEEN: Can you tell we were rocking out to the *Hamilton* soundtrack on our drive last night?

QUEEN OF SMUT: YOU GUYS I'M FREAKING THE FUCK OUT RIGHT NOW!!!

PROTEIN PRINCESS: She must be telling the truth—she's still talking in shouty capitals.

ALPHABET SOUP: Oh, good point, Gem.

YOU KNOW YOU WANNA: This isn't one of your books, Madz.

YOU KNOW YOU WANNA: Stop leaving us in suspense.

YOU KNOW YOU WANNA: *GIF of Joey Tribbiani saying, "I need an answer now."*

SANTA'S COOKIE SUPPLIER: Good use of a *Friends* GIF. I strongly approve.

MOTHER OF DRAGONS: The twins are going to be graduating high school before we find out what happened.

MAKES BOYS CRY: *GIF of woman spitting out water*

QUEEN OF SMUT: Okay. Here's what happened. Let me set the scene...

THE OG PITA: Forever an author.

SANTA'S COOKIE SUPPLIER: Shh…I'd read the phonebook if Maddey wrote it. Don't distract her from giving us words.

BROADWAY BABY: Damn, it's a good thing I excel at improv—otherwise I'd never be able to keep up.

DANCING QUEEN: Wrong! It's all those years you lived with me and Ella. We were good practice.

FIDDLER ON THE ROOF: *GIF of man waving his hand side to side saying, "This."*

QUEEN OF SMUT: So I'm in my office, working on formatting the newest hockey hunks book, listening to *I Never Expected You*…

MOTHER OF DRAGONS: Ooo, Stefanie Jenkins' book?

MAKES BOYS CRY: Oh, that Zach Jacobs! *fire emoji* *drool emoji*

ALPHABET SOUP: I love when he goes all growly alpha on Haylee.

PROTEIN PRINCESS: He can tell me what to do any day of the week.

SANTA'S COOKIE SUPPLIER: You sure about that, Gem? You seem to get all defensive when Chance tries to offer up suggestions.

BROADWAY BABY: True story. I thought you were going to dice him up and serve him with a side of potatoes last night.

FIDDLER ON THE ROOF: You and your damn potatoes. *facepalm emoji*

BROADWAY BABY: *GIF of dancing potatoes saying, "Taters gonna tate."*

DANCING QUEEN: May I offer up a suggestion?

THE OG PITA: *GIF of Wendy Williams looking interested*

PROTEIN PRINCESS: *groans* I can already tell I'm not going to want to hear this.

DANCING QUEEN: Did you ever think maybe if you served yourself up as his meal instead of one of your fabulous dishes, you guys wouldn't hate each other so much?

PROTEIN PRINCESS: OH MY GOD.

PROTEIN PRINCESS: HOW MANY TIMES DO I HAVE TO SAY IT?

PROTEIN PRINCESS: NOTHING IS EVER GOING TO HAPPEN WITH CHANCE JENSON AND ME.

YOU KNOW YOU WANNA: I love when we make you text like me. *smiley face emoji*

ALPHABET SOUP: And look at those shouty capitals.

MOTHER OF DRAGONS: Speaking of shouty capitals, let's hear the rest of Maddey's story before we dive back into another round of how Gem should jump on Chance's hockey stick.

QUEEN OF SMUT: Thanks, Jor. I swear *squirrel emoji* *Dory fish emoji*

THE OG PITA: To be fair, you distracted us with thoughts of Zach Jacobs, so…

SANTA'S COOKIE SUPPLIER: Hold up *open palm emoji* First off, we NEED to know what scene you were on when this went down.

QUEEN OF SMUT: After Haylee tries to make him jealous by showing up at the party with Chad.

ALPHABET SOUP: Oh I love that scene. It reminds me of how Gage reacted when he thought I was still with Jase.

BROADWAY BABY: OMG! Jase told me that story. Isn't that when you guys broke the massage table?

YOU KNOW YOU WANNA: OMG. Seeing you walk out from the back holding an ice pack on your ass is still one of my favorite memories of our friendship.

DANCING QUEEN: I think we need to hear this story.

MOTHER OF DRAGONS: Later. Let's finish hearing Maddey's first.

QUEEN OF SMUT: We are legit the worst. But it's okay—I love you ladies more than words.

MAKES BOYS CRY: We know. Now go on…

QUEEN OF SMUT: So ANYWAY…I'm in my office, and just as Zach is telling Haylee she is his and all that jazz, Dex comes barreling into the room like he was…I don't know…expecting to find a terrorist behind the door or something.

ALPHABET SOUP: Not to sound disappointed or anything, but why does that have you doing shouty capitals?

QUEEN OF SMUT: That's not the really weird part. Though, the way he seemed…jealous?…was strange. But no, we had this moment where I could have SWORN he was going to kiss me.

MOTHER OF DRAGONS: Oh shit! Girls night!

Chapter Seventeen

Dex

O ver an hour later, I'm still trying to figure out how this entire thing has gone FUBAR.

I almost kissed Maddey McClain.

I almost *kissed* Maddey McClain.

I'm a dead man walking.

All the training I've done to become a Tier 1 operator won't do anything to help me if my fellow Lost Boys find out what I almost did.

Maybe I can plead temporary insanity.

Except…

Fuck my life. Where the hell is my self-control?

The worst thing is, as soon as my worries over what her brothers would do to me recede, thoughts of Maddey push to the forefront.

What was she thinking?

Did she want me to kiss her?

Would she have kissed me back?

Did she even realize I was about to kiss her?

Then, because I have zero chill when it comes to Maddey, there's the X-rated turn my mind takes when the sound of water rushing through the pipes hits my ears.

Maddey in the shower.

Naked.

Hands roaming her body, brushing across those nipples that pressed into my chest, her hand slipping between her legs—

Fuck me. She might as well tase me in the balls again, because they are about to fall off they're so blue.

I wonder how she feels about shower sex. There are so many possibilities.

I could bend her over, her hands braced on the wall, and take her from behind.

I could lift her into my arms, press her against the tile as I drive into her while the water beats down around us.

I'm a SEAL; we do excel in the water, after all.

"What do you want to do today, baby?" Her melodic voice floats down the stairs.

Woof! Woof!

"It's a little late in the day to go paddle-boarding. Too many boats out now."

Woof!

"I know. I'm sorry. We'll go tomorrow, okay?"

Woof!

"We can go play with your cousins if you want."

Woof!

I don't even attempt to hide my grin as they amble their way in my direction, lost in conversation. And make no mistake, it *is* a conversation. Each of Trident's barks are practically English. The only other time I've seen an owner/canine connection like Tink has with her pup is with Bullet, our unit's Malinois.

Woof! Woof-woof!

"Yes I'll ask Chance to bring Pebbles and Bamm-Bamm too."

Woof!

I swear Trident just said *Yippie!*

"Who knew you were such a dog whisperer, Tink."

I shut the lid on my laptop, not wanting her to see the profiles of who we believe are our lead suspects in her case. She was so upset earlier, and I don't want anything to wipe away the beaming smile she has going on at the moment.

"You joke, Hook." She flashes me her dimples over her shoulder before going back to preparing her coffee. "But my boy totally understands me." She bends to scratch Trident behind the ears. "Right, baby? You know what your mommy is saying, don't you?"

The dog licks up the entire side of Maddey's face, and her responding laughter is music to my ears. I hold up my hands in surrender when she hits me with one of her *See? Told you* looks.

"You're insane, you know that right?" The quirk to my lips gives away how entertained I am.

"This isn't some *shocking* revelation or anything. You *did* grow up with me."

That's right. You did *grow up with her.* I should be court-martialed for the thoughts I've had about her.

I clear my throat and roll my shoulders back, needing to corral my errant thoughts. We cannot have another close call like earlier. I'm here to do a job, not do Maddey.

Maybe it will eventually stick if I keep reminding myself of that fact.

"I'm not sure what your G.I. Joe plans for the day are"—she circles a hand in the direction of the laptop on the counter—"but I'm going to Jake and Jordan's." Travel mug of coffee in hand, she starts down the hallway to the front of the house and calls over her shoulder, "You're welcome to join if you want."

I force my gaze off of the sway of her hips in her tiny cutoff shorts, and I don't notice the way her gauzy white top drapes off her shoulders or that the hem of it is high enough to show a hint of her toned stomach when she moves.

No. Nope. I don't notice any of that.

She chats with Trident the whole way, the pooch staying obediently by her side and hanging on her every word if his answering barks are any indication.

The dog picks up on her shift in demeanor a fraction of a second before I do. Maddey's steps come to a halt and all the joy is leached from her face as she riffles through the mail in her hands.

I'm at her side in an instant, my arm wrapping around her back and tugging her against my side.

I glance down, but there is nothing outwardly threatening about the nondescript white envelope and printed label with Maddey's information.

"Maddey?" She's like a block of ice in my arms.

"D-do you have gloves in your spy kit?" Her attempt at humor fails with the way her voice wavers.

"Yes." I hope the no-nonsense way I say the word reminds her that she isn't in this alone anymore. I've got her six.

"Can you get them and open this?" Barely pinching the envelope between her fingertips, she holds it out to me, watching it as if were a snake waiting to strike.

"You think this is from your stalker?" My head is on a swivel as if I expect to see the person inside the room with us.

"I don't know." She shudders, pressing into me harder. "But all the other notes I received were like this. Generic envelope, typed label, no return address—pretty much anything they could do to make it untraceable."

It is harder than it should be to let her go to grab a pair of gloves, but I do it. We need to know if this is a real threat. The rock in my gut tells me it is, but Maddey can no longer bury her head in the sand with this. It is time to face this head on.

Needing to keep her close, for her sake and for my own sanity, I thread my fingers through hers and tug her along with me.

Gloves in place, I take the offensive object and slip my

thumb under the edge. The tear of the paper is deafening in the otherwise silent room, our eyes trained on the action.

Gingerly, I pull the contents free, set the envelope off to the side on the counter, and unfurl the trifold paper. I drop it as if burned when I see the typed message.

> *Tsk, tsk, tsk, Madison Belle*
> *You know the only Beast that is supposed*
> *to be warming your bed is me.*
> *I am very disappointed.*
> *Don't worry…I'm really good at hunting.*

There's a gasp and then Maddey is suctioning herself to me again. This time I'm unable to appreciate how her soft curves feel molding to all my hard edges because I'm too busy seething.

There is so much wrong with what I've just read I'm not sure where to begin.

1. The letter itself.

2. It being delivered to her home. Yes, I know things coming here instead of her PO box was part of why I was called in, but it still bothers me.

3. The fact that this motherfucker not only called her by her real name, but also used her middle name.

4. The perversion of her Disney love.

5. That this fucker knows I'm staying here.

6. The threat now against me, though this is the least of my concerns. I *wish* this guy would come at me. I *long* to show him the error of his ways.

If all that isn't enough, the part that troubles me the most isn't the reference to Maddey and me having a sexual relationship. No, it's how the stalker is taking a turn for the personal, stating that Maddey is his and insinuating a sexual relationship with him.

Over my dead fucking body.

Chapter Eighteen

What in the actual fuck?

This is an entirely new level of fucked up. I can't even.

Sure, I told Dex the things I've received started to take a turn for the Maddey McClain versus the Belle Willis, but this is the first time I've actually been addressed as myself. To say it's freaking me the fuck out would be like saying Mickey is only a mouse—understatement of the century.

I have so many questions.

Who is this person?

Why are they doing this?

What is their endgame?

But the one running on repeat is: How does this person know about Dex staying here?

And don't even get me started on the whole *Misery*-turn of how I should be with this sicko. This is the first time in my life I'm grateful for my brothers' overprotectiveness, because if I didn't have Dex to literally latch onto at the moment, I might be a complete basket case.

My breathing is erratic and I can hear my pulse beating in

my ears, but with my arms wrapped around his washboard stomach like a vise, I'm able to stay just on this side of the panic line.

"I'm calling Justin and Paul," Dex says as he gently places the letter down.

If he's looking for an argument from me, he's not going to get it. This is no longer the time for me to be stubborn. Shit just got serious.

"And your dad."

Another nod. I don't expect them to be able to do anything more than they already have, but we need to utilize every resource.

"Go put some shoes on."

I bend my knee and point at the white Uptown sneaker wedges on my feet, my anklets sliding up my leg as my foot hits my butt. "Are these not shoes?"

Unless I'm on the beach or working out, if I'm wearing footwear, it has a heel, platform, or wedge.

"Sneakers, Maddey. Put on sneakers."

"Do you not see the giant swoosh on the side? These beauties are Nike, Hook." I have no idea where my sass is coming from. I chalk it up to the subconscious safety I always feel around him.

His eyes go to the ceiling, and if I had to guess, I'd say he is praying for patience. It's a look I'm very accustomed to seeing on him and my brothers.

You'd think they would know better after twenty-six years.

"Fine." Oh, look—he *can* be taught. "We're leaving."

That brings me up short. Yes I'm freaked AF, but I'm not going to be chased out of my own home.

"I'm not running away, Dex."

"I know." He smooths a hand along the side of my face, leaving it there to cup my cheek. Unlike when I swore he was about to kiss me earlier, the only thing I feel now is comfort. "That's not what I'm asking."

"You weren't really *asking* anything…"

"Smartass." The rigidity leaves his body as he chuckles. "Go upstairs and get your gun. We're going to make sure you really can shoot to kill like you claim."

Notice how he still didn't phrase it as a question? Damn alpha men. Why are they so hot?

Also, why do I find it so hot that he doesn't treat me like some porcelain doll? Even in the wake of the worst threat I've received, he's not locking me in an ivory tower. No, he's going all Shang to my Mulan, making a man out of me.

Half an hour later—all original plans canceled—we park in the lot of the gun range I've been familiar with for years. Jack McClain didn't give a damn that I was his only child born with a vagina; I started going to the range in high school just like my brothers.

Dex bringing me here isn't like a scene from a bodyguard trope where he's the big bad protector teaching the damsel he's charged with protecting to use a gun so she can take back her power. No, coming here is some kind of Mr. Miyagi lesson that I can take care of myself without him.

The spot behind my left boob flutters at how, even when faced with the worst of the "gifts" delivered to me, he believes in my capabilities.

I'm doing my best to compartmentalize my thoughts before my brain hits overload and fizzles out.

Jiminy has been doing the Argentine tango with my hormones since even considering the possibility of having a friends-with-bennies arrangement with Dex to end my *long* dry spell.

I get the impression Jiminy is still on the fence about what to do. My nipples, my clit, and my pussy—who hasn't had an up-close-and-personal experience with a real, live penis or fingers that didn't belong to me in far too long—are all holding up their scoring paddles at the idea of doing the horizontal mambo with Dex.

I have read a lot of FWB books and even written a few—I know how this scenario is supposed to play out. However, unlike a romance novel, there is no guarantee of an HEA in real life.

Didn't you already decide you aren't in love with Dex?

Yeah, didn't you go all Bill Engvall "Here's your sign" on your feelings not being "real" when you fell for Ryan?

I say jump Dex's bones.

throws confetti and spins around What's the harm in a few mutual orgasms between friends?

Still…

Could I do it? Could I sleep with Dex?

Holy shitballs it is *so* not helping that he is literally every cop/military/bodyguard book boyfriend ideal in his black t-shirt, khaki cargo shorts, and sneakers. The cotton is stretched taut across his back, molding to his shoulders, and cuts just above the bulge of his biceps. All I want to do is sink my teeth into the hard muscle and never let go.

Don't even get me started on his backward hat or how he has his black wraparound sunglasses resting on the rim. Seriously, why is that look so fucking hot? How is a girl supposed to keep her ovaries from exploding with all that panty-melting hotness?

I told you to stop fighting it.

Let him show you the world.

We get checked in, purchase our extra ammo, collect our safety gear, and make our way through the massive structure to the shooting range in the back. Dad prefers this facility to others in the area because of the wide range of practice areas they offer. In addition to the single person stalls we are headed to, there is also a virtual simulation theater.

There are only a handful of shooters in the range, and I follow Dex to the stall farthest from them and from the door, where it would be harder for someone to sneak up on us.

"Alright, Tink." Dex slides the case holding my 9mm onto the counter of the stall. "Let's see what you got." He loads one of the paper targets and hits the button to send it down the track.

We both slip on our safety glasses and noise-canceling headphones, and I get into position with Dex observing from behind.

Most civilians are nervous around guns, but as a Navy brat turned daughter of a police chief, I've been surrounded by weapons my entire life. The weight of it in my hand is a comfort.

I load the magazine, chamber a round, and take my stance. Feet spread hip-width apart, my left slightly in front of my right, I wrap both hands around the grip and extend my arms in front of me, making sure not to lock my elbows.

Shot lined up, deep breath in, I contract my finger, pressing the trigger and repeating the action six more times until I've emptied the entire magazine into my target's heart.

Flipping the safety back on, I set the gun on the ledge and pull the headphones from my ears to rest around my neck.

Dex recalls the target, the paper flying back toward us, waving in the breeze once it stops. A wall of heat hits my back as he comes up behind me, his tatted arm stretching alongside me to inspect the half-dollar-sized grouping I shot into the chest region.

"Impressive." It's embarrassing how close I am to melting at his compliment.

"Thanks." I keep my eyes on the target and not on the

inked flag in my peripheral. "I was gonna go for the head, but Dad always preached shooting for the heart because it's a larger target area if you miss."

"But you didn't miss."

I tilt my head back onto his chest, angling my chin to see him. "I was taught better than that."

"Of course you were, Baby McClain." His teeth flash in amusement.

"I'm not a baby," I grumble as he shifts to send the target back down the track.

"Oh, I know." I think that's what he says, but it's mumbled so I'm not sure if I heard him correctly or if it's wishful thinking.

He said it. He totally said it. Come on! Let's be part of his world, my lady bits cry as they push onto a rock with the waves crashing behind them.

"Head shots, Tink."

I repeat the same process as earlier but aiming for the head this time. As promised, I don't miss, the same tight grouping placed between the target's eyes.

"Very nice." He reaches for a fresh paper and hip-checks me out of the way. "Now let me show you how it's really done."

"So cocky." I giggle but move to the side.

"You have no idea, baby."

Wait…

What?

Is Dex…

No.

He's not flirting with me, right?

Oh my god I'm losing it.

I pull my phone from my pocket and sneak a few pictures. How can I not? I mean…just look at him.

There's a reason I love me a good military romance.

There's just something about a guy wielding a weapon to protect his woman that drops the panties.

Dex's confidence and competency in all things American hero are what wet dreams are made of. This right here is why I always paired my Barbie with G.I. Joe instead of Ken.

Unlike when it was my turn, he does both rounds before bringing it back. Then, displaying the thirteen-year-old-level maturity every man never grows out of, he holds the paper in front of him, beaming at the two tiny holes—barely larger than the bullet—in the paper.

"Okay," he says. "We know you can shoot when you have time to prepare and aim, but more likely than not, you'll have to shoot on instinct."

Warm hands take me by the hips, reversing our positions again. It takes considerable effort to focus on what he is saying and not on how his hands are large enough that his fingertips touch at the small of my back.

"This time"—his arms bracket my body as he loads a fresh magazine into my gun—"I want you to pick this up like you're grabbing it on the fly and shoot your would-be intruder."

Ooo, look at those forearms.

His forearms? Look at how well he handles his…equipment.

Speaking of equipment, do you feel *that? That's not an extra Glock in his pocket, if you know what I'm saying. *waggles eyebrows**

Hold on, let me speak her language. 'What's the issue, dear? Why are you holding back from such a man?'

Can we stop dancing around the subject by quoting lyrics from Frozen*? Listen, Madison…do the math. You are in the back corner of the range. Dex is hot and you need to get laid. The risk of getting caught having sex in public only adds to the hotness. Take off your shorts and do him already.*

Most people say they have voices in their head, and if Jiminy wasn't enough, I also have the privilege of my characters weighing in from time to time. That last one? That sounded suspiciously like the one Becky inspired me to write.

Seconds pass before I'm able to untangle the synapses in my brain enough to follow his directive. I lace my fingers, crack my knuckles, and shake out my hands.

Inhale.

Exhale.

I got this.

Bang! Bang! Bang!

My breathing is erratic as the paper makes its approach.

"*Damn*, Tink." Dex whistles through his teeth. "It's a good thing you only keep your taser under your pillow."

My shots may be more spread out, but all seven hit the chest.

"Again," he instructs.

The target is replaced and sent back down the line.

I load the 9mm, set it on the counter, wait a beat, then pick it up and empty the magazine.

This process repeats a dozen times before Dex halts me with a hand on the shoulder.

"Now I want you to do it with mine." He hands me a SIG Sauer P226. It is also a 9mm, but the grip handle is longer and the gun itself is slightly bigger than my own.

The recoil on both guns is low, but after firing more than two dozen rounds in such quick succession, my arms are getting fatigued.

"Now this." I eye the MK23 suspiciously. Both the SIG and this .45 caliber are weapons I know are in his arsenal with the Navy, but I also know he has to leave them at the armory when not on missions. "They're your dad's," he says to answer my silent question. "He wanted me to have what I was used to."

"So why are you having me shoot with them?" I point to the suppressor and laser sight attached above the barrel.

"Because if for some reason you are closer to my weapon

than your own, I need to know you are comfortable with it."

I note how he doesn't say anything about being able to handle it. The subject has never been up for debate with him.

Is that why I haven't fought him being here?

Between the added weight and awkwardness of the suppressor, the fatigue in my muscles, and the minor increase in recoil, my shots still hit the target, but they are sloppier.

"Here." With the headphones covering my ears, it makes hearing his instructions difficult, so he maneuvers my body instead.

Hands skim the backs of my arms, every hair rising in the wake of his calloused fingertips. He curls his fingers around my elbows, pressing to lift my arms an inch higher before continuing on down my forearms.

His front molds to every inch of my back, his knees bumping against the backs of my thighs, which clench at the familiar bulge resting on the top curve of my ass.

He shifts a headphone back, his stubble scratching along the shell of my ear and setting off all kinds of tingles I shouldn't be feeling.

"Like this." He adjusts my hold around the grip of the gun, curling his own hand around mine.

There's a low rumble in my ear so I know he's still speaking, but I'm lost in the subtle feel of the muscles pressed against me and the scent of the ocean invading my senses.

Once he's done maneuvering me like I'm his puppet, he shifts the headphones back in place and straightens.

I expect him to retake his spot at the back of the stall, but he doesn't. Instead his hands drop to my hips and he keeps his position behind me. He gives me a squeeze, telling me to shoot, but every cell in my body is too consumed by his near-ness to focus on anything else.

What am I supposed to be doing?

Oh, right—shooting.

I roll my shoulders back, not thinking of how he dips his fingers into the front pockets of my shorts.

I activate the laser sight—if I'm going to have toys, might as well play with them—ignoring how his thumbs run across my waistband.

I work to control my breathing, letting the scent of salt and sea ground me instead of making me turn around to lick the curve of his neck.

There's nothing I can do about my erratic heartbeat; the damn organ hasn't maintained a regular pattern since Dex invaded my house days ago.

One beat.

Then another.

Inhale through the nose.

Exhale out the mouth.

Pop! Pop! Pop!

I lower my arms after I empty the magazine. Dex doesn't move. With the exception of placing the gun down, neither do I.

Umm… *scratches head and looks around* Do you guys know what's going on?

Shh. Let them have this moment.

Anyone else think it's unfair we aren't actually real? Because holy crap I wish I could take a picture.

For reals, this is total Pinterest-worthy material right here.

Ooo, I hope she writes me a hot cop to bang.

Shit! I'm totally going home to write a cop into a WIP.

Yeah, gurl! Get it. Think of all the dirty possibilities. I mean…handcuffs!

I shake my head, chuckling to myself. If anyone knew what really went on inside my head, they would be fitting me for a straitjacket and reserving a padded cell.

I let my characters debate and brainstorm, twitchy for my keyboard.

Back and forth Dex traces figure eights on the part of my

midriff exposed by the hem of my shirt, my stomach muscles contracting with each pass underneath my belly button.

The color drains from my fingertips as I dig them into the metal counter, grounding myself in place instead of turning around and throwing myself at Dex.

Badum-badum, badum-badum, badum-badum, badum-badum.

Against my back, I feel his heartbeat echo each of mine.

His thumbs stroke.

Our breathing syncs.

Jiminy and the dozen other voices in my head battle it out over if there's any merit to doing something about this sexual tension that's brewing.

Sexual tension? Did I really just think those words in conjunction with Dex?

Those strong hands grip me, spinning me to face him. One of the curls from my ponytail is stuck in the stubble on his face, but I barely notice it falling as I'm knocked back a step from the banked heat swirling in those chocolate eyes.

There's a hint of pride there, but it's the raw possession lurking that has everyone in my brain cheering like we're at a Blizzards game.

He removes his ear protection, leaving the neon green headphones to hang around his neck before doing the same with my own.

"Tink." His hands come up to cradle the back of my neck, my hands automatically bracing themselves on his hard, *hard* chest when he tugs me closer, his eyes locked on my mouth.

His nostrils flare when I worry my bottom lip with my teeth.

I thought the moment we shared in my office was something, but this one right here puts it to shame. Sebastian is full-on singing "Kiss The Girl" as Dex inches closer.

"Hook." I exhale, rising up on my toes.

"Tink." His hold on me tightens.

Unlike in the movie, there's no crab and his helpers

singing to us. Instead, our soundtrack is the occasional echo of gunshots as, millimeter by millimeter, the space between us disappears.

This is it.

I'm going to kiss Dexter Stone.

His lips brush mine and—

Ring! Ring!

Chapter Nineteen

Dex

One crazy stalker note, two near kisses, and three McClains under one roof all added up to twenty-four hours of insanity.

After I was saved by the bell—or in this case, the ringing cellphone—from almost kissing Maddey for the second time in a handful of hours, the rest of yesterday was a whirlwind of activity.

Minutes after Maddey and I returned home from the range, Justin, Jack, and Paul arrived guns blazing—thankfully not literally—to discuss the latest developments.

We looped in the local LEOs, and after Maddey gave her statement to one of the detectives in charge of her case, she excused herself and hid away in her office for the rest of the night.

Thankfully the McClain men ignored the note's claim of me sleeping with the youngest member of the family, but it didn't do anything to help assuage the guilt over almost crossing a line I could never uncross.

The worst part?

If given the chance, I wouldn't just cross it, I would over-take it like it was the only thing keeping me from an HVT. To my heart, there's no higher value target than Maddey McClain.

After a mostly sleepless night strategizing the best course of action to finally catch this fucker once and for all, the only play we've come up with is to use me to draw him out. Honestly, I was shocked Justin suggested it. It's so not how he normally handles things with Maddey.

We still haven't figured out how the stalker even knows I'm staying here, but we will. The important thing is using his newly displayed jealousy to our advantage. When emotions get involved, people tend to get sloppy.

I loathe that this asshole thinks he has any right to Maddey, that he thinks she belongs to him when I know she's the other half of *my* soul. All I need is for him to make a move so I can prove it.

Trident perks up beside me, the dog surprisingly having stuck to my side instead of Maddey's since she's been sequestered away. My gaze follows his, and a moment later, the door to the deck slides open.

"Tinker Bell, where you at?" Jase Donnelly shouts as he steps inside.

"You know she hates it when you call her that." Ryan bends down to pet Trident when the dog rushes to greet him. I ignore the flash of jealousy I feel at how much the canine loves him.

"Duh! Why else do you think I do it?" Jase replies before shouting, "TINKER BELL!"

"Yes, piss off the deadliest Covenette—that sounds like a good plan." Jake edges his way past his brothers-in-law with baby Logan strapped to his chest, greeting me with a nod.

"Eh." Vince is the next to enter. "Let him talk shit. Person-ally, I could use the entertainment."

"Truth." Sammy makes a beeline for the coffee pot. "If she can tase him"—he hooks a thumb in my direction—"I can't wait to see what she would do to you."

"*Pfft.*" Jase waves them all off. "Tink loves me. She would *never* hurt me. I'm her triplet."

The guys all let loose a round of guffaws while I try not to lose it over Jase calling Maddey Tink. I don't have exclusivity on the nickname. Hell, her brothers helped coin it, and I've heard her friends use it from time to time, but being here, staying in her house, being called Hook more than Dex…

"Come on, Tink. Use those wings and fly on do—"

"I dare you to finish that sentence, Jason." Maddey pushes Jase back into the kitchen.

"You wound me, Madison."

"I'll be sure to send you a get well soon card, Trip."

The rest of their banter fades away as I take in what Maddey is wearing, or in this case, not wearing.

Where are her clothes?

She does *live at the beach.*

It really, *really* is a bad sign when the Admiral in my pants is the one being logical, but fuck me. How is a man supposed to think straight when Maddey is walking around like…like *that*?

To be fair, the black bikini bottom fully covers her heart-shaped ass and her top covers as much as her sports bra did the other day, but I was not expecting her to come down in essentially her underwear.

"Here, Madz." Sammy holds out a mug of coffee.

"This is why you're my best friend," she declares, taking a sip.

"Hey!" Ryan cries.

"You know you're my bestie, Ry." She pats the hockey captain on the chest as she walks past him. "But Samz has both seniority and caffeine right now."

"Burn," Jase and Vince say in unison.

"Bite me, assholes," Ryan retorts.

"Can we maybe keep *this* child of mine from learning

profanity from you puck heads?" Jake has his hands covering Logan's ears as the child sleeps, blissfully unaware.

"Don't worry, bro." Jase claps Ryan on the shoulder. "I'm pretty sure Logan hears worse from JD every day."

"Says the man who taught the twins how to say asshole," Jake adds.

"Not that I'm not happy to see you guys or anything"— Maddey leans back against the counter, and my gaze does *not* drop to the ring sparkling in her belly button—"but what are you all doing here?"

"I came for my running partner." Ryan pats Trident on the head.

"He didn't give me a choice." Jase points to Ryan.

"Holly had to work at Espresso Patronum today—no point in staying in bed without her." Vince shrugs.

"I'm just letting my girls get extra sleep by taking the little man out of the house," Jake says.

The topic jumps, multiple conversations happening at once, all of it typical of their group, and with as much crap as the guys give the ladies, they aren't much better.

Maddey, though? I've never seen her more at home than when she is surrounded by her friends. Witnessing her getting to experience these little pockets of normalcy amongst the chaos trying to invade her life is why I shot down Justin's suggestion of taking her back to Virginia Beach with me. Plus, they need someone here who can put their sole focus on helping catch this asshole.

"You staying here? Or are you coming paddle-boarding with us?" Maddey asks me over the rim of her mug.

"Do you think you'll be at risk in the middle of the ocean?" I can't help but tease. She's not hiding from what's happening anymore, and I can do my best to minimize the stress.

"Outside of sharks?" She pops a shoulder and smirks.

"No, but you are Aquaman—figured I'd give you the chance since the water is your domain and all."

"Nice." Vince holds out a fist to bump.

If we weren't standing in a kitchen surrounded by five of her friends, I'd throw her over my shoulder, haul ass to the ocean, and show her just how good my maritime skills are.

"Do you have a standard route you take?"

"Yes. It typically takes us an hour there and back."

I love that she anticipated my next question without me having to voice it.

"Go the opposite way."

Icy eyes bounce over my face then she nods. I expected her to fight me on the request, so I'm surprised she relents so easily.

"Let me grab my board and I'll meet you on the beach?" Sammy gives her a nod.

"See you next week?" she asks as Jase folds her into his arms.

"Nah, I'll be back tomorrow. Gotta see you put Cali through his paces."

"You're *such* a good friend, Trip." Maddey couldn't sound more sarcastic if she tried. Scratch that—if I told her that, she would find a way.

"You just want to watch him squirm under Griff's watch." Vince chuckles around his own hug.

"Please." Maddey rolls her eyes. "Griff is a total teddy bear, and Simone is stoked to be on a cover."

"That may be true, but even I'm glad you picked Cali as your victim, and I'm a happily married man," Jake says as Maddey places a gentle kiss on Logan's head.

"Yeah, yeah, we know you and Jordan are hashtag couple goals of the squad, but don't pick on Griff," Maddey scolds.

"Hey!" Vince and Jase toss their arms out in offense.

"You"—she points a finger at Vince—"may be perfect dirty talk inspo, but you can't claim couple goals until you can *at least* get your girlfriend to accept *one* of your marriage proposals. And you"—she shifts to Jase—"are still in the honeymoon stage. One step at a time there, Trip."

"If you weren't the happily-ever-after expert, I would fight you on this assessment, but I'll bow down to the queen…for now."

I can't get a read on the expression that crosses Maddey's face at Jase's statement, but I don't like it. It doesn't help that she immediately bends to Trident, her hair obscuring her face from view.

"You be a good boy and listen to Cap, okay?" Trident licks her face like usual.

"He's always good." Ryan gives Trident another scratch.

"I know."

"I'll bring him back after."

"I know that too."

Out of the corner of my eye, I see Sammy watching me watch Ryan and Maddey. He gives a subtle shake of his head when he notices me glancing his way.

Maddey is the first to walk out, each of the guys following closely behind. Sammy is the only one to hang back, rounding the island and leaning against it on the side closest to me.

"I take it you haven't given much thought to what I told you the other day?" He folds his arms over his bare chest, already dressed in the male equivalent of paddle-boarding attire—backward hat, Wayfarers on top, no shirt, and white board shorts with multi-colored palm trees.

"About…" I hedge instead of admitting how close to the mark he came the other night when he was being all cryptic.

"Fine." He pushes away from the counter. "If that's how you want to play it, I'm not gonna stop you."

"Sammy…"

He walks to the door but stops before sliding it open, turning back to eye me over his shoulder. "Look, if all you're gonna do is stand there and watch Maddey and Ryan like you're waiting for them to get back together, that's your prerogative."

My heart stutters and my stomach rebels at the thought.

"You may be used to seeing the world in shades of green in your night vision goggles and all that, but I think this particular green haze of envy you have going on is preventing you from seeing what is right in front of your face."

Chapter Twenty

Growing up in a beach town, paddle-boarding has long been my preferred method of exercise. It's also been one of my favorite means of escape—weather permitting—for when I need to quiet the noise inside my head.

Today is definitely one of those days where I could use the mental reset, but it's Tuesday, and Tuesdays in the summer are BFF-date day. As long as Sammy isn't touring with his husband and the Birds of Prey and I'm not on a strict deadline, we get together to paddle-board and creep on the local talent on the beach.

Still, alone time with my oldest and dearest friend comes at a premium nowadays, and I'm not gonna let myself get so caught up in my own bullshit that it keeps me from enjoying it.

"Will you spit it out before I go deaf over here?" Sammy splashes me with his paddle.

"I'm not saying anything." I return the favor, enjoying seeing him wobble on his board when the chilly water hits his skin.

Did he really think I wouldn't retaliate?

"Your mouth might not be, but the voices in your head are so loud even I can hear them." He stops paddling until we are standing side by side in the middle of the ocean.

I look to the waves rolling underneath us, the seagulls flying overhead, the wispy clouds blowing across the bright blue sky, and finally to Sammy waiting patiently next to me.

"And what is it you think they are yelling at me about?"

He hits me with one of his *Don't even try to play stupid with me, Madison* looks. He means business when his eyes call me by my full name.

"Dex—"

Oh, look—a cruise ship.

"Dex—"

Hold on. I need to wave to those nice people passing on jet skis.

Stop being a chickenshit and find your lady balls.

"Dexalmostkissedme," I say in a rush then add, "Twice."

"Hold up." One hand gets thrust forward with an open palm extended. "Flip it and reverse it."

"Don't go quoting Missy Elliot to me."

"Madison Belle, you know better than to skip the backstory. Now rewind, pull up a flashback, and give *all* the details. Because—*because* I could have *sworn* you just said Dex tried to kiss you."

I nod.

"Twice."

Two fingers wave inches from my nose, and I nod again.

"Dex? Dexter Stone?"

Another nod.

"The same Dexter Stone who is waiting back at your house?"

I'm going to turn into a bobblehead at this rate.

"Fuck me," he murmurs. "I was right."

Say what now?

"I knew he was in love with you."

"What?" I fall off my board, the blast of cold saltwater nowhere near the shock to my system that is the insanity that just came out of my best friend's mouth.

My hair sticks to my face as I scramble to fold my arms over my board. Water makes the view through the lenses of my aviators distorted, but I still see the way Sammy is clutching his stomach while he laughs at my expense.

"Wanting to kiss me and being in *love* with me are two entirely different things." I tread water as I try to make him see reason.

"That sexy SEAL wants to do so much more than *kiss* you, Madison Belle. If eye-fucking were an actual thing, he would have fucked you six ways to Sunday before you even finished your coffee this morning."

"Wanting to fuck me and being in love with me are also not the same thing." I swing a leg around and use my arms to hoist myself up until I'm sitting in a straddle position.

"Who's to say he doesn't want both?" A brow arches above the frame of his Wayfarers.

What the hell am I supposed to say to that?

I've barely wrapped my head around the idea that Dex sees me as anything other than Baby McClain; I can't even begin to fathom the idea that it could be more.

Jase called me the happily-ever-after expert, but outside the book world, that is a fraudulent title.

"It doesn't matter."

And it doesn't. I learned years ago that I don't know how to be *in* love. I love—fiercely if The Coven and the rest of my squad are any indication—but romantic love? The type where the hero and the heroine ride off into the sunset together and stand the test of time? That only exists for me in the stories I write and read.

I'm okay with it. I've made my peace. I'm surrounded by it enough on a daily basis to at least get to live vicariously.

"Maddey...you need to put yourself out there again."

Sammy softens his tone. "People break up. It happens. It's the circle of life and all that."

"Don't you try buttering me up with Disney."

He chuckles and reaches for me, tugging me in by the ankle, our knees bumping as the waves rock us gently.

"You also need to get laid. Stop telling yourself you're cheapening your relationship with Ryan by dating and maybe have a few sweaty sessions of meaningless sex. If the breakup had been so terrible, I wouldn't constantly have to battle it out with Ryan for the title of your bestie. You"—he pokes my chest—"are the only one who hasn't moved on."

He's right. I know it, and he knows it.

Still...

Where does that leave things with Dex?

Chapter Twenty-One

Dex

Jab. Jab. Jab-cross. Jab-cross. Jab-cross.

I hit the punching bag in Maddey's garage with enough force that the *swack* of my fists against it can be heard over the Birds of Prey song I have blaring from the sound system.

Jab. Jab. Jab-cross. Jab-cross. Jab-cross.

I need the physical outlet to help make sense of Sammy's parting shot. I'm not sure what it says about me as an operator that he can read me so well, but what is it he's trying to tell me?

Jab. Jab. Jab-cross. Jab-cross. Jab-cross.

"Did you know this is the first song Sammy produced for us?"

I whip around to find Sammy's husband, rock god Jamie Hawke, leaning against one of the support pillars. There's a smug smirk on his face, as if he knows he caught me unaware and is taking great pride in it.

"He's good at what he does," I say as I hit stop on the iPod. Sammy has gone on to produce two more albums with BoP since the one that led him to meeting his husband.

"He really is." Pride beams across Jamie's face. "But I didn't come here to gush about my husband."

He pushes off of the pillar and nods for me to follow, not saying anything else until we are seated on the lower deck overlooking the beach.

"I came to offer my help."

I arch a brow, not sure how a rock star thinks he has more to offer than the police officers in Maddey's family.

"No, no." Jamie waves me off with a laugh. "I'll leave the *Magnum PI* stuff to you, but I do have resources you can take advantage of since you aren't here in an official capacity."

Shifting back, I cross my arms over my chest and wait for him to explain. As a SEAL, I'm trained to use anything available to me to my advantage if it helps complete my mission. With Maddey's case at a virtual standstill, I'll take whatever break I can get, no matter the unlikely source.

"I know you don't really know me—"

"You love Sammy—that makes you family."

There's a flare of surprise in his purple eyes at the simple statement.

"Thank you. I know you've seen me more through a computer screen than in person over the years, but that means a lot to me."

My gaze follows Jamie's to where Sammy and Maddey are making their way up the beach.

"First, I want you to know if I thought we could have gotten away with it, I would have had guys protecting her." Jamie points at Maddey, who's now sitting side by side with his husband. "But Vince learned the hard way how easily she can suss out a security detail."

It's my turn to smirk as I recall when Justin told us how Maddey blew the cover of the security guys Vince tried to have watch Holly without her knowledge at the end of last year.

And now I'm shifting in my seat for an entirely different

reason. I'm really starting to question what it says about me that I get turned on by Maddey being such a badass.

"I've already paid a retainer for a small team to be dedicated to help with anything you need. A lot of the guys are ex-special forces so I suspected you'd be comfortable with them, but they won't be working in the field unless you feel you need the manpower."

"They were okay with that?"

"You are the only person Madz hasn't balked at having protect her. Trust me, we've *all* made countless attempts since this shit started. It's time we put a stop to it once and for all."

I cannot help but agree, and I thank Jamie for his support as he takes his leave.

Chapter Twenty-Two

Photoshoot days are some of my favorite, and I think a lot of it has to do with getting to use my closest friends as most of my models.

Today's is even better because we are doing an on-location shoot at Jake and Jordan's house, and those tend to turn into one of the shit-shows our squad is known for.

The thing I'm most excited for is the surprise guest who will be in attendance. Well, she's not a surprise for the shoot as she tends to come to any of the local ones she can, but I'm *dying* to see how Dex reacts.

I finish zipping up my strappy tan stilettos and adjust the band at the top of my strapless romper. The cotton material and lined pattern keep my outfit from coming off too dressy. I also needed something a little extra to help break me out of the funk I've been feeling under the weight of stress.

I'm thinking of revoking Sammy's BFF card because he is *not* helping the situation.

Am I attracted to Dex? Absolutely. Any woman with eyes would be.

Have I jilled-off to fantasies starring him more since he started staying under my roof? No comment.

Do I think Dex sees me as a sexual being and not Baby McClain? The jury is still out on that one. Yes, we had those two close calls where his mouth was almost on mine, but I feel like that was more situational than an *I need to kiss you now* type of thing.

The real question is if he does see me that way, what do I do about it?

I haven't decided, but I may or may not have chosen my sexiest white lace strapless bra and matching white lace cheekies when I got dressed this morning.

"You ready to go play with your cousins?" Trident's entire back half wiggles from side to side with his tail at the suggestion.

Because there aren't going to be enough humans there—you picked up on the sarcasm, right?—we will also have five canines to add to the chaos.

"You and Navy are in charge of keeping Stanley in line."

Woof!

"I know, but if anyone has a shot, it's the two of you."

Woof! Woof!

To be fair, Stanley is a good dog, but he's just over a year old and still acts very much like a puppy. Luckily for Jordan, he does love to imitate his older brother Navy and his cousin Trident when they are all together. And Pebbles and Bamm-Bamm—Chance's Great Danes—are the biggest mushes, so we won't have to worry about them.

I expect Dex to comment on me having a full-on conversation with my dog like he speaks English, but...nothing. Silence. Nothing but the click-clack of my heels and Trident's nails on the hardwood.

He's facing away from me, his back and shoulders doing that thing where they stretch the cotton of his white t-shirt, which looks as if it might rip like tissue paper if I were to touch it. The dark swirls of his tattoos show through like he's a coloring book with tracing paper over it.

"Dex?" My voice wobbles from the volatile tension filling the room as I take in the rigidity of his broad back.

He doesn't turn. Instead I could swear rage pulses off of him at the sound of my voice. My heart pogo-sticks into my throat. *Never* in my life have I witnessed him react like this.

His hands are clenched into fists on the table, balancing his weight on his knuckles while he stares at…something in front of him.

I try to peer around him, but his frame is too large for me to do so.

For as tough and lethal as I know Dex is—it comes with the territory as a SEAL—he never really shows those sides to me. He's always quick with a joke or smile. Even during the times my brothers would tease me, he always made sure to check in that I was good before joining in.

The lack of that reassurance now is concerning.

With cautious steps, I close the distance between us. "Hook?" I hope the use of his nickname will add levity to whatever has his back harder than stone—no pun intended—underneath the palm I've placed on it.

Slowly, he turns his head in my direction, his movements so robotic I can't even appreciate the hotness of his backward New York Kings hat.

The crazed violence in his brown eyes has me stepping back in self-preservation. I may joke about how he and my brothers are trained to kill a person with their pinky, but holy shitballs, someone get this man a scythe because he could be the angel of death with that look.

Trident whines, pressing into my side as he senses the tension.

Did I say I was concerned? Screw that—I've never been this scared in my life, and I think I'm going to be sick.

Every hair on my body stands on end, and I might be the first twenty-six-year-old to have a heart attack if the staccato of the beeps and the roaring in my ears is any indication.

Danger! Danger! Jiminy yells.

Gurl…what are you waiting for? Run.

Fuck that—get your ass upstairs and get your gun.

Go upstairs? She writes romance, not B-rated horror films. You never *run* up *the stairs.*

This is true. Look. *throws arm out, pointing* There's the door. Get out of here.

Saliva coats my tongue, and I need a paper bag before I hyperventilate.

Jiminy and my characters continue to toss out advice, but I barely hear it, let alone having the capability to follow it. Instead I stand rooted in place, waiting for my fight-or-flight instincts to kick in, but both those bitches are more than fashionably late.

They would never be given membership to The Coven, that's for damn sure.

"Hey. Hey." Warmth surrounds me and I close my eyes as Dex cups my face between his large hands. "Shit." His hold tightens. "Look at me, Tink."

White fills my vision. *Am I dying? Am I see the white light?*

"Maddey."

Should I go toward the light?

"Look at me, Madz."

I do have a 'Jesus is my homeboy' shirt in my closet—that should get me entrance into heaven, right?

"Look. At. Me."

The gruff command finally has me complying.

Oh look, the white I was seeing was only his t-shirt, not the stairway to heaven.

"Fuck, Tink. Don't scare me like that."

"*I* scared *you*?" I bring my hands up between us and punch his chest with the sides of my fists. "What the fuck do you think you did with your *I'm going to rip your entrails out* glare?"

"Shit." He snorts. "Only you."

My heart misses a beat for an entirely different reason. Damn Sammy for putting ideas in my head, because now I can't stop imagining Dex murmuring them while holding me in a romantic embrace and not trying to bring me back from the edge of insanity.

"What did I do?" I ask instead.

"Only you are capable of making me laugh when I'm feeling all 'entrail-ripping', as you put it."

His eyes lose that hardness and start to get that melty look I adore the longer he stares at me.

"Fuck, Tink."

Without warning, I find my face smashed into his ooo-let-me-grope-you chest, the familiar scent of the sea surrounding me like a comforting blanket and those equally drool-worthy arms banding around me like a vise.

"You're still scaring me." My voice is muffled while I resist the urge to bite the muscles doing the muffling.

Now is not the time to get distracted by my neglected libido. I'm a mature enough woman to recognize the severity of the situation.

His arms tighten when I try to pull away.

Gurrrl, where are you trying to go? A hot man has his arms around you —you stay there as long as possible.

Yeah, who cares about anything else? Enjoy this.

You know what you should do?

Don't waste your breath. I already tried telling her to climb that boy like a tree, and did she listen? No.

"Madz?" Dex interrupts the unhelpful voices.

"Sorry." I snuggle deeper into his embrace. I get the impression I'm going to need him to ground me for what's to come.

Chapter Twenty-Three

Dex

M addey wasn't far off in her assessment of how I'm feeling. If her stalker were standing in front of me, I would reach out and pull out his entrails through his ball sack before feeding them to him.

Our theory that my being here would spur him into action was correct. Not only has this been the fastest turnaround between gifts, this one also took on quite an escalation.

Fuck me. Thank god I started collecting Maddey's mail for her, because I can't even imagine how she would have reacted if she was the one to open this. Hell, I don't even want to tell her about it. If I thought I could get away with it, I wouldn't, but there are too many reasons why I need to tell her to keep it from her.

1. She has the right to know.

2. She has finally started taking the threat against her seriously, and I don't want her backsliding.

3. It would be a disservice to not tell her. My girl is stronger than that.

I don't even bother berating myself over the *my girl* thought because I'm too busy planning how I'm going to rip this asshole's fingernails off one by one.

The anger, the rage, the utter *fury* of wanting to burn the world down just to keep Maddey safe is finally starting to ebb with each sweet inhalation of coconut.

I hate that I scared her. I've come to realize I'm not the most rational person where she's concerned.

And this?

This is a whole new level of fucked up, one I'm still not sure how to process.

"Dex?"

I detest the wariness in her voice. I abhor that I'm only going to add to it.

I'm like a powder keg ready to explode at the first spark. Holding Maddey, her body brushing against mine with every ragged breath puffing out that mouth I still haven't gotten a chance to kiss, is not helping the situation.

I should let her go, take a step—or twenty—back, but I can't. If I release her, I'll lose the only thing tethering me to my sanity. Without her, there's a legitimate chance I will end up flying into the blind rage I was close to before she came downstairs.

"Something else came in the mail today."

She stiffens, and I want to punch myself in the face even though I'm just the messenger. I'd cut off a limb if I thought it would fix things. When she snuggles deeper into my hold, her arms squeezing me, fingers slipping beneath the hem of my shirt and brushing the skin of my lower back, I'm supremely grateful to have both my arms to keep her close.

"Show me."

I don't want to. I really, *really* don't want to.

"Tink…"

"Don't, Dex." She rests her chin on my chest, looking up at me. "I know you want to protect me and we both know I did my best to hide from this, but I'm done running. Show me."

There's my little fighter. Fuck me if this side of her isn't my favorite.

Keeping her anchored to me with an arm curved behind her back, hand splayed across it, I reach for the bubble mailer on the table. Crushing it in my palm, I will it to disintegrate in my grip, but to no avail.

With one last fortifying breath, I unfurl my fingers one by one to expose the red fabric. Balled up from being enclosed in my fist, the lingerie is unrecognizable until I hook a pinky in one of the straps and let it dangle from my finger.

Maddey sucks in an audible gasp, and my back burns as her nails scratch across it in an effort to get even closer, a feat that would require removing clothes to be made possible.

Whiskey. Tango. Foxtrot. Do not—I repeat, DO NOT start thinking about removing clothing, the Admiral in my pants warns me. He's right. Not to toot my own horn, but *toot toot*, I'm bigger than your average man, and thoughts like that would *easily* give away how I feel about Maddey with her held so close.

"What did the note say?"

All the color may have been leached out of her skin, but fire burns in her baby blues.

"What makes you think there's a note?"

"Don't fucking lie to me, Dexter." Her eyes now throw at me the daggers they were previously throwing at the lingerie. My balls experience a sense of táse-jà vu at her fierce determination.

I swallow down the lump of disgust that has formed in my throat, rolling my hips back when I see the way her eyes darken, following the movement of my Adam's apple. Maddey is the only one potent enough to affect me while preparing to relay such a murderous-thoughts-inducing message.

"It said something along the lines of how you'll wear this the first time you get on your knees for him." I leave out that he sent highlighted passages from some of her books for things they could act out.

The United States will negotiate with terrorists before I let this asshat pervert her work like that.

"And I thought *I* lived in a world of fiction." She reaches out to take the lace from me. "He doesn't even have good taste. If he's going to send me creeper gifts, the least he could do is send something that actually looks good on a woman."

I can't imagine anything not looking good on her trim curvy body, but again—not. The. Time.

"I need to call Jamie's guys and clue them in on this new development."

She jerks in my hold. "Jamie?"

"Yeah. He offered to have a few guys from the company BoP uses for security help with your case."

"You're the only one I trust to play bodyguard, Hook."

I crush her to me a second time, smoothing a hand across the back of her head and down her spine.

"I know, baby." Her simple statement means more to me than any medal I've been awarded in service to my country.

Chapter Twenty-Four

Dex has been hovering, and I'm shaken up enough to admit I *want* him close by.

I'm scared, terrified even. We've gone from Creepy McCreepster levels to felony sexual assault in only a matter of days.

It's a good thing the last nine months have trained me in the art of denial. Thank god, because if I didn't know how to relegate this insane shit to the back of my mind, I would have a better chance of my carriage not turning into a pumpkin at the stroke of midnight than getting any work done.

I'm also ridiculously overdue for a Coven night out.

It may have only been two days since I texted my girls in a panic over the first almost kiss, but so much has happened since then it feels like two years.

Jordan rushes me the moment I step inside her house, pulling me into a fierce mama bear hug without giving a damn about the baby squished between us. Life as I knew it changed the day Jordan and Skye stepped into our dorm room freshman year.

"Here." Jordan holds Logan out to a shell-shocked Dex. "Take him and go find Jake out back. He's got a beer for you, and I don't want to hear a peep about how you shouldn't drink—you *need* it. And you"—she tugs on my arm—"are coming with me."

Dex looks to me for help, but I simply tell him, "There's no point in arguing. Jordan always gets what she wants." It really is no wonder we consider her our group's de facto leader.

Dex reaches for Logan like he's a bomb and not a baby, and holy flying elephant Dumbo, I didn't think he could get any hotter—I've seen him in dress whites, dress blues, and full camo—but with a baby cradled to his chest in a white t-shirt and backward hat? Yeah, that could make a girl pregnant.

"Shit. It's a good thing Jake got fixed when the season ended. Otherwise I'd be having a fourth baby right now." I can't help but snort at how much Jordan's thoughts echo my own.

Arm linked with mine, I let her guide me to where our other Covenettes are gathered while Gemma makes margaritas.

"Talk about a book boyfriend come to life." Holly's gaze follows Dex.

"Shit, Madz. Please tell me you're planning on writing a single dad romance, because that"—Skye circles a finger at the door leading to the back yard—"was cover *gold* right there."

"For reals." Rocky nods emphatically. "I know I was cleared for sexy times, but Ronnie *does not* need to have a sibling so close in age."

"Fuck that." Becky, ever the devil on our shoulders, cuts in. "Like I told Rock when she was debating what to do with Octoman when he first moved into the building: you bang that man like a screen door in a hurricane."

"Mels and Ella agree wholeheartedly." Zoey holds her phone out for us to see their text convo.

"If you don't want to, I think I've served enough time with Wyatt that I've earned myself a hall pass," Beth muses with a tilt of her head. She and her husband, Gage's cousin Wyatt, have been a couple since high school.

"Yeah right, B. You know those James men are possessive as fuck," Rocky says to her cousin-in-law.

"True that." Beth holds out her glass for a cheers.

"To alpha men," the eight of us cheer in unison.

I let the coolness of the frozen margarita soothe my throat and the bite of tequila help ease away the stress of the morning. I would love nothing more than to get white girl wasted with my besties, but unfortunately I have to adult and work.

As if on cue, the doorbell rings and my photographer arrives. We discuss the feel I want for the cover and the different shots he'll take for teasers before heading outside to go over the details with Cali and Simone.

"I don't think I've ever seen this side of Cali before." Zoey hooks her arm around my elbow and pulls me into her side, whispering conspiratorially.

"Jase has already made about a dozen GIFs of Cali's nervous face," Rocky says.

"It's the best thing ever." Becky sidles up to Zoey's other side, proving once again why it's dangerous for the two of them to spend extended periods of time together.

"I'm all for picking on Cali—lord knows he deserves it—but I almost feel like it's an unfair attack on Griff," Gemma says, serving as our voice of reason.

She's not wrong. As formidable of a presence as Griff is with his bulging muscles and black ink covering almost every inch of his dark torso, the World Champion boxer is the biggest teddy bear of our group.

Hell, when he and Simone first started dating, he acted like a school boy with his first crush and not a twenty-five-year-old grown man. I may or may not have put some of that in a book.

Okay, who am I kidding—of course I put it in a book. It's pretty much understood that anything that happens is fair game for story inspiration. In fact, my fictionalized telling of Jake and Jordan's love story was my first bestseller, thank you very much.

We're halfway through the photoshoot—Griff scowling any time Cali checks and smirking the second he looks away—when Dex's surprise arrives.

"Oh no! I'm late? How can I be late? Madison Belle, did you tell me the wrong time?" Instantly I'm enveloped by a cloud of honeysuckle as strong arms pull me into a matronly hug.

To say Peggy Stone is one of my all-time favorite people is one of the highest compliments I can give. I mean, you know who my friends are.

"No, surprisingly we started early for once," I assure her as she holds me at arm's length, giving me a once-over and making sure I'm still in one piece.

"Don't worry, Pegs, we got all the good stuff on video," Holly calls out, cradled between Vince's legs on one of the lounge chairs surrounding the pool.

"I do love my fellow romance junkies." Peggy beams.

My text handle may be Queen of Smut, but Peggy Stone is the reason I discovered romance novels in the first place. Surrounded by all the testosterone that was her son and my brothers, she took pity on me and gave me my first escape. Some may argue twelve was too young to be handed my first Harlequin, but I've been devouring happily-ever-afters ever since.

"Mom?" Dex's deep voice has my hormones swooning like those triplets in *Beauty and the Beast* any time Gaston walks by. Those bitches need to chill when I have his mom in front of me.

"My baby," Peggy wails, launching herself at her son. Dex easily catches her, using those sexy SEAL muscles of his to hoist her into his arms.

I watch transfixed as Peggy gushes and fawns all over him. Her hands cup his face as I'm sure she tells him how much she loves him, has missed him, and thinks he needs to eat more because she swears he's wasting away. Spoiler alert —he's not.

Whenever I'm feeling down or missing my brothers and Dex more than usual, I pull up videos of soldiers returning home or surprising their families to feel better. Yes, I end up crying like a baby, but they are happy tears, I swear.

So when Dex bends to rest his forehead on his mom's, I need to bite down on my knuckles to keep from sobbing in public.

"You did this?" Emotion coats Dex's voice as he asks.

I nod, not wanting to give away how affected I am by witnessing their reunion.

"Why?"

Is he really asking me that?

I can't see his eyes behind his reflective lenses, but I can feel them on me. There's this innate sense of awareness that thrums through me, the hairs on my arms standing on end and goosebumps lining my skin whenever he expects an answer from me. It's a feeling I've grown accustomed to over the last few days.

Still…it doesn't explain how he could be asking this. He is Peggy's whole world. If he didn't spend more of his time traveling with the teams than at home, I'm sure she would have moved back to Virginia Beach to be closer to him.

I feel guilty enough that he's been in Jersey for *days* and hasn't been by to see her yet, too busy dealing with my crap. There wasn't a chance in hell I wouldn't make this happen.

"Ohana." The soft smile that curls on his lips when he picks up on my *Lilo & Stitch* family reference is a punch to the heart, and I need to look away and focus my attention back on the photoshoot before I do something stupid.

Something stupid equals launching myself at him similarly to the way Peggy did, except mine would end in one of those kisses we've almost had.

Chapter Twenty-Five

Dex

Living in Maddey's house these last few days has been like stepping through the wardrobe and entering another world. See what I did there? Look at me with the literary references.

It hasn't been much and I have previously spent some time with her friends over the years, but the casual way they accept me into the fold is mind-boggling.

Since walking into the Donovan home, I've been handed a baby, banished to a back yard, swapped aforementioned baby for a beer, served as a jungle gym for three toddlers, and listened to more trash talk than I thought possible.

Watching Maddey in her element, working with the photographer, her friends serving as her models—it's one of the sexiest things I've ever witnessed. Even now my gaze tracks back to where she's directing Cali on how he should hold Simone.

It's obvious why Maddey wants the pair for one of her covers. They make a striking couple with the hockey player's all-American boy-next-door appeal combined with Simone's sultry Tyra Banks resemblance; they would make anyone do a double take.

"Cali." Maddey drops her head with a groan. "Stop acting like English isn't your first language and nuzzle Simone's neck."

If you were to look up the word uncomfortable in the dictionary, Cali's picture would be next to it with the way he brings his face in closer to Simone.

"Should I tell Madz I've spent the last week telling Cali Griff will use him as his personal punching bag if he gets too *friendly* with Simone during the shoot?" Jase says out the side of his mouth.

"You do realize she's best friends with your sister, right?" Jake asks his brother-in-law.

"And?"

"And I think he's trying to remind you how your womb-mate is the queen of revenge plots." Gage points to Jase with his beer bottle.

"Motherfucker," Jase curses.

Gage chuckles. "Blue," he calls out to his wife. "Come take the baby before your bestie teaches him to curse like the twins."

Rocky makes her way over, liberates Ronnie from his dad, and gently bounces him while propping his head on her shoulder. "I would prefer my kid's first word *not* be asshole, best friend of mine."

"Sorry, Balboa." Jase holds his hands up in surrender, sounding anything but apologetic.

The rest of their bickering fades into the background as my gaze is drawn back to Maddey again when she starts to laugh. The action is so pure and unfiltered I feel my own lips pull up at the corners.

God she's a vision with her head thrown back, errant curls falling from her messy bun and brushing along the line of her neck exposed by her position.

Cali may be having a hard time nuzzling Simone as instructed, but I want to set up camp in the curve of

Maddey's neck...lick down the tendon running along the side, biting down and sucking where it meets her shoulder, marking her so the whole world will know she's mine.

Her laugh has always been one of my favorite sounds. It radiates joy in a way that makes you want to join in just because it's so goddamn infectious.

I've been doubting if I did the right thing withholding the second part of what the stalker sent, but seeing this, how easily she's been able to shake off her earlier terror, I'm glad I did.

I'm still unsure what my next steps are, but I'm going to have to take advantage of her being safe here, surrounded by her friends, to meet with Justin and Paul without her.

"Can you make sure Maddey stays here until I get back?" I ask the guys around me. She's going to rip me a new one when she realizes I went off without her, but I'm going to shield her as much as I can.

"She got another gift didn't she?" Ryan narrows his eyes, trying to read all the things I'm not saying.

I want to resent him for having been the person to hold Maddey's heart for years and being something to her I'll never be able to be, but he's too genuine a guy to make it stick.

Sammy may try to insinuate that there is nothing between Ryan and Maddey anymore, but I can't help but wonder if it's only a matter of time before they get back together. As much as it will gut me when it happens, I can't be mad about it. I've seen how he treats her.

I push to my feet, neither confirming or denying what he said. I'm calculating the best route of escape without being spotted when—*is that my...*

"Mom?"

"My baby."

Mom is a force to be reckoned with, so much so that almost everyone always refers to her as Peggy Stone. It's as if they need her full name to capture her essence. One of my favorite things about her is that her greetings always make me feel like a conquering hero. With her for a mother, it really doesn't surprise me that it's Maddey's badassery I find most attractive.

First Mom served as the epitome of a strong military spouse, holding down the fort at home while Dad fought for our country side by side with Jack McClain and the teams.

Granted, I was only five when Dad was killed in action, but even before that, I never felt like I was missing out on having a parent because Peggy Stone—see? even I do it—filled both roles so seamlessly.

Then when Jack McClain decided to leave the teams and move his family from Virginia to New Jersey to be closer to his extended family, she made the selfless decision to uproot her life so I wouldn't lose out on the only other family I had ever known.

"Look at you." Soft hands cup my face hard enough to make my lips pucker like a fish. "You're wasting away. Doesn't the Navy feed you?"

It's always the same whenever we see each other. Her being here now is everything. I probably should have swung by my childhood home before I ever went to Maddey's, but the SEAL in me who always puts the mission first overrode the mama's boy.

Yet in the midst of the shit-storm brewing in Tink's life, she made sure to make this, Mom being here, possible. It doesn't surprise me that she doesn't want to take credit for how meaningful this is. She only brushes it off, dropping the ohana line from *Lilo & Stitch* about how family means no one gets left behind.

Sunglasses shield Maddey's eyes, but I don't need to see them to know they are swimming with unshed tears when our gazes lock.

"Gemma!" Mom's shout breaks the weighted staring contest between Maddey and me.

"Yes, Peggy Stone?"

"I need you to cook up some of your heartiest dishes to stock at Maddey's, please. My boy is wasting away. He needs fattening up."

I roll my lips in to hold back a laugh. Thinking a child needs to eat must be in the official mom handbook or something, because she is always telling me I need to "fatten up" when she sees me. Granted, I may lose a little muscle mass when deployed, but I'm still over two hundred pounds. It's insulting for Mom to think I'm a lightweight.

"Anything for you, Pegs." Gemma looks me up and down. "But I think his physique is more than adequate."

"I don't know." Zoey steps into our circle. She's new to the group so there's still a lot I don't know about her, but I can tell she's trouble like Becky. "Maybe you should take your shirt off so we can give you a proper inspection, Navy boy."

See what I mean?

"I do so enjoy when The Coven gets a new victim to pick on." Jase tips his beer at me in commiseration.

"Truth." Vince taps his bottle against Jase's with an audible clank. "It's hard work being objectified all the time."

"Don't even try it, Muffin," Holly calls out with a laugh. "You were stripping down in my kitchen long before you even properly introduced yourself."

Holly's comment sets off a volley of insults and trash talk while Mom pulls me down to sit. Guess I'm not going anywhere for the moment.

Mom catches me up on everything—and I mean *everything* —I've missed since we last spoke. I don't mind. I know it's her way of feeling closer to me when most of my life is spent half a world away.

No matter how hard I try to keep it on my mother, my gaze keeps wandering over to Maddey. She's this intriguing combination of sex kitten in those sexy-as-fuck spiked heels and Diane Keaton in *Baby Boom* with one of the Donovan twins—don't ask me which one; they are too identical—braced on her hip while looking at the images her photographer is showing her on the camera.

"Dex, sweetheart?" The furrow in Mom's brow tells me I missed something. Those same dark eyes I inherited shift from me then out to Maddey on the pool deck. My back straightens as if I was called to attention. I don't trust the gleam I see in Peggy Stone's gaze for a second. It's too knowing.

She's never said it, but I get the impression Mom would love to have Maddey as a daughter-in-law. It's one of the reasons I've kept my feelings to myself. If she gets even a whiff of her lifelong dream becoming a reality, she will put together a target package more thoroughly than the best CIA operative.

Luckily, Mom's attention gets snagged by the shoot when Maddey says, "Christopher, can you act like you've had sex before?" Cali startles, but I can't tell if it's from the use of his legal name or the crack at his sex life. "You're in book club—you know what makes a hot cover. It's all about the neck grab."

"Speaking of book club…" Tucker cuts in. "When are we going to get another hockey book? You've been neglecting the best sport lately, Madz."

"Sorry to tell you this, brother-husband, but MMA is where it's at." Vince peeks his head around Holly to chime in.

"Bull—" Tucker catches himself before he finishes the curse. "The hockey contingent far outnumbers the fighter one, especially now that Nick took that coaching position in Lake Placid for the summer. Hockey for life."

"No way."

"Way."

"No."

"Oh my god." Maddey breaks up the childish debate. "Tuck, we've been taking a break from the hockey books because any time we read one, you all debate which teams would win in real life."

"We do not."

"You do too, and let's not forget how you guys almost came to blows over if Samantha Whiskey's Reapers would beat Maria Luis' Blades or if Pippa Grant's Thrusters would be the champs, and don't even get me started on Helena Hunting's or Maya Hughes' books."

Things break down even more after that, and a full-on debate over who has the best fictional hockey franchise and which players would make the All-Star roster ensues. This is exactly the distraction I need, and I slip out amongst the chaos. Mom will forgive me, but Maddey—she's the wildcard.

※

I find Justin and Paul on the back deck with beer when I arrive at my friend's house. It's probably a good thing he's drinking, because he sure as shit isn't going to like what I have to tell him.

"Where's Tink?" Justin tries to look around me for his sister.

"I left her at Jordan's." I accept Paul's offer of beer.

"You might want to hide the weapons when you get home, because she's going to be *pissed*." Justin's singsong tone is way too joyful for my peace of mind.

My friends have found way too much enjoyment in how Maddey took me down when I first showed up.

"Listen, asshole." I take a huge gulp of my beer, letting the cold liquid push down the lump that has formed in my throat. "This isn't a social call."

Both Justin and Paul jackknife up in their chairs, on alert. I keep silent as I pull out the two plastic baggies holding the copied pages of Maddey's books from the side pocket of my cargo shorts.

Passing one to each of them, I wait for their reactions, and neither disappoint. Eyes narrow, Paul does his best impression of the McClain jaw clench, and if steam could actually come out of a person's ears, they'd both be whistling like tea kettles.

"What the fuck?" Paul looks from the papers to me and back again.

"That wasn't all that came." The color drains from my hand as I choke the neck of my beer bottle. The passages may have been the thing I kept from Maddey, but I hate the implication behind the lingerie.

Who the fuck does this guy think he is? How fucking dare he think about my girl in *that* way?

The venom swimming in Justin's eyes as they meet mine reminds me that I also think of Maddey in a sexual way. It's something I've battled with for years.

Shaking off all the negative thoughts niggling the back of my brain, I take a deep breath and fill them in on the rest of what was delivered.

No one says a word, the silence only interrupted by birds chirping, kids playing in the neighborhood, and cars driving on the streets.

"This is the closest any two gifts have come together," Justin observes, and I nod.

"He's escalating," Paul adds, and I nod again.

They are both right, and I don't like it.

Justin jumps out of his seat and starts to pace. "We need to figure this shit out now."

Agreed.

"He's getting too close."

Also agreed.

"All it would take is one second"—he snaps his fingers—"for things to change."

Another silent agreement from me.

"My sister means the world to me."

She means the world to me too.

Oh shit.

I love her.

I thought I was in trouble battling it out with my attraction, but to have feelings—real, deep, make-her-my-forever type feelings—changes things.

"I promise you I will keep her safe." Conviction rings in each of my words.

Justin stops dead in his tracks, all his focus locking on to me. "I know you will. Of all the people in this world, *you* are the one I trust most with my sister."

The words hit like a punch in the gut. Maddey is the precious jewel of the McClain family—just don't let her hear you call her that. The McClains have always been like family, and to hear how highly they regard me means everything. I can only hope that opinion doesn't change when I make my move to make her mine.

Chapter Twenty-Six

I f I wasn't riding the high of a successful photoshoot, I would be acting more like Anger and not Joy from *Inside Out* over Dex pulling a Houdini and leaving.

I get that he's Mr. Stealthy SEAL Man and all that jazz, but if he thinks for *one* second I don't know *where* he is or *what* he is discussing, he has another thing coming when he gets back.

I also don't know what it says about me that I'm trying to keep my anger at the forefront of my mind because if I don't, I'm afraid I might be crushed under the weight of the disappointment I'm feeling.

Dex is the *one* person who treats me like I'm able to handle myself and don't *need* protection. Him dipping out like this? Someone needs to be taught a lesson about how actions speak louder than words.

Needing a moment to collect myself before I do something rash like taking the keys to one of the many cars parked outside and driving over to Justin's with my taser for an electric reminder, I excuse myself and head inside the house.

Since I've made the mature decision not to drive anywhere, I think I've more than earned the reward of tequila.

Ignoring the blender and margarita mix beside it, I grab the Patron XO Cafe from the fridge instead of the silver. A pit stop for a shot glass—I'm still a classy lady, after all—then I head for the living room instead of going back outside.

Carlee is video-chatting with Sean from hockey camp, and I plop down on the couch next to her so I'm not drinking alone. Okay, I mean that's only a technicality since she's in the room with me but isn't going to actually be drinking with me. Sure, I drank before I was twenty-one, but even I can agree nine years old is a little too young to drink.

I'm going to pretend throwing back shots like it's my job instead of authoring is *not* setting a bad example and corrupting the next generation. A girl has her limits.

"Hi, Wife." Sean greets me with my nickname when he sees me.

"Hi, Husband," I return, using my own moniker for him. Closing in on double digits, he's growing into a bigger charmer than any of the guys outside, but he's been telling me he's going to marry me since he was three.

If it weren't for the beauty to my right, I might have considered putting in the time and waiting for him to be legal. With the way my love life—or more accurately, my lack of one—has been going, I'm pretty sure I'll still be single in nine years. Alas, Sean and Carlee are destined for each other.

"Wife?" a voice asks, and it's then I notice a dark-haired boy sitting next to Sean on the screen. "You guys are that official?" He points at Carlee.

"Oh, I wasn't talking to Cars, Mav. Hold on." Sean slings an arm around the boy's shoulders. "Madz, this is Maverick. Mav, this is Maddey, Carlee's sister-wife."

"You and your family are so weird." Maverick shakes his head. "But I thought your sister's name was Jordy or something."

"It is. Maddey is one of her best friends. I'll draw you a family tree later." Sean holds up a hand, halting Maverick from interrupting. "Yes, we know they look a lot alike. You should hear the jabs Ry would take from Coach Parker and his teammates about it, but that's not the point."

"Nick holding up okay up there?" I toss back a shot. "Is he enjoying his vacation from The Steele Maker?"

Nick Parker—and yes we take immense pleasure in teasing him for having the same name as the dad in *The Parent Trap*—is one of the BTU Titans alums who switched to fighting out of Rocky and Vince's family gym after graduation. I may not have known a whole lot about hockey prior to dating Ryan, and sure, maybe Nick wasn't *Miracle* level, but even I could see his talent on the ice. He was the only one surprised by the prestigious Lake Placid camp's call to come coach for the summer.

"Dude"—Carlee and I both snicker at how Sean always seems to slip into calling us *dude* or *bro* when excited or serious—"I thought Ry was bad when he would go all Cap on us, but he's got *nothing* on Nick as a coach." His blue eyes widen when he realizes what he said, and I'm struck by how much he looks like his oldest brother. "*Don't* tell him I said that."

I toast him with my shot glass then toss it back, my belly warming as the coffee-flavored liqueur hits it for the third time. I can hold my liquor surprisingly well for a girl of my size, but even I'll be trashed if I keep up this pace. Honestly, though, I can't say I care too much.

I'm boomeranging shot number four for my Instagram feed when Skye bends over the back of the couch to put her face in mine.

"Oh no." She eyes the Yeti-shaped shot glass in my hand before bringing her gaze back to me. "What has you doing brother shooters?"

"Brother shooters?" I call to her retreating back.

Readers ask me all the time where I come up with some of the things in my books. I answer by taking screenshots of the infamous Coven Conversations. None of us are normal, and I wouldn't change it one bit.

"I've been friends with both you and Jordan long enough to recognize when the work we're putting in on a bottle of tequila is because of something the OPB brigade brought on." Skye fills her own Blizzards mascot glass to the brim when she returns.

The fuzziness from the alcohol means it takes me a second to work out the acronym, but I snort when the meaning hits me. Yes, there is a huge overprotective brother brigade in our group. Jordan and I may be the ones to suffer the most, but all the Covenettes fall victim to it whether related by blood or honorary induction.

We clink glasses and toss them back, my eyes closing as the happy buzz starts to set in.

"Dex left," I say, pouring us a refill.

"Ah." Skye looks around as if to make sure we are still one SEAL short but accepts the next round held out to her. "So we're getting you drunk so you don't do something stupid about him playing bodyguard behind your back?"

I give her a finger gun for her spot-on assessment.

"Okay then. Bottoms up."

Another clink and down the hatch it goes.

Ahh, that's better. I tap my teeth to make sure they are still there. Them going numb is always the first sign I'm well on my way to a good time.

"So this is where you're hiding," Jordan says, squeezing in between Carlee and me. "What are you doing?"

"Corrupting the youth," Sean says, making me realize I forgot all about him on video chat.

I snort, slapping a hand over my face when tequila comes out of my nose. Shit that burns. Jordan hits me with one of her mom looks that says *Don't encourage him*, but I can't help it—my husband is funny as hell.

"Holy crap that's trippy." Maverick's finger bounces

between Jordan and me.

"Fucking A," Sean agrees.

"Sean Patrick!" Jordan scolds. "I swear it's like you *want* Mom to ban you from my house."

"Don't worry, Jordy." Sean waves off her concern. "Mom knows I pick up way worse hanging out at Ryan's. Hockey players aren't exactly known for having the cleanest language."

"Or sailors." I snicker, recalling all the times Peggy and Babs, my mom, would scold Dad for cursing in front of us growing up.

Witnessing Jack McClain being threatened with having his mouth washed out with soap is still one of the best memories I have.

Oh what a potty mouth Dad has. Potty mouth. *hehe* What a silly saying. Why do they call it that? Is it because the language is dirty? Who comes up with stuff like that?

Then there's the word potty itself. What a fun word. Potty. Pot-ty. Po-t-ty.

"What the hell are you doing?" Skye digs an elbow into my ribs.

"Huh?" is my brilliant response.

"Were you mouthing the word potty?"

Was I? Oh shit. Three cheers for tequila. Hip hip, hooray!

Speaking of…

More shots.

I'm about to tip shot number whatever-I-lost-count-I'm-an-author-I-don't-math when a hand covers the glass before it reaches my lips.

"I may not be a bartender anymore, but I *think* we should cut you off." Skye eases it from my grip, ignoring my dropped jaw completely.

"Why don't you just shout 'Andy's coming' and ruin all my fun." I pout.

"As epic as it was when you had the Blizzards go viral

doing that challenge, when you start fist-pumping and singing LMFAO's 'Shots' to yourself, we know we're doing it for your own good," Jordan cajoles.

Wait…was I doing that? I look to my left, and *son of a bitch* my arm is raised. Tequila is so fun.

"I love you guys. You're my favorite." I put an arm around both my female besties and pull them into me.

"Oh man, I'm missing drunk Maddey—that's no fun," Sean says.

"Remember when she tried to give us 'The Talk' on New Year's?" I groan at Carlee blowing up my spot.

"You didn't?" The dip in Jordan's cheek tells me she's biting it to hold back a laugh.

I nod. I did. I totally did.

"Don't worry—I'll take one for the team and give it to the twins when they get older," I offer.

"Oh count me in on that one. I can't let you have all the fun when it comes to our goddaughters." I bump the fist Skye has held out.

Jordan is so lucky to have us as her best friends. Look at us taking on the burden of having to discuss the birds and the bees with her children. I'm like the fairy godmother of sexual education.

Ooo, that would make a great text handle.

"I want to say thank god Sean is my brother and not my son, because I can't even imagine the phone call Maverick's mom is going to be making when she hears her future fourth grader is being taught about sex by a group of relative strangers." Jordan falls back against the couch cushions.

"You say that like Mama D won't be calling you as soon as she hangs up," Skye points out.

"Nah, Top Gun's mom is cool," Sean offers, trying to help me out of the sticky situation I've found myself in. He's a good husband.

"Oh my god!" I throw my arms up and happy-dance in

my seat. "Can we *please* watch *Top Gun*? Tom Cruise is *so* sexy in a flight suit. And look at the next gen coming up with the good nicknames! I approve." I give Sean a salute.

Oh I'm in a mood. I narrow my eyes at the tequila, and the level of the brown liquor is lower than I thought it would be. Whoa boy. Dex's night is going to be interesting.

No, wait—I'm mad at him. How could I forget?

Maybe because you're drunk?

Oh, shut up Jiminy.

"Oh no."

"She's further gone than I thought if she's fighting with Jiminy out loud."

Jordan and Skye's conversation over my head tells me I spoke aloud. Oh well.

You know what? More tequila sounds like a fantabulous idea right now, but I'm gonna have to be sneaky about it.

Maybe if I…

Using my peripheral vision, I check my cohorts besides me and slide forward an inch. Another check then another inch.

I got this. They won't catch me. Dex isn't the only one who's stealthy. Stealth is my middle name.

Yeah, whatever you say, Madison Belle.

Another inch. Almost there. They aren't going to be able to stop me. One…more…inch.

Got it.

VICTORY!!!!

I jump from the couch, fingers wrapped around the squat neck of the bottle, which I clutch to my chest like it's my precious as I start doing the running man in place.

My girls give in instead of fighting the inevitable, and "Tequila" by The Champs starts playing from Skye's phone as they join me in my impromptu dance party.

Just like Aladdin got three wishes, I'll give you three guesses who walks in while I'm doing an *epic* sprinkler.

Chapter Twenty-Seven

U nlike earlier, as I approach the front door to the
Donovan home, I feel like I'm prepared to find a
tango strapped in an S-vest on the other side.

It was a risk to leave without telling her, but I'm trained to
take calculated ones daily and am prepared for whatever the
fallout will be—I think.

So when I come across three females in various stages of
doing the shopping cart, the lawnmower, and the sprinkler,
I'm not really sure how to react.

If the Patron bottle clutched in the hand by Maddey's face
isn't enough of a clue, the sloppy jerks of her outstretched
arm as she pulses it front of her while making the *shhh-shhh-
shhh-tick-tick-tick-tick* sound of a sprinkler would have given
her away. My girl is drunk.

Well this should be interesting.

"Hook!" She throws her arms up with a cheer. "Oh no."
She brings the bottle down, trying to hide it behind her hands
against her chest.

"What's wrong, Tink?" I can't stop my lips from curling
into a grin at her hand-caught-in-the-cookie-jar expression.

"We're drinking *tea-key-la*," she whisper-shouts.

"Last I checked, you're old enough to do so legally."

"Yeah…but…you're a pirate, Hook." Her eyes dart around the room, looking for who the fuck knows. "Pirates drink *rum*." Another whisper-shout.

Remember how I said my girl was drunk? I take that back —she's three sheets to the fucking wind.

Time to go.

With a shake of the head, I stalk across the room, liberate the tequila and pass it to a sober-looking Jordan, and toss Maddey over my shoulder in a fireman's carry.

"Whoooooooa." Hands smack my ass. "This might not be the safest position for you to have me in, Hook, but I'm not gonna complain about the view." Another slap, this one followed by a squeeze, *honk-honk* sound effect included.

Jesus. Lord give me strength.

With my bounty secured on my shoulder, I make a pitstop at the back door and whistle for Trident, the dog coming the instant he's called.

I wish his owner would be as obedient. Instead she's currently kicking her feet and jostling around, encouraging the chorus of cheers sent our way.

"Put me down if I'm too heavy," she says when I groan.

Her weight isn't the issue—it's the way the hem of her shorts rides up with the movements, giving me a teasing, ball-tingling glimpse of the bottom curve of her ass.

"Please, Madz. My rucksack weighs more than you."

She huffs and, in true Dory fashion, is quickly distracted by something else. Unfortunately, that something is me. More specifically, my t-shirt.

Cool air brushes along my lower back as she inches it up, her fingers walking up each vertebrae of my spine like steps as they are revealed.

"Stop that, Tink," I warn, holding the door open for Trident.

"Nope." She reverses the direction of her fingers, this time letting them dip under the band of my boxer briefs.

"*Madison*," I growl as I smack her ass.

Even in her prone position, her back arches and she lets out a hiss.

That was a tactical error.

Then, as if she wasn't just trying to drive me insane with lust, her little fists start pounding on my back in earnest while her kicks change from flailing to seeking a target.

Hasn't this woman abused my balls enough this week?

"Maddey." Like the ones before it, she ignores this warning too.

"You." Punch, punch. "Left." Punch. "Without." Punch, punch, punch. "Me."

There's the anger I was expecting.

"Madz," I soothe.

"Fuck you Dexter." I swing my hips to the left to avoid a nut shot.

"Maybe when you're sober." She's too intoxicated for my dirty promise to register.

"You left me." Punch, punch, punch, punch. "You fucking left me."

Rounding my truck so we're hidden from view of the house, I lift her off my shoulder, telling myself I don't notice how good her curves feel sliding down the front of me.

"How could you?" Now that she's on her feet, this punch connects with actual force, leaving behind a surprising sting on my pec.

"I did it for your own good." My thumbs ghost over the bumps of her hipbones, trying to soothe away some of her ire.

She's the most adorable hot mess I've ever seen. Her messy bun is falling apart, listing to the side with curls spilling out of it. Her cheeks are flushed from both the liquor and her indignation, the pink color extending down her neck and across the chest currently heaving with each inhalation.

She's got the classic McClain jaw clench going on, and her nostrils are flaring like a bull's. Her blue eyes throw icicles at me with her death glare, and it only gets worse as they narrow upon seeing how amused I am by the spectacle she is.

"You think this is *funny*?"

Punch to the chest.

"Think it's some *joke*?"

Shot to the ribs.

"You left."

Hook to the side.

"You went to Justin's to talk about *me*." Punch, punch. "With. Out. Me."

I register the shift of stance, locking onto her wrist before she can hit me in the face with an uppercut. Never one to give up the fight, she tries again with the other hand, but I snag that one as well, easily pinning her to the side of the truck.

"How could you, Dex? How *could* you?" Her voice breaks as she repeats herself.

"I had to." I risk digging myself in deeper.

"You were the *only* one who treated me like an equal."

She bucks against my hold, her stomach brushing against my dick each time. I adjust my grip, taking both her wrists in one hand to free the other to clasp her hip again and keep her lower half immobile.

"The *only* one who didn't treat me like some damsel in distress," she wails.

"That's because you're not."

A rock settles in my gut at her words. Of course I didn't treat her like a damsel—she's the furthest thing from it. I couldn't think of anyone who embodies the phrase 'tiny but mighty' more than Maddey McClain.

"Everyone else just wanted to lock me up in the tower with Rapunzel while they took care of the problem."

She attempts to free herself and growls in frustration when she can't.

Shit! She kicked me. Damn feisty pixie.

I step a foot between her legs, bringing our bodies flush. Our legs are scissored together, the cold metal of the car door a direct contrast to the heat of her center burning through the fabric of my shorts at the top of my thigh.

Her hips roll, and I'm pretty sure she doesn't realize she's grinding her pussy against my leg, but I do—oh boy, do I fucking ever.

Her breathing picks up pace, her nipples poking into my chest with each inhalation, the pressure of the hard tips never fully easing without an inch of space between us.

"You." She thrashes, her curls tumbling down around us as the elastic in her hair finally loses the battle. "*You* were the only who believed *I* could slay the dragon."

"Because you can."

I do believe she can. I've told her over and over I'm not here to play bodyguard. It's why I took her to the gun range. I know she can handle this, but I need *her* to know it as well.

"You lied to me."

I shake my head vehemently.

"You did! Maybe not explicitly, but by omission."

Fuck me. What happened to the happy drunk from the living room? She sounds too sober, is making too much sense for my peace of mind.

"You're *keeping* something from me."

"No I'm not." I am.

"You *are*. *Don't* lie."

I keep my eyes locked on hers, not looking away from her icy glare while I issue another denial.

"LIAR!" she shouts, voice echoing into the dark night, Trident whining with his owner's increased agitation.

"Tink—"

"Stop, Dex. Just stop." She hiccups. "If you weren't hiding something, you wouldn't have gone off without me."

I hate that she's not wrong, that in trying to do what I thought was right, I hurt her.

She chokes on a sob.

I've survived BUD/S, SERE training, Green Team, multiple deployments, and countless missions—but the sight of a single tear streaking down Maddey's cheek is what breaks me.

My fingers flex around her wrists, pushing them harder into the truck. I release her hip, grasping the back of her neck in pure possession.

My fingers twine their way into her curls, tugging on the strands until her head tips back with the force, angling her face up to mine.

I've fought this long enough.

My attraction.

My feelings.

The chemistry.

I've warred with my sense of loyalty to my friends.

I can't deny it any longer.

Maddey is mine, and it's time for her to realize it.

Hoo-Yah!

I slam my mouth down on hers, swallowing her gasp of surprise and owning her with a single kiss.

I lick the seam of her lips, tasting the salt from that tear before getting hints of coffee from the earlier tequila.

With a breathy sigh, she relents to my assault, all the fight draining as we become consumed by each other.

Fire spreads through my veins.

I don't give her the chance to deny me, to deny *us*. I fuck her mouth, stroking my tongue against hers the same way I will her clit. *Will*—not if, not even when. My mouth kissing the lips between her legs isn't an eventually; it is an actuality.

I am going to show her in every possible way imaginable how much I love her. And when we run out of those? Well, she's an author—I'm sure she can come up with a few creative ideas.

She rocks against me, this time not to get away, but to get closer.

Her tendons flex under my hold as her fingers search for purchase.

She may be submitting to my kisses, but she is my equal in every way. We belong together. Time to prove it to her.

Chapter Twenty-Eight

Sunlight streams through the glass doors of my bedroom, and all Seven Dwarfs start mining for diamonds inside my skull.

Ugh, tequila. I love it, but it doesn't always love me.

I groan and pull my pillow over to cover my face and block out the offensive rays.

Movement on the bed has me freezing as memories from last night start to materialize like images in a magic mirror.

Dex kissed me. Correction—Dex *owned* me.

What the fuck am I supposed to do with this?

There's another shift, and I realize the body next to me is furry. *Trident.* He flops his head on top of the pillow, smothering me a bit. I lift my head and drop it down next to his, snuggling into the soft fur of his neck.

"Who's a good boy?" I run a hand down his side, his tail thumping in answer. "Do you want to help Mommy out?"

I've always said my dog can understand English, and he's also more intuitive than most people. He only goes to further prove it by licking the side of my face instead of answering with his typical bark. It's because he knows the harsh sound would likely split my head wide open.

"Can you get Mommy a drink?" Another lick. "Water please."

I'm jostled and there's a thud as he jumps from the bed. Yes my dog is highly trained and could teach his own course on obedience, but he also knows a few fun party tricks—opening the pantry to grab water bottles is only one of them.

I scrub my hands over my face, trying to jump-start the synapses in my brain. From the feel of my hair, I'm sure I resemble Anna on Coronation Day.

Dex kissed me.

Dex flipping *kissed* me.

Breathe, Maddey. Just breathe.

Inhale.

Exhale.

I do my best to calm myself down when I recognize the familiar scent of salt and sea. *Dex?* A cautious crack of my eyelids reveals I'm alone in the room. Why do I smell him?

I'm not caffeinated enough to deal with all the questions swirling in my mind. Why didn't I train Trident to use the Keurig?

Lacing my fingers together, I stretch my arms overhead and freeze. What am I wearing?

Is this…

No…

Holy shit, I'm wearing Dex's shirt. Scrambling amid my cocoon of covers, I work to get my hands under them and find the only other thing I have on are my lace cheekies.

What the hell happened last night?

There was tequila—so much tequila. Confessing to corrupting minors. A dance party. There was a fight? *Oh, shit!* I hit Dex—repeatedly. Ah, that's what lead to *the* kiss. After that, though…blank. Why don't I remember what happened after? Did he literally melt my brain cells?

There's the clack of nails on the hardwood, and I'm

bounced as Trident leaps onto my bed, dropping a bottle of water onto my stomach.

Deep rumbling laughter sounds from above me, and my nipples—my braless nipples, I might add—perk up. I may not remember all the events of last night, but they sure as shit haven't forgotten what it felt like to be pressed against Dex's shouldn't-be-possible-to-be-that-hard chest.

"Need a little pixie dust, Tink?"

I'd scowl if I didn't think the action would add to the conga line dancing inside my head. I settle for flipping him off instead.

"What's wrong, princess? Can't think of a happy thought?" The laughter in his voice has me gritting my teeth. To think a part of me was feeling guilty over getting physical with him last night…now all I want to do is punch him again, preferably in his face this time.

"I asked you to get me a drink, baby." I scratch behind Trident's ears. "Not a Dex."

"What a mean thing to say about the person who brought you painkillers." There's the telltale rattle of a bottle of pills.

With *way* more effort than should be needed for such a simple task, I push myself up to a seated position, folding my arms over the covers bunched at my waist.

The starkness of my wardrobe against the kaleidoscope of color that is my bedding brings one of the many questions running rampant to the forefront.

"Why am I wearing your shirt?" I hold a hand out for my salvation—the Advil, not the man.

You sure about that one?

What the what?

"Because I put you in it." There's a territorial gleam in those dark eyes when I chance a glance at Dex, and holy shit, he's shirtless. Why is he shirtless? Fuck me.

No. None of that, Madison Belle. Do not think the words 'fuck me' in relation to Dexter Stone—EVER. We are just going to pretend that kiss last night never happened. Or better yet, feign not remembering it. Blame the alcohol.

"Why? And where is your shirt? Don't even try to say it's because I'm wearing it. You're staying here—I know you have other clothes with you. I've seen them."

"Why doesn't it surprise me that even hungover, you still talk a mile a minute?"

My insides flutter at another one of those manly chuckles, and I wonder what the hell is going on. Flutters mean feelings, and I don't have feelings for Dex. Right?

No. No I don't. It's just the intensity of the kiss combined with my hangover that is messing with my central nervous system. That's it. Anyone going through a sexual drought like mine would be on lust overdose after a kiss like that.

The possessive grasp.

The stinging hair pull.

The pinch of the chin to hold me in place.

Strokes of the tongue.

Nips of the teeth.

Talk about a kiss straight out of my Kindle crack.

"Well?" I arch a brow.

"Well what?" He shrugs, the action drawing my eyes to the rippling of those tempting muscles of his torso.

If Jiminy won't let us think the words 'fuck me', can we think 'lick'? Because I really, really think we should lick him. I mean, look at that ink along his rib cage. And it goes into the dip of that V. That V! Come to mama.

Fuck!

I need to focus—on the question, not the sexy SEAL.

"Why did you put me in your shirt?"

"After you reverse-Sleeping-Beauty-ed me—"

"I love when you use a Disney reference as a verb."

"—it was the easiest thing available to dress you in," he finishes, ignoring my comment completely.

With my gaze still homed in on that delicious—

*How do you know it's delicious? You won't let us lick him. *crosses arms and pouts**

Anyway... *side-eyeing those pesky voices* Since I'm still looking at it, I see the way his breathing changes, growing labored as if the memory of changing my clothes is enough to affect him.

"What? Are you so bored with your bodyguard assignment you decided to risk your life copping a feel?"

Why is the thought of missing out on the feel of Dex's hands running over my body, slipping my heels off my feet, unzipping my romper and pushing it down my body until it falls on the floor so disappointing?

"I was a perfect gentleman. I didn't even sneak a peek. Because, baby—"

I suck in a breath at both the endearment and how he bends, balling his fists and balancing on his knuckles, invading my personal space. The scent of the sea intensifies and a hint of minty toothpaste hits me as he brushes the tip of his nose across my cheek then down the shell of my ear.

"—when I get my hands on you again, it will be so much more than copping a feel."

Holy alpha, Walt.

My entire being liquifies. How the hell am I supposed to react to a declaration like that?

This is a complete one-eighty from everything I've ever believed to be true about our relationship.

He's still so close I feel his lips part as he goes to say something else, but it's cut off by Trident suddenly perking up. A few seconds later we hear, "Honey, I'm home."

I flop back with a groan, too hungover and undercaffeinated to deal with the craziness that is Tucker Hayes.

That's it—I'm staying in bed. These covers have accepted me as one of their own already. No need to get up; I'm okay with being part of their world.

Twenty minutes later, I pad downstairs in a pair of draw-string shorts with books printed on them and a white crop-top tank. Showering and brushing my teeth was pretty much the extent of the effort I took with myself, but the best thing about my friends is none of them will give a damn.

"Drink this." Rocky hands me a glass of I-don't-think-I-wanna-know the moment I step foot inside my kitchen.

"Isn't Gemma supposed to be the one handling my nutritional needs?" I eye the glass like my friend took her Harry Potter obsession too far and tried to brew me Polyjuice Potion.

"Yes, but I was the one they turned to when they needed to recover enough from a night of drinking to survive morning skate. Stop being difficult and drink." She stares me down until I do as I'm told. Who am I to refuse our resident physical therapist?

"Geez, who knew becoming a mom would turn you into even more of a hard-ass," I grumble, plugging my nose and taking a healthy swallow.

"She really does have a hard ass." Gage ambles over to join us, moving way more gracefully than a man of six-seven should be able to, and cups Rocky's butt with the hand not holding Ronnie.

God, there really is nothing sexier than a hot guy holding a baby.

"Can you save the foreplay for when you're not around people who aren't currently getting any? Not all of us are as disgustingly in love as you two," I say, stepping around them.

I'm joking—for the most part anyway. Just because I can't figure out what true love is for myself doesn't mean I begrudge anyone else having it. I love love. Hello—I write romance. At least I get to live vicariously through my friends as they fall like dominos into their happily-ever-afters.

"Madz, babe." Tucker slings an arm over my shoulders as soon as I'm close enough. "I keep telling you I volunteer as tribute to end your dry spell." Did Dex just growl? "Just ask Bubble how good I am."

He is damn lucky Skye isn't here to hear his comment. It wouldn't end well for Tuck if she were. For one, she *hates* when he calls her Bubble. And two, well…that's a story for a different day.

"Never gonna happen, M-Dubs." I pat his cheek a little harder than necessary. Soul sister solidarity and all that. "Plus, I don't need all the complications of sex in my life anyway."

I finish off Rocky's magic potion, which shockingly isn't gross, rinse out the glass, and load it into my dishwasher.

"Madz, Madz, Madz." Tuck shakes his head like he's disappointed. "When are you going to take my advice—"

"Never," Damon, another of Tucker's old teammates from BTU and the other player to switch to The Steele Maker, calls out from my living room, bringing my attention to him for the first time.

I'm not surprised to see him here. I grew closest with the guys who played on the hockey team with Ryan, but especially those like Damon and Nick who graduated the same year.

"Don't be a hater, Dame." Tucker waves him off before turning his attention back to me. "Anyway…what I was saying before I was so *rudely* interrupted." He waits a beat to make sure Damon isn't going to go for round two. When Damon continues to stay silent, he continues. "There is nothing complicated about sex. You slide a dick into a pussy. Simple as that." He inserts the pointer finger of one hand into the circle he's made with the other, simulating the action, and then wipes his hands together, illustrating how easy it is.

"And you wonder why Skye won't sleep with you again?" Rocky asks.

"I know you sleep with a lot of bunnies, but haven't you heard of a thing called foreplay?" comes from Damon.

"Maybe we should give him a highlighter so he can take notes for our next book club read," Gage offers, and I can't help but snort. He's been a part of our group for almost two years, but he's still one of the more reserved ones of our motley crew.

What is with all the growling coming from Dex?

"Yeah, Madz. Maybe you should be Tuck's Obi-Wan. Instead of teaching him the way of the Jedi, you can teach him the way of pleasing a woman before he goes all wham-bam-thank-you-ma'am." Damon falls over sideways, laughing at his own cleverness.

"*Annnd* on that note"—I spin on my heel—"I'm out."

I may be too hungover for the words to flow, but at least in my office I don't have to hear others comment on my lack of sex life.

Chapter Twenty-Nine

Dex

Deep down, a part of me always knew if I were to give in to my feelings for Maddey, even if for just a second, everything would change. What I wasn't prepared for was to have my entire world shift on its axis. With one kiss, that is exactly what happened last night.

For years she's held my heart without either of us knowing it, but with every whimper, breathy sigh, and low moan, she only burrowed herself deeper into me. She's in the fucking marrow of my bones.

I gave her the night, letting her sleep off the effects of the alcohol in her system before pushing the issue. It's bad enough I kissed her while she was intoxicated, but I justified it by telling myself if she was cognizant enough to rip me a new one over talking to Justin without her, she was sober enough for it not to be considered taking advantage. I simply *had* to kiss her.

Don't even get me started on the restraint it took for me *not* to cop that feel she joked about when I changed her clothes for bed. Her skin was pure silk underneath my rough hands when I eased her outfit down her torso and off her hips.

Thank fuck I had the foresight to put my shirt on her before I started to undress her, because the all-too-brief touches of the lingerie she had on under her clothes—lacy, delicate, sexy as hell—had me close to saying fuck it to my good intentions.

My self-restraint paid off in spades this morning. Rumpled, hungover, a riot of curly hair, she still managed to embody every fantasy I've had of her being mine. Okay, not *every* single one, but the PG ones at least.

When she sassed about why she was in my shirt, I brushed it off like it wasn't a big deal, though in reality it was just one of the ways I wanted to mark her as mine. It didn't matter that we were in her house, in a room with both a dresser and a closet full of her clothes. I wanted—no, *needed* to see what she looked like in something of mine.

Perfect—that's how she looked.

Maddey's friends didn't hang around long after she retreated to her office upstairs, and now hours later I scrub my hands over my face, frustrated by the lack of progress on identifying her stalker.

"Why can't we figure out who this guy is, Trident?"

Woof! Woof!

"I know he's smart, but there has to be *something* we're missing."

Woof!

"Don't worry, bud. I'm not stopping until I find it."

It doesn't escape my notice that one, Trident has started spending more time with me when Maddey locks herself away to write, and two, I'm talking to him the same way Maddey does. I can only imagine the hell I'll get if I start doing the same with Bullet when I rejoin the team.

It's nice having a sounding board, though. We need to catch a break. The way this asshole is only using snail mail to terrorize Maddey is making it infinitely harder to track his identity. The only thing we've been able to work out—a detail that only increases the threat level—is the guy is from New Jersey. Every time something comes through the mail, it has been processed somewhere in the state. Unfortunately, those locations have varied and changed each time.

As pissed as Maddey is that I excluded her from my conversation with Justin and Paul, I don't regret it for a second. The way my friend paled when he read the high-lighted passages and the intention behind them made me glad I went with my gut to shield Maddey from it.

I do hate that in protecting her, I hurt her, but I would make the same decision every time if it meant I could keep the darkness from snuffing out her light.

Trident's collar jingles as he turns toward the sound of Maddey's soft voice floating down the hall before she steps into view.

Her rose gold MacBook is open and cradled on an arm, her Mickey Mouse-printed Beats hang around her neck, and she has on a pair of black-framed glasses that give me all kinds of librarian fantasies.

If that isn't enough to have me shifting in my seat, the fact that she's still wearing that boner-inducing outfit is. Those tiny shorts show off her legs to perfection and come to a stop just under the curve of her ass, and the tank top exposes her toned belly and generous cleavage. They may be meant for comfort, but they look like sex.

She places her laptop down next to mine on the table, pats Trident on the head, and moves to the fridge while continuing her conversation on the phone held in her other hand.

"You're the one who likes to battle it out with Sammy over who my bestie is, not me."

From one sentence, I deduce she's on the phone with Ryan, and my inner caveman can't help but smack his club upon witnessing yet another exchange between her and the hockey player. I know it's irrational, but I can't help it. Maybe if he wasn't such a good guy, I wouldn't feel so threatened, but he had years with Maddey in a way I've only ever dreamed of.

She's quiet as she listens to whatever the hockey captain says, pushing the glasses onto the top of her head like a headband. I drag my gaze away from her before I start kissing her again. I'm in serious trouble because watching her do something as mundane as heating up lunch has me growing harder behind my zipper.

My eyes fall to the lit screen of her computer, and I can't help but take a peek at what she's been working on.

He groans, his eyes falling shut at the feel of my skin. I'm completely bare, no underwear to be found to avoid panty lines. Another groan when he realizes this, his grip on my ass tightening as he follows the line of my crack.

"Fuck, Princess." Lower and lower he travels. "You were naked under here all night?"

He buries his face in my neck, my body arching into him, rubbing against the hard-on now digging into my stomach.

"Panty lines don't really go with this look." I wave a hand down my body, but he doesn't see it because he's too busy raking down the pulsing vein in my neck with his teeth.

"Panty lines," he growls, his grip on my ass close to bruising.

"Jasper." Now I'm the one moaning, my head canting to the side to give him better access, my hands coming up to clutch at his lapels.

What the hell is happening?

What am I doing?

Shut up and just go with it*. I think I need to start taking applications for a new inner bitch.*

I say this, but do I stop him as he continues to travel south? No. Nor do I protest when he brushes my entrance.

"Fuck you're soaked." Each guttural word rumbles through me with a direct line to my clit, only adding to the situation he's discovered.

"N-Noble." A warning? A plea? I'm not sure.

Everything about me is one giant exposed nerve. My racing heart, my constricting lungs, the way my skin crawls at the thought of him touching me—all while feeling like I'm going to burst out of it if he doesn't.

"Jasper," he commands.

"Wh-what?" *I wheeze.*

"My name is Jasper. Say my name, Princess." *He bites my pulse point, flicking his piercing against it.*

My knuckles turn white with my tightening hold.

Say his name, say his name, *my inner bitch sings, like she's Destiny's Child.*

"Say it, Princess."

I press my lips together.

"Say it and you'll get a reward."

God, his words are like liquid sex.

Come on, Savvy. We love presents. Say his name.

How am I supposed to formulate words when the only thing I can focus on is the tap-tap-tap of his finger on my most sensitive area? He's toying with me. With his words, his touch—his presence is one big tease.

Saaaaaaavyyy, *Bitchy whines.*

I roll my eyes. Fine.

"Jasper."

I barely get out the last syllable before his finger plunges into me, the coming-from-behind angle delicious.

What am I doing?

I don't know, but hell if I want it to stop.

I give in. Shoving away the doubts, the worries that this is wrong, I give in to my wanton desires.

I wrap my arms around his neck, rising onto my toes to get closer to him.

Pump.

Pump.

Pump.

My pussy flutters, the walls of it doing their best not to let him go.

"Princess."

His hips rock forward.

"Jasper."

Mine rock back, riding his finger.

"Princess."

His hand fans out, another digit brushing my clit and his thumb stretching to press the rosebud of my ass.

It's naughty and dirty and if it's wrong, I don't want to be right.

Mo—

The sound of Maddey's laughter pulls me out of the daze I fell into, sucked into the story she told.

I blink. Not quite sure what it is I just read, but there are a few things I know to be true.

1. It was hot as all fucking hell.

2. I'm harder than I've ever been in my life.

3. Maddey and I will be reenacting it—the sooner the better.

I'm about to dive back in when I pick up on her side of the conversation.

"I need your help to break my writer's block on this scene, Ry."

The fuck?

Hold up. Time out. Writer's block?

My heartbeat quickens, every hair on my body standing on end, and the calm tunnel vision I'm only accustomed to feeling while staring down the barrel of my sniper rifle washes over me.

Writer's block? Writer's fucking block? She wants Ryan's help to break it in the middle of a sex scene? Over my dead fucking body.

My chair hits the floor with a bang, falling over from the force of me pushing out of it, and Trident barks at the sudden noise.

Startled blue eyes blink at me, and distantly I register her saying goodbye and hanging up as I close the distance between us with long strides.

No more messing around. Maddey is mine, and it's time I make that crystal clear.

I grab the back of her neck, squeezing with just enough pressure to have her pushing up on her toes to comply with my tug toward me. Her hands land on my chest for balance, but it's not necessary since I wrap my other arm around the small of her back and anchor her to me.

I slam my mouth down onto hers in a brutal kiss, this one making last night's claiming seem like a peck in a middle school game of spin the bottle.

My name is smothered as I thrust my tongue inside.

There are still so many things we have to figure out—her brothers, her stalker, my job, the fact that I live in Virginia Beach and she's in Jersey—but we can worry about all that as a couple.

This isn't some casual, *we'll fuck while I'm here then move on with our lives like it never happened* type thing.

Chapter Thirty

I have no idea what is happening. One minute I'm upstairs, doing a reread on a scene where my badass heroine submits to one of her bully-ish heroes, and the next Dex is kissing me—again.

I remember at some point between those two things, I called Ryan about getting access to The Ice Box—the arena that's home to the Blizzards—to help me work through some hockey writer's block I've been having, but I can't recall the minute details.

There's an urgency in the way Dex kisses me. It's like he's inside my head, channeling Jasper—my hero—and letting him bleed into his actions. It's rough, cocky, possessive, and all-consuming. There's no way for me not to respond.

The cold stainless steel of the refrigerator meets my back, but I barely notice it with the blanket of heat covering my front. I'm pinned in place, barely straddling the line of being crushed.

My scalp burns as my hair is pulled, tipping my chin up and exposing more of my neck for Dex's mouth to instantly lock on to, and distantly I hear my headphones hit the floor.

His stubble and teeth scrape down the side, leaving behind what I'm sure will be a wicked beard burn.

"*Mine*," he says against my skin.

I'm lost in Dex in a way I've never experienced before.

I hiss with every nip of his teeth then moan with every soothing lave of his tongue that follows in its wake.

"You're mine, Tink."

God! Why are those three words so hot?

My nipples are painful peaks and my tank is close to losing the battle against the way my breaths heave, sliding down fractionally at each brush against Dex's chest.

Growing up, I dreamed about kissing Dex more than pretty much anything else. As the puppy love of my youth faded with the growth of my feelings for Ryan, the thoughts of being kissed and riding off into the sunset with Dex for our happily ever after ended.

Dex may be my go-to sexual fantasy, but that's where it ends. Lust does not equal love.

So why haven't you had sex since you broke up with Ryan?

Can I GIF right now with the one that says "THIS" with the guy pointing up?

Yeah, Tuck has a point. Stop trying to complicate things and get some.

Oh shit! That is one scary thought. Please, for the love of all things holy, get laid. Tucker being right about anything *is one of the signs of the apocalypse.*

"Stop thinking." Dex seals his mouth over mine again, and I'm incapable of doing anything except following his command.

Wrapping my arms around his neck, I press the rest of the way up on my toes, rubbing against him like a cat in an attempt to get closer. I'll worry about the consequences later.

"Dex." I suck on his bottom lip and he rocks his hips into me, his erection digging into my belly. I want it. In my hands, in my mouth, inside me—I don't care. It's been so long since

I've seen a penis in person I'd have forgotten what one looks like if not for porn.

He plunges a hand into the back of my shorts, grabbing my ass cheek so forcefully there's a pull on the sensitive skin as it pulls away from the other.

I'm the one moaning, and I claw at the shirt I was disappointed to see he put on earlier and toss it to the side. As soon as the offensive garment is gone, I fuse myself to him again, my own tank finally succumbing and falling underneath my breasts. I don't bother wasting the time to remove the tank—*aren't you glad you took off you bra earlier?*—because Dex's long fingers have snaked their way underneath the lace of my thong and are curling around to the front in search of my center.

"Dex." My head falls back to the fridge with a *thunk* as two fingers slip inside me with ease.

"Are you wet because of me, Tink?" His fingers pump in and out of me lazily. "Or is it because you were writing dirty?"

My eyes fall shut and I dig my nails into his back, seeking purchase in the storm of sensation I'm lost in.

"Is this how you imagined it?" His thumb comes down, swirling through the wetness starting to coat my thighs and bringing it back to circle the pucker of my ass.

"Dex," I moan.

"Tell me, Tink." He repeats the process with his thumb for a second pass. "I want to make sure I'm doing it right."

Oh my god. His words register, and I realize he must have been reading the chapter I was working on.

"*Dex.*"

"You wrote about it, but has anyone actually taken you here?" He pushes his thumb until it slips into my ass, and I moan again at the fullness of the double invasion.

His other fingers wiggle inside my pussy, and I rise up on

my toes and fall back down with each slow but powerful pump of them inside me.

"Well?"

Pump.

"Has anyone had your ass?"

Pump.

"Hmm?"

Pump.

"Tell me."

Is he really looking for me to answer him right now? How does he expect me to formulate words while he finger-fucks me into oblivion? My orgasm grows closer with every movement of his digits. The only reason I haven't melted into a puddle on the floor is because his hold on me is absolute.

"Tink." I feel him smile before he bites down on my shoulder.

I roll my hips, chasing release. "No," I wail.

Like a tidal wave, my orgasm crashes over me. I couldn't even tell you where it starts. My clit pulses, and the walls of my vagina squeeze onto the long fingers scissoring inside it like keeping a death grip on them will prevent me from floating away.

"No one has fucked my ass."

Dex's fingers continue to pump as my cries echo off the walls, overtaking the sound of flesh meeting flesh and squishy wetness; I'm too far gone to be embarrassed by how audible the evidence of my releases is.

The sensitive, never-been-breached skin of an area that has previously been an exit-only situation burns in such a delicious way that has me wanting to reach for the kerosene to let it consume me.

My body bears down, riding each sensation for all it's worth. Light ricochets behind my closed eyelids like a spinning disco ball, every cell, hormone, and voice inside me dancing beneath it.

"*God* it's hot as fuck hearing you say 'fucked my ass'"—he increases the speed of his fingers—"but you left out the most important part of the sentence."

Huh?

I haven't even come down from the first manmade orgasm I've had in years and he wants to have a grammar lesson? I'd smack him if he wasn't already pushing me back up the hill for round two.

"Yet." He flicks my clit, and renewed pleasure splinters out like a web, shooting out to and up my spine. "You forgot *yet*." Flick, flick.

"Huh?"

My legs give out, and the only thing supporting me is Dex's grip on the back of my neck and his fingers inside me. His cocky chuckle almost has me tipping over again.

"Oh yeah, soak my fingers baby." He pumps then continues to speak like I didn't just shatter in his arms. "You forgot the word yet. The full sentence is, 'No one has fucked my ass *yet*.'"

My eyes snap open at that and meet Dex's now black ones. He doesn't mean…

"You're mine, Madz."

Thrust.

"I'm going to own every part of you."

A scissor and a pump.

"Like you own every part of me."

The thumb in my ass and the two fingers in my pussy plunge all the way in, holding their position and wiggling until I'm screaming through my third orgasm.

I'm no longer human, just one big pleasure point triggered to go off with the slightest twitch.

The lingering effect of my hangover combined with coming harder than ever before has my consciousness wavering. I think he says, "The only one who will be helping you through your writer's block is me," but I'm not sure.

Chapter Thirty-One

Dex

Tucking Maddey into bed after she passes out on me again is a lot harder to do the second time. Unlike last night, this time there is nothing blocking my view of her naked chest, her shirt having gone askew while I took her with my fingers.

Her lips are red and swollen from my kisses, made all the more prominent when they purse as she snuggles into her pillow.

I adjust her shirt and tuck the comforter around her shoulders.

Trident jumps onto the bed, and the moment he presses himself into Maddey, her arm drapes itself over him, the unconscious action the perfect display of how in sync the pair are with each other.

Smoothing her hair away from her face, I can't help but remember how the last time ended for me. How can she think I don't believe she can handle herself when she has proven from the moment I arrived she can?

Stepping back, I watch her sleep. Buried amongst her pillows and colorful blankets, arm thrown over her dog, face buried in his neck, both softly snoring, she is so damn cute it makes my heart ache.

I may spend more time away than at home, but what I wouldn't give to have this be the scene I come back to when I'm stateside.

I'm not sure how long I've been standing there watching her sleep when my phone buzzes in my pocket.

JUSTIN: Paul and I are stopping by. Please make sure all weapons are hidden from my sister.

ME: She's sleeping.

JUSTIN: Ah yes—heard about the tequila. See you in 10.

I should feel guilty about texting with fingers that are still covered in the scent of his sister, but I'm past the point of caring. Sure, a part of me wants to shout my feelings from the rooftops, but as far as my best friend is concerned, we will operate on a need-to-know basis. And Justin? He doesn't have the security clearance.

His message is a reminder that I have work to do. With one last glance at my girl, I leave her to dream—hopefully of me.

After a pitstop in the hall bathroom to wash my hands and adjust my very blue balls, I pull my shirt over my head to cover up the scratch marks Maddey left on my back then check in with my contact at Jamie's security firm. I understand why Maddey didn't want a security detail assigned to her, but I have found them to be invaluable in gathering backend intel.

Justin and Paul arrive while I'm combing through their most recent report on the analytics of Maddey's social media accounts. I had them run both the Belle Willis ones and her personal ones, not wanting to leave any stone unturned.

"Nice to see you're still in one piece." Justin drops into the chair across from me with a shit-eating grin on his face. I should have never told my fellow Lost Boys about Maddey and her taser. I supplied them with years' worth of ammunition for ribbing.

Trident ambles into the room, having heard the door, and heads first for Paul, who gives him a fresh bone, then lays himself down across my feet. At least I know the dog approves of me.

"How do you even know about last night?" I give Trident's head a scratch.

"We swung by Espresso Patronum this morning," Paul says, referring to Lyle's coffee shop up north near where they work.

"If you need to know what's going on in the world, find a Covenette." Justin offers a shrug.

"I don't know what Lyle was more upset about missing— Cali doing a photoshoot, or you carrying out a drunk Madz." I'll give Paul props for saying that with a straight face. If it had been Justin, there would have been another dig or two thrown in there.

Outside of a comment or two about the case, none of us say much while we go through the files that were sent over. I'm not sure what I was hoping to find, but the lack of *anything* is frustrating as hell. The internet may be a fount of information, but it also makes it easy for creepers like Maddey's stalker to keep their identity a secret as they troll behind their keyboard.

"Was she really pissed?" Justin jerks a chin to the ceiling.

"Yup." I feel the knife of guilt twist as I remember the lone tear that escaped while she did her best to beat me up. "What's worse is I made her doubt how capable she is."

"Fuck."

I nod. It's a delicate balance trying to make sure Maddey

is able to handle herself in any situation while keeping her from bucking the help she clearly needs.

"Did anything come today?" Paul's question has a fresh wave of anger washing over me.

"Yes," I say through gritted teeth. "More of the same as yesterday." I use a towel to pick up the bubble mailer and bring it to the table. "Highlighted passages from some of her books."

"Lingerie?" Justin slips on a pair of latex gloves to sift through the contents.

"No." I clench my jaw hard enough I almost crack a tooth. "But this time I was threatened in the highlights."

I circle my finger for Justin to flip the pages, waiting until he comes to the passage underlined in red Sharpie where one of Maddey's characters is hit by a car. I'm not explicitly called out, but it's the only section not done in blue highlighter and where the characters aren't having sex. It's easy to draw the conclusion that it's a warning for me.

With each day that passes and each gift that arrives, my loathing grows. His threats against me roll off my back like water on a duck. It's the terrorizing of Maddey, the messing with what's mine that is unacceptable.

"What are you going to do?" Justin asks.

"I'm going to find the fucker and make him wish he was never born."

Chapter Thirty-Two

I wake up from my impromptu nap feeling surprisingly refreshed. There's also a lingering sense of déjà vu. If I thought trying to process kissing Dex was going to be a challenge, what the fuck am I supposed to do now?

Maybe you should start with how that was the hottest sexual experience of your life and there wasn't even any penile penetration.

Did you really have to think "penile penetration"?

*Why not? *shrugs* It's true.*

Yeah, but...yuck.

Can you two stop arguing so we can talk about how unexpectedly alpha Dex is when he kisses?

*Whoa, boy. *fans self* Yes please. I mean, can we talk about that neck grab?*

Truth. That was hot AF.

Or the growly way he said, "Mine."

*Hold on. *hits delete button* We need to back up a second. We've totally skipped over the part where he claimed he is going to pop our anal cherry.*

Now that was hot.

*Agreed. *insert GIF of Ron Burgundy nodding with "Agreed."* My cheeks weren't clenching in reluctance—it was anticipation.*

throws arms in the air Bring on the butt stuff.

facepalms Do you really have to say butt stuff?

First you have a problem with penile penetration and now you're taking issue with butt stuff? Way to be a buzzkill.

I clearly need to find a way to relax and clear my mind, because my characters are out of control in there. My stomach growls, reminding me I never actually ate earlier.

Nope, you were too busy letting your brothers' best friend finger you in your kitchen to eat. Jiminy taps his foot at me. Nice to see he's still there, because he was super silent while the other crazies recounted the events from earlier.

If he's going to channel the Italian side of my bloodline and take me on a guilt trip, I'm definitely going to need sustenance.

Untangling myself from the sheets, I notice my dog is missing. For someone who is typically my shadow, I've seen less of him this week than I have his whole life.

Making my way downstairs, I find my fur baby gnawing on a bone at Dex's feet, and the sight makes my heart do a funny little flip.

"Feeling better, Tink?"

I'm struck dumb by the appearance of those twin parentheses that bracket his mouth whenever he lets loose one of his full-on smiles. They've always made me want to kiss him.

What's stopping you now? You've kissed him twice in less than twenty-four hours. Might as well go for the hat trick.

Shit. *slashes hand across throat* Don't speak in hockey references.

Yeah, don't make her think of Ryan. You know it only gets her all up in her head, and then Jiminy will come in and be the fun police.

Where's the "This" GIF when you need it? Because if that happens then she will get too Debbie Downer to jump on Dex's disco stick, and I really, really want her to jump on his disco stick.

Oh, Sammy would be so proud of that Lady Gaga reference.

bows with a flourish Thank you.

"Should I take offense to how often you zone out on me?" Dex says in my ear.

When did he get up? Shit, I guess I was zoned out.

"I need food," I say instead.

"I bet." He turns and pulls my bowl from earlier out of the fridge. "I put this away for you."

My cheeks heat at the reminder of *why* I didn't eat. Nowhere near being in the proper headspace to process *anything*, least of all…that, I ignore and evade, heating up Gemma's egg bake.

"Did you eat dinner yet, baby?" I lean across the island so I can see my pup, and I think I hear Dex groan behind me but can't be sure over the noise of the microwave.

"Yeah, I fed him. He was my dinner date."

I'm pretty sure I'm developing a heart condition. It's really the only thing to explain what the hell has been happening within my rib cage.

Beep! Beep! Beep!

The microwave saves me from having to analyze my feelings, and I dig into my food right there at the counter. Bite after bite, I shovel it in, barely even tasting the food. It's a crime, really, because Gemma's food is the best thing I've ever had in my mouth.

That's only because you haven't had Dex in your mouth yet.

A strong hand beats between my shoulder blades as egg slides down the wrong pipe at that particular thought.

Note to self: *Hey self, don't ever end a writing session in the middle of a sex scene. Your characters tend to be a little more out of control when they have blue balls.*

Speaking of…

I slide my gaze to Dex, eyeing him out of the corner of my eye. If he were a full-time member of book club, I'm sure his boys would be doing their best to channel their inner Rimmel and Ivy from Cambria Hebert's Hashtag series and cheer "Smurf balls!" after earlier.

Yeah, bitch. You left him hanging. That's not nice.

Ooo, ooo. *insert Stephanie Tanner "How rude" GIF*

Dex is up five nothing on you.

Five? I may not be the best at math, but I only counted three orgasms.

It's five because he kissed the stuffing out of her twice too.

Oh, good point.

Look at him. *points repeatedly at Dex* He's so sexy.

True. No one wears a t-shirt like he does.

That's high praise considering who we hang out with on the reg.

OH MY GOD! I shout at the voices in my head. *I am killing you* all *off because you are the* least *helpful people ever!*

Pfft. You would never. You love us too much.

Done with them, my meal—everything—I place my bowl in the sink and reach into my wine cooler for a bottle of Moscato. Drinking might not be the best decision, but I need something to help me deal.

"I'll be on the top deck in the hot tub if you need me." I grab the stone bottle chiller from the freezer and a silicone wine glass from the cabinet then head upstairs to change.

Once inside the safety of my bedroom, I pull out the first bathing suit I get my hands on—a white string bikini—adjusting the tiny triangles of the top so they hold my boobs in place enough that I'm not *Girls Gone Wild*-ing it.

After securing the ties on my hips, I gather the last of my survival kit—waterproof Kindle and phone already loaded with my chillax playlist—and use the French doors of my room to exit and climb the stairs to my rooftop deck.

Folding back the cover to the hot tub, I heft it to the side, press the buttons to raise the temperature, start the jets, and let the underwater lights provide all the illumination I'll need.

Twisting off the top of the wine bottle, thanking the geniuses who came up with twist tops instead of corks, I pour a glass, select Carrie Underwood's "Drinking Alone" on my playlist, set my Kindle aside, pull my hair into a messy bun, and slip into the warm water.

Shutting my eyes, I let the pulsing beat of the jets at my back work the tension from my body.

God...was it only days ago that I thought my karmic to-do list was out of hand? If I didn't know any better, I would think the universe was messaging my editor, because she *loves* to up the angst in my manuscripts.

I came to terms with Dex living in my house. To be honest, I think I more than earned a pat on the back for not fighting him—much—when I learned of his plans. But now this? How am I supposed to handle this?

Dex kissed me.

Fingered me in my kitchen.

Promised to take me to sexual planes I haven't experienced before.

Brought me so much pleasure I literally passed out from it.

Fine. I'm an adult, a grown woman—I can handle sexual encounters with the best of them. Don't even start with me about my lack of them lately; that's not the point here.

No, the point is I'm mature enough that I should be able to take Tucker's advice—though if you try to tell him I said so, I'll deny it—and have some uncomplicated, no-strings-attached, friends-with-bennies sex with a man I trust. Because at the end of the day, there are very few people I trust more than Dexter Stone.

But can I trust him with my heart?

The thought is enough to have me jolting up in my seat, water sloshing up the side of the tub from the violent movement.

My heart?

Who said anything about my heart?

Then again...

Dex claimed me, said I was his.

What did it mean?

What was he thinking when he said the word "mine"?

And what the hell am I supposed to do with how that four-letter word made me feel?

The rush of wetness to my panties? That's easy enough to process. There's the whole forbidden factor of him being my brothers' best friend. Damn me and my love for tropes.

The way my being settled? Yeah, that's the part I'm having an issue with. Maybe I can blame that on a trope too. I've long since gotten over my childish dream of us being a friends-to-lovers story, but the familiarity of years of friendship is the only explanation I can come up with.

"I want to say"—I inhale deeply at the sound of Dex's voice—"you told me you were coming up here to keep me from going all Rambo on you—as you would say—when I noticed you gone."

His voice grows closer with each word, and the scent of the sea increases seconds before I feel his presence beside me. Cracking an eye open, I see his hands clasped together. I follow the lines of corded forearms to bulging biceps and see him resting with his elbows on the edge of the tub, leaning over to encroach on my space.

Oh, and he's shirtless. Don't want to forget to point out that *very* important detail.

His brown eyes sparkle with laughter as they peer down at me, but I skate past them, down his back, and suck in a breath when I realize he's got on a pair of board shorts.

He's not planning on…

No.

Before I can even finish the thought, one of his long legs rises up and over and he's in the seat in the corner across from me.

"Now correct me if I'm wrong here, but aren't you supposed to run and hide in a cottage in the woods?"

I hate how easily he can toss out my beloved Disney references. It makes it supremely hard to stay mad at him.

"I'm having enough difficulty with the *one*"—I hold up a finger—"man in residence. I can't imagine how frustrated I would be if I had seven of them trying to keep things from me."

I flatten my mouth and raise my eyebrows, lending weight to my passive aggressive dig. Yes, I'm still salty over the stunt he pulled last night.

"Tink—"

"Don't, Dex." Water splashes as I throw up a hand to cut him off.

"Stop calling me Dex."

"Wh-what?" But he hates being called Dexter.

"You haven't called me Hook since yesterday."

Ahh, okay. I see.

"I only call you Hook when I like you, and I don't like you very much right now." I reach for my glass and take a large gulp of the sweet wine.

My nipples tighten when he chuckles. I should record the sound and sell it as a ringtone. I'd be a millionaire if I did.

"Oh, Tink." He reaches forward, snagging one of my feet and yanking me to him until I'm straddling his lap.

Well this is new.

This is a much *better seat than the one we were in before.*

Ooo, ooo. *claps hands* He's hard.

Can someone change the playlist to Ginuwine's "Pony"?

Something must be seriously wrong with me for voices inside my head to take over even as my fingers press into his chest and my nails dig into his skin as they curl.

Underneath my butt, his thighs clench, rocking me forward slightly while his hands hold me prisoner at the hips.

Goosebumps break out across my skin as the cool salty breeze from the ocean hits my torso, which is overheated after being submerged.

The *drip-drip-drip* of water sounds in the silence between one song ending and another beginning as Dex lifts a hand to tuck an escaped curl behind my ear. The gentle move is at odds with the heated way he scans the tiny top I'm wearing.

"*Fuck me*, Tink," he curses, a pained edge entering his voice. "It should be illegal for you to wear this."

Yes, fuck him.

Please, please do.

The hand still on my hip starts to move, skimming up my back in a sensual caress, fingertips tracing over each bump of my spine, the thin material of my top stretching tight across my beaded nipples when he hooks a finger in the string tied at my back and pulls.

My hips roll of their own accord, and I bite my lip to hold back a moan at how the hard length of him feels hitting my center.

"Don't bite." He swipes a thumb across my bottom lip, freeing it from my teeth and dragging it down, my lips parting at his mercy.

I still, not even breathing. The only movement comes from the bubbling water surrounding us.

Stupefied, I watch as his dark eyes fall from my mouth and flare when they track the movement of my throat as I work to swallow the lump currently in it. I just had to go and read a paranormal romance last week, didn't I? Holy Eric Northman—there's no way I can justify using an Edward Cullen reference here—he looks like he wants to suck my blood he's staring so intently.

"I know what you're trying to do," I say with another roll of my hips.

"Oh yeah?" His gaze snaps back up to hold mine. "And what's that, Tink?"

Is he taunting me?

"You're trying to distract me." I grit my teeth. "Make me forget your betrayal." This hip roll is met with another one of those make-my-brain-stupid, why-is-it-so-hot alpha male neck grabs.

"Betrayal seems like a bit of a stretch."

Thick soupy air fills my lungs as I inhale in an effort to re-center myself. "You talk a big game about how I can take care of myself, yet you cut me out."

"That's not what I was doing." Hurt and anger flash behind his eyes.

"Bullshit, Dex." I try to push away, but his grip on me is too resolute. "Your words say one thing, but your actions say the opposite."

The Tink Train chugs down the track at full speed, but I refuse to look away. "Are you looking for an apology?" he challenges.

"Not if you're not going to mean it."

He presses his thumb into the vein pulsing at the side of my neck, and my head falls to the side, allowing him better access. Staying on topic is difficult with my hormones joining in a conga line with the voices in my head.

"Dex."

"Hook." He increases the pressure of his thumb.

"Dex," I challenge.

"Call me Dex one more *fucking* time." He yanks me closer, a wave of water spilling over the edge behind him. There's not an inch of space between our lower halves.

Oh this poor man. With Jordan as one of my best friends, I've seen every episode of *How I Met Your Mother* more than once, so his words? They have me in full-on Barney Stinson "Challenge Accepted" mode.

I press in closer. Belly to belly, the hair of his happy trail tickles. Chest to chest, every rapid beat of his heart syncs with mine.

Stubble prickles my lips, and I breathe in the scent of coffee and mint. My tongue hits the soft pillow of his lips when it peeks out to wet my own.

"What are you going to do?" Our mouths brush with each word I speak.

"Don't test me, Maddey."

Ooo, now I'm Maddey. Interesting…

Walking my fingers up his chest, I scrape my nails along the short hairs at the back of his neck and tunnel my fingers into his hair. Tilting my head to the side coyly, I ask, "Why?"

"Because…" He wraps a hand around my messy bun, pulling on it so my head is bent to a full 180-degree angle. My pulse takes off faster than Lightning McQueen as he pulls harder, bringing his mouth to my throat. "The only time I want to hear you call me Dex for the rest of the night is when my cock is thrusting inside you."

Oh god.

"No, Madz. Dex, not God," he utters just like every alpha-hole ever written, and then he fuses his mouth to mine.

Chapter Thirty-Three

Dex

I f I didn't love this woman more than life itself, I'd strangle her. Madison Belle McClain is the most frustrating, obstinate, plays-with-fire person I have ever met—and that's saying something since my best friends are the Die Hard Trilogy.

I know she's mad at me. I understand her anger, and I don't begrudge her it. The thing that pisses me off is how she's keeping me at a distance because of it.

Every time she calls me Dex when I know she would usually call me Hook digs at me like a hot poker.

Not even the fact that she is straddling my lap, wearing a bikini that shouldn't be seen outside of a dressing room, skin flushed pink from the heat of the tub, water droplets falling in rivulets over the swells of her barely restrained breasts is enough to soothe me.

I'm done playing games.

I take her mouth with mine, and before the night is over, I will take the rest of her.

"*Hook.*" She sighs my name—fucking finally—as I trail kisses along her jaw and down her slender neck.

"That's it, baby."

I bite.

I suck.

I kiss.

Our bodies are pressed together so tightly there's an audible release of suction as I use the hand still wrapped around her hair to pull her back.

Her heavy-lidded eyes are the color of a twilight sky as they struggle to meet mine. Her lips are already turning red and swollen from my kisses, and though they'll be gone by morning, she's got the darkening of love bites all down the curve of her neck.

I bend, putting my nose against the marks I reluctantly didn't leave hard enough to last, and inhale. The chemicals of the hot tub aren't enough to wash away her sweet coconut scent.

"We are now getting to the point of the evening where you can call me Dex all you want, baby."

She said my apology would be empty, that actions speak louder than words. First I'll show her how I feel about her. Then I'll tell her.

After she's sated, I'll explain my thought process from yesterday.

From her shoulders down to the flare of her hips, I knead the muscles of her back, enjoying each arch that pushes her tits into my face. I need them in my mouth.

Skimming my fingertips up her arms, I lull her with each light caress, following the line of her collarbone and down the edge of her top.

She inhales deeply, her nipple brushing my palm in the process, and I need it.

With a thumb hooked inside each triangle, I peel them to the side until her breasts spill free and I'm eye to nipple with the prettiest pink tips I've ever had the privilege to see.

She's more than a handful, and I test their weight as I take each one in hand and push them together, leaning in and swiping my tongue across both pebbled tips before taking one into my mouth.

"*Dex.*"

This time I smile around the nipple in my mouth. I may not be thrusting inside her yet, but she's already getting lost in the pleasure only I can give her.

I keep my face buried in her chest as her hips start to rock in a way I doubt she's even aware she's making happen.

"Dex—" She breaks on a gasp, her hands clutching at my hair until my scalp burns as I suck hard enough to leave a mark on her tit where it can't be seen.

We're back to kissing, our tongues tangling for dominance. She shivers as I run my hands down her ribs and into the dip of her waist until I find the strings tying her bottoms together. I feel around for the tips and pull when I find them.

Smoothing the flat of my palm over her hip, I follow the curve to her ass, grabbing her cheeks and taking control of her thrusts.

Roll forward. Roll back.

Squeeze.

Roll forward. Roll back.

I splay my fingers, following her cleft, bared completely to me now that her suit is gone, until I'm met with her center.

Fuck me.

Even inside the jacuzzi, she's hot enough to rival the triple-digit temperature, so wet there's no way for the water to wash it away. The best part? It's all for me.

Without any preamble, I thrust two fingers inside her and hold on as her body instinctively pushes itself up on her knees, water sloshing around us.

In and out. I take her from the same angle I took her earlier.

"Fuck, baby."

Rises onto her knees. Falls back onto my thighs.

"Do you have any idea how sexy it is watching you ride my fingers?"

"Dex…"

"Don't stop."

Pump.

Pull out and spread her wetness on her asshole.

Thrust in.

Pull out, gathering more of her juices.

One more plunge inside and I curl my fingers to hit her G-spot at the same moment I press my thumb inside her ass down to the bottom knuckle.

"I love holding you in the palm of my hand while you fall apart."

I hold her close as she rides out the last of her pleasure, giving her a moment to come down. I don't need her passing out on me again. This night is far from over.

Hooking an arm around her middle, I lift her enough to slip from beneath her and position myself behind her then bend her over the edge of the tub.

Nudging her knees open with my own, I feel around the jets now facing Maddey's front until I find the one I need. Pushing through the resistance of the powerful stream of water pumping out of it, I push on the plastic lip until the jet is angled just right. When Maddey gasps, I know I've found it.

"That's it, baby." I run hands up and down her torso. "Let the water work your clit."

"Dex." I grab her hip when she tries to move out of the way.

"No," I caution. "Don't move." I reach around, framing her lips in the V of my fingers before pushing on her swollen nub. "Think of it as an extra hand." I remove mine and bring it back to her hip.

I make quick work of my board shorts, untying the string and ripping open the Velcro of the fly.

Her back arches to perfection as I drag the head of my cock through her wetness, the pulsing beat of the jets hitting my overly sensitive head as I tease her clit.

"Please tell me you're on birth control?" I ask. I have a condom in my cargo pocket, but I am loathed to use it.

"Yes."

Thank Christ.

"Do you trust me, Tink?" I line myself up at her entrance, silently asking permission to take her bareback. I've never done that before, but I don't want any barriers between us.

"Always, Hook."

Those might be my two favorite words in the English language. I wrap my hands around her waist, hers so much smaller than mine, my fingertips easily meeting over her belly ring. My thumbs find home in her sexy-as-fuck back dimples, and I work myself inside.

Inch by inch, I watch as my cock disappears inside the velvet heat of her pussy, gritting my teeth in an effort not to come from the vise-like grip it has on me.

"Fuck you're tight."

"Dex." Her head falls forward and she circles her hips, looking for purchase.

A few more pumps of my hips and I'm buried balls-deep, my chest heaving like I've done a ruck run.

"Dex." She swivels, and I lean back to watch my cock pull out and push back into her. "I'm so full."

That's what she thinks.

"Not yet."

I take her lazily, enjoying the show a little longer before I show her just how full she can be.

Reaching around her again, I run two fingers through her slit then bring them to her ass and push in.

"*Dex*," she squeals.

"Fuck, baby." I can feel my cock moving inside her through the thin membrane of skin separating it from my fingers. "Your pussy is tight as hell, but your ass is something else."

"Dex." Another gasp, followed by a long moan.

"Do you want me to stop?"

"*Stop?*" She flashes me a look over her shoulder. "Why the fuck would I want you to stop?"

I chuckle, resting my forehead between her shoulder blades, and place a path of gentle kisses there as I keep the thrust of my hips and my fingers easy. The pace doesn't matter because I can already feel the tell-tale flutters of her pussy around my dick.

"Fuck me, Dex." She pushes back again. "I need you to fuck me."

Reluctantly, I pull my finger from her ass. If she wants me to fuck her, I'm going to need both hands.

Gripping her to the point of bruising, I hold her close to the jets and pound into her with skin-slapping, water-splashing thrusts.

She comes but I keep going, not giving her a chance to come down from her orgasm this time.

Over and over I drive my hips forward. My balls draw up tight and I get that familiar tingle at the base of my spine. I'm going to come, but not until she does again.

Thrust.

Thrust.

Thrust.

Her walls ripple; she's close.

"Maddey."

She arches more, the dip of her back deepening.

"Maddey."

"Dex."

Two more pumps and she's coming; one more and I join her.

I keep her close as we ride out the pleasure together.

I loved her before, but now? There's no going back.

Chapter Thirty-Four

The theme song to Super Mario blares from my phone, and I curse myself for not switching it to silent.

"Why didn't I teach you how to fetch my phone?" I grumble to Trident, slapping a hand around willy-nilly in an effort to find the offensive object.

I feel the bed shift and then see Lyle's grinning face staring at me from the lock screen on the pillow next to me.

How did…

Trident's good, but not that—

Oh shit!

I bolt upright, whipping around to see the weight that was pressed along my back is Dex and not my dog.

Dex is in my bed.

Dex is shirtless in my bed. Only shirtless? Is he naked?

Wait…

Am I naked?

Gingerly, as if I'm anticipating finding a spider underneath them, I pinch the end of the comforter that miraculously didn't fall from my abrupt movements, squinting one eye shut as I peek under the covers.

Holy shit! I'm naked.

Yeah you are. *lying back in a beach chair, toasting with a piña colada*

Why bother putting clothes on when Dex was only going to remove them?

Don't call him Dex. Hook, remember?

Dex, Hook, Daddy—whatever you want to call him is fine by me.

Eww. Don't call him Daddy.

I don't know. *shrugs* I think he more than earned it the way he dicked her down last night.

Talk about motion in the ocean.

Screw that. Let's talk about the size of Navy boy's boat.

"I'd pay good money to be able to hear what goes on inside that pretty head of yours when you stare off like you're trying to see Neverland, Tink." Dex's voice, thick from sleep, has the voices in my head shaking my nipples like they are maracas.

Oh my god! I slept with Dex.

No, no. *tut-tuts and wags finger* You had sex with Dex.

Correction. *sits up, slides glasses down nose, and peers over the rim* Dex fucked the shit out you. Honestly, I don't know how any of us are still around with how many times he blew the top of your head off last night.

I clench my thighs, deliciously sore between them in a way I haven't been in years. Beard burn runs down the length of my body, and I spot a hickey on my boob. A smile twists my lips thinking of all the times Rocky would bitch about Gage's penchant for love bites.

The ringtone cuts off as the call is kicked to voicemail, only to start back up again a few seconds later. Lyle is relentless when he wants something.

I swipe to answer, thumbing it to speakerphone because I cannot even muster the energy to hold it up to my ear.

"Hey, Lyle," I say around a yawn.

"Dollface." The ever-present tinge of excitement in his voice never fails to bring a smile to my face. Yes his coffee is amazing, and now that Holly has taken over the bakery side of the business, the waistband of my pants is in danger, but it's the barista's gregarious, flamboyant personality that has me making the commute to Espresso Patronum when there are approximately a thousand other coffee shops between my home and there.

"What's up, boo?" Lyle lives for pet names, and I can just picture the goofy grin he's probably sporting right at this moment.

A strong arm wraps around the tops of my thighs, tugging me closer.

Someone doesn't like hearing you use a pet name with someone else.

Interesting. *taps chin*

It really is elementary.

Don't go quoting Sherlock Holmes.

What? *places hand on chest* Anyone can see someone—*side-eyes Dex*—is po-ses-sive.

Le sigh. Alpha men.

"When are you coming to visit?" Lyle's voice brings me back to the conversation I'm having with an actual human being.

"You and Kyle were just down here the other day." I flop backward onto the mattress, Dex shifting me to my side to spoon the instant I'm flat on my back.

This is nice.

"Yes, but I need you up here." I don't need video chat to know he's stomping his foot and pointing down to the ground aggressively.

"Why—" Anything else I was going to add to the question falls away as Dex starts to place kisses along the back of my neck.

"Because." There's a pause then his voice lowers to a

whisper. "Only you can sprinkle your fairy dust and make clothes come off without it sounding like sexual harassment."

"What?" I choke out a laugh then bite back a moan as Dex buries his face in the curve of my neck to smother his own. I appreciate the discretion. I'm not even close to figuring out what all this—and by 'this' I mean the fact that I let my brothers' best friend, my childhood crush screw me those six ways to Sunday—means, let alone the complications adding my people to the mix would bring.

"Don't you try to act all innocent with me, Miss Smut Queen—"

"Queen of Smut," I correct.

"Potato, vodka." He brushes me off with Vince's tried-and-true saying. "Now stop trying to distract me." God forbid. "What I'm trying to say is, I've never met a person in possession of a penis"—teeth bite into my shoulder and a leg is thrown over both of mine as Dex really struggles to hold in his laughter—"who has been able to say no to you."

"Isn't Jase the exaggerator of the group?" I question.

"I said don't try to distract me," he scolds.

"*How* am I distracting you?"

"You know what bringing up hockey hunks does to me. I get all flummoxed." He's fanning himself with his hand right now, I just know he is.

"Says the man who opened up a coffee shop across the street from a gym that trains boxers and MMA fighters."

"This from the girl who writes out of both said shop and said gym?" he counters.

"Touché."

A hand glides across my belly, making the muscles twitch. It's a reminder—as if I could forget—that I'm not alone in bed.

"*Sonofabitch*," Lyle hisses. "Damn you and your super squirrel powers—you got me off topic."

"I bet I can get you off," Dex whispers in my ear.

Yes he can.

He deserves a medal for how many times he got you off last night.

Like the Medal of Honor?

More like the Medal of Orgasm.

He should totally be voted in as the mayor of O-Town.

Truth. He is what liquid dreams are made of.

Great, now you got the song stuck in my head.

Me too.

Me three.

"My gift is my curse," I say to Lyle, arching deeper into Dex's hold. If Lyle doesn't hurry up and get to the point, we are going to discover a whole new meaning for phone sex.

"You're lucky I love you, bitch."

Oh, someone sounds like they're pouting now.

Don't be mean to our GBF.

Isn't Sammy our GBF?

A girl can never *have too many GBFs.*

Fact. Every strong woman needs to have a gay best friend behind her telling her how fierce she is.

"Don't get your panties in a bunch, Ly. Maybe you should ask Holly if you can borrow some frosting and let Kyle put you in a better mood."

"*Mmm,*" Dex hums against me. "Sounds delicious."

I reach back, blindly feeling around for his mouth to shut him up. I need to wrap this call up.

"What did you need my help with, Ly?"

"I need you to get your cute little ass up here, bat those baby blues of yours, and flash your dimples so people start stripping off their shirts."

"My shirt is off," Dex informs me, as if I could forget.

"You're ridiculous." I'm not sure which man I'm speaking to.

"Yet you love me anyway, doll. What does that say about you?"

"It's a well-documented fact that I'm not normal." I spend more of my day conversing with fictional characters than talking to people in real life.

"You got that right," comes from Dex, who flips me to my back when I pinch his side for the dig.

Braced above me, his arms caging me in, I get another one of those weird cardiac flips while taking him in. Bedhead, pillow creases slashing across his cheekbone, eyes a little heavy with sleep—he looks like the reason people started having morning sex.

"I gotta go, Lyle." I don't even wait for his goodbye before I end the call.

"Morning, sunshine." There's a smirk I'm used to seeing playing across those delectable lips, but the way he's looking at me is different.

"Ahoy, matey." I pull out my pirate humor, needing to break the tension of what is giving me pause.

I need to get out of this bed before he uses his magic wand to put a spell on me. Sure, he can bibbidi-bobbidi me into the land of rolling orgasms where the coming never stops and the party in my pants is the event of the century. I can handle that. My underutilized hormones fully support that, claiming Dex is my glass slipper and fits me perfectly. Well, maybe not *perfectly* if the tenderness I feel is any indication.

It's the affection, the adoration swimming in his choco-latey gaze that has my heart turning into a pumpkin.

Chapter Thirty-Five

Dex

Maddey may have been voted most likely to wish upon a star, but I'm the one who's having all their dreams come true.

Finally taking the crab's advice and kissing the girl? Check.

Finding out what she looks like when she comes? Roger.

Fucking her brains out in a hot tub—twice? Jackpot.

Holding her all night long as we slept? That was my favorite part.

There is absolutely no better way to wake up than with the woman you love in your arms.

After avoiding spending extended time with her since my feelings for her started to change, being immersed in her life now is a head trip. Lying in bed, touching her, feeling the way she reacts and responds to me while having a ridiculous conversation with one of her friends is an experience in and of itself.

It feels like our lives have been irrevocably altered in such a short amount of time—me realizing the depth of my feelings and throwing caution to the wind—but in reality, we've been a lifetime in the making.

Yet, as I look at my sleep-rumpled girl, I get a tingling sense that she is fighting what I already know to be true. I should have been prepared for it, but she still manages to slip out from under me and bolt for the bathroom.

The door shuts without the click of a lock—not that it would stop me—followed by the sound of the shower starting up.

"Let me talk to your mom and then we'll go out, bud," I tell Trident when he lifts his head from where he's sprawled out in a sunny spot by the glass doors.

I riffle through my crumpled bottoms on the floor, searching out the small packet of lube in the pocket, and I don't bother pulling on my boxer briefs since I plan on stepping right into the shower. It's cute how my girl thinks she can run from me.

Though it's a logistical nightmare with her having a stalker out there, one of my favorite things about Maddey's house is all the natural light the massive windows let in. Even now, she didn't bother turning on the lights.

"I should have locked the door." She keeps her head tipped back, face turned into the spray when I come up behind her and wrap an arm around her middle.

"Baby." I nuzzle into the space where her neck meets her shoulder. "I kick in doors for a living—a little lock wouldn't have kept me out."

"What if I told you I needed a minute to myself?"

"Not even then," I say unapologetically.

I'm done hiding from my feelings. I'm not going to let her run away from hers.

"Dex."

"What did I say about calling me Dex?" I suck her earlobe into my mouth.

"Can you be serious for a minute?" She sighs and I tighten my hold, mulling over my options. The time has come for me to lay all my cards out on the table.

The water beats down on us, the temperature cooler than I would have suspected she would like.

It might be the SEAL in me, but I've always thought Maddey looked cute wet. There's something about how the water sticks to her blonde lashes and the way her hair gets slicked back from her face, keeping it from being obstructed from view that I could stare at all day.

"You want serious?" She nods. "How's this for serious?" I spin her around to face me and pin her to the tile wall with my body, elbows bracketing her face on either side.

The rain shower head above keeps us wet, and I do my best to block most of it from hitting Maddey in the face so she can see me. Dropping my hands to cup her head, I use my thumbs to wipe away the droplets along the ridge of her brow, tangling my other fingers into her hair and tugging to tilt her face to mine. I need those icy eyes on me while I say the most important words of my life.

"I love you."

She gasps and shakes her head. "No you don't."

"The fuck I don't." I bring my forehead down to rest on hers. "I love you and have loved you for *years*." Even if I only just made the connection.

"Dex." She chokes out a sob, squeezing her eyes shut tight.

"Look at me, Tink." Forever passes before she does as she's told. "I. Love. You."

She shakes her head violently, and I move to cradle the back of it to keep her from banging it against the tile.

"You can't love me," she pleads.

"Maddey, I'm a SEAL—I'm not the type of person who likes to be told what they can and cannot do."

The skin on my elbows burns more the harder I dig them into the wall.

"You follow orders from command all the time."

Even while I'm trying to profess my love, she has to be a

difficult smartass. I anticipate lots of spankings and makeup sex in the years to come. Then again, if she was a shrinking violet, she would never be able to handle me.

"Now is not the time for jokes, Madison."

Her eyes flare, staring at me defiantly. "Then stop messing around."

"Stop trying to piss me off by intentionally being obtuse."

Out of the corner of my eye, I see her clench her hands into fists then unclench them.

"Look." Her shoulders roll back. "I get it." Does she? "We had sex. But I'm a big girl, Dex." She inhales deeply and blows it out before she continues. "Just because we have history doesn't mean I'm going to get the wrong idea."

What the fuck is she talking about?

"I don't need false assurances. I'm perfectly capable of separating sex from emotion."

If she thought what we spent more than half the night doing didn't involve emotion, she's out of her goddamn mind.

"If you're worried I'm going to go crying to my brothers because you didn't say you 'love me'"—I growl when she puts air quotes around the words—"don't be. I won't say anything. This"—she bounces a finger between us then circles it at the ceiling in the direction of her bedroom—"is none of their business."

Am I worried how the Die Hard Trilogy will react when they find out about me sleeping with their sister? Sure. I technically broke bro code, but after Justin's declaration, I'm more confident they will forgive me when they realize the depth of my feelings. Now if only I could get the youngest McClain to grasp the concept.

Chapter Thirty-Six

Dex loves me?
Did I hear that right? Nah, no way.
Or maybe I'm still asleep?
Though…

I haven't had a dream about Dex confessing his undying love for me in years. Maybe having sex jostled one of my old fantasies loose?

Yeah. That has to be it.

But…

If I'm dreaming, why would it include a random phone call with Lyle? I'm no Freud or anything, but I can't see how those would correlate.

That's because they don't.

Yeah, girl. You are not *dreaming.*

This is very much real.

*Oh my swoon. *fans face* I can't handle it. Dex dropped the L-bomb.*

*Ahh! *twirls and throws confetti* Dex loves us!*

stares off dreamily I just love a happy ending.*

My characters may be all heart eyes, toasting champagne,

and happy-dancing at Dex's declaration, but not me. I've read this story. I know how it plays out.

"I love you, Tink."

God! Why does he have to keep saying it?

I shake my head. "Please stop saying that, Dex."

"I do. And you know what? You love me too." A finger over my lips cuts off my denial. "Don't you dare lie to me, Maddey."

I shiver, and it has nothing to do with the water that still hasn't warmed and everything to do with Dex being all growly alpha man. His nostrils flare and the Tink Train is in full effect as he watches me with hard eyes.

Dammit!

Why does he have to be right? Yes I love him. Of course I do. It doesn't matter that it isn't by blood; he's been my family since before I was even a twinkle in my dad's balls.

Oof. Why are you thinking about your dad's balls right now?

Yeah, so not appropriate.

Stop trying to use it as a distraction technique.

Focus on the task at hand.

Fine. They want me to focus—I can do that. I can focus like a person has never focused before. It will be like when I get inspired by a scene and I knock out thousands of words of word vomit.

"You love me, and you know how I know?"

"You're being ridiculous." I wonder why he won't just let this go.

"I have a list, but we'll go with one of the more obvious ones."

Obvious? Is he kidding me right now? *Obvious*? Even when I thought myself in love, *no one* suspected it. Well…maybe Sammy, but then again, I didn't really keep my feelings hidden from him. It was like with Jordan and Skye; I told them because they were my vent sessions.

But obvious? Yeah, no. I don't believe I have any *obvious* tells, not then and certainly not now.

"This right here"—his thumb strokes across the frog prints tattoo curving along my hip—"tells me you love me."

"If that were true"—my gaze falls to where his finger is moving along the ink—"then I must be prepping for one hell of a taboo reverse harem romance, because I have prints for Justin, Tyler, Connor, Dad, and your dad too."

When I decided on this particular piece, I knew I wanted something to honor all the important frogmen in my life. I may have been too young when Dex's dad died to really remember him, but without him, Dex wouldn't be in my life. Plus, with all the stories I've heard about him from my dad and Peggy, I feel like I know him.

"Sure, it's not *exclusively* for me, but only *one* of them has a hooked toe."

Fucking hell. How did he notice that? It's barely discernible, only the slightest bend to one of the digits.

"That doesn't prove anything," I argue. Besides, I got the tattoo years ago, back when I was in my puppy-love stage—I know, I know, I'm an idiot—so it no longer applies.

"Oh no?" He arches one of his dark brows sarcastically. How is it sarcastic? Just trust me, it is.

"No." I bring my arms up to push him away, trying and failing to get some much needed space. The jerk only crowds closer, making it so any time either of us breathes, our chests brush with each inhalation. "I think you're suffering from Stockholm syndrome."

He chuckles. The bastard.

"Neither one of us has been kidnapped, Tink."

Grrr.

"Fine." I harrumph. "Under some delusional spell from living in such close quarters."

"You don't really live in a shoebox. Try again."

Is he smirking? Oh my god he's totally smirking.

"Look, Dex—"

"Hook."

"What?"

"Hook. I told you to call me Hook. My cock was buried balls-deep in you last night…" He puts his mouth to my ear, the chill from the water chased away by the blanket of heat that is his body. "You can't tell me you don't like me after that."

"Haven't you ever heard of hate-fucking?" I challenge.

"No matter how mad at me you get or how much you claim to not like me at a particular moment, you could never hate me."

"Don't test me."

"So spunky." He nips at my earlobe. "Just one of the many things that makes me love you."

I may not literally hate him, but the churning in my gut, the boiling of my blood, and the pounding beat of my heart tells me I'm giving it the good ol' college try.

Not gonna lie, part of me is jealous of how easily he can say the words. Why can't I? It's only three words, eight letters. That's nothing. That's barely even a tagline. So why? Why? Why? Why?

Fuck me this is Ryan all over again.

If my life were one of my books, I can only imagine how they would rip me apart in the reviews.

I should have never had sex with Dex.

Ooo, now that sounds like my kind of Dr. Seuss book.

Agreed. Think about it: Sex With Dex. *Instead of telling you all the places you could eat green eggs and ham—because who really eats green eggs and ham?—it could list off all the places you can do it.*

A car.

A counter.

Bent over the desk in the office.

A chair.

A couch.

Oh-em-gee the list is endless!

Yup, *definitely* shouldn't have had sex with Dex. It's like his dick was the key, unlocking a whole new level of ridiculous for the characters in my head. Orgasms are apparently like steroids to them, and now they're bouncing around like they are at a tea party with the Mad Hatter.

Honestly, I wish I could fall down the rabbit hole, because in Wonderland it's all *eat this* and *drink that,* but instead of making me big or shrinking me tiny, maybe I could find something that would help me actually be able to fall *in* love with a person.

Chapter Thirty-Seven

Dex

I had to go and fall in love with a McClain. Goddamn stubborn mofos, the lot of them.

I'll have to remember to follow up with their group's book club, because I'm pretty sure I'm not supposed to want to shake the woman I'm trying to tell I love. Then again, maybe it's common.

Shake her, strangle her, put her over my knee and spank her until she stops lying to me and to herself—all of those seem like viable options right now.

The thing I can't figure out is *why* she won't admit her feelings.

She loves me. I know she does. I've seen it in the way she looks at me, in how her body subconsciously angles toward me when we're in a group, and in how she stays close any time she's been spooked.

Every breathy sigh and pleasure-filled moan, each dig of her nails into my back to keep me close—when I'm bringing her pleasure, she's too caught up in it—in us—to hide.

Maybe that's what I need to do…

Spend as much time naked together as possible, let her body tell me all the things she refuses to say out loud.

Maybe if I do that, she'll be able to voice the words I know she feels.

It's a tough job, but someone has to do it.

Maddey McClain better prepare herself, because I'm coming in hot.

Bending my knees, I cup my hands under her ass and lift her into my arms. Spreading my feet, I use my body to support her, leaving my hands free to roam and claim.

I may be brute brawn and she a tiny pixie, but our bodies still fit together perfectly. Really, it's genetics' way of proving we were made for each other.

Gripping her by the nape, I cover her mouth with mine, feeling her melt under me. Her hands relent and stop trying to push me away, traveling up to lock around my neck.

"I love you," I say against her lips, her thighs squeezing my hips in response.

I kiss her chin, follow along her jaw and down her neck. She arches each time my lips make contact with her skin.

Down and down I go, sucking a nipple into my mouth as it is thrust against me. She mewls, the sting of her nails washed away under the cool water.

"I love you." I grind my hips forward.

"Dex." She meets me with a roll of her own. My erection slips between the lips of her pussy, sliding through her wetness and bumping along the hard nub of her clit.

"I love you." I smile against her skin when she growls.

"Stop." Another hip roll. "Saying." Another squeeze of her thighs. "That." I'm pretty sure she just drew blood as the ridge of my cock head flicks her clit again.

"Why should I, Tink?"

I keep teasing her when she doesn't answer right away.

"Because."

I wait for her to continue, but that's all she says.

"Wow, great argument. You're a real wordsmith, Miss Bestselling Author."

The death glare she shoots me has me hardening the slightest bit more, and I find her entrance and push inside. The contrast of the chilly water and the warmth of her pussy surrounding my dick is almost enough to bring me to my knees.

"I love you."

"Unless you're gonna talk dirty to me, keep your mouth shut."

Oh, my little Tinker Bell. It's like she stepped in ink, but instead of showing me the path to Pan's hideout, she's supplying me with the quickest way to Orgasmville. We can certainly stop at Dirty Talk Village on our trip to Poundtown.

"See this?" Instead of pumping my hips, I keep a steady press, waiting for her body to adjust. "The way you suck me in?" I keep pushing until I'm buried to the hilt. "Your body knows it loves me. Now we just have to get"—I run a thumb over her bottom lip, pinching her chin between my fingers—"this smart mouth of yours on the same page."

Her eyes flutter closed and she trembles, wet strands of hair sticking to the tile as she thrashes her head in denial.

"One day soon, this"—I lean in and suck her lip into my mouth—"will tell me what your body is already *shouting* at me."

She attempts another rebuttal, but her heels dig into my ass like she's wearing spurs and I'm the horse she's trying to encourage. *Giddy up, Tink—I'll be your motherfucking stallion.*

"You're mine." I'm hyperaware of every vein, every ridge of my cock as it drags along her walls with each lazy pull out and leisurely push in.

"You're wrong," she insists, but she clutches at me when I swivel my hips to hit that special place inside that takes her to infinity and beyond.

"You've been mine for years."

The great blue bikini incident may have been the catalyst for changing how I saw her, but she's always been mine.

"Even before we were old enough to realize it." I kiss the soft spot behind her ear. "Even when you were with someone else." I kiss her cheek. "Even before I recognized it for what it was, you were always mine."

Her lashes fan across her cheeks as she shuts me out by closing her eyes again. Bringing up Ryan may not have been the best play, and if they'd ended up together, I wouldn't have gotten in the way of that. What I need her to realize, though, is that my feelings are very real and aren't going away any time soon—as in ever.

"You're mine, Maddey."

"No I'm not."

This woman has so much to learn.

Unwinding her legs from around me, I slip from her heat, my dick flipping me off in the process. I ignore him and can't stop a triumphant grin at how she whimpers at the loss. Lowering her down, I keep my hands on her until I'm sure she's steady on her feet.

"You're mine and I'll prove it."

Taking her hand, I spin her to face the wall, pressing every inch of my front to her back. Lacing our fingers, I position us so my palms rest atop the backs of her hands, bringing our linked fingers up until I have her arms fully stretched above her head, and then I step us closer to the wall.

I place my feet between hers, feeling the smooth skin of her thighs on my quads as I spread her stance, grinding into the curve of her ass where it's pressed to my groin.

She's so sexy from this angle. The long line of her back, those maddening dimples at the base of her spine then the round bubble of her heart-shaped ass. My only issue with this position is I can't see her beautiful face when she falls apart for me.

Her skin burns against mine even as the coolness of the tile touches the insides of my forearms.

"Mine, Madz." I nip across the back of her neck. "Mine."

She attempts to push me away with another rebuff, but—surprise, surprise—it doesn't work. Instead I wrap a hand around both her wrists and run the other down the length of her body.

I grip her throat and place another kiss behind her ear with a whispered, "Mine," then drag my fingers along the bumps and dips of her collarbone.

Down. Squeeze a breast. Twist a nipple.

Down. Feel her abdominals jump and her stomach cave in.

Down. Trace the frog prints walking across her hip, swirling a finger over the one meant for me.

Down. Slip between her lips, press my thumb to her swollen clit, and thrust two fingers into her dripping pussy.

Her words deny me, but her body can't. Our connection is too strong, too primal to be ignored when we're close like this.

My dick is leaking pre-cum all over the curve of her ass while her cries echo against the walls with her climax.

Her hips roll and sway, her body searching me out as I continue to work her through her release.

I start to push her back up the hill as soon as she hits the bottom, pumping a few more times until bringing my arm back and gently slipping the same fingers that were inside her pussy into her ass, using her juices as lubrication.

"Dex." She gasps, pushing back into the invasion. Encouraged by her response, I take the opportunity to add a third to the mix.

It doesn't matter how many times I've fantasized about taking her here through the years; her every reaction subtly telling me she's down for a little backdoor action is what dreams are made of.

"Dex…*please*."

"Please what?"

Easy pumps.

"Please—" Her hands splay against the tile. "I need you in me."

Not want—*need.*

I scissor my fingers with a flex.

"Where do you want me?" I taunt.

"I don't—I don't care."

She rises up on her toes and lowers herself back down.

"Does your pussy want me again?" I nip along her shoulder, dragging my thick stubble across her skin.

"*Dex.*" Another plea.

"Or do you want me here?" Another pump. "In your ass." Another scissor. "Where no one else has had you?"

I'm not one of those guys who thinks a girl should be a virgin for her future husband. Hell, it would make me a fucking hypocrite to judge someone for indulging their sexual appetites.

But does it please me to know no one else has had her here? To know I can claim one of her firsts? You bet your sweet ass—pun intended.

"*God yes,*" she says, and it's more of a moan than actual words.

I reach out and snag the packet of lube from the built-in shelf I placed it on when I first stepped inside the shower. I don't want to hurt her, but I have teased and played with her here enough that her body has already started to adjust to having something there.

Still, it's going to hurt a little at first. Even with her currently taking three of my fingers, she's going to be stretched to her limits to accommodate my cock.

Pinching the packet between my teeth, I also grab the body wash and squirt it until it fills my palm. I inhale the sweet scent of coconut as I soap up her torso, thumbing her nipples, squeezing and weighing her breasts before moving the massage down the line of her spine.

Working up a lather, I spend another few minutes between

her legs, circling her clit, needing her as keyed up as possible to help alleviate the initial pain that will come when I breach her.

Finally, I rip the top off the packet, squirt it into my palm, and take my aching erection in my hand. The remainder of the lube is squeezed onto the top of her crack, smoothed into her cleft as I run my dick up and down it to make sure I'm fully coated as well.

"You know why you trust me to do this?" I place the tip of my dick at her rosebud but don't push. "Hmm? Do you?"

Slowly, easily, I shift forward, the head of my cock slipping inside with a hiss through Maddey's teeth. I hold still, giving her body a moment to adjust.

"Don't want to guess?" I thumb her clit as I push forward another few inches. "Just want me to tell you?"

Her head falls back to my chest, her back arches in the most beautiful curve, and her nipples kiss the wall, her lips parting with panted breaths.

She's maddeningly silent, but you know what she doesn't do? She doesn't pull away.

We work together, like we've been doing this for years and it's not her first time allowing someone to take her in one of the most intimate ways possible.

I release her wrist, lacing my fingers with hers once again, our knuckles digging into each other as she curls hers into a fist, bending my wrist so I can continue to hold her hand over the top of it while I finish pushing the rest of the way inside.

My body is on fire, my skin feeling stretched tight as her ass squeezes me like a vise.

Talk about choking the chicken.

What the fuck?

Fuck me, I've been spending too much time with Maddey if I can have that type of ridiculous thought float through my brain at a time like this. Then again, I can't stop the smile from overtaking my face because, *hoo-yah*, I'll take *all* the ludicrous thoughts if it means I *am* spending all my free time with the woman I love.

Propping my chin on her shoulder, I peek over it to watch the gorgeous sight of her body undulating against me. With my mouth close to her ear, I again ask, "So do you know why you trust me to do this?"

"Dex." She braces her free hand on the wall with a flat palm, rolling her hips back and forth between my dick in her ass and my fingers working her clit.

"No matter how big or small, you came to me if you needed anything." I kiss up and down her neck. "You trust me because I've always been your shelter in the storm."

Chapter Thirty-Eight

It's too much. And no, I'm not talking about the dick in my ass.

Are you cray-cray?

You have a dick in your ass.

You're giving him the Sacramento turtleneck.

The vegan Hot Pocket.

Dex is shooting for the moon.

Talk about plundering your booty.

Yeah, let's not act like this isn't something that needs mentioning.

Oh my god. For real, someone needs to fit me for a straitjacket and start renovating my room to have padded walls. How? How is it that the voices in my head can have an opinion while I'm having sex? And I'm not talking about plain ol' vanilla sex, either. Nope, we're talking holy-shit-I've-never-felt-so-full, how-is-it-even-fitting, why-haven't-I-done-this-sooner anal sex.

Like a dick up the poop-shooter isn't enough to have my head spinning, Dex won't stop saying he loves me.

Hold up. *makes T with hands* While that's all well and good, can we talk about the other thing he said?

Oh, yeah. I hope you were taking notes.
Hell yeah, that line was swoony as fuck.
He's your shelter in the storm.
Major heart eyes right now.
I'm totally that black and white GIF of the woman swooning.
Seriously. Add that shit to your next book.
You'll have the panties dropping for sure.

"I sure hope your characters are at least on my side." Dex chuckles then groans as he pumps into me again.

Because our history and his lickable body, roguishly handsome face, and declarations of love aren't enough. No, he has to go and get my weird eccentricities and accept them even in the middle of coitus.

Goddamn my defective heart.

Where's a fairy godmother when you need one?

Not wanting to give him any ammo to use against me, I keep my mouth shut. Well, not fully shut—sighs, moans, and pleas for more slip past my lips as Dex works me toward an orgasm unlike anything I've ever felt before.

Not gonna lie, when he first shoved his pork sword up my fudge-maker—okay, he didn't shove, but I'm allowed to be a little dramatic when I have something in a place I used to consider a restricted area—it hurt.

Ever the gentleman, Dex gave me the time I needed to turn the slight pain into pleasure beyond belief. The fullness, the flicks of my clit, then the two fingers that find their way inside my pussy—and I'm done. Shooting stars, fireworks, fairies sprinkling pixie dust; I'm coming, and a few thrusts later, Dex is following me just around the river bend.

After Dex hakuna-ed matata-s, we didn't linger long in the shower. It is one thing to deal with the chilly temperature while having a big hunky SEAL showing you exactly how far you will go like Moana; it is a whole other deal when that's not happening.

"Since when do you shower in temperatures that should require a wetsuit? I seem to recall when we were growing up you would take showers that were so hot steam would billow out when you opened the door. It was like you were filming a 90s rock video in there," Dex asks, looking far sexier than he should with one of my hot pink towels riding low around his hips. He gives a whole new meaning to the idea that real men wear pink because, holy Stitch, those pecs, those abs, the ink, those stupidity-inducing Vs—all of it…gah! Talk about happy thoughts. Give me my keyboard and let my fingers fly.

"The hot water heater must be on the fritz." I rub my curls with a towel. "I'll ask Declan to come take a look at it later. He's the handy one of the group, always fixing things around The Hightower apartments and such," I tell Dex, providing way more information than he needs.

I'm rambling. Why am I rambling? Shit, I'm nervous. Why am I nervous? This is Dex. I've never been nervous around him before. Not even when I crushed on him was I like this. What changed?

Umm…you slept with him?

Could you be *more sarcastic right now?*

Could you *stop channeling your inner Chandler Bing?*

What? *shrugs shoulders* It's not my fault. Blame Holly for upping the frequency rerun-watching.

And…no…it's not the sex that has her bumbling around like she was just handed a note that said, 'Do you like me? Check yes or no.'

That would be because Dex didn't ask. He rained down L-bombs like Hiroshima.

That was nothing.

What do you mean that was nothing?

Don't you screech at me. All I meant was can we talk about how he didn't ask her if she loved him back? Like… *fans self* He was all 'I know you love me' and went all Demi Lovato and was like, 'Tell *me you love me.' Talk about h-o-t-t hot! And before you ask, yes, the extra T was needed.*

"I need to find me a Cave of Wonders and get my hands on a lamp." Dex brushes a curl behind my ear. When did he get so close? "My first wish would be to hear what is going on in here." He taps my temple.

Why does he have to use Disney to wreck my walls like he's Ralph?

"It wouldn't work." I back away from his touch before it has me launching myself at him for another round, instead searching for my bikini from last night. "Genies love me."

"Both as mystical blue beings and as dogs." His lips twitch at the memory of his old husky. I miss that pooch.

"You should know better." I poke his forehead. "I'll always be one jump ahead." Spotting the white material, I scoop it up—only to have it snatched out of my hands. "What—"

"You are *not* wearing that."

"*Excuse* me?" He did not just do what I think he did, did he? I reach for the bikini only for it to be held out of reach. Sometimes I really hate being vertically challenged. "It's a bathing suit."

"Hardly." He scoffs.

"What else am I supposed to wear to go jet-skiing?" I wasn't planning on wearing that one, but now I almost want to out of spite.

"Not this." Eyes so dark they are almost black watch me in possessive frustration as he shakes the bikini in his hand before tossing it behind him.

"And who made you king of the world?"

"Leonardo DiCaprio." Dex's deadpan delivery combined with his stoic expression make me want to kiss him or hit him; I haven't decided which yet.

I vote kiss.

Yes! Yes! *claps hands excitedly* Kiss him and tell him you love him. Then maybe we can get back to the sexy times.

It would be an effective way to end this argument. No bikinis necessary.

Truth. They would only get in the way when you're trying to get frisky.

Will you fools behave? She's not going to tell him she loves him, and she probably shouldn't sleep with him again until she can figure out her feelings. Jiminy chimes in for the first time in a while, throwing some serious shade my way.

"You're not the boss of me, Hook."

"No, but if you think I'm going to let you out of this house in that"—he thrusts an aggressive arm behind him—"sorry excuse for swimwear, you are even crazier than you think you are."

"Ha." I let out a humorless laugh, doing my best to cover up how turned on this bossy side makes me.

"I dare you, Tink." He crowds me until the backs of my legs hit the wood of my dresser. I shamelessly check out the way the sinews of his forearms move as he cages me in with an arm one each side of me, his fingers going white with his grip on the edge of the top. "Try walking out of here wearing it and I'll call your mother and tell her that her daughter is prancing around the beach in a bathing suit that barely covers her tits."

Rolling my shoulders, I cant my head back and meet that determined you-will-do-as-I-say gaze of his. "Don't go threatening me with Babs." Besides, it's too bad, so sad for him—it wouldn't work anyway. I'm Mom's favorite—perk of being the only girl in a house full of testosterone.

"I'll do whatever I have to if it means you don't go parading around in something I can see the soft pink of your nipples through." He ghosts a thumb over one of said nipples, and I need to lock my knees from melting into a puddle like Olaf would have in summer without Elsa's magic.

"Wow, first I'm prancing, and then I'm parading. We really need to get dressed and go downstairs, because I'm going to need some serious caffeine if I'm going to have enough energy to do all that." I slip into annoying little sister mode, hoping it will help put some distance between us. Too much has happened in the last thirty-six hours; I can't process it.

Just like that, those parentheses pop out and his eyes soften as he smiles down at me. I'm purposely ignoring the subtle shift I see in the depths of those dark eyes.

Turning, I hip-check the giant pain in the ass out of the way and grab a teal bikini from the drawer. The back ties with a string and the top is like a halter around my neck, but Mr. Caveman over here should be pleased because the front covers the girls in a full panel of material with only a small strip of open zigzags at the very top. My tan line game is on point with the variety of styles I shift between.

Not wanting to encourage another round of nookie, I slip the boy short bottoms on underneath my towel and get the top into position, tightening the tie in the back once I lose the terrycloth.

Pretending I don't feel the weight of his gaze is a feat in and of itself. Has he always looked at me this way? Have I just been a straight-up Dory about it, noticing only to promptly forget?

Inside my closet, I tie a sarong around my waist, adjusting it so it's knotted at my left hip, leaving the gap to expose my left leg as the gauzy material floats down to the ground like a maxi skirt.

Slipping into a pair of teal flip-flops since it's a beach day, I tie my hair into a messy bun, grab my beach bag, and am ready to go. No muss, no fuss.

Thankfully, Dex is dressed by the time I step out of my closet, but the way he wears a plain white t-shirt and simple pair of black and gray board shorts isn't really any better for my sanity than the towel.

Having intimate knowledge of what he looks like under all that only makes him more tempting than the spindle of a spinning wheel. Keeping my distance until I can make sense of everything jumbled up inside me is going to be one hell of a challenge.

But like Dory says, 'Just keep swimming.'

Walking over to the French doors leading out to the deck, I open one and gesture for Trident to go out. "Go head, baby. Go do your thing and meet me downstairs for your breakfast."

The house is eerily quiet as Dex falls into step beside me and we head downstairs.

My gaze snags on the gallery wall running down the length of the staircase, following the visual representation of how defective my heart is when it comes to love.

I lock onto the framed shot of Ryan and me at Jake and Jordan's wedding, both of us looking dapper in our formal wear—me in my bridesmaid gown, him in his tux—beaming smiles stretching ear to ear on our faces. We were so happy, but when push came to shove, I threw it all away.

I felt so much guilt about how our relationship ended that in the years since, I haven't been able to bring myself to sleep with someone else and have barely even dated.

Yet look how fast you jumped into bed with Dex…

Dammit, Jiminy.

A guilt trip is the last thing I need this morning.

Yeah, you dumb cricket, don't slut-shame her.

You act like Dex was some rando in a bar.

He's special.

I stumble down the last step at what they are insinuating. They aren't wrong per se; Dex is special, but he's not *special* special. A strong arm wraps around my middle to steady me, and my body—not on the same page as the rest of me—melts back, enjoying the familiar embrace.

I'm so conflicted about how to feel and what to do I can't even. Sex isn't complicated my ass. I'm punching Tucker the next time I see him.

The *flop-flop-flop-flop* of my sandals echoes down the hall. There may be a storm brewing inside me, but outside is the most perfect sunny day illuminating my home with a warm glow.

I push the button on my coffee maker, but nothing happens. I check the plug, try pulling it out and putting it back in, but still nothing. Then I realize why it seems so quiet —there's no hum of the refrigerator, no breeze from the vents of the air conditioner.

"Is the power out?" I ask, moving to flip the switch closest to me and getting nothing.

Dex's brows form a dark slash as they merge together in contemplation. The immediate transformation from my Hook to super SEAL Dex is staggering. The way it has me instantly on alert is enough to override the panic I'm sure would normally set in from thinking of him as *my Hook*.

He starts to move around the island to where his laptop is and stops short. If I thought his earlier change was scary, it has nothing on this version that snaps his back up ramrod straight, nostrils flaring, hands clenching into fists so tight they turn white. The Tink Train is pulsing harder than I've ever managed to get it, his jaw is clenched like he's a McClain and not a Stone, and his eyes narrow like he's about to shoot lasers out of them.

Murderous death glare is too tame of a description.

What is he looking at?

I start to turn to follow his gaze but stop at his harsh, "Don't."

Swallowing thickly, I start to shake. I've never been one to follow orders, especially ones that are barked at me, but Dex has *never* been like that with me. For him to do so now only adds to the severity of what is happening.

My eyes bounce around the room, looking for anything that is amiss, but whatever it is that has Dex's attention is only behind me. I wait for him to pass before I disobey orders —are you really all that surprised?—and turn around. Unfortunately, he has a should-be-on-a-romance-novel broad back, so I can't see a thing.

Worry slams into me when he stops at the doors leading to the deck. "Trident," I cry, my feet already moving of their own accord.

"He's fine." The dark edge to Dex's voice does little to reassure me that's true, and I take another step. "Madison, stay there." The use of my full name roots me to my spot.

This is bad. Bad, bad, bad.

Chapter Thirty-Nine

Dex

To go from the highest of highs in the shower to the lowest of lows when Maddey mentions the power's out is enough to give a person whiplash. The way I have her security system setup, both Jamie's firm and myself should have been alerted the second it cut off. The fact that it didn't isn't a good sign.

Talk about an understatement.

Looking past the beach babe vision standing in front of me, I catch sight of something that wasn't there before.

Motherfucking cocksucker asshole.

Fury burns through my veins as I try to make out the details from a distance. Unfortunately I can only tell there are pictures taped to the glass of the outer wall, not what the subject matter is.

Maddey attempts to check out the situation, but I need to keep her as far away from it as possible. There's no missing the flash of hurt on her beautiful face at how I command her to stay, but she'll get over it. Her safety is paramount, and she's not some precious snowflake that will crumble from a few hurt feelings.

Each step feels like walking across broken glass, not

wanting but needing to know what the latest thing her stalker has left is.

"Fucking hell."

My heart stops then takes off like a runaway train as I take in the different snapshots.

"What?" Maddey rushes toward me, her curvy body pressing into my back, trying to see around me. I was able to hold her off when she first panicked over Trident, but I knew she wouldn't heed my warnings once she heard my reaction.

A hand falls to the middle of my back, and I force down the lust that bubbles up from the simple touch. Being around Maddey has always messed with my central nervous system. Having had her, knowing what it feels like to be inside her, seeing her fall apart in my arms—it all just increases our connection by a million.

She doesn't move to go around me, letting me dictate when the reveal is made.

I shift, not wanting to let her see. This is so much worse than the highlighted passages of her books. That was a perversion of her work; this...this is an invasion of her privacy—our privacy.

"Dex?" Her voice is small, weak, fearful—so unlike the Maddey I know and love. I fucking hate it.

Reaching behind me, I feel for her hand and lace my fingers with hers. I bring her around and keep her tucked close to my side so I feel as well as hear the sharp breath she sucks in when she takes in the pictures taped to the glass.

"Oh my god—is that—is that...is that *us*?" she asks with a screech.

I fight back a wince by squeezing her to me tighter. I hate this, fucking hate it. It's not because this is the *last* way I wanted her brothers to find out I slept with their sister—though, let's be honest, I wasn't looking forward to that particular conversation—but because of the pure terror radiating from my girl as she wraps both arms around my middle and buries her face in my chest.

There's so much to do, so many questions that need answering, but I can take a minute to hold on to the trembling woman in my arms.

Her warm breath hits me in puffs. Rolling my shoulders forward, I curl my body to envelop her deeper into my embrace, leaning down to rest my chin on top of her head, staring down a shot of us kissing in the hot tub last night.

I hate that they are displayed like a play-by-play recap of every intimate moment we shared.

It starts with a shot of Maddey by herself, loose tendrils of hair falling around her face while she leans her head back with her eyes closed. When I first found her just like that, I had to pause to appreciate the simplicity of how serene she was in that moment.

The next is a shot of me leaning against the side of the hot tub and her looking up at me. There was no way to miss how she checked me out—even now I'm internally flexing like a bodybuilder at the memory—but the picture captures the exact look from Maddey I was telling her about. If it wasn't evidence of the sicko who is obsessed with her, I would pump my fist in the air at having tangible proof of her love for me.

There are a handful of the more innocent shots. Maddey sitting in my lap right after I pulled her onto me, trying valiantly to look mad at me but the tilt to her lips giving her away. Me pushing hair behind her ear. Another of me brushing a thumb across her bottom lip. From the angle of the shots, you can't see my face, but even in the dim lighting and through a telephonic lens, there's no missing the flare of heat in Maddey's icy eyes.

It's as I continue down the line that the urge to put my fist through the window gets stronger.

My hand wrapped around her hair, her eyes shut as my mouth trails down her exposed throat. The kiss, her arms circling my neck, her fingers clutching at my hair. I can still feel the sting from how she yanked on the short strands.

Her head flopped forward as I suck on her bare breasts. Her rising onto her knees as I fingered her.

Then finally a shot of her bent over the edge of the hot tub with me fucking her from behind, her naked body—which is only meant for my eyes—on display.

"I need to take them down," I say, but she doesn't make any move to release me.

Her shelter in the storm.

"Tink."

"Give me a minute," she mumbles into my chest.

She can have all the minutes. I don't care that the longer I look at the pictures, the closer I am to smashing everything to smithereens. If my girl needs to hold on to me longer to feel secure, she can take all the time she needs.

"Okay." She blows out a breath. "Let's do this." She straightens, pushing her shoulders back, ready to take on the world.

There's my little fighter. Fuck she's hot when she gets all bring-it-on-I-got-this.

"Ho. Lee. Shit." Her back hits my front as she takes in the full scope.

She's silent as she continues to look at each picture in turn. A silent Maddey is never a good thing. Sure there are the times I can tell it's because she's lost in a world of her own making, but more often than not, when she's quiet, she's plotting.

"I know I'm supposed to freak out—and don't get me wrong, I am—and I'm struggling to find the words to express how violated I feel, but is it wrong that I think we are totally hot?" She reaches out to touch the one of us in the throes of passion.

Only my girl can find smut inspiration from something like this—except I know her well enough to know she's deflecting. The slight tremble vibrating in her voice and the way she flinches at the sound of Trident running up on the deck are dead giveaways.

"Let the dog in." I nudge her toward the door when she doesn't move. "Feed him his breakfast while I take these down and call Justin."

She stops with her hand on the handle, turning to look at me over her shoulder. "You do realize he's going to castrate you for this, right?"

***

Distraction is the name of the game, and I could play it professionally.

After Trident's culinary needs were met, I brought Maddey with me to check out what happened to the power, not wanting to risk being away from her. It was an easy fix of flipping the breaker back on, but the concerning part is how her stalker was able to get into the garage where the box is located without detection.

Once the most pressing matters were handled, I forced Maddey to sit at the kitchen counter with a cup of coffee while I made us breakfast.

"Eat." I slide a plate loaded with bacon and eggs across the counter.

"I'm not hungry." She attempts to push it away, but I stop her.

"Eat anyway." The fear and adrenaline from earlier are masking her appetite, but after the workout I put her through last night and again this morning, she needs the calories.

"Why?"

Can't she do as she's told this one time?

"You need to eat if you're going to have enough energy to plan what our next course of action is."

"Does that mean you'll finally clue me in on what you kept from me?"

Goddammit. I stab a forkful of eggs with more force than necessary. I knew she wouldn't let me leaving her behind to see Justin go. She's already attempted to draw it out of me a few times. Doesn't make it any easier to have to tell her about it.

"Hold on," I instruct before running upstairs to grab the copies of the printed excerpts. We left the originals with the police for their file but made sure to have copies on hand for when Maddey forced the information out of me.

I don't know what kind of arrangement Justin and Paul have with their captain—I'm sure it has a lot to do with strings pulled by Jack—but I really hope it doesn't take them too much longer to get down here. I have a feeling I'm going to need all the protection I can get.

Without ceremony, I drop the papers next to her elbow. Grabbing my mug, I lean against the counter across from the island, crossing my legs at the ankles and sipping the lukewarm coffee while I wait.

Thankfully she finishes off her food before tentatively lifting the small stack.

Her brows grow closer together with each flip of the page.

I remain silent, letting her take it all in on her own time. Every now and then, her eyes flit up to meet mine, only to return to reading.

The sound of paper crinkling fills the silence from it crumpling inside her strangling grasp.

With an eerie calm, she sets the stack down and looks my way. Nerves prickle under my skin, and I'm hyperaware of her every tick as she stares me down.

A full minute passes before she finally speaks. "Why did you keep this from me?"

There's no point in lying now. I put my feelings on the line this morning; holding back now would only serve to piss her off more. I can handle her ire, but what I don't want is for her to act out irrationally because of her anger.

"I didn't like the idea of your work being used against you." Her eyes soften at the admission, and I can no longer keep my distance. I need to be near her. "Everything your stalker has done makes me want to rip him limb from limb, but this"—I stab a finger at the excerpts—"perverting your words"—another stab—"makes me want to do it with rusty tools."

Coconut floats toward my nose as she sways in her seat, a hand braced on my chest, the muscles flexing under her touch. I circle an arm around her and pull until the few inches between us are gone.

Dropping my chin to rest on the top of her head, I inhale, letting her ground me. I may have told her she sees me as her shelter in the storm, but she's always been my anchor.

Training, missions, deployments—Maddey was always there if any of us needed her. She's practically a one-woman USO.

"I'm sorry I kept this from you." I trail my fingers up and down her silky back. "I was trying to protect you, but I only ended up being the one to hurt you instead."

Again, she's silent.

I don't move. I continue to embrace her, seeking comfort in the feel and scent of her. The longer I hold her, the more emotion starts to creep in, and I come to the startling realization that I'm scared. My entire world is in my arms...what if I can't keep her safe?

Woof! Woof!

Trident's sudden bark startles Maddey, and I straighten to see Justin and Paul entering. Both of Justin's brows rise as he takes in the scene in front of him, but I don't address any of the questions I see burning behind his eyes.

Dad, if you have any pull with the big man upstairs, please let

Tink's prediction of castration be wrong. I would really like to give
Mom those grandbabies she wants one day.

Maddey bites her lip, swiveling to her brother then to me
and back again. The worry, the fear, the pure uncertainty
swimming in the pools of her pleading eyes douses any of the
primal urges I typically have when I see her take her lip
between her teeth.

"Madz?" Justin rushes her, taking her by the shoulders
and holding her out for his inspection.

She's pale underneath her summer tan, and there's a
constant flare to the outer corners of her eyes as if she's in a
horror movie checking to see what lurks in the dark.

"What happened?" This time Justin directs the question to
me as Paul moves in closer, Trident close to his side.

"Why don't we all sit?" I gesture to the living room
instead of the kitchen table where we typically sit.

I get the feeling Maddey is seconds away from crumbling.
Guiding her to the round reading chair, I whistle for Trident,
and he settles in to snuggle at her feet. Knowing the dog will
serve as emotional support for her while I do the heavy lifting
is enough to ease a little of the weight I'm feeling.

Justin and Paul take opposite ends of the couch, and I
settle across from them on the ottoman, resting my elbows on
my spread knees, looking for the fortitude to get through this.

The time for games is over. It's not that I wasn't taking the
task of helping figure out who Maddey's stalker is seriously,
but this new threat takes us to DEFCON 1.

"At some point during the night, the power to the house
was turned off." Two stone statues face me as Justin and Paul
take in the information.

"You're just telling us now?" Confusion laces Justin's tone.

"We didn't know it happened until we woke up." They're
both silent as they process all the things I'm not saying.
Everything that has happened with Maddey and the things
I've implemented during my stay to help put an end to all

this, they have been a part of. They are well aware that the system should have sent out an alert when disabled.

"What did your contact say?" Paul asks, referring to the security firm.

"They are running diagnostics on the system, but the early assessment is it's because the power was switched off at the house and the system itself wasn't attacked. That might be why it never triggered."

"Wait." Justin holds up a hand. "What do you mean switched off at the house?"

"The breaker box itself was turned off."

"*What?*" Justin and Paul say in unison, and I nod.

"That's not the worst part." I look over at Maddey, waiting for her to meet my eye. The *Good luck* quirk to her lips and arch of one of her brows has me giving her one of my own. My girl doesn't let anything keep her down for long.

I also get the impression leaving me to handle this by myself is payback for me leaving her out two days ago.

From behind me, I pull out the Ziploc bags we stored the pictures in to help preserve any potential evidence. There are only two—Maddey alone in the hot tub and me talking to her from outside it—in the bag Justin takes. Maddey thought it was best to keep the ones that gave away the details about what went down between us from Justin.

I tried telling her I didn't care, but she convinced me that wasn't the best plan. She reminded me that though Connor is the brother with the shortest fuse, Justin's temper is going to be tested enough with everything else he's being hit with.

She also tried to say there was no point in telling them about something that had an expiration date. I let that particular comment go for the time being; we have enough to deal with at the moment. I'll tackle setting her straight on us after she's safe.

"These were taped to the wall this morning." I point to where they were displayed for our viewing pleasure earlier.

Justin and Paul move closer together, studying every detail, looking for clues. I can tell the instant they come to the same conclusion I did.

Their gazes go from the pictures, to me, to Maddey, to the ceiling, and back down to the pictures.

"Come on." Justin jumps to his feet, not bothering to wait for anyone to respond before walking out the door.

We all follow, not saying a word as we take both flights up to the rooftop deck. Justin circles the hot tub, looking from it back to the bag of pictures still clutched in his hand.

"You were here?" He points to where Maddey sat the night before.

"Yes." Maddey takes a step closer until her shoulder brushes my arm, relaxing the instant we make contact.

"Have you met the renters?" Paul points at the house to our right.

"Yeah. That one is a big family having a reunion vacation. And that one"—she switches to the house on the left—"is a bunch of college kids. They were funny when they realized the other house next to theirs is filled with hockey players."

My suspicion is that whoever the stalker is broke into the house on the right for his surveillance. What worries me most, though, is that I doubt last night was the first time he's done it.

Chapter Forty

"Oh best friend of mine, where you at?" Sammy's voice shouts from below us.

There's so much that needs to be done if we're going to catch the stalker, but I refuse to allow the asshole to intrude on Maddey's life more than he already has. He does not get to take her joy, and spending the day with her friends is one of the things that brings her the most of it.

Knowing my girl the way I do—and knowing her previous track record—I opted to lay my plan out for her, tacking on the request for her to let me carry it out without her.

Hence the call to Sammy.

I'm hoping her oldest and dearest friend will be able to convince her she needs the break from her fucked-up reality.

"Sammy?" Maddey leans over the railing to peer down at the men making their way up the stairs to join us on the top deck.

"Hey, babe." Sammy pulls her in for a bear hug, closing his eyes as he squeezes her extra tight. I didn't give him all the details of what went down when I called him, but he knows enough that he's taking a moment to reassure himself she really is okay.

"Dollface!" Lyle cries, placing a smacking kiss on her cheek. The first true smile crosses Maddey's face at her friend's gregarious greeting.

The more subdued Jamie and Kyle hang back while Lyle spouts off a rant about all the half-naked men they will get to ogle today. *I'd be worried if he weren't such a happily married man.* Instead I know it's all in the name of "research" for Maddey's books. I've borne witness to so many novel-related conversations this week that if the Navy considered knowing *all* the things that make a perfect book boyfriend a usable skill, I'd be able to add it to my qualifications.

Sammy shoots me a *How is she really?* look over the top of Maddey's head, and I give him an *Our girl is stronger than she looks* one right back. His sudden bark of laughter tells me how true that is.

"Why are you guys here?" Maddey asks, bouncing her gaze around the group.

"Weren't you listening?" Lyle clutches his hands over his heart. "You wound me, doll. Jet-skiing!" He singsongs the last word.

"I can't anymore." Maddey shakes her head.

"Well I'm not taking no for an answer." Lyle takes one of her hands, and she sends me a pleading look over her shoulder.

"Tink." I close the distance between us and rest a hand on the small of her back. "I promise I will tell you *everything* we discuss and plan today." I spin her around so we're face to face, letting her see both my sincerity and my vulnerability. "You deserve to have some fun after everything we discovered this morning."

"What about you?" Those baby blues blink up at me.

I bring a hand up, acting like I'm brushing a strand of hair out of her face for an excuse to cup her cheek. "That's not what I'm here for."

And it would do you good to remember that, my conscience scolds.

"Hook—"

"Go." I shake my head. "Have fun and decompress." I bend so my mouth is at her ear and only she can hear my next words. "Just make sure *I'm* the one giving you inspiration for when you're writing dirty." I hold back my pleased smirk at her quick intake of breath.

Sammy's doing his best impression of the cat that ate the canary while Justin watches me quizzically. Ignoring them both, I tell Maddey I'll swing by for her later. Thankfully, she heads out with her friends, leaving me behind to take care of business.

I wait for the sound of footsteps to fully fade before rejoining Justin and Paul at the railing facing the rental to the right.

"There were more, right?" Paul asks after a beat of silence. Damn him for being such a good cop.

The uncertainty of how Justin will react to finding out about me sleeping with his sister has my gut churning like rough seas, but I'm hopeful once he hears the extent of my feelings he won't kick my ass too bad. At least I only have one of the McClain brothers to contend with. Those odds are a little more in my favor.

Elbows on the railing, hands clasped in front of me, eyes staring at the ocean, I say, "It was only pictures that he left…"

"But…" Justin prods.

"But he also got about a dozen shots of Maddey and me together." I finally turn my head to meet Justin's eyes.

"Together?"

"Yup."

"You mean…"

Deep breath in.

Swallow the lump in my throat.

Time to rip off the Band-Aid.

"Maddey and I slept together."

"Doesn't sound like you did much sleeping," Paul says under his breath, and I shoot him a *Be cool, bro* plea over my shoulder. Justin hasn't said anything, but there's no reason to poke the bear—or in this case, the ex-frogman.

I wait, heart in my throat, blood roaring in my ears, feet braced for the punch I expect is coming my way.

"Just?" I question, not quite sure how to react to him suddenly laughing and shaking his head.

"Con is going to be *pissed*," he gets out between his chuckles.

Only Connor?

"Thank you." He claps me on the shoulder.

"You're *thanking* me?" Okay, Maddey's crazy has officially rubbed off on me and I'm hearing the voices that are in her head. That's the only explanation I can come up with.

"For sleeping with your sister?" Paul asks. At least I can take comfort in the fact that I'm not going crazy because he clearly heard the same thing I did.

"No." Justin waves his hands back and forth. "We're just going to pretend you two are like a *Leave it to Beaver*-era type couple who sleep in separate beds because you don't have sex. I'm thanking you for giving me the opportunity to tell Con he owes Ty a hundred bucks."

This can't be his only reaction. For eight years I've battled my attraction, worried about what it could cost me if I gave in. I know it was a comment from him that gave me enough confidence to take a chance, but…this? That's it?

"You're not pissed?" I need to clarify while bracing for the other shoe to drop—or be shoved up my ass.

"Are you only sleeping with her to get your rocks off while you're here?"

"No." The answer is automatic. "I love her."

He shrugs. "Then we're cool."

That was a whole lot easier than I thought it would be.

"Okay." I clap my hands together. "Let's catch us a stalker."

Chapter Forty-One

The Lost Boys Group Chat

JUSTIN: Oh man. Con you better pull up your Venmo account.

CONNOR: What the hell do I need to pay for while deployed?

JUSTIN: You owe Ty $100

CONNOR: What??

TYLER: Ooo, I love free money.

CONNOR: Bullshit.

JUSTIN: Nope. It's true. Do you recall a certain bet we made about 3 years ago when the 3 of us were all together?

CONNOR: Umm… *thinking face emoji*

DEX: Justin…

JUSTIN: Ah…speak of the pirate.

TYLER: Hold up.

TYLER: *GIF of Britney Spears looking over her shoulder with a knowing smile*

CONNOR: I can't believe you just used a Britney GIF. No…wait…scratch that—yes I can. You ARE Tink's favorite.

TYLER: *GIF of Snow White dancing with the words 'Haters gonna hate'*

CONNOR: Ugh, Disney. There's NO getting away from it.

JUSTIN: Can you two idiots stop for a minute? I have news!!!

DEX: Just…

JUSTIN: Stop glaring at me from across the room. I didn't kick your ass—let me have my fun.

DEX: *GIF of Kramer saying, "That's true."*

JUSTIN: Okay, okay. *rubs hands together* Drum roll, please *drum emoji*

TYLER: You are clearly spending WAY too much time with Madz and her Covenettes because you forgot how to get straight to the point.

DEX: I'll be over here making a fresh pot of coffee. It'll be nightfall by the time you're done.

JUSTIN: Aren't you two SOOO funny. Keep that shit up, Ty, and maybe I won't tell you that our dear sweet Hook here finally made a move on his Tinker Bell.

TYLER: SHUT UP!

CONNOR: NO WAY!

TYLER: BOO-YAH. *HIP THRUST* TOLD YOU ASSHOLES HE LOVED HER.

CONNOR: THIS IS BULLSHIT!

DEX: Wait....

DEX: Hold on…

DEX: You guys knew?

TYLER: I did for sure. Justin was on the fence, and Connor was straight up in the land of denial. Which works for me because now I'm a hundred bucks richer.

TYLER: *GIF of man making it rain dollar bills*

CONNOR: It's $100, not a million. Chill, bro.

DEX: How?

TYLER: You act like I don't see you with your shirt off A LOT. Did you really think I wouldn't spot the silhouette of Tinker Bell hidden in the ink on your shoulder?

DEX: Shit.

TYLER: Nah. It's cool, bro.

CONNOR: HOO-YAH! Now the title is gonna be OFFICIAL! Brother-in-law status.

Chapter Forty-Two

Allowing Dex to send me away so he and the guys could work on a plan of attack went against every independent instinct I have, but even I'm woman enough to admit it was a good idea. I didn't realize how close I was to being one talking teacup away from getting hauled off to the looney bin with Belle's father.

Except, if I had a teacup like Chip in my life, I think I would be too entertained to worry about all the things I'm purposely not thinking about.

Like stalkers who are peeping Toms.

Having the most erotic sexual experiences of my life with my brothers' best friend.

Or how that same best friend, who also happens to be my old childhood crush, is in big, fat, stupid, why-can't-I-figure-it-out-for-myself love with me.

"So…" Sammy plops down on my left while Jordan and Skye settle in on my right.

"So…" I don't turn, instead keeping my gaze trained straight ahead where Tucker and Jake are helping the twins build a sandcastle.

"Don't make me go all 'Lucy, you got some 'splainin' to

do' on you, Madison Belle. Just spill the deets on the sweet nothings Dex whispered in your ear to get you to come with us today."

"You do realize in the almost week Dex has been here, you've Madison Belle-ed me more than you have all year, right?" I peer at him over the top of my sunglasses.

"Well if the glass slipper fits…" He gives me a nudge at his cleverness, and if I wasn't trying to avoid answering his question, I would give him props for it.

"Sammy, don't pick on her," Jordan chides, slipping into her mom role effortlessly.

"Yeah," Skye echoes, but she ruins the girl-I-got-your-back facade by adding, "At least not until she tells us if she hopped on Dex's magic carpet and let him show her the world."

Over my head, Sammy reaches out a fist for Skye to bump, and my pained groan is like a siren call for Becky and Zoey to skip—literally skip—over in our direction. Any time the two get even the barest whiff of trouble, they are there like cats with catnip.

I adore how the number of female friends I have keeps expanding. After going without girlfriends for so long, every addition to The Coven makes my heart happy. The fact that Melody's friends—like Zoey and Ella—feel comfortable enough with us to hang out when she's not here speaks to the specialness of our squad.

"What did we miss?" Becky's eyes alight with potential mischief.

Skye fills her in, only to have her tilting her head like Trident does when confused. "But Dex is a man."

"*Yeah* he is." Zoey waggles her eyebrows, causing us all to snicker.

"Don't distract me," Becky mock-scolds.

Oh, please distract her. Please save me from the I-know-it's-well-meaning-but-I-just-don't-have-it-in-me-to-deal-with-it inquisition.

"Anyway, like I was saying…" Becky huffs. "Dex is a man,

so wouldn't the carpet reference be more suited to Madz, and his would be more like…" She struggles to find the right words. "Sliding down his flagpole?"

"Oh, good point," Skye concedes, leaning forward to rest her elbows on her knees. "So, Madz, tell us—did you Jolly your Hook's Roger?"

"Now that's a good one."

"Oh yeah."

Becky and Zoey both agree and share a three-way exploding fist bump with Skye.

You see why the voices in my head are the way they are, right? My friends are *insane*. I also wouldn't trade them for the world.

I sit back and listen to the chaos around me, making all kinds of mental notes for all the book material they are giving me. Damn Dex for being right.

What if that's not the only thing he was right about?

Ignoring the taunting voice of Mr. Annoying Jiminy, I rest my head on Jordan's shoulder, going back to watching how her girls are squealing as Tucker chases them with clumps of seaweed like he's a monster.

Toddlerdom has thinned them out from when they were cute pudgy babies, but as they run to enlist Damon, Deck, and Ryan to join their cause, I can't help thinking they look like Peggy Bundy with how their hips shimmy.

"You doing okay?" Jordan asks, keeping her voice low enough for us to stay in our own little bubble.

"I don't know," I answer honestly, and I feel her nod, but she doesn't comment.

One of my favorite things about Jordan is her ability to know when to push and when to just let us be. It's probably why she's become the matriarch of our crew. Don't get me wrong, just because she's not a bossy know-it-all doesn't mean she doesn't interfere if the situation warrants it—Jase and Melody are a prime example—but that's a story for a different day. Still…she's a pillar of support for us.

"I'm just a phone call away if you need me." See what I mean? "It doesn't matter the time."

Honestly, if anyone could help me with what I'm going through, it would be Jordan. Just because she knew the identity of the person who harassed her back in college doesn't make what happened to her any less serious than what is happening with me. She's also seen me through all my stages of feelings for Dex, but there's that ever-present guilt about what happened with Ryan—her brother—that prevents me from using her as my sounding board.

Instead, I accept her silent support and let the smell of the sea, the gentle crash of the waves, the heat of the sun on my skin, and the sounds of my friends enjoying this beautiful summer day soothe me.

If only I could stay in this perfect little bubble.

Chapter Forty-Three

Dex

T he sun is still hours away from setting and already I feel like I've been up for days. While we managed to install a number of new protective measures when it comes to Maddey's house and the now independently powered security system, it still frustrates the fuck out of me that we are no closer to figuring out the stalker's identity.

We dealt with the cops, turning over the new evidence—not allowing Justin to see the *other* pictures—and talking about this latest development in the case. The police will add periodic drive-by patrols to the neighborhood, but I don't have much hope that it will be a fruitful endeavor.

If having an active SEAL staying inside the house hasn't been a deterrent, what makes anyone think the occasional cop car passing by will?

I haven't stopped kicking myself for allowing this fucker to get the drop on me. There have even been a few points throughout the day when I've let the occasional doubt creep in, wondering if I'm distracted by being personally involved, but then I remember this is Tink we're talking about—it was always personal for me, with or without the sex.

One of the other changes I made was to pull in the security firm to have a slightly more active role in the investigation, and I also had them supply me with a tracking device small enough for Maddey to keep on her person.

I've done all I can; now it's time to get my girl. Shockingly enough, she's kept me apprised of her itinerary as it changed throughout the day. Then again, for as resistant as I've been told she was before I got here, like Jamie said, she hasn't balked once at my directives. Hell, the only time she gave me an issue was when I left her out to talk to Justin and Paul the first time. Even today, she didn't give me much of a fight once I promised to keep her in the loop.

This is how I find myself walking the short distance on the beach, two doors down from Maddey to where the hockey guys share a house. Why a bunch of guys who make millions share a house, I have no idea.

On the way, I study my surroundings, taking an extra close look at the house rented by the college students, but there is no way the stalker used that one to take the pictures. The angle is all wrong.

Plus, the number of people I can see hanging out of the various decks at the moment would make it hard for anyone to be sneaking around. It wasn't all that late when Maddey and I had our hot tub romp, and there's no way all of them were down for the night then. The families sharing the house to the right? That makes more sense.

Unlatching the gate, I step into the fenced-off yard. There's a group of the fighters playing corn hole off to my right, and I see most of the hockey players spread out around the lower deck with a sprinkling of Covenettes in both places.

Trident lumbers down the steps to meet me as I make my rounds to greet everyone, and I bend to scratch his ears and ask him where his mama is. He takes me to where my favorite beach bum sits on one of the lounge chairs, Mickey Mouse headphones around her neck, those I'm-going-to-need-her-to-wear-them-for-me-in-the-bedroom glasses pushed up like a headband, small horse—er, Great Dane—sitting in her lap, ignoring the MacBook open in front of her as her attention is focused somewhere else.

"A little hard to be writing dirty with your laptop all the way over there," I tease, only to have a hand wrap around my forearm the best it can and yank me down.

Electricity sparks from everywhere her skin makes contact with mine, and I'm instantly hard. It hasn't even been twelve hours since I've been inside her and already I'm counting down the minutes until I can do it again.

"*Shhh*," Maddey cautions, keeping her hold on me.

"What?" I lean in close to whisper in her ear, letting my nose brush along the shell of it, smiling at her quick intake of breath.

"Because…" It's her turn to move in closer, her lips skimming my jaw as she speaks. "I'm trying to listen and I can't hear when you're flapping your lips."

"You didn't seem to mind how I flapped my lips last nig—" She pinches said lips together so I look like a duck.

"Careful, Hook." She arches one blonde brow. "These guys are friends with my brother. You don't want one of them running to tell Justin about how you had your wicked way with me in my jacuzzi, do you?"

She's like an adorable little kitten when she tries to be tough. My smirk turns predatory.

"Don't forget the kitchen, your bed, and of course, the shower this morning." She gapes at me like a fish, but I haven't even gotten to the best part yet. "Plus, Just didn't care when I told him. In fact…Con has to pay Ty a Benjamin because of it."

She rears back. "My brothers bet on if you would get me into bed?" Each word comes out slow and measured as she finally gives me her full attention.

"No. Ty bet Con I would finally admit to being in love with you and make a move." I'll take every opportunity afforded to me to drive home the fact she insists on denying.

Her eyes pop wide before jerking back around to watch Gemma and Chance arguing in the corner of the deck. Chance's Great Dane Bamm-Bamm—I can tell by the lack of gray spots mixed in with the black and white—snorts unhappily as Maddey rocks him out of his slumber, but she settles him by running a hand down his back.

Not wanting to push too hard and have her retreat from me again, I ask, "Why are you spying on your friends?"

"Because those two"—she makes a V with her fingers and points—"are enemies-to-lovers gold, and until they admit they want to fuck each other's brains out, I'm going to let them inspire some material for one of my favorite tropes."

"You mean you aren't the *only* one refusing to admit their feelings? *Shocker*."

"Shut. Up." Guess she didn't appreciate my sarcasm.

There's no stopping the laughter spilling from my lips as I move around the zoo animal—pardon me, the giant dog in her lap. The gap in her sarong grants me easy access to her leg, and I trail my fingertips along the back of her calf on the way to her ankle.

Maddey tries to free the limb from my hold, but the weight of Bamm-Bamm on her middle prevents her from doing so.

Separating the strands, I find the clasp I'm looking for on the third, opening it to remove the Tinker Bell anklet that sits in the middle of the five wrapped around her slender ankle.

"What are you doing?" Eavesdropping forgotten, she's completely focused on me as I slip the new charm next to the one of her nickname-sake.

Pinching the end of the delicate chain between my thumb and forefinger, I lay the piece of jewelry in my open palm, displaying the charms to her. She looks first at the slightly bent form of Tinker Bell puckered for a kiss, and then to the miniature jar filled with blue glitter the same shade as her eyes. On the jar, it reads 'Faith, Trust, & Pixie Dust'.

"I found this in a shop a few years ago," I explain as she runs a finger gently over the tiny script.

"Why'd you wait until now to give it to me?" She glances up at me briefly before letting her gaze fall back to the charm.

"It didn't seem right." Time for the hard part. "But…"

My palms start to sweat as I struggle to get out what I need to say. I can't have her rejecting the gift when her safety could depend on it.

"But?" she prods.

"I've also hidden a tiny tracker inside."

"Like a GPS chip?" I nod. "Smart."

What? That's it? No argument? Just acceptance? What is with the McClains reacting like I least expect today?

"What?" she giggles. "Did you expect me to fight you?"

"Fuckin' A."

"It's a good idea. Thank you for telling me and not doing it behind my back."

"Maddey." I drop my hold on the anklet to cup the side of her face. "I'm sorry I hurt you by talking to Justin and Paul without you the first time."

"I know. I already forgave you for that this morning when you told me why you did it."

"This also is in no way an indication of me thinking you can't handle yourself." I refasten the clasp. "This is just me making sure I'll have your back no matter where you are."

Chapter Forty-Four

From the Group Message Thread of The Coven

MAKES BOYS CRY: Do I have to start clapping my hands and saying, "I believe, I believe," to get you to come out of hiding, Madz?

MOTHER OF DRAGONS: Skye, be nice.

YOU KNOW YOU WANNA: Umm...

YOU KNOW YOU WANNA: Jordan...

YOU KNOW YOU WANNA: You've MET your bestie, right?

ALPHABET SOUP: Well if that isn't the pot calling the kettle black, BFF of mine.

PROTEIN PRINCESS: Seriously, Beck. Rock isn't wrong. You and Zoey are the BIGGEST shit-starters.

DANCING QUEEN: Guilty *does shimmy dance*

SANTA'S COOKIE SUPPLIER: OMG she really is shimmying.

BROADWAY BABY: I feel compelled to add that my boyfriend is also guilty of this crime.

FIDDLER ON THE ROOF: What about Cali? He's not an angel.

THE OG PITA: I think all those boys who claim they are brother-husbands do worse than any of the stuff they try to pin on us.

SANTA'S COOKIE SUPPLIER: This is true. I caught Vince and Tuck whispering in a corner earlier. When they saw me, they had total caught-with-a-hand-in-the-cookie-jar expressions on their faces.

MOTHER OF DRAGONS: Please keep them away from my house. I just got all the kids to sleep and I would really like to jump my husband without having to worry about having the party in my pants crashed.

ALPHABET SOUP: Seconded. Having my brother walk in while naked with Gage is not my favorite experience.

THE OG PITA: Didn't that only happen once?

ALPHABET SOUP: And that was more than enough, thank you very much.

MOTHER OF DRAGONS: Brothers *sighs*

ALPHABET SOUP: *GIF of Steve Buscemi toasting with teacup saying, "I hear you, sister."*

MAKES BOYS CRY: HOLD UP!!! Where is the other one who

loves to bitch about her brothers? MADISON BELLE MCCLAIN don't make me come down there.

QUEEN OF SMUT: Geez. Take a chill pill, Skye. You guys bitch about me leaving you hanging and needing to write faster, but when I try to go into my cave and do it, you bitch about me not texting back fast enough. Which is it that will please you?

MAKES BOYS CRY: Sarcasm—SHOCKER.

QUEEN OF SMUT: Don't EVEN TRY to act like that isn't the official language of The Coven. But whatever. What did you need?

MAKES BOYS CRY: I want to know what happened with Dex.

QUEEN OF SMUT: Not quite sure what you mean.

MAKES BOYS CRY: Don't play dumb. We let you get out of having this conversation earlier, but not now.

MOTHER OF DRAGONS: Skye...

MAKES BOYS CRY: Don't act like you didn't pick up on how our girl was acting.

YOU KNOW YOU WANNA: *GIF of Michael Jackson eating popcorn*

DANCING QUEEN: Oh, good idea. They have popcorn in this house, right?

SANTA'S COOKIE SUPPLIER: In multiple flavors.

ALPHABET SOUP: Thank god I just fed Ronnie. I'm going to need wine for this *wine glass emoji*

QUEEN OF SMUT: I don't want to talk about it, but I WILL talk about this scene I've just written. Let me tell you…it is enemies-to-lovers perfection thanks to a little inspiration I got from my FAVORITE source today.

YOU KNOW YOU WANNA: Ooooo

YOU KNOW YOU WANNA: *GIF of woman clapping her hands in excitement*

YOU KNOW YOU WANNA: *whispers* She's talking about Gemma and Chance.

PROTEIN PRINCESS: *GIF of Amber in *Clueless* saying, "Whatever."*

BROADWAY BABY: Wait.

BROADWAY BABY: *GIF of Zach Morris calling for a timeout*

BROADWAY BABY: You and the sexy SEAL? Wow *head exploding emoji* Jase has been holding out on me.

DANCING QUEEN: Maybe with information, but not with that D, though.

FIDDLER ON THE ROOF: That's what she said.

MOTHER OF DRAGONS: Gross.

THE OG PITA: Can I just say how much I FLOVE that you all are a merry band of squirrels?

QUEEN OF SMUT: And with that, I'm switching to airplane mode.

Chapter Forty-Five

Too conflicted about everything that has happened and the emotions I can't even get a grasp on, I spent the night hiding out in my office writing. I was able to keep my girls at bay—surprisingly—by turning off the service on my phone, but my reprieve is about to come to an end.

Today is book club.

Which means my friends are going to come busting into my house like Genie putting on Prince Ali's Welcome to Agraba parade.

Also...I miss my puppy, though I don't blame Trident for ditching me. Admittedly, I'm boring when I'm a chickenshit. Seeing him stretched out across Dex's feet—again—gnawing on bone—again—hits me in the feels.

Talk about being the perfect book boyfriend.

Even man's best friend approves.

Yeah, bitch—why, why are you purposely giving yourself blue clit when you have Mr. Incredible ready and willing?

Ooo, we might need to rename him from Hook to Mr. Incredible. I like.

Yeah, Mr. Incredible Peen. Boom. Mic drop.

"Wow." Dex's dark eyes find me as soon as I step into the kitchen, melting my insides, and the jingle of Trident's collar serves as the soundtrack of the moment. "You ghost on me for the night, hibernating like Baloo, only coming out for the bare necessities, and *still* you're lost in your head on me."

Dammit, Dex. Stop using Disney against me.

"Nice shirt." Those parentheses pop out as he reads my 'I don't have a dirty mind. I have a sexy imagination.' crop top.

"You ready for today?" I ask just as Gemma walks through the door loaded down with two giant insulated bags.

"Hellooo." She drags out the word, using more syllables than needed for one greeting, eyes filled with mirth as they bounce between Dex and me.

"Need help?" Dex is already on his feet.

"I got this." Gemma places the bags on the island with a ladylike grunt. "But if you want to help the guys bring the rest of the stuff over, that would save me another trip."

"There's more?" He eyes the numerous dishes being uncovered.

"Aww." Gemma sets the oven to preheat, plastering a dreamy expression on her face. "I always forget what it's like to have a newbie join us for book club."

I hide my smile behind my coffee mug, not wanting to give away how amused I am by getting to witness the rarity of Dex being uncertain.

There's a slight crinkle around his eyes when he looks my way. He's trying hard to hide it, not wanting to remind me of the dark stalker cloud hanging over our heads, but he's nervous about leaving me alone unprotected.

"Go." I shoo him toward the door. "You'll be gone less than ten minutes, Justin and Paul are already on the way, and I'm sure your mom will be here any second. Honestly, I'm surprised Gemma beat her here."

"My mom is coming?"

"Duh." This time I brave reaching up and putting my

hands on his hard, I-want-it-to-pin-me-to-a-wall-again chest and push. "She's pretty much our president since she's the one who got me into the smutty smut I love so much." I waggle my eyebrows and add a wink for good measure. If I'm lucky, I'll be able to use over-the-top humor as a barrier.

"You mean I have to listen to my *mom* discuss her favorite parts in the latest lady porn you just read?"

"First off"—Gemma puts a hand on her hip, holding a spatula up with the other—"I love that you used the term 'lady porn'. Then again, with Peggy Stone as your mom and you two"—the spatula waves between Dex and me, food splattering on the floor, which Trident quickly takes care of— "playing hide the salami, I shouldn't be surprised."

"*Gemma!*" I shout, scandalized. I'm going to kill her.

You can't kill her. If you do, who's going to feed you? It's annoying when Jiminy is right, and I'm sure my cheeks are as bright as the sun with how hot they feel.

"Turn your phone off all you want, Madz. You're a Covenette—you know you can't hide from a Coven Conversation."

This is true, but I much prefer one of the guys being the topic of them, thank you very much.

Strong arms wrap around my middle, tugging me back until I feel that chest I just want to lick along my back. The scent of the sea has my eyes closing to properly breathe him in.

"You're telling me our girl here was kissing and telling?"

Delicious shivers skitter down my spine from the stubble brushing the side of my neck when Dex nuzzles into me. If the gesture didn't feel so good, I would elbow him in the gut.

"Our girl…" Gemma sighs dreamily.

My friend is a sight. Her dark hair is in its perpetual messy bun, canting to the side, her spatula is clasped in both hands as she looks over it with heart eyes, and she's wearing a *Hunger Games* quote shirt that reads 'I have zero interest in these Capitol people. They are only distractions from the food.'

"Don't even start." I point an aggressive finger at Gemma, and she tries—and by tries, I mean doesn't even attempt in the least—to act all innocent.

I turn and shove Dex out the door before Gemma can say anything else. I have a feeling this isn't going to be your typical book club.

Chapter Forty-Six

Maddey's home is starting to feel like Mary Poppin's magic bag, but instead of being stuffed with anything the nanny might need, it's full of people.

Holy shit the number of bodies in here is staggering.

It has been over an hour since the last arrival made their appearance, and they have yet to discuss a book.

My girl has been in a huddle with my mom pretty much since she stepped in the door. I've kept my distance, because if I were near them, there would be no way for me to keep my recently declared feelings from showing. If that were to happen, Mom would have a wedding planning binder out before I could say hoo-yah.

"Do you guys actually talk about books during this thing? Seems to me it's just an excuse for you all to get together and eat," I say to Sammy and Jamie, who are to my left.

"After a week, you really think we are the type of group that needs an excuse to hang out?" Sammy shoots me a look that says *Get your head out of your ass, Stone.* Gotta say, he has a point.

"We're just waiting for Jase to call then we'll get started,"

Maddey explains, shooing Trident and Navy away from sniffing the food laid out on the ottoman. The dogs have been good, not taking any of the food easily in their reach, but they sure have been begging.

"I don't know." Rocky stands off to the side, swaying back and forth while holding Ronnie. "Maybe we *should* start without him. I can already hear the ridiculous things he's going to say when it comes to Jason Orson."

"And Mels saying *I can't even*," Zoey calls out.

"Good thing she's at the theater," Ella adds.

It is a marvel of modern day science how a group of this size can all fall on the same wavelength and carry on the same line of conversation even when you think they aren't paying attention.

The flat-screen on the wall lights up with a picture of Mr. and Mrs. Potato Head kissing, and Maddey answers with a "Hey, Trip" followed by all kinds of greetings and nicknames being tossed out.

"Sorry. I had to see Mels off first," Jase says after a solid minute of exchanging salutations.

"And by 'see her off'"—Cali hops over the back of Jase's couch, taking the empty spot to join the call—"he means shove his tongue down her throat."

Another minute goes by as the process starts all over with Cali's arrival on the screen.

"I just want to start off by saying I don't give a fu—" Jase cuts off the curse when he spots his nieces in the room. "*Fudge* how good Jason Orson looks in *the* towel. My ass is the best ass of all the Jasons in the world, and hockey butt trumps baseball butt any day."

"Totally called it." Rocky jerks a chin at the TV.

"Come on, Balboa." Jase stands and turns so his ass is facing the camera. "You work with the athletes." He points to his butt with both hands then cups it from underneath. "You trying to tell me this isn't better than baseball butt?"

"Can you save your questions about your ass for your own woman?" Gage grumbles.

"Oh, relax, Octoman." Jase waves him off. "I was only asking in a purely clinical sense. If I were fishing for compliments, Lyle would be my go-to person."

"You know it, handsome," Lyle cheers from somewhere behind me, and Jase points finger guns at him, sound effects included. "Take your pants off so I can *really* get a good look."

I shake my head, biting back laughter. These people always make me feel like I've fallen down the rabbit hole and stepped into the craziness of Wonderland.

"Have I mentioned lately that I'm so happy I left my old book club for yours?" Mom says to Maddey, who laughs and holds the Oreo in her hand higher so Trident can't lick it.

"How could we not have you, Peggy? You have the *best* book recs." Maddey whistles for the two dogs to follow.

The argument over baseball butt versus hockey butt continues as Maddey gives each dog a scoop of food to keep them from begging for scraps.

"For as much as I love Jason Orson, Knox Gentry is still my fave book boyfriend of Meghan Quinn's Brentwood baseball series," Maddey says as she retakes her seat.

I probably shouldn't be jealous of her talking about a fictional character, but I am. I'm sure part of it stems from not being able to be her *real* boyfriend because of her refusal to admit she loves me.

While I sit and stew over unwarranted emotions, the discussion and debate rages, topics changing in the blink of an eye. With Maddey's one comment, they are now talking about three books instead of one.

For fifteen minutes, I make a valiant effort to follow along, but eventually I shift my focus to watch the dogs play. It's a damn good thing I did.

Chapter Forty-Seven

Book club.

Typically it's a controlled type of chaos, but today we are in rare form. It doesn't help that *The Lineup* is the third book in the Brentwood baseball series by Meghan Quinn, one of my favorite authors and human beings. When we read all the books in a series, things do tend to devolve quickly.

The guys take things *way* too seriously. It's one of the reasons the girls and I actually have a separate club where we still get to read the hockey books I've had to eliminate from this one and the bully romances we are all addicted to.

It should come as no surprise that sports romances are the bulk of what we read for BC, but if the boys keep fighting like children, we're going to run out of sports to read about. In my personal opinion, I like *all* the uniform bottoms.

Baseball pants and how they are tapered? Yes, please. And yes, baseball butt is a thing, and it is glorious.

Hockey pants themselves don't really allow a person to appreciate how amazing the hockey butt—also real—is because of the padding, but when a player wears them without a shirt on under their jersey so you get a peek at their abs when they lift their hockey sweater—oh boy, that's something special.

Football pants are a thing of skin-tight, drool-worthy perfection.

And I would be remiss if I didn't mention those tiny shorts our fighters wear.

Sign me up for all of it.

Poor Dex looks lost while most of our squad argues—nicely—over fictional characters. I've been watching him—as discreetly as possible so Peggy doesn't get any wedding bell ideas—every chance I get. There's been a furrow between his brows for at least five minutes, but it smooths out when he turns his attention to Trident and Navy ambling back into the living room.

During hockey season, Jake and Jordan usually host book club at their home, but in the summer we alternate between houses. The times we all cram into my house, Navy is typically the only other canine to join to help keep the crazy at tolerable levels.

Except…

The longer I watch my two favorites labs, the more I feel a furrow form between my own brows.

"Trident, baby?" The kernel of uneasiness in my gut increases more the longer my dog doesn't come running. "Trident come here, baby."

Nothing, not even a lift of the head.

I'm out of my seat, the coldness of the hardwood floors barely registering when I drop to my knees and cup my puppy's head in my hands, raising his face to mine.

Pressing my nose to his, I notice a glassy sheen in his brown eyes. Something is most definitely wrong.

I only just finish thinking the thought when Navy falls with a plop, Trident falling a second later, his weight tipping me to the side.

"OH MY GOD!" *My baby.*

There's the shuffle of feet and bodies, but I'm not paying any attention to it as I cradle my dog's head in my lap, rubbing him viciously to rouse him, but to no avail.

Jordan is next to me in an instant, doing the same with Navy, and I'm sure the panic swimming in her hazel eyes mirrors what must be swirling in my blues.

What do we do?

What do we do?

What do we do?

"Tink." The simple weight of Dex's hand on my lower back is enough to quell the hysteria so I can assess.

Heartbeat: pulsing against my palm.

Breathing: a little slow and labored.

No foaming of the mouth or anything, so I don't think they got into something poisonous. There is a considerable amount more drool, though; the front panel of my denim cutoffs is already soaked.

Okay…what next?

The vet?

No, the animal hospital. They will be better equipped to handle anything—but it's half an hour away.

Think, Maddey. Think.

"Justin," I cry out.

"Madz." My big brother is down at my side in a flash. "What do you need?"

"Please tell me you drove the Charger today." He and Paul don't always drive separate, but I'm hoping they did today. I need the advantage the after-market lights and siren will provide to get my baby to the doctor as fast as possible. "Thank god." I breathe a sigh of relief when he nods.

"Let's get them loaded," Jordan says, shifting out of the way for the guys to lift the dogs.

"I'll call the animal hospital." I run for my phone on the counter.

The ringing sounds in my ear as I follow behind Justin

and Dex carrying Trident and Ryan and Jake with Navy. When the call connects, I give all the pertinent information.

Jordan links her arm with mine, and side by side, we watch as they get the dogs loaded into the vehicle. I move to climb in with them, but with a professional hockey goalie, a Navy SEAL, and two dogs closing in on a hundred pounds, it's too tight of a fit for me to squeeze in.

"Here, Madz." Ryan holds open the passenger's side door when he notices my predicament.

I shake my head. Even though it goes against every maternal instinct I have not to be with my baby during his time of need, there's no way I would be able to help carry him. It's more important for him to have those who can help him than for me to be close to him, especially with how frantic I am.

"You are *not* driving yourself," Dex orders, and I'm too worried about Trident to bristle like I normally would.

Why are they still here? They should be gone already.

"Fine." I whip around, searching for a solution. "Paul, will you drive me?" He may not have his cruiser, but I'm hoping having a cop driving will at least mean he'll speed.

With haste, I close the distance to Paul's SUV and open the door. Standing on the runner, forearms braced on the hood, I see Justin's Charger is *still* here. "Happy?" I lock eyes with Dex, and he gives me a nod. "Now go!"

Chapter Forty-Eight

"Trident is going to be fine, Madz." Paul reaches across the center console, trying to comfort me by patting my leg.

I'm beyond consoling at the moment, a complete basket case with every worst-case scenario about what is wrong with my baby flashing through my mind like a movie reel. It doesn't help that I'm in a different vehicle than him.

Yes, I know I was the one who suggested the carpool arrangements. As much as it hurts, I would make the same decision every time if it meant my kid (Trident) and my nephew (Navy) got to the vet that much sooner.

At least I'll be joining them, whereas poor Jordan had to stay behind because of her human children.

"Justin is driving with both lights and sirens, so they will be there in no time, and you called ahead to the vet, so they are expecting them. Everything will be alright." Paul pats my knee awkwardly, but I appreciate the attempt at comfort.

Rolling my head along the headrest, I give him my best attempt at a smile and pull out my phone to text Dex for an update.

QUEEN OF SMUT: How's my baby?

HOOK: I'm good.

QUEEN OF SMUT: NOT the time for jokes.

HOOK: No change. Still unconscious, breathing a little labored. I know you're freaked, but it's also a good thing their symptoms haven't worsened.

That may be true, but Trident is so much more than simply my dog. I'm perfectly okay with being one of those crazy dog moms; I'll wear that badge with pride.

HOOK: *picture of Trident's head cradled in Dex's lap, paw in hand*

HOOK: I got him, Tink.

I don't know if it's because of the words or the sight of Dex literally holding my dog's hand, but tears spring to my eyes and start falling down my cheeks like twin rivers big enough for Pocahontas to step into while singing about the colors of the wind.

"Oh, Maddey." Paul reaches over, fumbling around inside the glove compartment until he pulls out a handful of napkins and hands them over.

"I'm sorry," I mumble around blowing my nose like a foghorn.

Poor Paul. This has to be the most uncomfortable situation for him to be in. Sure, he comes around our group with Justin on occasion—we are the type of people who will welcome anyone who isn't an asshole (Tucker and Chance notwithstanding) to hang—but he hasn't been fully initiated. For him to be the one stuck with me when I'm a bawling mess with snot running out of my nose who's unable to formulate coherent sentences? Yeah, someone drew the short stick.

"You have nothing to apologize for. I know how much you love your dog. It's perfectly understandable to be upset."

"You know…" I let out a humorless laugh. "I was just thinking how unfortunate it is for you to be the one stuck with me when I'm like this." I circle a finger at all the fabulousness that is me at the moment. Can you hear the sarcasm? I am the perfect picture of ugly crying here. "But if it were any of the other guys driving me, they would be giving me shit."

"Not your brother," he counters.

"*Especially* my brother." I tuck a leg underneath me as I turn in my seat to face him. "For real though, Paul…thank you."

His keeps his gaze on the road as he navigates us around shore traffic, but it flits to me a few times. "Your brother is my partner, and you're his sister. He's got my back, and I have yours."

As annoying as their overprotectiveness can be at times, one of the things I've always loved and valued about my brothers and those they work with is their brothers-in-arms mentality. With my dad now a police chief, I have experienced a lot of the same with his guys. It's nice to see Justin got paired with such a like-minded person for a partner.

I flip my phone over and over in my hands, desperate for something to do, way too fucking antsy to sit still but needing to be in a car to get where we're going. I should text the girls to distract me, but I'm past the point where a Coven Conversation will do anything.

My foot beats a *tap-tap-tap-tap-tap* on the floorboard, and I've taken out and redone my ponytail a few dozen times.

Flip the phone.

Tap the foot.

Redo ponytail.

Over and over I repeat these steps, needing an outlet for all the anxious energy coursing through me.

"Maddey." Paul's calming tone washes over me. "You need to try to relax. You won't be any help to Trident if you send yourself into a panic attack before we even get there."

He's right, I know he is, but it doesn't make me feel any better.

"If you have a panic attack, I'll be forced to pull the car over to help you work through it before *you're* the one passing out." He chances another glance at me. "And if I do that, it will only delay our arrive at the animal hospital."

That gets my attention. Delays are *not* acceptable. Paul is already pushing the speed limit, but I'm tempted to ask—to *beg* for him to go faster.

Doing my best to channel my inner Rocky and all the yogi breathing she has taught me through the years, I work on getting myself under control.

Breathe in…the car eats up another mile toward our destination.

Breathe out…the *thump-thump-thump* of the wheels spinning under us.

Breathe in…a glance at the clock on the dash.

Breathe out…doing my best to calculate how much longer our drive should be.

"If you need something to drink, there should be a bottle of water in the door." I flop my head to the side and scrunch my brows together, causing Paul to chuckle. "When my adrenaline is pumping, I get crazy cotton mouth. Figured I'd offer in case you were the same."

Feeling around inside the cutout of the door panel, my hand meets the soft plastic of a water bottle inside the cupholder.

The crack of the seal opening interrupts the silence, and I guzzle the whole thing down in one go that would make any beer-chugging frat boy proud. I even go as far as crushing the bottle against my forehead because…well…I needed to do something, anything to distract me, and the move made me laugh.

Jesus Christ this whole thing is going to end up taking years off my life. How the hell do Jordan, Rocky, and Beth handle feeling this way? It's gotta be a million times worse for them since they actually birthed their babies, whereas I picked mine from a breeder.

Shit! How the hell am *I* supposed to handle procreating?

Well, young whippersnapper, you'll never have to worry about that if you keep running away from your feelings like you've been doing.

She doesn't need a man to have a baby.

This is true. There are plenty of attractive turkey basters out there.

I ignore the voices, not having the energy to deal with them right now. Honestly, I'm surprised they were even able to butt in on what is happening.

Continuing my breathing, I shut my eyes and lean my head against the cool glass of the window.

Hold on, baby. Mommy's coming.

Chapter Forty-Nine

Dex

The moment we arrive at the animal hospital, two technicians whisk both dogs and the four of us humans to two exam rooms. I don't know if it was Maddey calling ahead or the two star hockey players that prompted the expedited service, but you aren't going to hear a complaint from me.

The rooms they've taken us to are connected, and we have the door between them open so we can get updates in real time.

Have you ever seen a lion at the zoo? How it paces back and forth in its cage or behind a glass wall? Now imagine that times four—that's what we look like. Justin and me in one room, Ryan and Jake in another, probably making both veterinarians and their techs nervous while they work.

We've been here ten minutes and Maddey still hasn't arrived. Yes, Justin drove with the lights and sirens on, but I highly doubt Paul is obeying traffic laws, not with Maddey in the car. My girl would bat her lashes and flash her dimples to get here as quickly as possible.

We were texting earlier but she hasn't checked in for a

while, so I pull out my phone to give her an update. Those three bouncing dots never come. *Weird.*

I try calling her, but it goes straight to voicemail. Did her phone die?

"Just?"

It takes a few seconds for my best friend to take his eyes off the dog sleeping on the table and lift them to me. "Hmm?"

"Can you call Paul? I think Tink's phone died or something, and they should have been here by now."

"Yeah, sure—right. Good point." He's so distracted I'm surprised he actually does it.

My pacing stops so I can focus on the side of the conversation I can hear.

"Hey, man, just checking in to see where you're at." There's a pause while Justin waits for his partner to answer then he says, "Oh, shit."

My whole body goes on alert at the curse. *What's wrong? Is my girl okay?*

"What happened?" I move in closer to hear both sides of the conversation.

"They got a flat," Justin answers. That's not good. I can only imagine how much Maddey is bouncing off the walls— or in this case, the interior of the car—at the delay.

"How are the dogs?" Paul asks before grunting, obviously still in the middle of changing the tire.

Justin relays the little bit we know, but the only thing I can focus on is the clawing need I feel to talk to Maddey.

"Do you know why Maddey isn't answering her phone?" I cut in.

"It must have died from all the texting she was doing with the girls." Makes sense. Their group chat blows up incessantly, as if most of them don't see each other every day. "Let me go so I can finish this up and we can be on our way before Maddey decides to tase *me*." Even with the seriousness of the situation, Justin rolls his lips in to hold back a laugh. "I'll have her call you guys as soon as I'm done."

"Sounds good, man. See you soon." Justin pockets his phone, and I resume my pacing.

I hate this. Fucking *hate* it.

I should have dragged Maddey into the car with us. I don't care how much she reasoned with me or pleaded; I shouldn't have given in. The dogs would have been fine. Hell, she's barely bigger than they are—she wouldn't have taken up *that* much space.

She's never been able to charm me before, so why did I let her now? With so much still up in the air, this is the *worst* time for me to have done so.

I've yet to get her to admit her feelings for me.

There's the whole issue of us still not knowing who her stalker is.

Wait…

Holy shit!

What if…what if this was all some sort of elaborate play so this motherfucker could get to Maddey? It's barely been two days since the guy had the balls to set foot on her property and leave those pictures of us in the hot tub, and what if the pictures weren't the only thing left behind?

Fuck!

I throw my hat to the side and start to yank on the ends of my hair.

Fuck, fuck, fuck, fuck.

Paul needs to hurry the fuck up with that tire because I need to talk to Tink right fucking now. I'm not going to feel better until I have direct confirmation that she is okay.

Relax. She's with Paul. He's a cop—he'll be able to protect her if anything happens.

That's just it though…it's *my* job to keep Maddey safe.

Chapter Fifty

My head is pounding worse than the night tequila and I had a fiesta, and my mouth feels like it did that time I let Tucker talk me into trying to do the saltine challenge.

Burying my hands in my hair, I dig my fingers into my skull in an effort to massage away the deep ache in it. What the hell happened?

A gentle rocking starts to lull me back to sleep then everything slams into my consciousness at once.

Trident and Navy acting weird then collapsing without explanation.

The mad dash to get out of the house and get them to the animal hospital.

Dex sending me a picture of him taking care of my baby.

Paul trying to keep me from having a panic attack.

And then…

Nothing.

It's just one big blank void.

I bolt upright, clutching my head again when the world around me spins. Seriously, what happened?

Cautiously, I blink my eyes open, and…where the fuck am

I? The room I'm in is only big enough for the bed I'm on. The door is cracked, and I scoot forward to peer out into…a… galley? I'm on a boat?

Oh, I love that song. Let me grab my flippy-floppies.

No, I say sternly, cutting off the voices before they can begin. This is *so* not the time for them to be butting in. I have to figure out what the hell is going on.

The first thing I do is search the covers, smoothing them out, lifting them, tossing the pillows on the floor—anything that could hide my phone—but I come up empty.

I'm too goddamn fuzzy to think straight, and when I manage to do so, all I come up with are questions, not an answer to be found.

Where's my phone?

Why am I on a boat?

Whose boat am I on?

What time is it?

Based on the fading light outside the small window above the bed, time has passed, but I'm not sure how much.

Holy shit! I'm pretty sure I was drugged.

A sick realization slithers into my belly and makes my skin crawl. Did my…did my stalker finally get me?

I feel frantic but my movements are sluggish, and I'm starting to realize it definitely has to do with being drugged. I pull my leg from under me and slap a hand on my ankle, searching. When my fingers brush the stack of anklets circling it, my heartbeat speeds up. I feel around until I find the familiar shape of Tinker Bell hanging off one of them, but my pulse doesn't slow until I hit the new addition from yesterday. The miniature mason jar Dex added is still there.

Okay, good. I'm still trackable.

Where's Paul? Is he okay?

Fuck me I need to stop with the questions and come up with a plan. Time to think logically.

Digging my knuckles into my brow, I take a few deep

breaths and will myself to get it together. I need to control the chaos.

First things first. I've already deduced that I've been missing for an undetermined amount time, but there's no way Dex and Justin aren't already scouring the earth to find me. Well, they won't really have to scour since whoever took me didn't remove my tracker.

There's also the whole I'm on a boat thing. Whose boat am I on? Why am I even on it, and where we are headed? I know we are moving because I can tell by the rocking of the hull and the sound of the waves *shoosh-shoosh-shooshing* against the sides.

Taking stock, I try to suss out what type of vessel I'm on. From the lack of a motor and the faintest sound of fabric rippling in the distance, I suspect it's a sailboat.

The conclusion also fits with the cabin setup. There are stairs leading to the top deck straight across from the end of the bedroom. To the right of them I see a bathroom, and to the left is a tiny kitchen area. Closer to me there are two chairs and a small table between them, also to my right, and large bench-style seats surround a kitchen table on three sides.

I hate the thought of having to sit here and wait around for someone to come rescue me, but without my phone, I don't have any means to communicate with anyone to relay the small amount of information I can supply.

The funny thing is—not *ha-ha* funny, but ironic funny—if it is my stalker who has me, they *clearly* don't know me as well as they claim to. What person in their right mind takes a person who has former and active SEALs protecting them on a boat?

I'm pretty sure in the guidebook on how to become a stalker, the first thing is that they aren't *in the right frame of mind.* Jiminy, ever his helpful self.

This is true, though. Plus, how many times this week has

Dex told me 'SEALs do it better in water'? Guess it's time for him to put his money where his mouth is.

In all seriousness—or as much as I can manage; I am still me, after all—whoever has me made a major tactical error. It *so* doesn't help their case that I will *literally* have John McClain (pretend it's the correct spelling for the story's sake) as one of the people coming to save me with his fellow frogmen.

Recon—I need to get the lay of the land and assess everything so I know what I can use to my advantage. Actually, scratch that—I need a weapon. Maybe the kitchen will have something suitable.

I wobble when I push to my feet, still a little groggy from whatever I was dosed with. The room swirls around me as I take a few cautious steps, but after a few seconds, it passes. I'm really starting to worry about what happened to Paul. If I was drugged, does that mean he was too? And what did they do with him? I swear to god, if this asshat hurt Justin's partner…

As badly as I want to ransack the cabin to find something, *anything*, I know I need to slow down before I act. I want to keep my captor from knowing I'm awake for as long as possible.

My blood roars in my ears and I hold my breath as I ease open then close each cabinet door.

Nothing. No cutlery, no plates, not even a cup in sight.

My exploration yields me bupkis. A bottle of liquid dish soap is the most lethal thing I can find after checking every nook and cranny of what is essentially my dungeon.

Where's the frying pan when you need one? Hell, at this point I'd settle for a dinglehopper. I'm confident I could do some significant damage stabbing the tines into a meaty thigh.

The movement of the boat starts to slow, and then I hear the sound of metal clanging.

Oh my god we've dropped anchor.

That can only mean…

Spinning in a circle, I survey the cabin to make sure there's no evidence of my snooping and scramble back to the bed. Slipping back under the covers, my head hits the pillow at the same time I hear a foot hit the first step. Maybe if I feign sleep, whoever is coming will continue to leave me alone.

I just need to hold on for a little bit longer, because one day my prince will come—or in my case, my pirate.

Chapter Fifty-One

Dex

When we first arrived, the vet was able to deduce that the dogs had been drugged with a sedative, but we needed to wait for bloodwork to confirm if they would need to stay overnight for observation.

The chaos over the exams and trying to work out how they were even drugged makes time pass in a haze of worry. The pungent scent of multiple animals and the cacophony of barks and meows fades when I finally check the time and realize another hour has passed since we spoke to Paul.

One hour. Sixty minutes. Three thousand, six hundred seconds have gone by without me once noticing Maddey is *still* missing.

Fuck me. How could I not have noticed?

Whipping my phone out of my pocket, I quickly dial Maddey's phone, only for it to go to voicemail—again.

"Justin! Call Paul," I demand, cursing myself for not thinking of getting his number myself.

He does as I ask, his head swiveling from side to side, going as far as to step through the adjoining door to check that Maddey and Paul are in fact still not here as he waits for his call to be answered.

"No answer." The grim expression on Justin's face matches the one I'm sure is on my own.

Every worst-case scenario there is starts to play like a movie reel inside my brain. Every molecule inside my body freezes, and my gut screams that something isn't right.

Now is not the time to give in to the panic. I need to be able to think logically.

Ignoring and overriding is essential in my line of work, but I've never had the person I love above all else be my mission. There's a niggling feeling in the back of my mind that it is my feelings that led to this.

"Can you have his phone pinged?" I ask—then it hits me.

Fuck I'm an idiot.

I allowed myself to be so blinded by the panic I almost forgot I have my own way of tracking Maddey.

Her anklet.

I need to stop acting like a goddamn tadpole and be the brilliant frogman I am.

Distantly I hear Justin on the phone while asking Ryan to call Jack to see if he can send a unit to check out the pinged location since his precinct is more local.

The weight of three sets of eyes fall on me, but all my focus is waiting for the tracking app Jamie's guys installed to open.

Each flip of the hourglass feels like days as I wait for it to locate my girl, all my fingers and toes crossed she's even still wearing it.

"What are you doing?" Justin asks.

I ignore him as every ounce of my being homes in on the satellite imagery zooming in.

"Dex?" Justin tries again.

"I'm trying to find Tink." The global view of the United States closes in, the generic blocks of green and blue coming into focus.

"What do you mean you're trying to find Tink?" Ryan's

tone is snippy, but I ignore it and keep my focus on the buildings coming into view.

"I put a tracker on her. I can't believe I almost fucking forgot about it." Blue becomes the prominent color on the screen.

"Shit, man. You better hide her taser because she will *not* be happy when she finds out you bugged her without her knowledge," Justin declares, having relayed the information on Paul's location to his dad.

As the image on my phone zooms in, it doesn't look like where we were told Paul is, and it really sets in that Maddey's stalker *does* have her. Closer and closer the image gets, and when it stops, it's in the middle of...the ocean? Did this fucktard really take her on a boat?

"She's on a boat." I hand the phone over to Justin.

"Meet me at the harbor." Jack McClain's strong and angry voice rings out in the exam room, and it's then I realize Ryan switched the call over to speakerphone.

The four of us are on the move, complying without comment and running for the parking lot.

"Dad?" Justin asks, gunning it the before the doors are even fully shut.

"Jamie has a speedboat we can use. I'll loop in the Coast Guard and local LEOs, but if you think I'm waiting on them to mobilize to get my daughter, I messed up raising you, son."

●

Chapter Fifty-Two

My ears strain to gather any details they can since I have my eyes closed, feigning still being under the effects of the drugs. It's the only advantage I have at my disposal.

A maritime rescue may just be another day ending in Y for my guys, but it puts *me* at a supreme disadvantage. Even if I can overpower and subdue whoever it is that has me, I literally have nowhere to run.

The pad of footsteps gets louder the closer this asshat gets to me, and it takes every ounce of self-control my body has not to let my fingers give in to the twitch I feel to reach for a weapon I don't have. (The soap doesn't count.)

The sensation of eyes focusing on me makes my skin crawl, and I need to concentrate on keeping my breaths slow and steady when all I want to do is pant, I'm so uncomfortable.

Over the last few days, I've been undressed by Dex's eyes more times than I can count. The difference is, when he does it, I feel sexy and cherished at the same time. It also makes me want to actually strip out of whatever clothes I have on and jump his bones, whereas this assmonkey makes me want to bathe in a vat of bleach to rid myself of the memory.

The bed dips as he sits. Allowing myself to roll with the movement is one of the hardest things I've ever had to do because it means my body is just that much closer to someone who has absolutely no right to be near it.

The urge to open my eyes and get a look at the person who has been fucking with my life for the last nine months is strong—like *I'm pretty sure Gage could crush a person's skull with his bare hands if he tried* strong—but I resist.

It feels like spiders crawl across my skin when he reaches out to brush back my ponytail from where it has flopped over my face. He. Has. No. Fucking. Right. To. Touch. Me.

He lets out a sigh, and even my overactive writer's brain doesn't want to know what he's thinking. I just want to get away, find out if my dog is okay, and get back to Dex's arms where I feel safe.

He's my shelter in the storm.

Damn, Hook was right.

Pressure falls to my back as he leaves his hand there. Thank god he put me under the covers earlier; I'll take whatever barrier I can get.

Deep slow breath in, followed by a deep slow breath out.

In.

Out.

Inhale.

Exhale.

I wait him out, continuing my charade. The longer I can get away with it, the less time I have to interact with and potentially fight off my stalker, and the greater the chance Dex will get here before anything happens. Because Dex *will* get here. The only reason he wouldn't already be on his way is because he is taking the time to evaluate every angle, every chance of me getting hurt before making his move.

If it weren't for how dire my situation is, I would pop

some of the popcorn I came across in my search for weapons to have on hand for when Dex gets here.

Bad guys don't mess with my Hook and live to tell the tale.

Wait…did I just think of him as *my* Hook?

Well, shit. That's new.

"I wish it didn't have to come to this."

Oh.

My.

Fucking.

God.

I know that voice. You have got to be fucking kidding me. Him? No fucking way. This has to be some sort of sick joke.

Holy shit. Did you suspect him?

Nope. Did you?

Not even a little bit.

Talk about a plot twist.

"I was hoping you'd be up by now so we could talk."

Talk? He wants to talk? What does he think we're gonna do, sit down and have a tea party? I don't care that growing up I always wanted to attend one of the Mad Hatter's shindigs; this is *not* that.

"I guess I didn't factor in how tiny you are when I was measuring out the dosage of the sedative."

At least my suspicion about being drugged was correct.

With the way he's sitting, not really touching me except for the hand resting on my back, it makes me fairly sure he didn't do anything to me during the block of time I'm missing, which comforts me slightly.

How did he manage to drug me though?

None of this makes *sense*.

Chapter Fifty-Three

Dex

Jack is already waiting for us by the time Justin pulls into the parking lot at the marina, tires squealing, not giving a fuck that he's parked crookedly across multiple spaces.

The frown of all frowns mars his face, the wrinkles bracketing his mouth and lining his forehead more pronounced than I can ever recall seeing as he adjusts the straps of a bulletproof vest.

"My guys found Paul's phone smashed on the ground in a small pool of blood next to his car, which was abandoned on the side of the road. The passenger's side window was smashed and the door was left ajar." Jack's update only causes bile to rise in my throat. I choke it down, needing to remember my girl is no damsel, and if anyone stands a chance of surviving being kidnapped unscathed, it's my Tink.

Will she survive unscathed?

What if she's tied up? Or drugged?

"If this guy wanted Maddey, why take Paul? It's got to be a risk to have a cop with you, right?" Ryan asks as I pull on the vest offered by Jack while Justin does the same with the one from his trunk.

"Unless he's using him to keep Maddey in line," I say as the startling possibility hits me like a sledgehammer.

Shit!

That's actually a really good plan. Maddey's bleeding heart and fierce loyalty would have her doing anything possible to protect those she cares about, and if Paul is already hurt from them clearly being taken by force, that instinct is only going to be heightened.

"Are you sure this is the best plan?" Again, Ryan is questioning. He didn't let the sound of the sirens on the drive stop him from voicing his opinions about Jack's plan for us to handle this ourselves.

"Yes," I answer curtly. I'm getting sick and tired of his bullshit.

"I still think you're going to need backup."

We'll have it.

"That's what the Coast Guard is for," I say through gritted teeth.

"Then why aren't you waiting for them?"

"Because." I refuse to add anything else to my explanation and take off running toward Jamie's speedboat. I can't believe he thinks I would allow Maddey to be in her stalker's clutches for even *one second* longer than necessary. "We'll be fine."

The wood of the gangplank scratches my knee as I bend down to untie the rope from where it secures the boat.

"And we're just supposed to be okay with that?" He shoves me when I stand, but I hold my ground.

I shouldn't hit the guy. Tink kept him in her life as her bestie so I don't think it would do me any favors to deck him, but I really, *really* want to.

"Yes."

"That's not good enough." If he shoves me in the shoulder one more time...

"It'll have to be."

Ryan scoffs. "I can't believe you would put her life in jeopardy just so you can play hero by yourself."

That's it. I'm done.

"Fuck you." It's my turn to offer my own shove, this one with both my hands to his chest, causing him to stumble back two steps.

"Fuck you." He returns the words *and* the push.

The other guys move to break up the fight brewing, but I wave them off. This needs to happen, and it needs to happen now.

"I'm done with your fucking bullshit, Ryan. All you've done is bitch and ask questions that do nothing to help and will only end up costing us time."

"Well if *you* actually kept her *safe*, I wouldn't have to question this too-little-too-late plan you're concocting."

It's not my plan, but I don't bother mentioning that.

I did keep Maddey safe.

It's not my fault she was taken...right?

Do I regret not forcing her to come in the car with us? Sure, but what the hell was I supposed to do when she was in a blind panic and set the terms?

Plus, she was with Paul, a cop—a member of the SWAT team. He's highly trained. Who wouldn't think she would be safe? How were any of us supposed to know the stalker would make a move on her with someone like that with her?

What pisses me off the most is how Ryan is making me doubt my own feelings. Time to shut that shit down.

"I'm only going to say this once, so you better fucking listen." I square up against Maddey's ex. Yes, I've been intimidated in the past by all the could-have-beens she and Ryan share, but I'm done. "I love Maddey."

A hush falls over everyone else, but I'm not speaking to them. This is between me and Ryan and that's it. No one else's opinion matters.

"You may have loved her first, but I'm sure as shit gonna

love her last." For the first time in hours, something essential inside me settles. I've always said Maddey is my anchor, and admitting that I'm going to marry the hell out of her in front of some of the most important people in her life only serves to dig that anchor deeper into my heart.

"Now, if you're done questioning the validity of the plan created by three men who have collectively done over a thousand maritime missions"—I move around him—"I suggest you shut the fuck up and get out of our way so we can bring *my* girl back home."

Chapter Fifty-Four

With the effects of whatever he drugged me with still lingering in my system and the gentle rocking of the boat, my plan to feign sleep worked a little too well—I actually did end up sleeping. I hate that I don't know how much more time has passed other than guessing based on the fact that there's still a sliver of light in the sky.

Staying alive is my number one priority.

Dex is on his way. I have no proof that this is true, but I know it is. It's elemental.

I also need to be conscious of not hitting this guy's crazy switch and having him go *Fatal Attraction* on me before help arrives.

Reaching for every iota of control I have in this asinine situation, I blink my eyes open, giving the fog a second to clear and allowing the wood paneling of the walls to come into focus before pushing myself to sit up.

The blankets pool around my middle, but I don't make a move to get out of the bed. I'll come across as less of a threat if I make myself seem as vulnerable as possible. Feeling around, I find the rounded edges of the soap's squeeze bottle. What I wouldn't give to have a more formidable weapon.

Sucking in a fortifying breath, I lift my head and meet the familiar pair of gray eyes watching my every move from one of the chairs in the galley.

Betrayal bubbles into the back of my throat as I watch him rise from his seat. I have to work to choke it down. My heartbeat kicks with each step he takes to close the distance between us.

Why?

Why did he do this?

How could we *not* see this side of him?

Seriously! How did we miss this?

Him.

Him!

The longer I go without blinking, refusing to take my eyes off him for the millisecond the action would take, the angrier I become.

How could he do this to me?

"You're awake." The pleased tilt to his lips only adds to my ire.

Fuck him.

I hope someone puts a bullet in him.

"How are you feeling?"

"Like you care," I snip.

Shit! Not part of the plan, Madz. Remember? Play nice.

"Sorry," I offer, trying to sound as sincere as possible. "I'm not the nicest when I have a headache." I massage my temples as if I don't know the throbbing under my skull is because this asshole drugged me.

"I can give you something for the pain if you would like."

Yeah, so you can drug me again? I don't think so. Thankfully, I keep those thoughts to myself and only shake my head.

"Do you want anything to eat?"

I give another shake. It's been hours since I had any food

and normally I would be tipping the scales into full-on hangry mode, but my stomach is too full of knots to be able to put anything in it without it coming right back up.

"Are you sure?" He brings his arm around and gestures to the kitchen table now set with a tablecloth, dishes, and even a small vase with a single rose in it.

Does he think we are on some date?

Yeah, right.

There's only one thing I want from him—answers. It's about time I got them.

As if waiting for a cobra to strike—an appropriate analogy since he's such a snake—I watch as he takes a seat on the end of the bed when I make no move to get up.

How *dare* he act like this is any ol' day.

Fuck him and his creeptasticness.

Fuck his betrayal.

"Are you sure I can't get you anything? I packed some of your favorites."

I hold up a hand, cutting off any more false platitudes. I don't need them. I need answers.

"Why?"

He blinks as if *I'm* the crazy one, as if *I'm* the one not making sense.

"Why?" I ask again.

"Why what?" He reaches out to cup my knee through the covers, and my nostrils flare at his audacity.

"Why are we on your boat?" I can't believe I didn't recognize it earlier when I was looking for weapons.

"Because I know how much you like it. You've always had a blast on it. Plus, you're constantly saying how much you love being out on the water." One of his hands comes up to the side of my face, his thumb stroking across the curve of my cheekbone, and I legit throw up in my mouth a tiny bit. "It's really no surprise you have an affinity for the sea since you're a Navy brat."

I hate that he talks like he knows me.

"I was hoping we could enjoy a romantic sunset dinner, but I miscalculated and we missed it."

Guess that explains why he dropped anchor, though it's not like I'm going to point out that flaw in his plan. If being stationary will help put an end to this...date from hell, I'll take it.

I do have another question.

"Why did you do it?" I ask.

"Do what?"

Oh my god I'm going to hit him. If he keeps this shit up, I am going to do it. I'm only human after all.

"Cut the shit." I fist the blankets to keep from actually hitting him. "Why did you stalk me?"

"Stalking is such an ugly word."

Yeah, because the shit you put me through was pretty?

Don't you guys even start with me right now. I'm a bit too busy trying to process this situation to worry about making sense.

"What was the point of sending me"—I swallow down the bile as I choke out—"gifts?"

"I needed a way to get past your walls."

"My *walls*?" He really is insane.

"How's a guy supposed to compete with Ryan Donnelly, of all people?"

Ryan? *Ryan?* What?

"Ryan and I haven't been together for almost three years—what does he have to do with anything?"

"Yeah, but you two always hang out."

"We're friends."

Ryan had been in my life for years before we ever dated. I'm so confused, and all it's doing is making my head hurt more.

"What does he have to do with anything?" I ask, trying to make sense of this.

"You never dated anyone else. At first I was afraid you were still hung up on him—"

"I broke up with him."

"—but then I thought, what if you just didn't realize there were other guys out there who were interested?"

That's it. I can't take it anymore.

Finally giving *in, I prop my elbow on my knee and massage my forehead in my upturned hand.

"And you thought scaring me would accomplish this?"

Cray-cray. *Totally* cray-cray.

"At first I didn't mean to scare you."

"At *first*?" I screech.

Rein it in, Madz.

"It was meant to be cute." He shrugs. "You know...like secret admirer type stuff."

He's cracked.

"Then when you didn't respond to any of them, I had to think of something new. When I realized how concerned everyone got any time you received something, I thought maybe you would turn to one of us to protect you."

Yup. He's completely off the reservation.

"Why?"

"So you would be safe."

"No." I wave a hand in the air. "Why would you go to all the trouble in the first place?"

"Because I love you."

WHAT?!

Nuh-uh. No way. No how.

He takes my hand in his, and creepy-crawlies spread across my skin as he runs a finger over the top of my knuckles. I want so badly to jerk it away, but as unhinged as he is, I'm afraid to set him off.

"And I'm sure, if given the chance, you would fall in love with me too."

What.

The.

Actual.

Fuck.

I can't even.

One plus one does not equal happy couple when one of those in the equation is a complete psycho.

Scaring a person into thinking they need you to stay alive is not love. It is not something that can be forced by an adrenaline rush.

That's not love.

Love is…

Love is going to bed thinking of the person even when you were with them all day.

Love is wanting to share good news with them when you get it.

Love is being there for the bad even if you can't be there physically.

Love is sharing all the stupid stuff that makes you laugh or think of them just because.

It's needing to be near them because their presence alone is enough to make you feel better.

It's finding excuses to touch them in the most mundane ways because the physical contact settles something deep inside you.

It's joking and teasing and giving each other crap.

It's accepting their weirdness just because.

It's knowing when to push and when to not, being able to read each other and give them what they need.

Holy motherfucking shit-balls. I love Dex.

I'm *in* love with Dex.

Then, as if written by Walt himself, there's a clatter of rushed steps and Dex is there. Flanked by my dad and my brother, all three with guns drawn, taking in the scene in one swoop.

Like magnets, our gazes snap together, my blues meeting

those chocolatey browns that start to melt just the smallest bit as they take me in, satisfied I'm in one piece.

While Dex's attention is on me, Justin's is on my stalker. He must not have recognized the boat either, because his voice practically comes out in a whisper of shock.

"Paul?"

Chapter Fifty-Five

Dex

The narrow doorway into the cabin below makes it impossible for a sneaky breach, and the layout of the Catalina 355 sailboat prevents us from scoping out what we are about to walk into. Going in blind is never a preferred method, but it is what it is at this point. My entire world is down below deck; there is nothing that will keep me from her.

I can't hear anything over the rush of blood in my ears, my heart beating a battle cry of *Tink-Tink-Tink*. My gut and my soul urge me to rush, to plow full steam ahead, but I wait for Justin and Jack to fall into formation with me.

There's a tap on my shoulder and we storm the cabin, me running point, Jack to my right and Justin to my left.

Jack clears the tiny kitchen space and Justin handles the bathroom while I sweep across honey-toned wood accents and white furniture. Then, like a heat-seeking missile, my eyes lock onto Maddey sitting in the middle of the bed in the sleeping quarters near the bow of the boat with…

"Paul?" I distantly hear Justin say before his partner's presence fully registers.

Tension drains out of Maddey's beautiful face as she takes in my sudden appearance, but the worry is back in a second when she slides her gaze to Paul on the bed in front of her.

I scan every inch of her I can see, searching for any sign of injury. There are no bruises or blood, and she's not restrained at all. That right there is a mistake.

But...Paul?

Fucking *Paul* is her stalker?

How the hell did I miss that? He was right under our noses the entire time. Was Ryan actually right? Did I allow myself to become distracted by giving in to my feelings for Maddey?

"Justin, my man, nice to see you, but you're kind of interrupting right now." Paul keeps his tone conversational like he didn't just pull a gun on us.

"What the fuck, Paul?" Justin is seething as he takes another step closer. "It was you? You're the asshole who has been tormenting my sister this whole time?"

"I wasn't tormenting her." There's a genuine look of offense on Paul's face.

"What the fuck do you call what you did then?" It's Jack's turn to move in.

"I was only trying to show your daughter how much I care about her."

Is this guy for real?

"By scaring the shit out of her with your so-called gifts?" I taunt as I inch closer to my baby. Paul is too busy concentrating on justifying his actions to pay attention to the fact that we're closing in on him.

"Those were tokens of love." The volume of Paul's voice starts to rise.

"Love?" Justin scoffs.

"We have a connection." Paul continues as if he didn't hear Justin. "Maddey's always the one inviting me to join you guys, but you're my partner. I needed a way to make you see that your sister and I were meant to be."

"So...you started to stalk Maddey to...what? Swoop in and prove you could protect her, and you thought I would just be like, 'You know what? You should date my sister.'?"

If that was really his plan, Paul obviously doesn't know all that much about his partner.

"Don't you look at her." Paul turns his attention to me when I chance a glance at Maddey.

Needing to keep his attention on me and not on my girl methodically shifting on the bed, I comply. I have no idea what she thinks she's doing, but the determined set of her jaw and the calculating gleam I saw in her eyes tells me she has a plan.

"This is all your fault, you know." Paul's eyes harden as he stares Justin down.

"The fuck?" In my peripheral, I see Justin's hands flex around the grip of his gun.

"It was love at first sight for me the first time you brought me around your family, but out of respect for our partnership, I waited. I took the time for you to really get to know me so you would *know* I'd be a good match for Maddey." He lets out a humorless chuckle that has every hair on my body standing on end. "You had to go and call your *precious* Dex to ride in and save the day when you should have trusted me."

A shudder runs through me at the thought of what would have happened if Justin had actually done that—if he'd entrusted Maddey's safety to the same person putting her at risk.

"Do you have any idea what this last week has been like for me? Having to sit there, not saying a word while he"— Paul gestures to me with the gun, the willy-nilly way he flops it around making me nervous it will discharge—"put his hands on her in front of me? Listening to them call each other Hook and Tink like they are pet names?"

"Those have been their nicknames for each other since we were kids." Justin tries to reason. "Dex has been friends with our family since birth."

"Some friend." Paul scoffs. "You're so blinded by your so-called friendship with him that you don't even care that he's giving that friendship a giant middle finger by screwing your sister every chance he can get."

"Watch your fucking mouth," I warn. I wish I could just put a bullet in him and be done with this. Too bad shooting him will only cause all kinds of legal complications, even with him having a gun trained on us.

"You come in here, distracting her with your dick, and she can't realize she loves me."

Because that makes sense.

"She doesn't love you," I counter.

"She does."

I shake my head. "She doesn't."

"She *does*," he shouts.

"No." The low, calm tone I use is at direct odds with his agitated yelling. "She loves me."

I don't give one fuck that she hasn't admitted to it; I know she does.

"No, no, no, no, no, no," Paul chants, starting to unravel.

"She does." Two more steps and I'm now in the middle of the cabin.

"No." He whips his gun around and the room sucks in a collective breath.

Time stops and every muscle in my body locks. Staring down the barrel of the 9mm myself barely even fazes me, but seeing it pointed at the love of my life has me quaking in my metaphorical boots.

The thick black border around her pale irises becomes the most prominent feature of her face as her eyes flare wide like saucers.

"Tell him," Paul demands.

"Tell him what, Paul?" Maddey speaks like she's talking to a child.

"Tell him it's *me* you love." He waves the gun in her face.

Two more steps and I'm coming to the end of the kitchen table, only stopping when the gun swings back my way.

"STOP!" Paul screams, coming completely unhinged. He can rage all he wants; the important thing is the gun is on me and not Maddey.

The reprieve doesn't last long. "Tell him, Maddey." The barrel almost smacks her in the face when he whips it back around. "TELL HIM!"

"No." Her shoulders roll back as she stares down Paul and his gun, her hand clutching something I can't make out and coming to her stomach.

What is she doing?

Is she insane?

Doesn't she know it's okay to lie when your life is in jeopardy?

I just *had* to go and fall in love with a McClain.

"It's because of *him*, isn't it?"

Maddey follows the path of the gun as it swings back to me.

"ANSWER ME!"

Back to Maddey.

"This has nothing to do with Dex."

Back to me.

"Of course it does. He's here and now you're confused again."

Back to Maddey.

"No."

"No?" Paul arches a brow and comes back to me so I'm once again the target. "Maybe I should just shoot him and eliminate the competition."

"NO!" Maddey screams. Something arches through the air as she jumps from the bed and launches herself at Paul.

Gunshots echo in the small space, and I wait for the tell-tale pain.

Chapter Fifty-Six

Dex

I fucking hate hospitals. The smell, the sounds, the lingering sense of death that permeates the hallways. Intellectually, I know they do good, know they heal and help fix the broken, but none of that hits home as I pace the tiny waiting room while a team of surgeons work to save Maddey's life.

I may not be a big believer in serendipity, but the way the Coast Guard's Maritime Security Response Team showed up seconds after Maddey was shot might just convert me.

Blood...there was so much blood. What the hell was she thinking?

The skin on my hands is raw from washing it—her blood —off of them, but it doesn't stop me from rubbing them together. The sting of pain helps ground me in the moment.

"No!" Ryan's shout has everyone, including me, looking in his direction. "Don't tell me to calm down, JD."

I've been keeping my distance from the hockey captain since the rest of their group arrived at the hospital. Any time I've met his gaze, he's looked at me like I just told him Bauer stopped making his favorite hockey stick.

"Why are you still here?" He steps around his sister and

into my space. He may have a couple of inches on me, but I'm bulkier and a whole lot more deadly, so he doesn't intimidate me.

I don't dignify his question with a response, having had enough of his shit earlier.

"Get the fuck out of here."

"That's not gonna happen." I cross my arms over my chest.

"You don't deserve to be here. You're the reason they had to pull a bullet out of her. Maybe if you had spent more time actually working on finding out *who* the stalker was and less time working on how to get into Maddey's pants, we wouldn't be here right now." Ryan shoves my shoulder, but I don't react.

Acid churns in my gut, wondering if he is right. Sure, what I've been doing with Maddey is so much more than getting into her pants, but did it pull my focus? Was I trying so hard to get her to admit her feelings for me the same way she did for him that I lost sight of the true reason I'm here? Is that how Paul slipped through the cracks?

"I don't know why the fuck Just even called you"—Ryan points to Justin behind me—"because *clearly* you being here only made the situation worse." He slams a fist onto the closest chair, the sound reverberating through the room. "You should have never fucking called him," Ryan says over my shoulder, speaking to Justin this time.

Do not punch Tink's bestie, I tell myself when Ryan shoves me again. *If you harm a hair on his stupid, annoyingly perfect hockey head, she is liable to tase you in the nuts again.*

"Fuck!" Ryan punches the chair again. "You're just some asshole with a hero complex."

I'm able to keep myself from jumping off the cliff of anger, but the longer he berates me, the more I worry that he might be right.

Chapter Fifty-Seven

What kind of Shakespearean tragedy am I living in where I finally realize I'm in love with a man, only to have him be held at gunpoint by a psychopath?

The headache that was starting to fade earlier is now back in all-Seven-Dwarfs-digging glory.

In the distance, I can make out the sound of deep male voices…arguing?

Is Paul still trying to say I'm in love with him? When is he going to get a clue?

In addition to the headache still raging, there's a throb in my shoulder that is both blinding and hazy around the edges.

I go to bring my hand up to check on the spot causing me pain, but then something pulls the skin on the back of it.

"Madz?"

Sammy? Why does he sound so…relieved?

Bitch, open your damn eyes and get some answers.

With considerable effort, I lift my lids to see my partner in crime hovering over me.

"She's awake," he shouts over his shoulder then turns his caramel eyes back to me, scanning me from head to toe.

A door slams against a wall followed by a rush of foot-steps, and then I'm surrounded by hulking figures.

I pay them no mind as I try to process what I can. Looking down, I take in the blue and white material of a thin cotton hospital gown, and sure enough, an IV is taped to the back of my hand.

Machines beep from somewhere off to the side, but aside from the IV, I don't feel like I'm connected to anything else.

Questions come at me from all angles, but I ignore them as I follow the line of the white blanket tucked in over my lower half and up to where the snaps of the gown are open at my left shoulder. White bandages are wrapped around the joint, so aside from telling me I'm injured, I can't make anything else out.

Wait, if I'm injured…

Does that mean…

What about Dex?

Did Paul shoot him?

Frantically, I search the faces around me.

Sammy, Mom, Ryan, Jordan, Skye, Jamie…I lose track after that as person after person I love crams into the room in a way I'm sure the hospital frowns upon.

Except…

Where's Dex?

Justin and Dad also aren't here, but I'll worry about them later. Right now I *need* eyes on Dex.

The heart monitor starts beeping out of control as my panic starts to climb.

Where is he?

Why isn't he here?

Did Paul shoot him?

Dex. Dex. Dex.

Beep-beep-beep.

"Madz, calm down."

I think it's Mom who tries to get me to do so, but I can't.

Dex. Dex. Dex.

Beep-beep-beep.

"D—" My throat is sore and my voice comes out all scratchy, so I clear it and try again. "Dex?"

"He's gone," Ryan answers.

NO!

No. No. No. No. No.

Beep-beep-beep-beep-beep.

No, he can't be.

Paul killed him?

Dex. Dex. Dex.

Beep-beep-beep.

"What?" I cry.

No. No. No.

Beep-beep-beep.

I can't have lost him.

"Paul killed him?" I barely manage to get the question out as I fear giving voice to my greatest fear will make it true.

"What? No." The voices from around the room answer all at once.

"You said he was gone," I say to Ryan.

"Jesus, Madz." He runs a hand through his already disheveled hair. "I didn't mean *gone* gone. I just meant gone from the room."

"Hook." I try to shout, but my throat feels like it was scraped with razor blades. I don't care about the pain. I need him. "Hook! *Hook!*"

Tears stream down my face and the heart monitor beeps out of control while I continue to yell for Dex.

Then finally, *finally*, coming in behind a doctor in dark blue scrubs and a white lab coat, rushing into the room, he's there, filling the doorway with his large form.

The doctor is all "What's going on here?" and "You can't all be in the room at once!" but I don't hear a word because

I'm too busy trying to read the deadened expression on Dex's handsome face.

"Guys, let's give them a minute," Jordan says.

"We can check back after the doctor does her exam," Mom adds.

Dex turns to leave, and I rush to say, "Not you, Hook."

I spot Peggy hovering behind him as he shifts so the others can exit the room, and thankfully, he stays.

He stands in the corner, arms crossed with eyes that might as well be rock there's so little emotion in them. He watches the doctor run through taking my vitals and checking the wound underneath the bandage.

She tells me I was shot in the shoulder, I had to have surgery to repair the damaged artery, and they have me on antibiotics to treat possible infections. I have months of PT ahead of me, but I'm lucky I survived the blood loss.

Despite the headache raging in my skull, I decline the offer for more painkillers. I have a feeling I'm going to need *all* my wits about me to handle Broody McBrooderson in the corner.

"Hook—"

"Don't."

"Don't what?" I'm confused.

"Don't call me Hook."

I give him a *Really?* look, but my head hurts too much to hold it long.

"First you're all *Call me Hook* and now you don't want me to?" I go for a hint of humor to cut through the forcefield he is trying to put up around himself.

"I don't deserve to be your Hook anymore."

Lord give me strength, I don't have it in me to deal with stupid right now.

"What the fuck are you talking about?"

"I'm the reason you're in that bed." He stabs a finger at where I'm propped up by flat hospital pillows.

"Yeah, you are." His shoulders fall and his head drops forward. It's like I'm watching Jake and Jordan's bouncy house deflate when we pull the plug. "If it weren't for you, God knows where I could have ended up with Paul."

Dex's dark gaze snaps to mine, and I suck in a breath at the spark of hope in them.

"If not for you putting that tracker on me, Paul could have had us anywhere before you figured out *he* was the stalker."

"I should have seen it coming."

How? None of us did. He was hiding like a wolf in sheep's clothing, right under all our noses.

"Why?"

"Because."

That's it. That's all he offers as an explanation.

"Justin didn't suspect him—why should you have?" I try again.

"Because."

Ugh! Where's my taser when I need it?

"Stop blaming yourself for something that isn't your fault, Hook."

"Maddey—"

"No." I slash a hand through the air, the IV pulling enough to make me wince.

Dex closes the distance faster than a man of his size should be able to, taking my hand in his and inspecting where the needle pierces. Satisfied I didn't cause myself any more bodily harm, he drops it—much to my disappointment.

"You are *not* the reason that lead to me needing to be in this bed."

"You were *shot*, Maddey."

"Were you the one who shot me?" I arch a brow, every one of the voices in my head crossing their arms and tapping a foot since I can't.

"No, but Maddey—"

"*Stop* calling me Maddey. I'm Tink." This time I ignore the pull as I point to my chest then thrust my arm out at Dex. "And you're Hook."

"Mad—"

"What did I fucking *say*?" I'm about to lose my shit in the most epic, red-faced Tinker Bell tantrum ever to be had. "Tinker Bell." My thumb bends from the force of me putting it on my chest before I point at him again. "Captain Hook."

The IV loses the battle against me throwing my arm out all willy-nilly and warmth trickles down my wrist, but I ignore it. I'm too fucking pissed off to be concerned about blood. The good doctors replaced what I lost, so I have some to spare while I set this stubborn idiot straight.

"Do you need me to speak in terms you understand? Should you and I complete our own AAR?"

There's the teeniest, tiniest tilt to his lips at the mention of the after action reports the SEALs fill out after missions. Navy brat for the win.

"How did I get shot?"

"Maddey."

I growl. Like legit growl.

There's another flicker of a lip tilt, but all amusement fades again as he tracks the red spot forming on my blankets from the stream dripping off my arm.

"*How*...did I...get shot?"

He still doesn't answer. Instead he grabs a handful of paper towels and applies pressure to the puncture site.

"Tell me what happened." I need him to say *out loud* that he didn't shoot me. Even though the details are fuzzy for me, I know he didn't, but it's *him* who needs reminding of the fact.

"Paul threatened to shoot me," he answers, almost reluctantly.

That part I remember in all its technicolor glory. Another growl sounds from the back of my throat. When I finally get my hands on Paul, he better watch out. You do not threaten what's mine and get away with it.

"You went all *yippee-ki-yay* and launched yourself at Paul, spraying him in the face with *dish soap*." He makes his feelings about my weapon of choice perfectly clear.

What was I supposed to do? It was the only thing I had to work with.

"His shot went wide from your surprise attack, so it hit you instead."

Well that gives a whole new meaning to the saying *I would take a bullet for you*. Look at me taking things in the literal sense. My shoulder screams at me as if to say *Yeah, thanks for that—bitch.*

"Luckily the Coast Guard showed up and we were able to get you back here in time for surgery."

"What happened with Paul?" I let out a pained groan as I jerk upright, a sickening thought hitting me all at once. "Oh my god—what about Justin? And Dad? Are they hurt? Is that why they aren't here?"

The Tink Train pops out, and I know what he's about to say isn't going to be good.

"Paul is dead. Justin shot him when his gun went off, and he and Jack are fine. They are dealing with all the fallout and paperwork."

I should feel bad that someone lost their life, but I cannot scrounge up much empathy right now.

"But not you?"

"They left after you got out of surgery to give their statements. I was just waiting for you to wake up so I could say goodbye before I left."

"Goodbye? Left?" My eyes bounce around the room, searching for answers. "What the fuck are you talking about?"

"Maddey—"

"I swear to *God*, Dexter Stone, you call me Maddey one more fucking time, I'm putting you in the bed next to mine."

"Your room is a single."

"Now is *not* the time to be cute."

I want to hit him; it's such a shame I'm too injured to do so. I need to remember to ask Rocky—or better yet Gage since he's the professional—to do it for me later.

"We *just* went over this. *You* are not the one who put me in this bed. When you showed up, you promised to slay my dragons and catch my crocodile." I roll my hand and reverse our grips so now it's my hand on his wrist, and then I pull. "Guess what, Hook? You did just that. No more ticking clock to be heard."

The chug-chug-chug of the Tink Train tells me he still wants to argue. Time to push it off the tracks.

"I love you."

He rears back in shock—which is ridiculous since *he's* been the one telling me I've loved him since long before I was able to realize it.

"You were right. I love you."

He frees himself from my hold and takes two steps backward. Where the fuck does he think he's going?

"Don't you *dare* walk away from me, Dexter Stone."

He stops but doesn't return.

"You heard me, right?"

He stubbornly stays too far away for me to touch.

"*I. Love. You.*" There are those melty chocolate eyes I love. "Now stop acting dumb, be a good book boyfriend, and kiss me."

I hold my breath, waiting for him to comply

He closes the distance and slips a hand behind my neck, gripping it in that possessive way that makes my panties wet. His thumb wraps around until it rests on the vein pulsing away—not that he needs it because the heartbeat monitor is blowing up my spot, telling him *exactly* what his nearness does to me.

The frustrating man still doesn't kiss me. We're nose to nose, our lips close enough to brush when he speaks, but not enough to fully touch.

"You love me?" he asks.

My eyes cross trying to hold eye contact, and I nod.

"You're *in* love with me?"

Another nod.

"You want me to put my ring on your finger?"

"And your babies in my belly...if your boys are able to handle it after my electrocution," I add cheekily, because he still won't kiss me.

"Fucking hell, Tink."

There it is.

"Kiss me, Hook."

The tip of his tongue brushes across my lower lip when it peeks out to wet his.

"I'm going to do so much more than kiss you, Tink, so much more than all those things you just asked for." A quick peck then he's back in the same maddening position. "I'm going to give you the best damn happily ever after you've ever seen."

And he seals it—*haha, I'm so punny*—with a kiss.

Dex

Epilogue 1

Ten days later

For as long as I live, the sight of Maddey surrounded by a mountain of colorful pillows and sea turtle bedding will never get old.

After three days spent in the hospital, the staff was more than happy to see my girl leave. It wasn't her—Tink was a model patient—but the constant stream of visitors with a side dish of drama that drove them insane.

Sure, they mollified the staff by having the professional athletes visit the pediatrics floor and cheer up sick children, but there were more than a handful of noise complaints that started to outweigh the good.

With only a few days left on my three-week liberty, I stare down at the only person fierce enough to demand I get over myself and just love her.

And I do. I love her so fucking much.

The memory of her, curls a wild mess, hospital gown falling off one shoulder, arm not supported by a sling waving wildly in the air while she put both Ryan and me in our place still manages to give me a semi. I'm a sick fucking bastard for being turned on by being scolded, but that's what my baby does to me.

Under Maddey's watchful and don't-you-dare-test-me eye, the hockey captain and I kissed—not literally, much to Lyle's disappointment—and made up.

I think learning about some of the details of Paul's elaborate abduction of Maddey helped as well. It's unfortunate most of what happened we will never know because they died with Paul.

The jingle of metal sounds to my right, and I look down at Trident as he sits on my foot, taking up his own vigil.

"You ready for this, bud?"

The wet stroke of a tongue licking across my forearm is his answer.

Now or never.

With a jerk of my chin, Trident jumps onto the mattress and snuggles into his mom's side. Following his lead, I round the end of the bed and pull my girl to spoon against me.

Unfortunately, thanks to the feathers of a million geese in the way, I don't get to enjoy the feel of the soft curve of her ass against my dick. The Admiral has been feeling a bit neglected with Maddey on the disabled list.

"*Mmm.*" Maddey stretches, her back arching in that delicious way that never fails to turn me on.

"Hey there, Sleeping Beauty." I nose her curls out of the way, breathing in the sweet scent of coconut as I kiss along the back of her neck.

"Have I ever told you how much I love when you use Disney references on me, Hook?" she mumbles sleepily.

"A time or two." My hand fumbles with yards of fabric as I try to snake my way under it so I can hold a person and not a duvet.

She growls in frustration at not being able to stretch back and touch me with her injured shoulder, having to settle for stretching out her other arm to pet Trident.

I track the movement of her hand up and down the dog's side. She may be annoyed at her failed seduction attempts, but snuggling up with her and the pooch is my second favorite thing to do in this bed.

This...this is what I want to come home to every time I return from a mission.

"I don't want to hurt you, Tink." I drop the gentlest of kisses to the stitches keeping the bullet wound closed.

So close...I came so close to losing her, and it still keeps me up at night. The guilt and the blame also manage to creep up on me, but whenever they do, Maddey is there to put me back in my place.

Justin is a whole other issue, but I trust their squad to bring him around in my absence.

"Well if you won't give me the D, can we at least do something fun today?"

Remember how I said she was a model patient? Yeah, well that shit stopped once the medical professionals were no longer in charge of her care. If it weren't for my mom and Babs forcing her to sit her ass down and let others take care of her, Maddey would have ripped her stitches open within twenty-four hours of being home.

"Of course, Tink. I have big plans for us today." *Bigger than you'll guess.*

"Really?" The hopeful lilt to her voice has me chuckling, but the way she grinds against me suggestively has it breaking off into a groan.

"Not those kind of plans." I grip her hip to still her efforts at tempting me into fucking her when we're supposed to be behaving. "I'm going to spend the day kicking your ass in Mario Kart, babe."

Her sudden bark of laughter has Trident lifting his head to see what he missed, and the jingle of his collar reminds me what my real plans are.

"I think your refusal to fuck me has your semen backing

up and causing you brain damage, Hook, because if anyone is kicking *anyone's* ass in Mario Kart, it's me."

This is true. Even with an injured wing, she and Princess Peach still dominate the tracks.

Neither of us move, preferring to laze it up in bed. With my job, I won't have as many of these mornings as I would like, so I need to make the most of each one I can get.

I continue to place a path of kisses down her neck and along the top of her back, reveling in every shiver my stubble elicits.

Trident flops his head back, giving me a look that says *Are you gonna get on with it already?* If it were possible, I would swear he was biologically Maddey's, because damn, the dog is as much of a ballbuster as she is.

"I think someone is feeling neglected." I gesture to Mr. Impatient.

"It's because he agrees with his mommy that you're being a fun-sucker." Maddey scratches behind his ear, turning Trident into a pile of doggy goo.

Thankfully, my wingman is smart enough to flop his head around sufficiently to have her hand falling to his collar. Like she always does, Maddey hooks her fingers under the Pluto-printed Kevlar.

With our bodies pressed together, I feel as well as hear her suck in a breath.

"Dex?" She always drops the Hook whenever she's startled.

"Yeah, Tink?" I feign nonchalance while internally shaking in my skivvies. My entire future hinges on how this moment plays out.

With a small hiss of pain, Maddey pushes up to sit, patting her lap for Trident to drop his head into it.

As her delicate fingers work to separate the tags from the string tied alongside them, I move to follow, peering over her shoulder.

"Dex?" She unties the string. "What is this?" The ring is pinched between her fingers as she holds it out to me.

"It's the ring my dad proposed with." Those icy eyes lock onto me as I take the simple round diamond ring from her.

"This was Peggy's?"

I run a thumb around the thin halo of diamonds surrounding the center stone. It's not the most elaborate of rings, but Maddey is a hopeless romantic. The sentimentality gives value to it in a way additional carats couldn't.

With a nod, I slide off the bed and drop to a knee. She likes when I talk Disney to her, and well, I'm about to Disney it up in here.

"Madison Belle McClain...you have been my happiest place on earth for as long as I can remember."

"Why did I never think of that as a euphemism for my vagina before?" She smacks a hand to her forehead. "I'm so disappointed in myself."

I arch a brow and barely manage to hold back an eye roll.

"Do you think maybe you can refrain from being a smartass until *after* I get through my proposal?"

"You're proposing?" She feigns shock with a hand to her chest. She's all baby blue eyes and flashing dimples, and fuck me if I don't want to strangle and kiss her at the same time.

You sure you want to spend the rest of your life with her?

You're goddamn right I do.

I had to go and fall in love with a McClain.

Sensing I need the backup because his mom has *never* made things easy for me in life, Trident jumps down to join me. Sitting his butt next to my bent knee, he holds a paw out like he's the one asking for Maddey's hand in marriage. He gives me a look that says *I got you. Let's do this.* I'm buying him the biggest damn bone possible.

"Anyway..." I wait to see if she will interrupt again before continuing. "You and me, Tink, we're a tale as old as time. I always knew you were a girl worth fighting for." I run a finger over the slight scar by her elbow where bullies caused her to bleed years ago, a nod to the moment she told me was when she first thought she fell in love with me.

"It may have taken me until a few years later to have my *This is love* moment, but you always had hope that one day your prince would come—even if you tried to be all *I won't say I'm in love* when I first tried being part of your world."

With each princess I tick off on my list, the light in her eyes continues to grow.

"So what do you say, Tink?" I place the ring in front of her finger. "Why don't you let me explore this whole new world with you and marry me?"

Tears fall from her eyes, and she gives me a watery smile.

My heart is in my throat as I wait for her answer. Trident, less patient than me, smacks our joined hands with a paw.

"You approve of Hook as a dad, bud?"

Why am I not surprised she's deferring to the dog?

Woof! Woof!

Yup, *definitely* buying him the biggest bone at the store.

"Come on, baby. Say yes. Be my forever happy thought."

Maddey

Epilogue 2

Because I'm a person who's easily distracted by shiny objects, the gorgeous ring on my finger is not something I'll be able to wear when writing.

It's so pretty.

If you decide you don't like it, can I have it? Asking for a friend.

You do realize we aren't actually real so you can't "wear" it, right?

Semantics.

"Did you know you've been doing that for close to an hour?" Dex braces his elbows on the arm of my favorite reading chair, where I'm currently wiggling my fingers to make the light dance in rainbow prisms.

Dragging my gaze from my engagement ring, I turn to look at my fiancé—*eep, oh my god I still *can't* believe it*—and give him a dreamy smile.

"Don't make fun."

His face softens when I pout. "I'm not." He places a kiss on the top of my head and, not gonna lie, I totally swoon a little. "I'm just glad you like it."

"I love it, Hook." The significance of whose ring this is

makes it all the more special. "I can't believe Peggy gave you her ring."

"She loves you." He shrugs those shoulders I just want to bite. "She handed it to me and said, 'Now don't go being a stupid ass again and fucking this up' and capped it off with a smack upside my head."

Peggy Stone is my hero.

If it weren't for her, who knows if Dex would be here as my fiancé. I'm not talking about how she got jiggy with her husband and nine months later twenty-eight years ago she pushed him out of her hoo-hah. If she hadn't been there at the hospital keeping her son from running away, I wouldn't have gotten the chance to tell him to stop being an idiot.

"I'm kicking myself for not proposing sooner," he muses.

"Because *ten* days of officially being a couple was the *longest* wait ever."

"I've been waiting a lifetime for you, Tink." My eyes fall shut as he cups me behind the head and strokes a thumb across my cheek. I love these moments where he's possessive yet gentle. "Even when we fought it, you were always mine and I was always yours."

WHY AREN'T YOU TAKING NOTES RIGHT NOW?

Don't yell at her.

Why not? Are you listening to him? This is teaser-line gold.

Can you idiots shut up? I'm trying to listen.

"I take it your characters approve?" He chuckles and drops a kiss to the tip of my nose before pushing to stand.

Ooo, look at all those muscles.

And all that ink.

Can we lick him? He is our fiancé now, so doesn't that mean we get to lick him whenever we want?

Usually. *crosses arms and pouts* But he's been holding out on us.

Yeah, he won't give it up. *gives the evil eye*

Dex only shakes his head at my lack of a verbal response and holds out a hand for me to take.

"I made a fresh pot of coffee with the beans Lyle dropped off yesterday. He called it some kind of beach bum blend. No idea what's in it, but it smells like something you would like." He steers me in the direction of the sweet aroma coming from the kitchen. "You get caffeinated, and I'll get the Nintendo cued up."

I might just have to keep him.

Might? Did you already forget you accepted his proposal? Marriage typically means you keep the person until death do you part. Oh, Jiminy is feeling feisty today.

I fill a to-go cup in hopes it will help keep the coffee warm while I get lost in the racing world of Mario and his friends.

Leaning back against the counter, I take a minute to really let the scene in front of me unfold. There's a diamond I never imagined I would get my shit together enough to have the right to wear on my finger, and the man who put it there is sitting on my couch pulling up my favorite video game while my dog chews on a squeaky toy across the room. There are still so many decisions we need to make, but I'll enjoy this moment of domestic bliss for as long as I can.

Bending over the back of the couch, I wrap my good arm around Dex from behind, looking up at the pick-your-avatar menu on the television.

"Tink." He sighs when I kiss the silhouette of Tinker Bell hidden amongst the stars of the American flag decorating the back of his shoulder.

"I still can't believe you have this."

Or that I never knew he had it.

"Come here."

I make my way around the couch and settle onto his lap. There's more than enough room for me to sit on the cushion behind him, but dammit, I'm horny and he is holding out on me. If the semi I feel poking me in the ass is any indication, he's as hard up as I am. I just need to push his buttons enough to make him stop worrying about hurting me long enough to have an orgasm or two.

"I told you"—he runs a thumb along my own Tinker Bell on my collarbone—"you're my anchor. I got her there so you can always watch my six."

From the day I penned my first novel, Dex has always been my go-to book boyfriend inspiration. Sure, most of it was based on his sexy SEAL looks, but oh my Jane Austen, this man sure knows how to sling the swoon.

With a kiss to his scruffy jaw, I spin so I'm cradled in the V of his legs, letting his broad torso serve as my backrest. Mini wheel controller in hand, I feel those strong arms come around me.

Scrolling through the menu, I select Princess Peach, and Dex is King Bowser. With my foot, I connect to the Bluetooth speaker on the ottoman, and almost instantly, trash-talking voices fill the room.

"I don't care what you say, you losers are going down," Cali taunts.

"The only person going down is Sammy after *I* win again," Jamie retorts.

"*Jesus*, guys," Jordan hisses. "Sean and Carlee are logged on." Even through the line, I can tell she's rubbing the bridge of her nose.

"Maverick is playing too," Sean singsongs.

"I'm going to be kicked out of the PTA for being complicit in the corruption of minors."

"You're not in the PTA, wombmate." Jase chuckles. "The girls aren't in elementary school yet."

"Your friends are insane, you know that?" Dex whispers so only I can hear.

"You sure you want to marry me? It's a package deal."

The Sunshine Airport level zooms into view as each of our

avatars lineup at the starting line. The stoplight goes from red, to yellow, to green, and we're off.

We concentrate on driving through the airport, dodging baggage carts and airplanes as we battle it out for first place.

I'm lining up my shot with a red shell when Dex finally leans in to say, "Tomorrow."

"What?" I'm so stunned by what he's implying, Princess Peach hits a banana I could have easily avoided.

"Tomorrow." I fall back another place in the race. "You." A kiss behind my ear. "Me." A nudge and another drop in rank. "A courthouse." Stubble drags along my jaw. "You as my wife before I head back to Virginia Beach."

All thoughts of playing the game cease and I drop my controller as I spin in his arms, looping mine around him, ignoring the pull of my stitches.

"What do you mean before *I* head back? Don't you mean we?"

I don't like the implication. We're going to spend enough time apart thanks to his job as Mr. I Help Save The World And No One Knows—I'm not going to waste the time we are both on US soil by not being in the same state.

"I'm not going to take you away from your life when I'm gone more than I'm here."

Boys are dumb, and this one—the one my stubborn, defective heart decided is the one for us—is the head of the class.

I'll admit, it took me long enough to realize my feelings, but it's like as soon as I did, this stupid, stupid man has been trying to...what? Run away?

Oh, my poor, sweet, foolish Hook.

He's so lucky I love him.

And that I was raised by a SEAL. The only easy day was yesterday, right?

"You do realize I can do my job from anywhere, right?" I already explained to him how I don't have a mortgage—the why a fact he had to come to terms with.

There's a pinch around his sweet eyes, but he gives me a nod.

"And how, sir, do you expect me to continue to be able to write dirty without my inspiration?" I thread my fingers through the hairs at the back of his head.

"Tink." He nuzzles into my touch, and much to my blue clit's pleasure, his hips also surge up into me.

Ooo, gurl! You about to get your seduction on.

Yes, yes. *claps hands* Let's get laid.

You know what would help? *waggles eyebrows*

Things always end up taking an interesting turn if I take my characters' advice, *especially* when one of them sounds like Lyle.

Still…I'll take all the help I can get.

Calling out to disconnect the call, I have the speaker switch over to Ginuwine's "Pony" like they so helpfully suggested back in the hot tub.

"Maddey."

Oh, he must be serious if he's switching over from Tink. It doesn't stop the roll of my hips as I channel my inner Channing Tatum. Disney movies aren't the only ones I watch.

"Dex." I moan his name in that way I know makes him lose control.

There's a clatter as his controller falls, followed by a bruising grip on my hips as he wraps his hands around them. I suck in a breath, worried he's going to put a halt to my advances—again. Much to my surprise—and the shaking of my nips and the cheering of my clit—he doesn't.

Back and forth, I roll my hips.

Rising and falling, he grinds his up.

The mesh of his athletic shorts does nothing to take away from the sensation of having him beneath me. Each glorious inch of his cock is felt as he parts my lips through the thin material of my boxers. The ridge around the head flicks my clit with each up and down wave we make.

"Maddey."

I dig my nails into the flexing muscles of his back.

"Yes to tomorrow." I kiss his cheek. "Yes to the courthouse." I kiss his jaw. "Yes to being your wife as soon as possible." I flick his earlobe and suck it between my teeth. "But I *will not* agree to not going with you."

His head drops, our temples resting against each other as we each take in ragged breaths, our lower bodies continuing to undulate.

"So please stop talking nonsense and fuck your very-soon-to-be wife on the couch."

With a strangled sound coming from the back of his throat, Dex pulls back, cupping my face with both hands like I'm the most precious thing in the universe to him. It's not a hard hold, but it is commanding. "Fuck, Tink."

"That's what I'm trying to say, Hook." His gaze drops to my mouth when I lick across my bottom lip. "Stop holding out on me and fuck me."

"I don't want to hurt you."

Fucking Paul. If he weren't already dead, I would kill him for putting this crisis of confidence in my man.

"My shoulder is fine." Mirroring his hold, I bring my hands to his face and drop my forehead to his. "Please, Dex. I need to feel you...*all* of you."

His dark lashes fan across his cheekbones, his nostrils flare, and his chest expands enough to brush my nipples, but I read the moment for what it is—his surrender. To me, to us. To finally letting go of the last of his doubts.

As badly as I want him to throw me down and bring out his I-own-your-body side, that's not what I get.

With just his fingertips, he skims my body, down my neck, over the curve of my shoulders, pulling the thin strap of my tank down my arms with the utmost care.

My nipples pebble into hard points as the air-conditioned air hits them when my shirt falls to my waist.

Down, down, down he continues his path.

Tickling along my rib cage, he then tracks the band of my shorts and across the tops of my thighs. He reverses direction, his thumb hooking into the hem bunched at the juncture of my legs until he finds my center.

He drags his finger through my wetness right away thanks to my lack of underwear. I'm a withering mess of need as he torments me with his lazy actions.

"Dex," I plead.

"Easy, baby." With me still in his lap, he rises enough to lower his shorts and free his erection. "As much as I want to throw down and fuck until we both pass out from pleasure, we are going to take this nice and easy."

The loose material of my boxers makes it easy for him to pull it to the side and fit himself at my entrance. My eyes roll to the back of my head as he pushes inside me, moving so slowly it feels like it takes hours before he's buried to the hilt.

He anchors himself to me with an arm wrapped around my middle and his hand gripping my neck in that way that has me dripping around his dick.

Forehead to forehead, breaths and rapid heartbeats in sync, we give and take pleasure.

There's a sheen of sweat coating both our bodies as we clutch each other.

"I love you," I cry out as my orgasm slams into me with intensity.

"I love you," Dex echoes as he follows me over the cliff.

Sated, I sag forward.

Snuggled in the crook of his neck, the comforting scent of the sea filling my lungs, I marvel at how my Hook ended up being the plot twist I never saw coming.

Want to know what it's really like in Maddey's head? Or how Trident feels about his new dad? Continue reading. There also may be a third surprise.

The BTU Alumni Squad will be back in 2021. Add BTU6 to your Goodreads TBR.

Is 2021 too long for your next BTU Alumni fix? Jordan and Lyle have cameos in the #UofJ Series Looking To Score, Game Changer, and Playing For Keeps.

Are you one of the cool people who writes reviews? Writing Dirty can be found on Amazon, Goodreads, and BookBub.

Remember that excerpt that pushed Dex over the edge? Well good news. Savvy King has forcefully shoved BTU6 out of the way and will be my first release of 2021. This Untitled Royalty Crew U of J Spin-Off Novel will be releasing March/April 2021 and is available for preorder.

Bonus Epilogue- Characters

Okay, okay, okay. First things first, we have to say we love our creator.

This is true. Without Maddey, none of our stories would ever be told.

But is it really too much to ask that she listen to the fantabulous advice we give her?

For reals, because if she did, homegirl would have gotten laid hella sooner.

Jiminy: If she listened to you fools, she would have ended up in jail—or something—more times than I can count.

Oh look—it's Cricket Buzzkill.

Yeah, if you didn't butt in and guilt her all the damn time, she wouldn't have gone through such a dry spell before SEAL Sexy Pants came along and Beyoncé-d it up in here.

Hell yeah he put a ring on it.

Dance party! *pulls up Beyoncé playlist*

Okay, so now back to the good stuff.

Yes, yes. *claps hands*

Holy Kindle-melting, panty-ruining hotness does her Hook know how to inspire some primo smut.

You know what my favorite thing about Miss Tink marrying Dexter with the good dick is?

What is with the Beyoncé kick?

Are you complaining about talking about Queen B?

holds hands up in surrender Never.

Anyway…

You were about to tell us the best part about marrying the rocket launcher smuggler.

And I'm going to guess it isn't all the orgasms, because that seems too easy.

It is. That would be a total gimme.

Jiminy: Geez, no wonder her Coven Conversations are a hot mess—she can't even keep you guys in line. There's *no way* she would be able to when she's combined with whatever craziness goes on in the minds of the other nine of them.

blows fart noise on hand Stop being boring.

Anyone have any Raid? We seem to have a pest problem.

And to think, I was trying to be serious over here, and the cricket can't resist ruining my flow.

Jiminy: Can you really blame me? There are days I have to ask myself if you fools even know the meaning of the word serious.

Hardy-har-har. Okay, well before you decide to get on your high horse again and stop me, here goes. *clears throat* Dex is great because he 100% accepts us talking to Maddey at all hours of the day.

Oh, yes. *nods emphatically* And he finds us hilarious.

Umm…that's because we are.

Yup. You know the acronym NSFW?

Not safe for work?

That's the one.

Well we are what you call NSTEODAWLTU.

Okay, now you've lost even me.

Not safe to eat or drink anything when listening to us.

snaps and points Totally us.

Jiminy: You guys are going to age me prematurely.

Ehh. *shrugs shoulders* At least we know Hook and Tink's happily ever after will never be boring.

Bonus Bonus Epilogue- Trident

Trident

I know some people like to make fun of my mom and think she's crazy for talking to me the same way she does all her super-awesome Covenettes, but let me set the record straight right now. You might as well call my mom Dr. Dolittle because, duh, I understand her.

She's the best. She is literally the best hooman ever.

Well…my Aunt Jordan is a *really* close second.

At least she was until my new dad came into the picture.

The guys are almost as much fun as the girls. Sammy always pets me, Ryan takes me for runs, Jake lets me chill out, and Jase holds it down with giving me treats when Mom isn't looking.

But new Dad? He makes Mom smile in this weird goofy way no one else can. He's also kind of a badass.

Uncle Justin is cool too, and he keeps me sharp by taking me to see the lady who teaches all the real heroes—the K-9 unit.

But back to Dad…

He gives really good head scratches, knows how to pick

out the best bones, and has comfy feet. You might not think this is an important attribute, but when you are a dog who likes to lay across them, it matters.

Plus, it's nice to have someone to hang out with when Mom has to retreat into her writing cave.

He's not as fluent in dog speak as Mom, but he holds his own, and it's nice to have a wingman I don't have to worry will try to take the bitches like when Navy and I are on the prowl.

"Trident, baby, are you ready?" Mom calls, coming out of the bedroom.

Woof! *Ready*

"Who's better than you?" She crouches down so she can scratch both my ears at the same time.

Woof! Woof! *No one*

"That's right, baby. No one."

I sit to bask in her praise, shoving my nose into her neck and breathing in her sweet scent. Dad says she smells like coconut. I like coconut—he gave me some the last time he was home. What I don't like? How after they ate the coconut they went and did that thing that always makes me leave the room.

I know I'm not her hooman child, but a kid does *not* need to see his parents naked.

"What do you say we go pick up Dad?"

Woof. *Sure*

"Don't pout," she scolds.

It's not my fault. I'm super excited Dad gets back from deployment today, but when he's home, there's so much less space in the bed.

"Come on, baby." I wait for her to slip on her American-flag-print high heels that match the bandana she tied around my neck.

She grabs the keys to Dad's truck, holds the door open for

me, and rolls the window down so I can feel the wind blow through my fur then we set off for the airfield.

Mom sings along to the radio as we make a quick detour to Starbucks—coffee for Mom, puppuccino for me—and then we are pulling into the parking lot to wait with a bunch of other people.

Mom lets me run to say hi to the hoomans we know, and when I'm done getting my pets, I jump up onto the open tailgate and lie down next to her in the bed of the truck.

I put my head in Mom's lap; it's quite a feat with how she's bouncing in her seat, but I start to drift off when she does that thing where she rubs my ear over and over. I'm only a dog, but I don't think coffee was the best choice for how hopped up she is.

I don't know how long we wait—I'm a dog, we don't wear watches—before Mom lets out a squeal I think I'm the only one capable of hearing.

She jumps to stand, using the height of the truck to her advantage.

Mom's excitement is always contagious, so of course I join her in her search.

My tongue hangs out the side of my mouth and I can already taste the bone Dad will get for me so he can do all that gross naked stuff with Mom.

Hmm…I wonder if Uncle Tyler would have a slumber party with me tonight.

"*Squee!*" Mom hops down from the truck, and I have to scramble to keep up as she takes off across the tarmac and launches herself into Dad's arms.

They do the whole thing where they try to eat each other's faces. Why can't they just sniff butts like us normal people… normal pooches? Whatever.

"So, what?" Uncle Tyler pulls me in for a pet. "He wifes you up and you forget all about your brother who *also* returned home from deployment?"

Mom does that thing where she holds one of her paw's fingers in the air but doesn't stop kissing Dad.

"I'm telling Mom you flipped me off."

"Way to sound like an adult there, Ty." Mom giggles, unsurprisingly not concerned about the threat. Mom is my Nonna's favorite—after me, that is.

Want to know another reason I approve of Dex as my dad?

Even with Mom wrapped around him like Lucy and Lacey when they try to ride me like I'm a horse—those silly girls; Pebbles and Bamm-Bamm are much better for that—he bends down to give me a hello scratch.

"Hey, bud." I lick his face. "Did you keep Mom in line while I was gone?"

Woof! *Duh*

"Good boy."

As a group, with Dad still carrying Mom, we make our way back to the vehicles.

I leap into the truck bed and supervise Uncle Ty's loading of the bags.

"Ugh, Madz, *really*?" Uncle Ty acts like he's going to be sick as he pinches the poster Mom made but forgot to hold up because she was too busy being icky to remember it.

"Don't hate on my craft skills. Skye helped," Mom says between kisses.

Dad finally lifts his head long enough to look over at the 'Stone, report for booty' sign done up in red, white, and blue puffy paint. (At least that's what Aunt Skye said the colors were.)

"Your wish is my command, Tink."

Uncle Ty buries his face in my side with a pained groan when Dad squeezes Mom's butt. Doesn't he know that's not what you're supposed to do to a butt?

"Why am I not surprised you own a pair of patriotic heels, Tink?" Dad lifts one of Mom's feet after he sets her down on the tailgate.

"Any excuse to go shoe shopping, huh, sis?" Uncle Ty chuckles like he's the funniest hooman.

"I'll have you know, smartass"—Mom waves a hand over her shoe like she's that pretty lady on *Wheel of Fortune*—"I *already* owned these. My Uncle Sam wardrobe really grew during the Olympics."

"Are you sure you want to be married to her?" Uncle Ty brings his hands to his chest. "I promise I'll still be your best friend even if you change your mind."

"Yeah, asshole." Now Dad chuckles, but he never takes his eyes off Mom. "This is my favorite McClain right here."

And they're back to kissing.

Bonus Bonus Bonus Epilogue

WARNING

This Bonus is only for those who are curious to know how Ryan's proposal and the breakup went down this is it. I wrote it for the die hards. It did get me hella shouty caps from the betas.

Maddey

Almost 3 years ago

I look up at the familiar building as Ryan shifts the car into park. Though I didn't actually attend Brighten Tynes University, I did spend a considerable amount of time at the Titan Arena.

"Umm, Ry?" I question, unsure why we are here. This is not where I expected him to take me when he said he had something fun planned for us tonight. Dating the golden boy of the NHL can have its challenges when it comes to going out in public, but a hockey arena? The same one he graduated from? Yeah, that's just a recipe for disaster.

"Yeah, Bucky?" Ryan smirks before shutting the door and coming around to my side.

"Nope." I wave my finger side to side, cutting him off before he can really get started.

"What?" He feigns innocence, pushing the button for the tailgate. When it rises, I see both our sets of skates in the back.

Still not telling me *why* we are here, he drapes the skates over his shoulder, links our hands together, and leads us inside.

"It's my fault for letting us read Teagan Hunter for book club, but we are *not* stealing the nicknames for us. I don't call you Cap like everyone else does, so don't even *try* calling me Bucky."

"Fine. Ruin all my fun, Madison."

I roll my lips in to keep from smiling. I hate being called by my full name, but for some reason, Ryan gets away with it.

The heels of my stilettos echo down the empty hallway as we follow the all-too-familiar route to the rink. We pass the epic murals depicting Titans in play, photographs of both current and past players, and the entire glassed-in wall of trophies and accolades the team has accrued.

The sights aren't anything new—save for the most recent signed and framed Team USA Hockey jersey that's been added to the collection—but the absence of people is what has my head on a swivel. Yes it's the summer, but the arena is always available to those who stay in the area year-round.

The need to ask why we are here burns the back of my throat, but I manage to hold it in. A thumb smooths across the bumps of my knuckles, and I give the hand holding mine a squeeze, silently telling him I'm along for the ride.

The lighting inside the arena is dim with only half the lights switched on. I'm not used to seeing such a cavernous building shrouded in shadows. Between that and the cold air that keeps the ice from melting, I shiver.

Ryan being Ryan, he notices and drops an arm around my shoulders, tucking me close to his side. There's a hint of a smile playing on the edges of his lips, and it makes me wonder what he has planned.

Metal clanks when he lifts the handle of the door that grants us access to the team bench to sit.

Ooo, question. *raises hand*

Why are you raising your hand? This isn't a classroom.

Shut up. Anyway…do you think we're finally going to get to check having sex in the locker room off the boom-boom bucket list?

If that's what Ryan is planning, why are we inside the arena?

You know Ryan—he's a gentleman. Maybe he's going to wine and dine our girl first.

I'm so lost in the musings of the voices inside my head—I'm not crazy, I'm an author, and it's hard to get my characters to shut up—it takes me longer than it should to spot the setup at center ice.

Shit! Our dating anniversary isn't for a few weeks, but is this some type of anniversary thing? Why else would he recreate the on-ice picnic from our first date?

Trying not to let my panic show, I accept the pair of tube socks Ryan holds out and start to switch out my pumps for my skates. Why the hell can I write romance novels with the dreamiest romantic gestures in them but always feel like I'm coming up short as a girlfriend in real life?

After making sure the laces are nice and tight, I adjust the socks until they are secured above my knee. The high cotton will offer protection against the cold of the ice, and it's no surprise Ryan thought to bring them. Sundresses are great for the season, but not so much inside an ice rink.

Ryan taps on his phone, and a few seconds later Jessie Ware's cover of "A Dream Is A Wish Your Heart Makes" starts to play through the arena's sound system. I arch a brow but only get that playful smirk I love so much in return. Look at him earning bonus points by catering to my Disney-loving heart.

He hoists himself over the half-wall separating the bench

from the ice effortlessly. I'm sure he's done it so many times in his life it's muscle memory, but it doesn't make it any less hot. How do you not appreciate the bulge and flex of muscles?

Personally, I could watch Ryan move all day and never get bored. It's one of the reasons he's one of my go-to inspirations for book boyfriends when I write.

Oh yeah, he gives the perfect swoon.

I approve of anything that inspires a scene where we get some.

You mean like the chapter she wrote last night when she was thinking of Dex?

Do you fools really think you should be bringing up another man when she's with Ryan? Jiminy—my aptly named conscience—scolds.

He's right.

I suck for letting thoughts of my brothers' best friend creep in when I'm with Ryan.

Shaking off...everything, I focus on the world's best boyfriend in front of me. Ever the gentleman, he's already holding open the small door so I can step onto the ice without having to hop the wall like him.

Reaching for the hand he's holding out, I lace our fingers together, and the blades of my skates glide over the smooth surface of the ice. Taking my other hand as well, Ryan spins so he's skating backward, tugging me along for the ride. My skills have vastly improved in the years we've been dating, but they are amateur compared to Ryan's. Skating comes as naturally as walking to him, if not more so.

Trusting him to not let me fall, I scan the arena around us, my mind always making mental notes for what I could use in a book.

As the first song ends and Pentatonix's rendition of "Can You Feel The Love Tonight" begins, Ryan skates us over to the blue and yellow checked blanket. Carefully, I step onto the plush material, eyeing him warily when he doesn't join me. My confusion only grows when he stops me from sitting.

"Ry?" My brow furrows.

He shifts his feet, his skates wearing grooves into the ice from the back and forth motion.

Why is he acting weird?

My gaze drops to his chest, ogling it as it expands with a massive inhalation. I should probably be trying to figure out what has him so worked up, because that was obviously a breath for fortification—*what the hell does he need fortifying for?* —but my attention is more focused on the way his muscles test the limits of his cotton shirt.

"Madison."

My gaze snaps up to his, locking with his deep blues. Why do I feel like I should be the one bracing myself?

Ice scrapes, and Ryan drops to one knee.

My heart skips into overdrive like we were racing each other around the rink instead of skating at a leisurely pace like we were.

He's not doing what I think he's doing, is he?

He releases my right hand, taking my left in both of his.

No.

No, no, no, no.

He clears his throat.

Oh my god. He's really doing it.

"Madz." He gives my hand a squeeze. "I've thought of a million different ways to do this, ranging from the simple one of asking you in bed one morning to the most epically grand of flying us to Disney World and doing it during Mickey's parade, but none of them felt right—and in the case of the mouse, it would have be too public."

He's not wrong about that. Jordan, his sister and one of my best friends, would lose her shit with Skye, her business partner and another bestie of mine, over the internet gold of a public proposal in the happiest place on earth. It would totally turn into a mob scene.

Aren't you glad you aren't in public right now?

Not the time, Jiminy, I snap at my conscience.

Anyone have a clue how I should handle this? Sleepy, Sneezy, Doc, Grumpy, Bashful, Happy, Dopey? Anyone?

Gah!

The dwarfs are just as useless as the cricket.

You do know I'm not actually *a cricket, right?* Damn Jiminy. My conscience is lucky it isn't an insect. If it were, I have a five-inch hot pink stiletto I would be introducing it to.

What the hell am I supposed to do?

Even my characters are suspiciously quiet.

"So." Ryan's voice brings me out of my crazy musings. "I finally settled on coming back to where it all started." He jerks a chin at the arena.

My chest twinges, and I wonder if it's possible for a person my age to have a heart attack.

I know everyone has been expecting this—especially after his sister married her own college sweetheart so soon after graduation—but I am not prepared.

As terrible as it sounds, I've never even pictured us getting married. Whenever I've thought about Ryan and me as a couple, that's all we were—a couple, us.

I'm not sure if I'm ready for this—for things to change.

No, that's a lie. I'm not sure if I *can* do this.

Do I love Ryan? Of course I do. He's become so much more to me than just my boyfriend; he's one of my best friends. We have so much fun together. We make each other laugh, and he treats me like I'm a heroine in one of my books.

So why don't I want him to ask me to marry him?

"I love you so much. I've been in love with you pretty much from the beginning of us dating. My heart beats for you, Maddey."

That—that right there is why I'm dreading what is about

to come next. Because while I can say I love him, I'm not really sure if I'm *in* love with him.

For years I thought I was in love with another man. Now that I'm older and have witnessed one of my best friends fall head over heels, I can see that what I've felt for Dex was only puppy love born from a childhood crush.

I mean, Kirstie Alley had the right idea in *It Takes Two*. The person you marry should make you feel that can't eat, can't sleep, reach for the stars, over the fence, World Series kind of love.

Hmm, maybe the fact that my go-to love quote refers to baseball further proves I'm not meant to be with a hockey player.

Still…no matter how hard I've tried to change it, there will always be a small part of my heart that belongs to *him*.

Dexter Stone.

Not my boyfriend.

I'm totally that character readers want to throat-punch.

"Will you marry me?"

Ryan's handsome face is so hopeful. His love for me radiates off him.

I want to say yes.

I want to say yes *so badly*, but Ryan is too good of a person for me to say yes if I can't give him all of me. He deserves someone who will love him completely.

And…

And as much as I wish things were different, that person is not me. If it were, I wouldn't be picturing how this might play out if it were another person in his place.

My eyes sting, filling with tears. As the first one falls, so does his expression.

He knows.

Randomness For My Readers

Whoop! Welcome to the craziness that makes up my mind. Out of all the characters Maddey's internal thoughts are as close to how it is for me to live with the BTU Alumni in my head.

I hope you enjoyed Maddey and Dex's story, and for those of you have been with me through the others, thank you for trusting me to give Madz her HEA with someone who wasn't Ryan. I hope I did her HEA justice, and I promise our faithful Captain will get his own.

If this was your first book of mine, you can see Maddey and Ryan as a couple—and the reason for the shouting lol—in *Power Play*. Curious to learn the story of Rocky bruising her butt? Find out in Tap Out. Find out what *really* happened in the kitchen of Espresso Patronum in *Sweet Victory*. Wondering about the potatoes? Puck Performance has the answer.

So now for a little bullet style fun facts:

* I love my Disney. Good thing because Disney+ is forever being used because of the mini royals.

* Dopey has long since been my favorite Disney character but Stitch and Pascal are super close seconds.

* Of the classic Princes, Prince Phillip and Prince Eric are my faves because they fight for their women and Prince Eric loves his dog!

* For those of you that hang out with me in my reader group you know I fangirl it up. And the hockey romances discussed by the BTU Alumni Squad are hangs down some of my faves.

* Same goes for Meghan Quinn and her books!

* The We Love Disney album has some of my favorite covers of Disney songs.

* The audiobook Maddey is listening to isn't a real audio but it *is* a super amazing, dirty alpha, rip your heart out read by one of my closest friends and author Stefanie Jenkins *I Never Expected You.* I am a huge fan of her books even though i should invest in Kleenex when I beta read for her. And in her upcoming release of *I Never Let You Go* there may be an appearance of your favorite BTU Alumni romance author and a few of her friends…just saying!

* The excerpt that pushes our boy Dex over the edge of control is from a book—if you're in my reader group you've heard it being talked about—we refer to as kindle crack. It is now officially my first 2021 release. It is still Untitled and will be a Royalty Crew U of J Spin-Off Novel that you can PREORDER HERE! Savvy the heroine as a side character in my #UofJ series. releasing this fall. You can read them all for free in KU Looking To Score, Game Changer, and Playing For Keeps.

* I know I was yelled at for messing with the dogs—but I couldn't *really* do anything bad. I am totally one of those people that care more about the dog in the movies than the people. You should have heard me in the movie theater back in the day when I saw *Independence Day* and worried about them leaving Boomer in the car until he was safe.

* Some of the texts the Covenettes send to Maddey when

they are mad at her leaving them hanging with her writing come straight from texts I've gotten from my betas.

* Soliders coming home videos to their families and their pets are some of my favorite things to watch on the internet.

* The *Twilight* and *True Blood* books are some of my faves so they needed a shout out in Maddey's brain.

If my rambling hasn't turned you off and you are like "This chick is my kind of crazy," feel free to reach out!

Lots of Love,

Alley

Acknowledgments

This is where I get to say thank you, hopefully I don't miss anyone. If I do I'm sorry and I still love you, just you know, mommy brain.

I'll start with the Hubs—who even though he gave me crap **again** that *this* book also isn't dedicated to him he's still the real MVP (but maybe I earn points this time because he *is* mentioned in it *shrug*)—he has to deal with my lack of sleep, putting off laundry *because… laundry* and helping to hold the fort down with our three crazy mini royals. You truly are my best friend. Also, I'm sure he would want me to make sure I say thanks for all the hero inspiration, but it is true (even if he has no ink *winking emoji*)

To my Beta Bitches, my OG Coven: Gemma, Jenny, Megan, Caitie, Sarah, Nova, Andi, and Dana. Our real life Coven Conversations give me life.

Thanks to Stef for being one not only a sounding board, but a beta, and for lending me Zach Jacobs and scenes from *I Never Expected You.*

To Jenny (again) my PA, without her I wouldn't be organized enough for any of my releases to happen. Thank you for being the other half of my brain and video chatting all hours, damn our timezones and letting me break your heart over and over with this book. You know I live for your shouty capitals.

For Jess my editor for always pushing me to make the story just that much deeper. Some of those shouty capitals are in your honor lol but I do love that you only ramp up my evilness and you are stuck with me for life.

For Caitlin my other editor for entering my crazy and making sure my words sparkle. I am so happy we found each other.

To Gemma (again) for going from my proofreader to fangirl and being so invested in my characters stories to threaten my life *lovingly of course*…especially since I broke your heart over ending #Radz long before you even knew I broken them up.

To Dawn for giving *Writing Dirty* it's final spit shine.

To my street team for being the best pimps ever. Seriously, you guys rock my socks.

To my ARC team for giving my books some early love and getting the word out there.

To Kylie and Jo and all the girls at Give Me Books for always helping me spread the word of my books.

To every blogger and bookstagrammer that takes a chance and reads my words and writes about them.

Thank you to all the authors in the indie community for your continued support. I am so happy to be a part of this amazing group of people.

To my fellow Covenettes for making my reader group one of my happy places. Whenever you guys post things that you know belong there I squeal a little.

And, of course, to you my fabulous reader, for picking up my book and giving me a chance. Without you I wouldn't be able to live my dream of bringing to life the stories the voices in my head tell me.

Lots of Love,
Alley

For A Good Time Call

Did you have fun meeting The Coven? Do you want to stay up-to-date on releases, be the first to see cover reveals, excerpts from upcoming books, deleted scenes, sales, freebies, and all sorts of insider information you can't get anywhere else?

If you're like "Duh! Come on Alley." Make sure you sign up for my newsletter.

Ask yourself this:
* Are you a Romance Junkie?
* Do you like book boyfriends and book besties? (yes this is a thing)
* Is your GIF game strong?
* Want to get inside the crazy world of Alley Ciz?

If any of your answers are yes, maybe you should join my Facebook reader group, Romance Junkie's Coven

Join The Coven

Stalk Alley
Join The Coven
Get the Newsletter

Like Alley on Facebook
Follow Alley on Instagram
Hang with Alley on Goodreads
Follow Alley on Amazon
Follow Alley on BookBub
Subscribe on YouTube for Book Trailers
Follow Alley's inspiration boards on Pinterest
All the Swag
Book Playlists
All Things Alley

Also by Alley Ciz

BTU Alumni Series

Power Play (Jake and Jordan)

Musical Mayhem (Sammy and Jamie) BTU Novella

Tap Out (Gage and Rocky)

Sweet Victory (Vince and Holly)

Puck Performance (Jase and Melody)

Writing Dirty (Maddey and Dex)

Scoring Beauty- BTU6 Preorder, Releasing September 2021

#UofJ Series

Cut Above The Rest (Prequel) <—Freebie for newsletter subscribers.
Download here.

Looking To Score

Game Changer

Playing For Keeps

Off The Bench- #UofJ4 Preorder, Releasing December 2021

The Royalty Crew (A #UofJ Spin-Off)

Savage Queen

Ruthless Noble- Preorder, Releasing June 2021

About the Author

Alley Ciz is an internationally bestselling indie author of sassy heroines and the alpha men that fall on their knees for them. She is a romance junkie whose love for books turned into her telling the stories of the crazies who live in her head…even if they don't know how to stay in their lane.

This Potterhead can typically be found in the wild wearing a funny T-shirt, connected to an IV drip of coffee, stuffing her face with pizza and tacos, chasing behind her 3 minis, all while her 95lb yellow lab—the best behaved child—watches on in amusement.

facebook.com/AlleyCizAuthor

instagram.com/alley.ciz

pinterest.com/alleyciz

goodreads.com/alleyciz

bookbub.com/profile/alley-ciz

amazon.com/author/alleyciz